Singleholic

Katherine Bing

HANSIB

Published by Hansib Publications in 2009

Hansib Publications Limited
P.O. Box 226, Hertford, Hertfordshire, SG14 3WY, UK

Email: info@hansib-books.com
Website: www.hansib-books.com

A catalogue record for this book is
available from the British Library

ISBN 978-1- 906190-15-6

Printed by CPI Cox & Wyman, Reading, Berkshire RG1 8EX

For Mummy and Daddy
who are extraordinary.

And for Brett
who keeps me sane.

Acknowledgements

Much gratitude is owed to the stars who helped me: Biyi Bandele, Sarah Barlow, Alphege Bell, Cliff Berry, Carol Bewick, Charlie Bishop, Jennifer Bullock, Wyndi Bullock, Derek Bowen, Val Burton, Saqib Chaudhri, Abdallah Chihk, Kamau Crawford, Amy Elnas, Sarah Georgiou, Paul Goodwin, Amy Grant, Lani Guinane, Jo Grimes, Dan Hind, Cat McNeil, Diane McVey, Dawn Metcalfe, Gilbert Morris, Tua. Nefer, Guillaume Orhant, Karen Palmer, Zac Philipps, Aliza Pollack, Emily Rudgard, Milan Selassie, Christine Singh, Kwame Springer, Karen Smith, Tricia Taylor, Alex Wheatle.

Thanks also to the stars at Hansib for making this into a real book! And a special thanks to Maynard Eziashi, who is the brightest star of all.

Prologue

Alcoholics, chocoholics, workaholics, shopaholics: everyone has an addiction.

This time I thought I'd clinched it. Coffee-coloured, hard-bodied Djamel, complete with a sexy mole on the chin - he was the man I would marry. So what if I had to take the kids to the local Brixton mosque when in return I had a sex-god whose old-fashioned habits meant he opened doors and pulled out chairs for me? Had it all planned. A Muslim wedding: men on one side, women on the other; and the bride isn't the only one wearing a veil. It would have been fabulous.

'What do you mean, it's over?' I gulped, sitting on a tatty sofa in Djamel's front room. 'We can find a compromise.'

'Compromise? I won't compromise on this. I'm a Muslim. You don't seem to understand what that means.' Djamel ran his long brown fingers through his short wavy black hair. 'I'm not saying you can't be friends with Manuele. But you can't meet up with him alone.'

'But I've been friends with him for fifteen years!' I grabbed hold of Djamel's arm. 'He's just my friend for goodness' sake. And you're always busy working. It would mean I'd never see him. He's my friend. You're not being fair.'

'Yeah, well my family think I'm crazy to have put up with this for as long as I have. It's been five months!' He tore his arm away. 'I'm sorry, Sarah. I'm already compromising by going out with someone who isn't a Muslim. You won't meet me halfway.'

'Halfway? I won't meet you halfway? I've stopped eating pork. I've given up drinking wine around you. I even said that I would be willing to call our first-born Mohamed!' I leapt off the sofa. 'But I draw the line at giving up my male friends. I just can't do it!'

'Look, Sarah, I'm not asking for much.'

'OK. OK. What if I only meet Manuele in public places?'

'No.'

'And what if I promise to only see him for an hour at a time?'

'The choice is yours, Sarah: either you drop Manuele or you drop me.' Djamel paused, patting my shoulder. 'Remember, you're not getting any younger. You're about to turn thirty.'

I could feel the heat in my cheeks. My blood vessels drew tight as I threw his hand off me. 'What is it with everyone and age? I don't care how old I am! I draw the line at Manuele!'

'Then I'm drawing a line through us.' Djamel shrugged, stuffing his hands in his pockets, and showed me the door.

Failure #66. Had it all planned. That is until Djamel hurled me back into my quicksand sea of singledom, quite possibly to be banished here forever.

Chapter one

I jump out of bed and run to the mirror. Another man bites the dust and fate conspires to have me turn thirty a week later. OK. OK. OK. Don't panic. In the mirror I see a relatively attractive woman staring back: tall and slender (well, sort of, if I turn my bottom at a certain angle). I'm even quite sophisticated; well, I would be if I took off my pyjamas. Think, without Djamel I can wear sexy clothes again. Yeah, that's right. Who needs him? I'm only thirty. No big deal.

If I were thiry-one, different story. I'd be thirty-something: game over. But for now, I'm still in the game with a chance to find Mr Right. And Djamel is so Mr Wrong. Soon I'll be Mrs Sarah Somebody. Friends even tell me I'm in my prime. That's right. Prime City.

What I need is a plan: a plan to meet *The One*. But where the HELL do I start? Jesus. How do I make myself irresistible? Especially when my bottom is the size of France?

OK. OK. OK. Calm down. Just have to find a way to meet loads of men. Then they'll be queuing at the door. Black ones, white ones, brown ones. Who makes the better husband anyway? And who's better in bed?

Bloody hell. I've been staring at the mirror for half an hour. Jesus. Wasting my time while my guy is out there roaming the streets, looking for love, looking for ME. Gotta get cracking. Gotta get out there.

Rule Number ONE: Gotta get out of the house.

Rule Number TWO: Gotta get out of these bloody pyjamas.

Standing on my sanded floorboards, I open the wardrobe

door. Like all my furniture, it's Ikea chic, and the door only opens halfway. I delve into a drawer and find a few sexy-looking black t-shirts; sexy because they're tight; tight because I've had them ten years. When I bought them at the age of twenty, they were loose. Then, somewhere around the age of twenty-five, they became snug. Everything's blurry between snug and now. But tight is good. My boobs stand out. Must make the most of my assets. They look great squeezed into a bra. Out of a bra? They're more of a liability.

I grab one of my grey suit-trousers off the hanger, the one that gives me shape. I glance back at the mirror: brown olive skin, snug grey trousers, tight black t-shirt, tousled dark brown hair and thirty. Passable. Damn right I'm passable. Yeah. I'm better than passable. Djamel doesn't know what he's missing. After all, even Fiona and Shrek managed to find each other. And I'm not hugely fat with massive warts. I'm not missing any essential limbs, all of my teeth are intact and most importantly, I'm not GREEN. What more could a guy want? Deciding that he'll want a better-dressed version, I slam the front door and head for the West End.

MAKE LIGHT OF THE DARK

My eye catches the Estée Lauder sign in the cosmetics department of John Lewis on Oxford Street, and I find myself being drawn uncontrollably inside. A saleswoman jumps up from behind the counter.

'Can I help you?' she coos, smiling. She has straight blonde hair done in that flippy style, which must have taken hours. Her dark pink lipstick, flowery chiffon scarf and crisp white shirt have me thinking of Barbie or better–those Bratz dolls.

'Well, I saw your sign about that product for dark circles under the eyes, that's all. Does it work?' I blush and slip my hair round my left ear. 'I mean, uh, does it actually get rid of dark circles?'

The woman grabs my face as if I'm a mannequin in the window, twisting me from left to right and left again, peering up, down, sideways, umming and ahhing. I feel like a rat in a science experiment.

'Certainly, Madam. It will do wonders for your circles,' she says stroking my cheek. 'But looking at your face, you could do with a moisturiser as well.'

How forward! I already use facial moisturiser. So maybe it isn't Estee Lauder material, but it's still moisturiser. So what if it's some £3.99 jobbie from Boots? It works. Doesn't it? The nineteen-year-old pushes a mirror in front of my face.

'As you can see, Madam, you've had a little too much sun over here.' Her thumb drags across my forehead. 'And your smile lines are quite noticeable now.' Picking a bottle off the counter, she continues. 'A moisturiser would do wonders for you.'

Bitch. I hope your teeth turn green and fall out. Did Djamel put you up to this? You may be nineteen, honey, but you're not all THAT you know. I bet you wish you weren't so flat-chested, you short, stunted Barbie-Bratz-Bitch from hell. Your skin may be smooth now, but just wait till YOU hit thirty. You'll be worse than me; and when you're sixty, HA! Isn't white skin meant to wrinkle faster than brown skin? YEAH. I wish I could be there to gloat.

Traumatised and feeling sick, I attack the sampling products in front of me. By the time I've finished, I've spent a fortune. My heart thumps in the pit of my stomach. Imagine: £123! I examine my fancy peach paper bag: two pots of cream, one for the day, one for the night, and a container of serum to cut five years off my face. The Barbie-Bratz-Bitch looks extremely smug. Have I lost my mind? Is vanity taking over my life? No matter. It'll make me beautiful. The Barbie-Bratz-Bitch said so.

'Sarah! Sarah, Darling! How are you?' It's Georgina. Must hide. No. She's my dearest friend. She's lovely, kind, and happy.

There's nothing to dislike about her. She's blond, beautiful and a brilliant GP. She doesn't need expensive moisturisers. Why is there nowhere to hide?

'Fancy running into *you* here.' Georgina pokes me in the shoulder as I dangle my tiny bag behind my back. 'This is the last place I would have thought to find *you*. I've been buying some body creams for *pregnant* women.' She pronounces the word 'pregnant' as if it's some prestigious award. 'I'm hoping that this should do the trick of preventing those unsightly stretch marks. How ghastly,' she shouts, cupping her face in her hands. Her sleek golden shoulder-length hair bounces over her white knit turtleneck as if she's in a Timotei shampoo advertisement. 'I'd hate to appear like a raisin when this is all over. John might never look at me again!'

John is Georgina's delightful orthopaedic surgeon husband. Tall, dark and handsome, he is so attentive and adoring of his wife. Had John been Barbie's man, instead of poor old Ken, Mattel might never have felt the commercial pressure to give Barbie other boyfriends. Georgina and John are the perfect couple. They make me want to vomit.

'Oh, Sarah, darling,' Georgina gasps, 'have you recovered yet from that dreadful Djamel?'

I turn slightly pink. 'Yes, yes, I'm fine. He wasn't dreadful, you know, he was nice.'

'Nice? Nice how? My goodness, when I think of what he did to you. Breaking up with you because you have male friends. How ludicrous. Who thinks like that nowadays?' Georgina indignantly flips her hair back, her wedding rock sparkling on her finger.

'Lots of people. He's a French-Algerian Muslim, that's all. It wasn't Djamel's fault.' I say, defensively. 'He was lovely to me. I was the one who refused to convert.'

'Never mind; forget him. You are going out tonight to celebrate, aren't you?'

'Well, not exactly. I thought I'd stay in.' I desperately search for an explanation. 'Thirty isn't a number you want to advertise, is it? And there's this great movie on Sky that I've been meaning to see.'

'A FILM ON SKY?' spouts Georgina, shaking her head in disbelief. 'Don't be silly, Sarah. You are definitely NOT staying in. You'll come round and have dinner at our house. We're already having people over.' She strokes my arm. 'You'll have fun. I promise. Just look at me,' she purrs, gesturing at herself. 'I'm turning thirty next month and I'm not a bit worried.'

Suddenly it dawns on me. Georgina's married and pregnant, has a life she loves and a husband she loves even more. She has a full-time job, can find time to shop for luxuries on a Saturday afternoon and can whip up a superb dinner party for her wrinkled thirty-year-old singleholic friend. Maybe Djamel was right. If only I were Jewish so my mum could introduce me to a number of eligible bachelors. Or if I were Indian, the whole community would find me someone. But who's ever heard of the mixed-race community? What mixed-race guy wants to meet his mixed-race other half? My mum is Jamaican and my dad is English. In the eighties I was 'half-caste', and in America I'm 'bi-racial'. Whatever. I'm black. Or am I?

'I'll expect you at eight. OK, Sarah?' Georgina kisses me on both cheeks. 'Don't be late. Oh, and put something sexy on. I'll invite that single friend of John's, Greg. I know you hate being introduced to men, but who knows,' she sings, shrugging her shoulders, 'perhaps you'll hit it off.'

I only hate it because it looks so desperate. 'Greg doesn't believe in God, does he?' I whimper.

'No sweetie, don't be silly.' Georgina yells, darting out the doors. 'He's a doctor!'

I walk along Regent Street towards Covent Garden, looking in shop windows. The fancy cakes in a French patisserie keep me distracted until my thoughts wander back to Georgina and her perfect life. Damn. Is my life so different? She's five foot seven; I'm five foot eight. She's a doctor; I'm a teacher. Mind you, she has a little button nose and large blue eyes like a cocker spaniel while I have a tummy in desperate need of tightening. Georgina is every guy's dream. She also has a stunning mews house in Knightsbridge, while I have a flat in Brixton. But I like my flat, and I like Brixton. Georgina thinks I'm crazy to live in Brixton. But I like the mad people shouting about the end of the world by the tube. Good to know some people are more whacko than me.

The perfect outfit in Jigsaw's shop window jumps out at me. I stroll in crossing my fingers, and snatch a size fourteen off the rack.

I glance at the mirror. Youpee. It fits. Prime City. This black, sexy, off-the-shoulder one-piece is exactly what's needed for this evening's nightmare dinner. I need to be irresistible tonight. Now I'll be the catch of the century. Greg won't know what hit him. Thanks to Jigsaw, I'm actually starting to look forward to it.

Chapter two

OK, you're going to be fine. Posture; think posture now. Head up, shoulders back. Imagine a cord is attached to your spine, pulling you upwards. Or, as I once read in *Marie Claire*, just imagine you don't have any clothes on. Think NAKED. That's it, Sarah. You're doing well. Remember, you look divine. Nearly there. A few more steps. OK. There's the front door. Go get 'em.

Two small trees hugging the door rustle in the wind. I pull at my dress riding up my thigh and ring the doorbell. I hear chatter and finally someone fumbling at the door. It's Georgina's husband, John.

'Sarah, darling. How lovely to see you. I'm so glad you could come.' John's chestnut hair has grown slightly, giving his conservative image a warmer edge. He bends down and kisses me on both cheeks. No stubble there. 'Happy birthday!' he says, petting my shoulder. Oh, God. Please tell me they haven't told the others it's my birthday. Please tell me they don't all know I'm thirty. Please God, let me die.

'Oh, really, John, it's so good of you and Georgina to have me over at such late notice.' I say hesitantly. 'Don't worry about it being my birthday. Let's pretend it's an ordinary day, OK?'

John is the perfect husband. Not only is he better looking than Ken; he is life-size and made of flesh and blood. He'll understand. He's sensitive like that. He just has to understand. John takes my coat and leads me out of the hall towards the front room. The house is immaculate. Georgina has pricy paintings on the walls, bookshelves packed full of classics and

13

the latest intellectual bestsellers. There are freshly cut flowers in vases, and all of the furniture is solidly expensive. The house simply smells *posh*.

'Sarah, we couldn't possibly ignore your birthday. Your thirtieth is a once-in-a-lifetime event...to be celebrated in style,' John says, condescendingly.

Forget suicide. Murder is the better option. Who the hell do they think they are, for goodness' sake, with their perfect house, perfect marriage and perfect pregnancy? Why do they have to rub my nose in it? Fuck. Fuck. Fuck. Why can't I be back in my jammies in front of the television with a tub of Häagen-Dazs?

We enter the front room; John slots a white wine in my hand and introduces me to a variety of lovely couples. 'Simply dreadful what's happening in Iraq, isn't it?' comes from one corner of the room. 'Have you seen the new Chanel perfume ad?' sounds from another.

'Georgina rang Joyce and asked her to come,' John whispers, cringing. 'You know, the black nurse at her surgery...But I'm afraid she was already booked.'

Understanding what John means, I blush. 'Oh, don't worry; I'm used to being the only *exotic* person at parties,' I trill, 'and at least I'm not the only single woman.' Georgina invited her friend Emma, a colleague from work. She isn't especially attractive, mousey stringy hair, but nice and friendly and very well-balanced. She has the distinct advantage of being twenty-eight of course, but let's not hold that against her.

Georgina is the most gracious of hostesses. She remains stunning while surveying the cooking, and swanning amongst her guests. John looks after the drinks. They're a fantastic team. He keeps asking her to sit down and take a rest, given her condition, but she won't hear of it and continues her heroic hostessing. I wonder if I might ever become the same: organised, responsible and settled. Will I ever finally get to be a grown-up too?

I'm in the middle of talking to Georgina's Italian friend Massimo and his German wife Katia about their trilingual four-year-old's relationship with his nanny, when the doorbell rings. 'Hi, Greg,' I hear John say. My heart skips a beat, then starts to race. Maybe he's the Prince Charming I've been searching to play grown-ups with. So I do what any other sensible girl would do: I escape to the loo. As my heels clap against the matt oak floor, I catch a glimpse of him. He's tall with dark short hair, wearing a black tailored jacket, white shirt with cuff-links: quite attractive really. He and John might even pass for brothers.

Georgina only sets me up with white guys. I have other friends who only set me up with black guys. It's equal opportunity all the time with me. Georgina would love to have more black friends. If only they spent more time shopping for scarves in Gucci, then she could meet them.

OK, out comes the lipstick. Why is it that whenever a woman feels nervous, she takes out her lipstick? Curling up in the foetus position I understand, but dabbing red on to our lips? Whatever. Focus, Sarah. Focus, or you'll screw up the lip line. That's it. You're looking fabulous. Remember: you're gorgeous, bloody gorgeous. Greg won't know what hit him when he sees you in this outfit.

I feel like I'm going to war. And in a way, I kind of am. I'm at war with that biological clock that ticks in all of us. TICK TOCK TICK TOCK. As I struggle with the door, I can hear it ticking. TICK TOCK TICK TOCK. Jesus. It's getting louder!

After what seems like an eternity, the door finally opens. I'm so nervous, I'm beginning to work up a sweat. Then I spot the grandfather clock. TICK TOCK TICK TOCK. Thank goodness. Calm down, Sarah. You're fine, just fine. Just get back to the front room. You're going to be fine. Georgina dashes out of the kitchen. 'Sarah, darling! I've hardly said a word to you all evening. What a lovely ensemble,' she exclaims, flicking my dress, 'you do know how to find the most original things, don't you? How are you? How's school? Have you recovered from Djamel?'

I know which question I have to avoid answering. Problem is how to do it. 'Oh, I'm doing very well. Life is great at the moment. And you, Georgina?' I twirl my hair about. 'How's the baby's room coming along?' She's off. Problem solved. She goes on interminably about the colours of the walls, the one they wallpapered, the size of the cot, the type of changing table and the variety of educational toys. Then she tells me that they're trying to find a Chinese nanny to give the baby a head start in life. A Mandarin speaking baby; I'll have seen it all.

'*Ding-a-ling*.' Saved by the bell: Georgina's oven timer. 'Goodness.' Georgina rolls her eyes. 'Already? Time flies when you're having fun. But before I get that, let me take you through to the front room, and introduce you to *Greg*.' She shakes her head, smiling as we walk. 'I just *know* the two of you are going to *adore* each other. I just *know* it!'

Oh, God. Another dilemma: what if I disappoint her? Gosh. There he is: Valentino himself. My knees start to give in. But Georgina, being such a dear friend, has me by the arm and holds on steadfast. Yes, that's right. A pregnant woman, carrying a whole other human being inside her has to help ME to stand up. We approach three figures. There's Greg, John, and Emma, Georgina's colleague.

'Greg, this is Sarah.' Georgina grips me round the shoulders.

'She's my dearest childhood friend. And, Sarah, this is Greg, one of John's colleagues. He works at the hospital as a general surgeon.' Turning to Emma and John, she says, 'You already know Emma, of course.'

'Of course,' I say, nodding. 'Very nice to meet you, Greg.' I hold out my hand. He takes it, squeezing ever so slightly.

I immediately go to work on the chit chat. The four of us discuss the weather initially, following with the glorious sights that London has to offer. When I start to get bored of the truly inane, I start criticising New Labour for not understanding educational issues.

'Politicians have no idea what real schools are like. Not that it's their fault,' I say, determinedly.

'What do you mean?' Greg asks, politely.

'When they visit schools the impression given is always false because teachers and pupils put on a show,' I explain, stealing the opportunity to smile specifically at Greg. 'Then they make fundamental decisions about education policy based on these false impressions. It's quite scary really.'

Emma leans in. 'Yes, it's the same with hospitals. That's why nothing ever changes.'

Greg and John nod and we continue to discuss the dreadful state of the public services in Britain. I describe how it's my plan to help transform inner-city schools.

'Inner-city kids deserve better, and I like being a small part of the struggle.'

Greg takes a sip of his wine. 'Sounds like you really enjoy your job. You're lucky.'

Yeah. If only I could be as successful in my personal life as I am in my professional life. Does one negate the other?

'I suppose I am, but sometimes I feel guilty for not being in a seriously tough school. Now and then I think that to really make a difference, I should be battling it out with major problem cases.'

'Nah. That'd be the same as me saying I should only work in tough hospitals. The rich need medical care too.' Greg howls, smirking. 'My favourite patients are the rich older women. They're so easily impressed and they always give me boxes of chocolates.'

We laugh and discuss the virtues of older women. A little later, when Georgina calls us to sit down to dinner, I dash over to the large mahogany table, eagerly expecting to be told that I am sitting next to Greg. Georgina is certain not to let me down and does as my mind telepathically urges. Greg immediately pulls out my chair, and I, feeling elated, sit down gracefully to dinner.

Emma is sat to Greg's left, while I am to his right. Dinner lasts some time, and Greg and I chat intermittently. We admire the grand lilies at the centre of the table, and we compliment Georgina's fine taste in silverware. Georgina's cooking is also superb, and everyone praises her incessantly. Greg is clever, charming and cute. I am having such a good time that I forget to feel my usual twinge of envy. Sure, I don't know that much about him, but he seems to be exactly what I'm looking for. I'm surprised at how right Georgina has got it this time.

'So, what do you like most about teaching then?' Greg asks.

'The kids. They're perceptive and fun. They notice things that I don't,' I say, chuckling. 'Yesterday some of them told me how cool it was that I live in Brixton. They said I was an honorary gangster. I was kind of flattered.'

Greg laughs. 'They must like you.'

'Yeah. I suppose they do. I like them too.' So this is what it is to feel comfortable and at ease: heart in my chest beating smoothly. If only it could be this way all of the time.

'Attention, everyone!' exclaims Georgina, standing, clapping her hands. Everyone looks up. 'Today is Sarah's thirtieth birthday!' she yells, lifting her glass in the air, 'Happy Birthday, Sarah darling!'

Fuck. Freeze. So much for feeling at ease. People mutter birthday wishes in my direction, smiling, cooing, trying to appear excited. I must seem uncomfortable because Greg gives me a sympathetic look, and then, most surprisingly, he touches my arm.

'Don't worry; I'm single and *thirty-four*. It could be worse.'

YESSS! When Georgina subsequently brings out a birthday cake with enough candles to burn down Buckingham Palace, I'm not phased in the slightest. I stand up, smiling as everyone sings 'Happy Birthday', do a slight curtsy, make a wish, and blow them out with one massive WHOOSH.

Dinner finished, we move to the front room. I notice Georgina and John having what seems to be a serious word inside the kitchen. But I am distracted when I overhear Greg making his apologies to various people, saying goodbye. I start to panic and spring over to where he is standing.

'You're not leaving already, are you?'

'I must, I'm afraid,' Greg winces, pointing to his watch. 'Early start tomorrow. Must get some sleep. But it was a pleasure to meet you.' He holds out his hand.

You mean that's it? You spend the whole evening talking to me, being charming and witty, sending out all sorts of bloody signals, and then 'poof' you disappear? I'm damned if I'm going to give up that easily.

'Well, it was a pleasure to meet you too. In fact, why don't we exchange numbers and meet up for coffee sometime?'

You go get 'im, Sarah! This is the twenty-first century after all. Women are allowed to be forward like that. Wise old Gandhi insisted: 'If you don't ask, you don't get.' And he got married. Didn't he?

'Sure. That would be nice,' he says, smiling.

Bingo. I *knew* it. He's just shy, that's all, shy. White English men are the most awkward men on the planet. What can you expect with a role model like Prince Charles who thinks 'sexy' is telling a girl he wants to be her tampon?

We exchange numbers and say our goodbyes. Then he disappears out the front door.

Youpee. Now I'm counting down the days until our next encounter. Nothing quite like teaching a shy guy how to be wild and crazy with only *you*. Gosh this is going to be fun. Ha! Can't wait. Djamel, shmamel. I'll be laughing all the way to the altar.

· Later that night, I lie in my aluminium double bed feeling pleased with myself. I stare at the spotlights on the ceiling. I started off the day feeling mournful at the thought of turning thirty, and now I've returned with a future husband. Georgina was right to drag me out. That's it: no more Sky movies for me. I'm the new Sarah, Goddess of the Night. Men will be falling at my feet.

I turn over and try to fall asleep faster so that Sunday can hurry up and get here. Can't wait to begin DAY TWO in my life as an energised and happy thirty-year-old.

Chapter three

'AARRGH! WHERE ARE MY FUCKING KEYS?' I'm standing at the red front door of the main house in the rain, shouting so loud that the net curtains twitch in the ground-floor flat. Deirdre, my seventy-year-old neighbour, is disturbed by all the fuss.

Gosh. Mustn't let her see me. Don't want her to worry. I move out of Deirdre's view and spill the contents of my bag on to the porch and sieve through. Nothing. Bloody hell. You always do this, Sarah. What the hell is wrong with you? Why can't you remember stuff like everyone else? Why are you such a moron?

Deirdre's window creaks open. 'Sarah? Is that you, Sarah? Are you OK?' Bloody hell. Poor old woman can barely walk and I have her opening windows in the pouring rain. I jump in front of the window. 'Deirdre, sweetie! I'm fine. Just on my way out.' I lie, pushing the window towards her. 'Now close the window before you catch a cold.'

Deirdre's small and fragile. Her hair is pinky-black from the dye she uses to retain her youth. It's tied in a bun at the back of her head. Her chocolate-brown wrinkled skin is riddled with age spots; she wears a turquoise blue cardigan with rolled-up fraying sleeves. Squinting, she nods.

'OK, dear. Thank you for the milk and eggs you dropped off the other day. Look after yourself in this dreadful rain.' Her clipped English accent – presumably learnt in a posh school in Barbados – trembles as she closes the window and pulls the curtains shut.

21

I peer at my watch: five thirty p.m. As a precaution against my scattiness, I keep a spare set of keys at Jacquie's house, which is only ten minutes away. But she won't be home so early. She's a glamorous writer for the *Guardian*. She's the only black British female foreign correspondent working for a broadsheet newspaper.

The rain turns into a downpour. It always does when I'm wearing a skirt. A silver car tears past booming 50 Cent so loud it vibrates as the rain hits the hood. I scamper to the casual café at the end of my road. It's Portuguese and always full of Brixton's Portuguese community. I run past the boarded-up house next door, which has heaps of old furniture abandoned outside. Looking up, I think I see someone move in one of the windows. I shake my head, wiping the rain water from my eyes. Silly me. No one's lived there for ages. Abandoned by the council years ago, the house has a real tree growing through the roof.

By the time I reach the café, I resemble a drowned gremlin. My shoes and coat are soaked through, and I can barely see for all the water pouring into my eyes. If I could see, I might have noticed the new step by the entrance on the inside. Instead, I push open the glass door with a huff. In doing so, my foot hits the step, and away I go, flying with pure and perfect humiliation. Fortunately the floor breaks my fall and I finish up on my knees and elbows, with my bag's contents spread out before me.

And I thought it couldn't get any worse. You see, a woman with a boyfriend would never find herself in this kind of predicament. Firstly, a woman who is not stupid enough to wake up at thirty without a man would never be so daft as to lock her keys inside her own flat. Secondly, even if by some strange twist of fate she managed to do so, she would only have to call Prince Charming to come and rescue her. I have no Prince Charming. I'll never be rescued. And now I'm flat on my face, soaked to the bone, with all the world looking and taking pity on me.

'My goodness. Are you OK?' I feel a man's hand gently grab hold of my arm attempting to help me up. I can't see him; my hair is in my face, and I'm so wet and flustered and so very, *very* embarrassed.

'Yes, yes, I'm fine…just fine.' I push his arm away. 'I'm OK, really, I'm *OK*,' I snap. What I really want to say is, 'No, I'm not *OK!* Do I look *OK?* I've just made an utter fool of myself and I'm so wet that I can't stop trembling. And you know what else? I turned thirty *fucking* years old five days ago and things have been going downhill ever since. I'm never going to get married and my poor mother will never have the chance to have grandchildren. I will be the biggest disappointment of her life and I will die a failure. He lets go of my arm and moves towards my bag. 'Well, let me help you with this then.' He begins returning things to my bag. I in turn fumble around trying to help him by gathering the bits closer to me. In the disarray, I flinch at my torn tights, and then I see his face. It's a smooth and rather nice-looking face. He has blond floppy hair and piercing blue eyes. A prettier less rugged version of Brad Pitt with Hugh Grant's lost and confused look in *Four Weddings*. Scrumptious.

Dammit. Why do I look like such a mess? This guy is CUTE. I might have caught his attention if I didn't look like I'd just flushed my head down the toilet. My old grey suit jacket hugs my shoulders awkwardly and I try to straighten it by pulling it down over my worn red striped skirt. I scramble around on the floor. I look up and notice something in the man's hand. 'Lawd 'ave mercy' is what my mother would have said. This perfect stranger is holding my Always ultra-thin maxi-pad. Thank God I'm too cold for the heat in my cheeks to show. Even a *tampon* would have been better… At least that would have shown style. You know, sophistication. Jesus Christ, SARAH, what Goddess of the Night wears *maxi-pads*? Why didn't I pack a slim little tampon in some fancy box that snaps shut? Maxi-pads are a sure sign that their owner wears grey limp grandmother-type knickers. Maxi-pads are a key sign that their owner is as single as the Pope. The fact that I have maxi-pads says it all.

Rule Number THREE: *Gotta ditch all unsexy maxi-pad paraphernalia and all unsexy underwear.* The stranger makes no mention of the embarrassing item in his palm and returns it to my bag. When he finishes rescuing my bag, he makes another attempt to help me stand. Having calmed down, this time I let him. And when our eyes meet, I have to lean a little harder on his arm.

'Oh, I'm so sorry…uh…Oh, really. You're too kind.' I gulp, twisting my hair around my left ear. 'Thank you so much…um… I mean…really. No, really. Thank you. I'm just so silly really. So silly. Thank you. I mean thank you for your help…' Shut up, Sarah. Just shut up, you prat. You're laughable. Try to smile. Come on, you can do this. Think 'ATTRACTIVE'. Think 'GODDESS'. Come on, stand up straight. Think 'NAKED'. I try my damnedest to look sexy and the stranger tilts his head. 'The pleasure was mine,' he says, winking and strides out into the rain.

BUT WAIT. I want to shout it out, but my vocal cords won't work. WAIT! I'm single, you know. We could go to the cinema sometime, and I could throw my bag down and you could save it all over again. We might be SOULMATES! But he can't hear the shouting in my head. He continues walking to the High Street in his long black overcoat and black boots, holding a newspaper over his head. Failure #68. Jesus Christ. I'm such a disaster. No wonder I'm single. No point in crying over spilt milk is what my father would say. Yeah, maybe he's right. And I still have to get into my flat.

I sit down at a rickety table in the corner with matching wobbly chairs, take out my old Nokia phone and ring Jacquie. She says she'll leave work early for me so I should expect her in half an hour. After popping to the loo to dry off a bit, I order a hot chocolate and sit sipping, while playing over the scene with the blond stranger in my mind.

'Sarah!' Jacquie shouts, bounding up to me, arms open, as if she's discovered a battered puppy. She's clearly worried about me. She pushes past the table, nearly knocking over my hot chocolate, and gives me a big hug. I must look truly pathetic to warrant such concern. 'Oh, Sarah, you've done it again, haven't you? How many times have I told you to hang your keys up on a nail by the front door?' Jacquie says, sitting next to me. 'You can't keep going on like this, now can you?' I feel like crying. She's right. No, I can't go on like this. I thought I'd be married with children by now, having discussions about whether we should hire a German Mandarin-speaking nanny. How did this happen to me? How am I still single?

Jacquie's thirty-five and glamorous. Her make-up is always perfect, even when it's pouring with rain. She wears braids, and her skin is a smooth rich black. She looks like a tall Lauryn Hill minus the dreads. As usual, she's wearing a burgundy sharp suit with heels, and could appear on the cover of a black woman's magazine. Her classic Armani suit screams power, sophistication and grandeur. Totally career-oriented, Jacquie doesn't care about not being married. She thinks children get in the way. At least that's what she says. I suspect she puts all her energy into work because she's given up on men. Of Jacquie's many relationships, some have been disappointing. And ALL women instinctively want to have children. Yeah. We want a family with 2.4 children and a white picket fence, at least we do deep down. Anyone who claims any different is just lying. But look at what Jacquie's failed relationships have done for her career! I used to wonder whether Jacquie owed the male species a huge thank-you for having made her into such a success, not that I'll ever tell her that. In fact, if she had any idea I dare harbour such ideas, she'd probably stop speaking to me altogether.

As I am obviously rattled, Jacquie resigns herself to a long heart-to-heart and calls the waiter over.

'My, you look fine today,' she says, looking him up and down. 'Can we have a couple of hot chocolates please?' The young freckled Portuguese boy blushes, assuring us that he'll have them for us instantly. The boy gone, Jacquie takes a deep breath in preparation for her pep talk and dives in.

'Sarah, you're a fantastic person. Don't worry about the keys.' She waves her hand in the air. 'Everyone forgets things. It's no big deal. You should really give a spare set to that old neighbour of yours.'

'But I don't want to bother her.'

'Don't be silly, Sarah. With all you do for that woman? Her shopping, her dry-cleaning,' Jacquie rolls her eyes. 'She loves you disturbing her. She's old and lonely for goodness' sake. Don't look so down. Remember: you're an excellent teacher, your mum and dad love you, your friends love you, and you're going to be fine.'

'Yes, but *Greg* doesn't love me,'

'Greg? Who's Greg?'

'He's this dashing guy I met at Georgina's house, on my birthday, a friend of John's, you know, her husband. We exchanged phone numbers; now it's Wednesday, and he still hasn't called.'

'Since Saturday? Hey, no big deal. He'll call. Just give him time.' Jacquie pauses. 'Is he white or black?'

'White'

'Oh.'

'Oh?' I say worriedly. 'What does that mean?'

'It means you have a problem. Had he been black, I'd say give it another week and then start to worry,' Jacquie explains, cocking her head back in that way that only *real* black women can do. 'You know black men and their "black people's time" thing and their "I'm so *cool* that I don't *need* to ring you" attitude. But a white guy? At Georgina's house? Uh-uh.' She wags her finger at me. 'You have a problem…Sounds like these white guys are as bad as the black ones. I thought they were meant to be more committed and responsible…You know, they buy flats and invest in stocks while black guys buy BMWs and still live with their mothers.'

We both laugh. 'Yeah, because a black man's car is his QUEEN,' I joke.

'Uh-huh,' Jacquie agrees, nodding. 'But black men are so fine. If you're going to go out with a white guy who, let's face it, should be called PINK rather than white, and who would no doubt let his dog, if he had one, sleep in his bed…you'd never see a black man doing THAT…yuck…then there'd better be some advantage to it. I just don't get it with these guys who ask for a woman's number and then don't bother calling. Why ask in the first place?' Jacquie yells, wincing. 'Do they really need to score a woman's phone number just to feel like a man? Bloody hell.' She puts her chin in her hand. 'Men are such weaklings. And Greg is clearly the biggest weakling of them all. Forget about him, Sarah. There are more fish in the sea.' I listen to Jacquie's tirade against poor Greg and begin to feel a little guilty.

'Well, he didn't *exactly* ask me for my phone number.'

'What do you mean he didn't exactly ask for your number?'

Jacquie peers at me and moves a little closer. 'Sarah? Sarah, tell me that you didn't ask him for *his* number.' I cut Jacquie off and explain that of course I didn't ask for his number. That would have been far too bold.

'I simply suggested we exchange numbers, that's all.'

'You did WHAT?' Jacquie screams, jumping up, throwing her hands in the air. People look round.

Well it's not like I've decided to become a lesbian. No need to overreact.

'Have you completely lost your mind, Sarah? No wonder he hasn't rung. You're so naïve.' She groans, putting her hand on her forehead. 'He never had any intention of asking for your number in the first place. He just felt awkward when you asked, so he agreed. Of course he's not going to call you!'

Jacquie plonks herself back down. Clearly, this is not the time to tell Jacquie that in addition to my request to exchange phone numbers on Saturday, later on Monday, I sent him a text saying that I was looking forward to hearing from him. Is that bad? Should I have waited? Did I come across as too keen? I just thought he might have lost my number, that's all. I wanted to make sure that he had it. It was just a little text. It isn't like I rang him or anything.

Jacquie looks at me suspiciously. 'I know what you're thinking. This is the twenty-first century and women should be able to ask a guy for his phone number.' She sighs. 'You think I'm totally overreacting. But the fact of the matter is that he hasn't called, has he?' She has me on that one. 'Neither will he ever call. Had he wanted to call you, he would have asked for your number. Yeah, I know. You're thinking, but what if he was too shy? Yeah, right.' Jacquie sneers, rolling her eyes. 'If a man likes you enough he'll move mountains to get you. Even the shyest of guys could have asked Georgina for your number at some later date.' She leans in, whispering. 'Haven't you ever read *The Rules*, Sarah?'

'Rules? What rules?'

Jacquie holds her face in her hands, shaking her head, exasperated. 'Not rules, *The Rules*. You don't know *The Rules*? Sarah, where have you been? And you actually lived in America when you were a child too!' Jacquie screeches, rolling her eyes again. '*The Rules*, Sarah: that book written by those two American women. Basically, it's a book telling us modern women how we need to be if we ever want to get a man.' Aha! I knew Jacquie cared about this kind of stuff! 'Not that I am ever *looking* for a man of course; but you have to keep up with what's trendy when you're in the media business like I am.'

Gosh. I clearly have no idea. People are actually writing books about women like me! More to the point, they're giving advice about how to become as little like me as possible.

Jacquie looks longingly at the door, clearly wanting a cigarette, and dispenses more advice. 'Take it from me, Sarah: NEVER ask a man for his phone number. If he doesn't ask you, then he just doesn't like you enough. Notice I said *enough*. This guy Greg probably liked you. Maybe he spent the whole evening talking to you. He just didn't like you *enough*, OK?' Jacquie taps my arm. 'And this doesn't mean that you're the most unattractive person in the world. It just means that you didn't do it for him, just like the thousands of guys who ask you out on Brixton High Street don't do it for you. Sometimes the shoe fits and sometimes it doesn't.'

Jacquie continues for a while about the peace of mind this 'new' way of thinking will give me, and I listen intently. I start to wish for a pad and pen to take notes. White, black and brown boys, they're all the same: none want to be chased. We talk through past relationships, short ones and long ones, recalling the beginnings, and we try to determine who did the chasing. We conclude that it was always me. I begin to see a pattern: none of my relationships have ever really taken off, and neither has anyone truly *adored* me.

'Men never lose the numbers of women they adore,' Jacquie squeaks, rubbing my hand. 'By behaving as you do, Sarah, you're guaranteeing yourself refused entry on to that pedestal that we women love to inhabit.' Pedestal? What pedestal? 'Remember that Greek actor you went out with last year? What was his name?' Jacquie lifts her eyes to the sky and frowns. 'Oh, yeah: Costas. Sarah, you were always chasing after him, trying to make him happy, and he just took you for granted. Remember?' Yeah. Failure #45. 'Course, I can't blame you for liking him. He was delicious. I love the Greek islands...jam packed with young beautiful Greek boys who aren't used to seeing black women. Yum.' Jacquie squeals, lighting another cigarette. 'And what about that guy Paul the year before...you know, the one with the two cats? He dumped you too.'

Thanks, Jacquie. But he only broke up with me because he hated my freezing cold feet in bed. Well, that, and because I preferred white wine. We could never agree on a bottle over dinner. Well at least that's what he said.

'Oh, and then before Paul...who was it again? Oh, yeah, that light-skinned good-looking boyish one...who broke up with you because he thought you were too serious about him... remember? Not to mention your most recent heartbreak with Djamel.' Jacquie sighs. 'Have you ever seen *me* chase a guy?' I shake my head. 'Have you ever seen *me* get dumped?' I shake my head again. 'Have you ever seen *me* in tears over a guy?' OK. I get the point. 'Men can only ever see their woman as a prize if they've been able to pursue her, work for her, and finally feel they've won her.' Jacquie clenches her fist, holding it up. 'That's why the men who most adore us are always the men who we aren't interested in.'

Apparently, in some twisted way, men actually enjoy being turned down because they need to participate in the chase. Roaming around in my past, I begin to feel silly. I've been going about my man-chase in entirely the wrong way.

Rule Number FOUR: *Gotta let men do the chasing*. After all, I'm a Goddess. Men *should* be doing all the chasing. Remember that, Sarah honey: Goddesses do *not* chase.

We finish our hot chocolates. Handing me my keys, Jacquie kisses me on the cheek. She has an early morning flight to New York. As we walk out the door and into the street and Jacquie lights a cigarette, I decide that the text I sent to Greg will be one of those little secrets I'll never tell, not ever, not to anyone, and certainly never to Jacquie.

Chapter four

I love *The Rules*. *The Rules* have saved me. If I knew that rules would be so liberating, I wouldn't have wasted my teenage years rebelling against my parents.

I spend the next few weeks getting out of my pyjamas, getting out of the house, and getting men to ask *me* for my phone number. Tampons now line my bathroom cupboards. Every Saturday afternoon, I go to an art gallery or a museum on my own. Every Saturday evening, I go to a bar or nightclub with friends. I meet all sorts of men...white, black, brown...short, tall, talkative, quiet. I'm on a mission. I perfect the art of looking attractive *and* approachable. I become an expert at tossing my hair from side to side and cutely tucking it behind my ear. I learn to catch a man's eye seductively while not looking too desperate; always reminding myself that Goddesses do *not* chase.

I meet a variety of pricks, jerks, and the simply boring. But then one Saturday afternoon, I decide to abandon the galleries and go shopping instead. Revamping one's entire wardrobe is a big job and I've only just begun. Having thrown away most of the unsexy contenders, my undergarments are few and far between. I walk up the escalator in Selfridges towards the lingerie department. The store seems even larger than I remember, with women posted at every corner, asking customers to try perfume. The Christmas tree at the centre of the store is magnificent, filling up half the room, dazzling with lights and ribbons. As I climb, I stare at it in wonder. At the top of the escalator I am distracted by the dozens of concessions on women's clothing.

A velvety pair of black bell-bottomed trousers catch my eye in Max Mara and I tear them off the hanger while whipping round to find the changing rooms. As I rotate, the trousers fly into a man's face. 'Whoah!' He puts his hands out and steps back. But he knocks the mannequin beside him and it starts to sway. I dive towards the mannequin to save it before it hits the ground. Instead, I throw myself at the man. The mannequin crashes to the floor. We find ourselves next to it, face to face, me leaning against him, him against a rack of clothes.

Jesus. Jesus. Jesus. He's the most beautiful thing I've ever seen. He's black, black like Wesley Snipes-black with Samuel Jackson's cheeky grin. Tall with a shaved head and a chiselled type face... the kind of face which surely belongs on the big screen.

Right Sarah: don't screw this one up. Now concentrate...think 'GODDESS'...think 'SOPHISTICATED'...think 'NAKED'. It's difficult for the mind to compute when the body is leaning up against a total stranger, surrounded by havoc. But I have to try. Much is at stake. How often do I have the opportunity of being so close to a beautiful black man with a shaved head? I try, and smile awkwardly. He smiles back. 'Boy, I've heard of women throwing themselves at men, but I didn't realise that this was how it's done.'

Match Point. I feel his arms move around my waist, and take hold of me gently. He pushes me up straight and then looks to me for help in standing up himself. His hands still around my waist, I slide my hands behind his back and pull him towards me. We end up standing pressed against each other, in the middle of the chaos, arms intertwined. His arms are strong and his torso tight. I begin to wish I used my gym membership a little more often. He gazes down at me from above and draws me into him as one might do before a kiss.

'Well that was quite an adventure.' He licks his lips. 'We'll have to do it again sometime.' Then he lets go of me and walks away. Deuce. SAY SOMETHING SARAH! COME ON! Just say something for god's sake! He's moving further and further away. Soon it'll be too late. But my mouth won't move. I stand there like a statue, willing myself to speak without success, about to chalk this up as Failure #69.

But then an extraordinary thing happens. He stops at the counter to talk to one of the saleswomen. He's about six foot and built like a footballer. Images of that Gap model Tyson shoot through my head. He points to the fallen mannequin. They both laugh a little. I start to gather hope. Maybe he isn't leaving after all. He turns around and walks towards me. Match Point. He's wearing a tight-fitting navy t-shirt and wide-cut Diesel jeans. My old frayed Levis make me want to dive under the clothes racks. He has a bit of saunter to his walk; a saunter that only the truly self-confident can pull off.

Thirty seconds to make myself presentable…shit. Thirty seconds to calm down, and get ready to be delightful. I'm trying hard to remember the art of tossing my hair and looking seductive, but my brain won't work and I keep brushing myself off as if I'm sweeping crumbs off my lap. Fuck. He's getting closer. Fuck. WHAT DO I DO? Where's Jacquie when you really need her? Come on, Sarah, just be calm. CALM, Sarah…CALM. He's not going to bite. He's just a man. A very good-looking man who can't possibly ever be interested in a girl like me…sure…but he's still just a man. So calm the *fuck* down.

'Hey there.' He twists his head to the side. 'Quite an adventure, eh? You look a bit shook up. Are you OK?'

'Yes. Thank you.' I nod. 'Thank you for helping me up. I'm so sorry for the trouble. I'm a bit clumsy sometimes.' I'm so proud of myself that I begin to smile.

'Ah, don't worry about it. Clumsy is cute…especially on a girl.' He scans the store. 'I was looking for a present for my sister, a nice top of some sort. But I'm not very good at this kind of thing.' He winces slightly. 'Uh…perhaps you might help me as a kind of redress for all the pain you caused me a moment ago?' I laugh.

Game, Set, Match.

'Yes of course I'll help you. What kind of top would she like? How old is she?'

We stroll around the store, looking at women's clothing. 'She's my BABY sister,' he explains, 'but she doesn't think she's much of a baby any more. She's going to turn thirty. And she's having kittens over it.' He shakes his head. 'So I need to find something that will make her feel sexy. She's gorgeous of course, but you women have such a thing about age.'

'She's thirty? Really? So am I!' I place my hand against my chest. 'I just turned thirty ten weeks ago. But I'm not so bothered about it.'

'Oh? So you're a baby too. I just turned thirty-five last week,' he says chuckling. 'Just wait until you get to *my* age…'

He's the perfect age, perfect height, perfect colour. If truth be told, I prefer them black. Can't betray the race. I want to belong to the club. With a white guy, I walk down the street and black guys stare in disgust. Need to be robust to deal with that.

I glance over at my treasure and admire his beautifully formed head, allowing my eyes to wander slowly over his chest and arms down to his hands. OH MY GOD. They're in his pockets. His hands are in his pockets. You're so god-damn stupid, Sarah. Why didn't you look for a wedding ring? He's bound to be married. Everybody's married these days. What thirty-five-year-old man is still single? Jesus. Now I can't tell… Can I ask him to take his hands out of his pockets? Can I? No. Of course I can't. Then what can I do? How will I know? He must be married. He has to be. I panic and start tearing clothes off the racks for his sister. He interrupts. 'Maybe you could try these things on for me?' He points at the clothes in my hands. 'You look like you're probably about the same size.'

WHAT? Jesus. What if I look FAT? What if he hates me? Oh God. I need to bow out of this gracefully.

'Well, I don't know if that's such a good idea...I really should get on with my shopping.'

'No, please don't go; I would love you to try these clothes for me.' He brushes my arm. HIS HAND is out of his pocket. Focus, Sarah. Look to the ring finger. Come on. Is there a ring there? I peer at his hand. NO. No ring! GOAL. Wait a minute. You bloody idiot. That's his right hand. The left is still in his pocket.

I take a deep breath and enter the changing rooms. I put on a skirt and top. The skirt is pink though it means to be peach, is too tight and is riding up my thighs. My bottom looks HUGE. The top is bright yellow and cut in a way that makes me look large and lumpy. I turn to the mirror. I look like an Easter egg. I can't step out there like this. One look at me and even if he isn't married, he'll pretend to be. How the hell have I got myself into this?

I walk out of the changing room, and he looks up expectantly and frowns. Maybe I should turn around and run back into the cubicle? Just hide. No problem. Stay until closing time. No need to come out. He's bound to get bored and eventually leave. He places his hand against the back of his head and cringes. 'Well I don't think it's very flattering, do you?'

Oh God.

'Nah. Take it off. Who makes these clothes anyway? If they don't look good on you, then they won't look good on anyone.' He points his index finger at me. 'Must remind me not to buy stocks belonging to those designers: they're bound to go bankrupt soon.'

Oh, isn't he lovely! I nod in agreement.

'Yes, my bottom looks a bit big in this.' Wish I could swallow the words back down my throat.

'Don't knock it. I'm a black man.' He laughs. 'I'll take

Jennifer Lopez over Gwyneth Paltrow any day.' I giggle and like a fish to water, I fall into my role, naturally trying on different clothes. Coming out of changing cubicles, twisting round to show off the various items, I make Julia Roberts in *Pretty Woman* look like an amateur. As we shop, we chat about all sorts of things. He's easy to talk to and we get on without effort.

'I haven't started my Christmas shopping yet. Have you? Where do you plan on spending Christmas?' I ask. 'I have to be up in Belsize Park with my parents for a week. I only hope I survive it.'

'I plan to go to Nigeria for two weeks,' he explains enthusiastically. 'I'm Nigerian; well I was born in London, but you know what I mean. My parents have retired in Lagos, so I'm going to visit them.'

I wonder if his wife is going with him? Or girlfriend? Does he have a girlfriend? Dammit. His hand is still in his pocket.

'So have you always lived in London?' I ask.

'Nah. Spent four years studying in Boston.'

'Really? Wow. I used to live in New York when I was younger. How'd you like it?'

'You know, I really enjoyed my time in Boston, but I prefer London. It's more multicultural and more relaxed.' He flicks a pair of trousers on a nearby rack. 'I'm an investment banker for JP Morgan. You know? They make me work day and night and I want to relax in the little time I have to myself. Not that it ever happens.'

'You must take breaks sometimes, don't you?'

'No, not really.' He shakes his head, 'No point in doing something unless you do it well. At school I had to get the top marks and today I have to find my sister a present. Hence your involvement…I knew that success would be inevitable with the help of your expertise…I decide on my goal and then do whatever is necessary to achieve it.'

Does he really think I'm indispensable?

We approach Selfridges' main entrance doors, and the conversation comes to its natural end. Bloody hell. Maybe this is it. Maybe he's married after all. His hand is still in his pocket. Maybe he only needed my help to find his sister a present, and now he'll abandon me alone and single, to stay like this forever, to spend the rest of my life fighting off Bridget Jones' Alsatians.

In front of the doors he pauses, and turns to face me. 'You know, I don't even know your name.'

'Oh yeah, well it's Sarah.' I hold out my LEFT hand. 'It's been a pleasure.' Out comes his. He takes my hand and holds it gently. As he slowly withdraws, I glance down quickly to take note of the ring finger. TOUCH DOWN. No ring. Now let's just hope he doesn't have a girlfriend. He looks to the doors. Remember Jacquie's wise words: You're a GODDESS. Let's wait and see if he likes you *enough*.

Oh please God, please God, please let him like me *enough*. I'll do anything…anything you want. Do you want me to give more money to charity? I'll go and find a beggar outside right now if you want. I'll give him all the money I have…Just *please*, *please* let this man like me enough to ask for my phone number.

He takes my hand and gently pulls me in, placing a soft kiss on my cheek. 'I'm Chibu. And the pleasure has indeed been mine. What a great afternoon. First this gorgeous woman literally throws herself at me, and then she kindly spends the afternoon helping me buy my sister's present.' He pauses and points his index finger. 'The number one question of the day, however, is whether or not she's going to give me her phone number.'

WAHEY. Prime City…He asked me. He likes me *enough*! Thank you, God. Thank you. Thank you for saving me from a life of solitude and misery.

I fumble around in my bag for a pen. I pull it out triumphantly. Chibu smiles, pointing to the mobile phone in his hand. Jesus.

Here I am trying to look cool, but with one false move, I manage to demonstrate that a man asking for my phone number is a rare occurrence. The last time I exchanged phone numbers with someone in this way, mobile phones didn't even exist.

Chibu makes no mention of my faux pas and punches in the digits as I recite them. 'Right,' he announces smiling, 'thanks for a lovely afternoon.' He winks. 'I'll give you a call soon.'
'I look forward to it,' I exclaim, taking one final look at his beautiful black head and I walk back into the store to do some more shopping.

'Ladies' Night' starts to play throughout Selfridges and as I walk amongst a selection of very expensive food items, my step picks up pace. I feel like dancing on clouds. As people push past, I step out of the way, smiling from top to toe. I hold my head high and the world is brighter than ever. As I slip past one of the security guards, he smiles at me.

'Good afternoon! Great day, isn't it?' I shout out.

'It is indeed, madam.'

I need to tell someone what happened. I've just met my Prince Charming and there's no one to tell! Remembering that I have my mobile phone, I dig into my bag and pull it out. I ring Georgina. 'I've met the man I'm going to marry! He's divine and I can't wait for you to meet him.' I skip through the store, yelling, with people pausing to stare at my excitement. 'Georgina, he's so cute! You have to see him. I can't believe that he's interested in *me*. I mean, he's *so* out of my league.'

'Oh don't be silly, Sarah. Nobody's out of your league. You're beautiful. You're intelligent, interesting and incredibly fun. He's lucky that you're interested in *him* quite frankly.' She pauses. 'Anyway, this might be a good time to tell you what I've been dreading telling you for the last few weeks.'

'Telling me? Dreading telling me what? What do you mean?'

What could Georgina not want to tell me?

'Well Sarah, remember that friend of John's: Greg?' She sighs. 'The one I set you up with and who you quite liked? The one who never rang you?'

'Yes yes yes. Of course I remember him. Failure #67. Why are you bringing him up now?'

'Well, it's just that I hear he's going out with Emma,' she says hesitantly.

'Emma?'

'Emma. You know: my colleague from the surgery. Apparently they had a lovely time that evening on your birthday and then a few days later Greg rang John and asked him to ask me for Emma's phone number. Ever since I've been feeling terrible because I tried to set the two of you up.' Georgina swallows, taking a deep breath. 'I'm such a bad friend...I'm so sorry, Sarah. Please don't hate me.' My skip turns into a standstill. My smile disappears. I lean against the wall by one of the back entrances to the store. 'Of course I don't hate you. It isn't your fault. And Emma's nice. So if Greg likes her, well, I wish them all the best.'

My mind is working overtime, thinking about the evening at Georgina's house. When Georgina introduced me, Greg was already talking to Emma...And she sat next to him throughout dinner. Jesus Christ. No doubt I was interrupting them all evening. Then to top it all off I asked him for his phone number.

Suddenly I'm hanging by my fingertips from the roof of a sky scraper, the crowd looking up is urging me to jump. They point at me, laughing uncontrollably; some of them are even doubling over, tears rolling down their faces—should I let go?

'Sarah?... Sarah? Are you there?'

'Yes, yes, still here,' I mutter.

'Don't worry, darling. It doesn't mean anything. Greg and Emma have lots in common, both being in medicine.' She insists, eagerly trying to pep me up, 'And Greg is so shy, whereas you're so confident and together. You would have walked all over him.'

Me…confident? Together? My toes turn in slightly as I bend my knees. 'Georgina don't worry. It's not a problem. Anyway, I've met Chibu now. So Greg is a thing of the past. I don't mind about Emma.' I hesitate slightly. 'Really, it's OK. So don't worry. Look, I must dash. I'm meant to meet Manuele for coffee in Covent Garden in twenty minutes.'

We say our goodbyes and promise each other to meet up soon. I throw my mobile into my bag and dash to the tube. I play over my birthday evening several times in my mind. The more I replay it, the more I feel a fool. Jacquie's right. I've learnt my lesson with this one. My face breaks into a grin. Hopefully never again will I have *reason* to ask a man for his phone number. Hopefully, thanks to Chibu, by this time next year, I'll have an engagement ring on my finger, and I'll be sending Greg and Emma an invitation to the most fabulous wedding of the century.

Chapter five

Bloody hell. Why am I always late? I sprint into a cute café in Covent Garden's piazza and look around worriedly. The café is warm and welcoming, with sleek wooden tables, each with a flower in a tiny vase, oozing stylish informality.

Manuele's a sexy, suave Italian who speaks perfect English with a hint of an accent; he's a thirty-three-year-old Shell marketing exec who drives a sexy new VW bug, is loaded with cash and has an ego the size of China.

There he is, short black hair, slight shadow of a goatee, tight red t-shirt and jeans, sitting at the corner table, talking to a very young blonde beauty. I should have known he wouldn't have any trouble entertaining himself. Catching sight of me, he stands up and strolls over.

'Ciao bella.' He wraps his hands around my shoulders. 'Come stai?' Pulling me in, he kisses me on both cheeks.

'I'm well…I'm well. Who's the blonde?' I smile mischievously. He rolls his eyes, showing his palms to the heavens, claiming his innocence.

'Who knows? I was waiting for you and she came and sat beside me. These women never leave me alone…We will go back to the table and she will ask to see me again. By next Saturday, she will be in my bed.'

In ten minutes, this man, who I am very much ashamed to call my friend, has effectively claimed that he can have sex with this girl at the snap of his fingers. What really pisses me off is that he's probably right.

We order a couple of cappuccinos at the counter and return

41

to the table. I place my bags under the seat. I notice Manuele's copy of the book *Enduring Love*. As we sit down, the girl stands up, behaving exactly as Manuele predicted. She giggles and gives him her phone number, cooing and batting her eyes. Ugh. I hope I wasn't that way at her age. Mind you, I feel sorry for her. My darling friend is about to chew her up. Poor thing.

As the leggy blonde tosses her hair back and forth, I start to wonder. These girls are silly after all: they only like Manuele because he's good-looking and rich. Yeah. She's only twenty-two. What does she have to worry about apart from the occasional pimple? I'm facing a destiny of loneliness and she's playing a game. If it weren't for all those *damn* twenty-two-year-olds throwing themselves at our eligible men, there'd be plenty enough for us thirty-something women. Why don't they stick to men their own age? I hope Manuele breaks her heart.

Manuele's snazzy phone is sitting on the table. He picks it up. 'Like my Blackberry? What's your address?' He pushes the buttons as I reel it off. It begins to ring. He gapes at it in horror. 'Take it Sarah. Take it. She'll want to see me tonight. Say that I have gone to the toilet. Say anything.' Manuele presses his teeth together. 'Just answer it for me!'

He shoves the phone in my hand and pushes it up to my ear, pressing the green button.

'Uh... hello?'

'Who is this? Why are you calling my phone?' says a man, huffily.

'I didn't ring you. You rang *me*.'

'You think I was born yesterday, do you?' he snarls. 'What are you doing ringing my phone?'

Manuele crumples his brow.

'I'm sorry, sir,' I stammer, turning pink. 'You must have the wrong number. I'm sorry.' I hang up and look suspiciously at Manuele as I hand him back the phone. 'What's going on? Why is he accusing you of ringing him? You expected it to be a woman, didn't you?'

'Oh, it's nothing, Sarah.' Manuele laughs nervously as he turns the phone off. 'Don't worry about it. Like you said, it was probably the wrong number.'

'Yeah…maybe. But what'd he mean when he said I thought he was born yesterday? Manuele, what's going on?'

'Nothing.' He runs his fingers through his hair. 'Don't worry about it.'

I'm not sure whether I should believe him, but he interrupts my suspicious thoughts.

'I'm seeing this gorgeous Russian girl tonight. She is so sexy. Can't wait to get her back to my place.'

I scold Manuele as usual, and he laughs, saying if only I had eyes for him, he would settle down and have babies.

'You know we Italians love black women.'

'Yeah I do. That's why I'd never touch you with a bargepole!' I snigger. 'Why would I go out with you? You're a lying bastard. I'd have to be mad.'

I've never known Manuele to have a serious girlfriend. His only goals in life are to earn stacks of cash, have loads of girlfriends, indulge in cocaine and wear designer clothes. He tilts his head to the side and fingers his cigarette packet. 'So Principessa, what's new in your life?' Manuele has been calling me 'Principessa' ever since that film *Life is Beautiful*. I've obsessed for so long about finding a man who might tell me 'Buongiorno Principessa' that he thinks it his duty, as an Italian, to act out the part now and then.

I tell him all about Chibu, his chiselled face, shaved head and our crazy shopping spree at Selfridges. 'He's just perfect. Perfect. I suppose we might even get married in a couple of years and then we could have children soon after. Not sure how many though…'

'Basta, basta Sarah…What are you saying? You hardly

know this man. For all you know, maybe he is just like me.' Manuele shrugs. 'Do you think that blond woman believes that I am a scoundrel? Of course not. She thinks she will marry me next year, just as you think you will marry this guy.' He laughs. 'What is wrong with you women? You are all the same, Italian or English, fat or thin, ugly or beautiful. Why do you only ever think of marriage? Why not have some fun instead?'

Did he *really* just say 'have some fun'? What's fun in sleeping with several different people a month?

I try to make Manuele see the light. 'Because "fun" is lying in on a Sunday morning, sharing out the newspaper, and laughing together over an article.'

'Yes, exactly. I did that last Sunday with Sophie. Tomorrow I'll do it with Katya.' Manuele grimaces. 'That way the sex always stays good.'

'Noooo…you dimwit. The whole point is that it's meant to be with the *same* person *every* week. Forever and ever.' I bang the table. 'Sex with the same person doesn't have to be boring. There are lots of different positions you know.'

Manuele nods in agreement. 'Sure there are. Just like you can feel in touch with your moral side when reading the *Guardian*, but when your revolutionary impulses are crying out, you can read the *Independent* and on days when you're feeling pissed off with the high rate of taxation, you can read the *Telegraph*.'

'Yes, exactly, Manuele!' I clap my hands gleefully. 'You can stay faithful to the quality broadsheet newspapers without getting bored!'

'Problem is, Sarah, sometimes men have a deep desire to take a peek at *GQ* and other times we want to get dirty with *Playboy*. And as much as *The Times* may try to imitate the tabloids, it's never going to be a substitute for the real thing.'

'Oh, you're insufferable! Don't you want to fall in love?'

'Love? It doesn't exist. Hollywood made it up so that it

could sell more blockbuster movies.' He rolls his eyes. 'You will spend the rest of your life looking for this "love", never find it and at the end you will realise you wasted your whole life.'

POW! Upper cut into the ribs. Is he right? What if love really doesn't exist? Several world religions don't believe in love. Maybe these billions of people have it right. But there's no way I'm giving in that easily.

'No! You're wrong!' I wave my finger in Manuele's face as he stares longingly at a smoker having a cigarette outside. 'Love is not love which alters when it alteration finds or bends with the remover to remove. Oh no, it is an ever fix'ed mark that looks on tempests and is never shaken...'

'You're quoting Shakespeare now?' Manuele taps his head. 'Bella, I worry about your sanity. You need to relax. You are only thirty. Look at me, I am thirty-three!'

Bastard. It really bugs me the way men who are older than me claim to be in a worse position age-wise. As if anyone could care less what age a man is. In fact, the older he gets, the *more* attractive he gets. WE GALS on the other hand, just get wrinklier and wrinklier. Remember how in *Sense and Sensibility*, Emma Thompson played opposite Hugh Grant as his love interest? Seven years later, *Love Actually* cast Hugh as the romantic lead, but poor Emma was demoted to middle-aged wife whose husband no longer found her attractive. Yeah...A thirty-year-old woman is probably equivalent to a thirty-eight or thirty-nine-year-old man. Single men start to worry when they approach the big 4 – 0. Not that they have anything to worry about of course. Let's face it, the older they get, the larger their pool of choice women. We girlies, however, have a much harsher deal.

A fit of nausea overwhelms me. The room starts to sway. I grab on tightly to the arms of my chair.

'Sarah?...Sarah?...Are you listening to me?' Manuele taps his cigarette packet. Opening up my eyes, I return to reality.

'Sorry, Manuele,' I gurgle, blinking, 'what were you saying?'

'I was saying that you should try to find a date on the Internet.'

'Sorry?'

'The Internet, Sarah , you could meet a lot of men this way.'

'The Internet? But isn't that for real SADDO people who can never meet anyone?'

Manuele raises his eyebrows as if to say: 'Yes?...And?' I sidestep Manuele's left hook and try to come up with a devastating return blow. But all I can think to do is change the subject. 'How's the novel?' I tap the book on the table.

'This one is brilliant. You must read it. This guy is involved in a bizarre accident where a man falls off a hot air balloon and is killed.'

'And it's called *Enduring Love*?'

'Yes. Because the book is about his relationship with his girlfriend...how it deteriorates because of the accident.' Manuele licks his lips. 'It is excellent. I will lend it to you when I am done.'

Manuele loves books. I've never known him to be without one. While his own romantic life is devoid of any meaningful feelings, he seems to experience them in books instead. I pick up the book to take a look, when the café door opens, letting in some cold air.

'OH MY GOD!' I grab hold of Manuele's sleeve and bite my lip. 'It's HIM. Oh my goodness. It's actually HIM.'

'Him? Him who?' Manuele looks around inquisitively. 'The guy from Selfridges?'

'No no no.' I twist his face back towards me. 'The guy who saved my bag in the rain.'

Manuele has no idea what I'm talking about. But he can see I'm smitten. 'So go talk to him then.' He turns and looks pointedly at the blond stranger commanding that I move. I begin to concentrate hard on stirring my nearly finished coffee, deliberately ignoring him. 'Sarah?' Manuele shakes me. 'Are you listening to me?'

'*Look*…he probably won't even remember me. So shut up,' I plead. 'He might hear you.'

Manuele swivels round to look at the stranger who is standing in a queue in front of the counter, his back to us. The stranger is tall and his blond hair is shining in the light. Jesus. *Come on, Manuele…Please don't embarrass me.* But Manuele continues to stare in his direction. My heart beats faster. Manuele looks ready to say something. We have to leave the café. I have to get us out of here. I scan the place quickly, devising an escape. I whisper precise instructions:

'*I'll walk out first, quickly, and then you follow behind. Hopefully he won't even see us. It'll be fine. As soon as we're outside, we turn right and head straight to the tube…no talking until we're safe. OK?*' Manuele stares at me as if I'm mad. But there's no time to waste. I grab his things off the floor, and shove them into his lap. The stranger's still waiting to be served. His back's facing us. It's now or never. I put my plan into action and head for the door, bending at the waist, as if I'm sneaking out. I can feel Manuele behind me. The stranger continues to face ahead. We are paces away from the door. The sun is beaming brightly on to the piazza outside. Freedom is in sight.

Suddenly, I feel Manuele's hands on my shoulders. He grabs hold of me tightly whispering 'Now be cool Bellissima.' Then without warning, Manuele shoves me forward in the direction of the counter, and promptly springs out the door. Paralysed with fear, I fly towards the counter in silence. Luckily, I screech to a halt, my shoulder only brushing against the stranger. He turns around. Oh God. I'm cornered.

'Oh. Hello,' he stammers. 'You're the one who threw open her bag all over the floor of that café in Brixton, aren't you?' Oh God…What do I say? Shall I pretend it wasn't me? No, Sarah. Keep it together. Now be cool. Just as Manuele said. Be COOL. Remember…you're a GODDESS. Stand up straight. Think 'NAKED'.

'Yes, it was me all right. I regularly visit cafés and throw open my bag. It's a shrewd trick I use to meet good-looking men.'

He laughs, and so do I. Yesssss. Full House.

'So, the name is Sam.' He winks. 'And you are?'

'Sarah. Hi. Nice to meet you.' We shake hands and move closer to the counter. When the waitress asks for an order, he asks me what I want, and then orders two coffees. We sit down. I immediately note that his ring finger is bare, and he has a couple of silver rings on his other fingers. We speak of the rain on the day we met, of the new step that I tripped over, and of how fashionable Brixton has become. He's an artist and he also lives in Brixton.

'What I love about Brixton is that there's a real mix of people there now.' He contemplates the ceiling. 'I like the multicultural aspects of it. Fifteen years ago, there weren't that many white people, but nowadays I think they outnumber the black ones…Not so many of you lot pushing in front of the bus queues any more.'

I chuckle. 'Yeah, you may be right, except for the kids I teach…I'm a teacher…they'll push in front of anyone! But with so many of you white lefty artist types, the clubs are packed with a bunch of people who do that head-banging thing when they dance.'

Sam laughs. 'Yeah OK, point taken. So you're a teacher. Cool. I love Brixton. The last time anyone spoke of race riots was in the mid-nineties. Funny how some people are too scared to go south of Pimlico, eh?' Sam laughs. 'Well, maybe they'll change trains at Vauxhall, but that's as far south as they go.'

'Whenever I walk down Coldharbour Lane amongst "the hood",' I whisper, making quotation marks with my fingers, 'the drug dealers never speak to me.'

'Yeah, well, that's because you're a woman, and more importantly a black woman. They ask me if I want to buy something every time I walk down there. Can't blame them though.' He shrugs his shoulders. 'We middle-class white guys are their prime market. If it weren't for us, they'd probably go out of business!' Sam's eyes open up. 'Don't you just love the market? Especially on Saturdays?'

I nod reluctantly. 'I suppose so; I go there now and then. But my favourite Brixton hangout…I must admit, is the mini Sainsbury's by the tube.' Sam laughs out loud. Can't tell him WHY I like Sainsbury's though. Can't tell him that I love the great selection of READY MEALS. Can't tell him I buy ready made meals for two reasons: the first is clearly so I won't starve, but the second is because it's a *key* place to meet eligible single men. At the market, you only ever meet beggars and women pushing buggies.

Sam is cute and witty. His smooth face, blond hair, boyish charm, and smile are to die for. However, as usual, there's a 'BUT': his clothes. His big black boots and black overcoat make him look a bit like one of those rock artists from the 1980s minus the long hair. His black cotton trousers are shapeless and covered in zips and his black t-shirt sports the red face of Che Guevara. I begin to wonder whether I might be able to influence him in this area…a few key Christmas and birthday presents…some sharp shoes, and hey presto, no more need for black boots. Hmm…This one will need some serious work.

'So do you prefer teaching the boys or the girls?' Sam asks, coyly.

'Well, I like them both, but I think boys are easier to teach. They don't hold grudges the way girls do. If they get angry, they just have a fight. Girls can be really manipulative.'

Sam laughs. 'Sounds like some things never change!'

Sam explains that like me, he's a member of Virgin Active gym in Clapham. While we like trendy Brixton, 'The Rec', short for Recreation Centre, is too 'street' for either of our tastes. Raid the Rec at prime time, and you could set up a jewellery shop with all the collected gold.

'Sometimes I feel guilty for going to Virgin Active,' I explain. 'Feel like I'm not being true to my people or something. It's like I'm saying the Rec isn't good enough for me, but it is for other black people.'

'But you're an individual,' Sam retorts. 'You should be able to work out where you want.'

'Yeah I know. And I so love the towels they give you there. Can you imagine them giving towels out at the Rec?' We laugh. 'Clearly I'd abandon all my principles and sell my soul for a bit of convenience.'

'I love the gym. I'm there at least four times a week. It's so invigorating; especially the sauna. I can't go without it.' Sam gulps down his coffee. 'Hey, how come I've never run into you at the gym before?'

Shit. Maybe it has something to do with the fact that I'm never there.

'Must be that we go at different times.' I pause, thinking carefully. 'I tend to go in the late evenings.'

'Really? But so do I!'

Fuck.

Sam draws his eyebrows together. 'When were you last there?'

Jesus. Now what do I say? Do I lie? 'Well, I'm not sure, let me see…' I start to count on my fingers as if I'm counting the days. As I count, I skilfully brush my hand against my coffee cup, tipping it over.

I jump up as the remnants of coffee dribble on to the table. 'Oh my goodness!' I shout. 'I'm sorry. I'm so clumsy.' Sam hurries to the counter to grab some paper napkins.

Once he's finished mopping up my mess, I leap up.

'Thanks a lot. Sorry about the mess. I suppose I should be going now.' I smile.

Sam stands up like a gentleman and insists on walking me to the tube. We push open the café door and walk out into the crisp air.

'Great to be able to meet you properly this time. You were so cold and unfriendly the first time we met, I didn't dare ask to see you again.'

'Cold and unfriendly? What do you mean? I was very polite to you.'

'Yeah, polite, cold and unfriendly. I was helping you with your bag, but it felt like I had you at gunpoint.'

Hmm. I suppose back then, I didn't know how to look approachable. In front of Covent Garden tube, Sam asks for my number and I'm an old hand at it. I wait for him to take out his mobile phone, then recite the digits at an appropriate speed. Sam squeezes my hand gently.

'Good to meet you.' He gives me a nod of the chin. 'I'll ring you soon.'

'Yes,' I beam, 'very nice to meet you too.'

I sit on the Victoria line, feeling satisfied. In one day I've given my number out to two potential suitors. My new lifestyle is coming along well. We've just passed Pimlico, heading south to Brixton, when I notice one of the advertisements above the small older Chinese man sitting opposite me: 'Love and Friends: The Internet Dating Agency for Thinking People.' Hmm. Maybe Manuele's right. Maybe I should try out different avenues. What if neither Sam nor Chibu ring? Yeah…'thinking people'…I'm one of *those* kinds of people, aren't I? I've heard thousands of stories of people meeting on the Internet and finally getting married. So why not *me*? As I stare at the poster, I sense a presence in the next carriage, as if someone is watching me. Maybe it's some delicious thirty-something guy?

I get up and peer through the connecting door, but no one's there. Now I'm imagining things. I return to gazing at the Internet sign and the Chinese man in the seat opposite. He's wearing a wedding ring. I wonder whether his wife is taller than him. I wonder whether he's happy. He's wearing a funny silver jacket that's too small for him. I wonder whether his wife bought it. No doubt he met her when he was fifteen. Maybe her parents introduced them back home. Then they immigrated to Britain some thirty or forty years ago…to open up a restaurant…planning a better life for their children. He's never had sex with anyone else. I wonder whether he and his wife are soulmates? And I wonder what he would think of *me* logging on to the Internet to find a soulmate for myself?

He glances at me and smiles. Yeah…Just as I thought. He doesn't think it's such a bad idea either.

Chapter six

The 'Love and Friends' webpage is colourful and upbeat. It prompts me to continue. I sit feet up on top of my beech computer desk in my bedroom and click to view some of the members' profiles. Right. Type of man? Well, let's see, say between the ages of thirty and well...forty? Yeah, that sounds about right. His marital status? Oh...well, tick the single box, oh and also the divorced box. Divorced is OK, isn't it? WIDOWED? Am I so old that my potential suitors might be *widowed*? OK, let's tick that one too. Why do they have a box saying 'MARRIED'? Why would I want to meet a guy who is already *married*? That would mean that he couldn't marry *me*.

I scroll through the dozens of profiles. Some are accompanied by a picture. No ogres or weirdos: just ordinary guys looking for love...just like me. Maybe London is the problem. So many single people, but we just can't meet each other. Yeah. What do I have to lose? I create a profile page and upload the best photo I can find of myself. Finished, I scroll down, reading through:

FIRECRACKER

Wild, wacky and wonderful. Pretty Princess seeks charming and clever Prince to whisk her away, or at least help her to find her keys. I can't cook or clean, but I am heaps of fun and a little hard to handle, for you guys who like a challenge. Favourite film of all time is Amélie because it shows that oddballs can also find love.
Occupation: *History teacher in a secondary school in South London. I'm even head of my department. Imagine that!*

Education: *BA in History*

Religion: *Used to believe in God but I've been single for so long now that I'm convinced He doesn't exist.*

Languages Spoken: *Some French and a little Italian.*

Music Enjoyed: *All sorts really. Classical, R&B, Ella Fitzgerald.*

Sports and exercise: *I am a member of Virgin Active. I never go. Well, sometimes I go and use the Jacuzzi.*

Interests and activities: *The cinema. And Sky movies. And reading trashy novels. Oh, and walking and travelling.*

Animals and Pets: *I like dogs. And I have a teddy bear...my best friend. Need I say more?*

Newspapers and magazines: *The* Guardian *and the* TES.

Books: *Those Shopaholic novels are great.*

Favourite Films: Casablanca. Breakfast at Tiffany's. Amélie. Waiting to Exhale. The Way We Were. Sense and Sensibility. When Harry Met Sally. Crash.

Enjoyable evening out: *Cinema, Theatre, Restaurant.*

Favourite Dishes: *I love all types of food. If only I could cook!*

Ideal Holiday: *Beach holidays and I like walking and exploring – especially with someone else!*

In another life: *Audrey Hepburn.*

The photo of me is reasonable. I don't look like a superstar, but I'm attractive enough to inspire a few replies. Well, at least I hope I am.

Right. Now my heritage, simple enough; seven choices: White, Hispanic, Mediterranean, African, Afro-Caribbean, Oriental, Asian, and Other. OK. Maybe it isn't so simple. Am I White or Afro-Caribbean? Well I'm not white...obviously. I must be Caribbean then. So I must be black. My cursor starts to slide to the Afro-Caribbean box. But I've never even *been* to Jamaica. I pause. It has to be 'Other' then. OTHER? What am I? An extra-terrestrial? But what else can I choose? 'Other' it is then. Maybe I'll get lucky and get zapped by Will Smith or Tommy Lee Jones.

I'm hungry. I go to the kitchen and open up my dreary plywood cupboards. The kitchen's in need of redecoration. Staring back at me are old pots of jam, some cans of baked beans and a few bags of unopened rice. Dammit. I don't want to go to Sainsbury's now. It's dark and cold outside and I'm having fun with my computer. About to shut the cupboard, I catch sight of one forsaken can of minestrone soup. Brilliant. I can have some dinner after all. I put the soup on the stove, return to the computer and discover a message. Already? Boy, this thing sure works fast.

Message from 'King Arthur'*: Hello Princess. Perhaps you might accept a King instead of a Prince? You are the far side of irresistible and I wish to know whether I might send my chariot for you. I am eternally in your service, Arthur.*

He's funny. Reading the rest of his profile, I discover that he's single and thirty-six. He's a barrister and lives in Waterloo. He loves long walks and the cinema. His father is Scottish, his mother English, and he grew up in North London. It's always hard to tell from a photo, but he seems of average height, brown short hair, a kind of younger version of Tony Blair with a slightly bigger nose. To the question 'Who would you have been in a past life?', he writes 'Plato'.

Dear King Arthur, Firecracker thinks it most exciting to meet a King instead of a Prince. Is your chariot drawn by two horses or four? And where will it take me? And why Plato? Sarah

His reply arrives almost instantly.

Message from 'King Arthur'*: My Lady Sarah, I am afraid that my chariot is only equipped with two horses but I assure you that it will provide the most luxurious and exciting of voyages. You need only say when, and it will be at your door to whisk you far far away. Arthur PS. Plato was very wise and loved the law.*

Gosh. This guy's a fast mover.

Your Highness, I could not possibly meet you when I know so little about you. Tell me more about yourself so that I should decide whether or not our meeting might be fruitful. Sarah

This time, his reply takes a little longer. To pass the time, I flick through the dozens of cards from school kids on the table. I open the largest one, which has a massive four-leaf clover on the front. *'Dear Miss…You're the best History teacher. No, you're the best teacher full stop. Thought you might need the four-leaf clover for good luck seeing as we have our exams next week and you always say that if we fail then that means you fail too. Jacob. PS. I'll come back and visit.'* How sweet. Jacob got an A in the end. Never thought we'd get there. Gosh, what if the kids were to find out about me and the Internet? Ugh. I look back at the screen.

Message from 'King Arthur': *For my Lady Sarah – her wish is my command. I am thirty-six and I would like to meet a nice and generous person who is interested in something long term. My work keeps me busy. I am in criminal law, not corporate. So unfortunately I am not rich like some of my friends. Hence only two horses on the chariot. However, what I lack in finance, I make up for in charm. I go to the gym two or three times a week and I cycle and go walking on the weekends. What about you? Arthur*

I write about the children at school and how I love teaching them. I write about my hatred of the tube and my love of buses. And I explain that this is my first time communicating with a total stranger on the Internet.

Message from 'King Arthur': *Dear Sarah, Yes, it does take getting used to. I have been doing this for some months now. I have met some nice women but no one who I have really connected with. But everyone has been very polite. It has been wonderful to meet so many interesting people who I would never normally get the opportunity to meet. I am tired of only* *ever meeting barristers and solicitors. Especially as so many of them are men! Arthur*

After a few emails, I discover that Arthur lives in a fabulous flat next to the South Bank which he inherited from his grandfather. How fantastic is that? I rush my reply.

Dear Arthur, The South Bank is my favourite part of London. The beach is especially nice in the summer. Do you hang out there much? Sarah.

Message from 'King Arthur': *Dear Sarah, I love it there. Sometimes I wander up and down the banks of the Thames for hours when thinking about a particular case. Recently, I've been thinking about this young man who I've now defended three times in court. He's always getting caught for petty crimes and he won't stop. He isn't much older than your pupils. Do any of your pupils ever end up in trouble with the law? Arthur*

I'm about to explain how I once visited Brixton prison to get one of my pupils out of trouble when suddenly I smell burning. OH MY GOD. The soup! I dash to the kitchen and find the sorriest sight of burnt soup on the old kitchen gas stove. Now I'm burning soup. I'm actually BURNING canned soup. What the hell is wrong with me?

Too furious with myself to indulge in food, I return to the computer, my stomach rumbling. Arthur and I continue to email each other discussing politics, and current films. I discover that his favourite restaurant is in Brixton. It's Ethiopian and he thinks it exquisite and unique. I look up at the wall clock above my bed. Ten p.m. Jeepers. I've been on the computer for hours! Gosh. Getting to know Arthur has been a good thing. Meeting Chibu earlier in the day at Selfridges seems like ages ago. I've also stopped obsessing about him. This Internet dating thing hasn't been so bad. Arthur and I finally say goodnight and bizarrely, we also write: 'See you tomorrow' even though we have no plans to meet. I've made a friend and I'm happy.

I start to draw the sheer long white curtains which protect

the front room from the neighbourhood's eye. I notice a figure below on the pavement by the boarded house next door. He's wearing a hood and scarf and he seems to be searching in the hedge. Wonder what he's searching for? He looks up at my window. Gulp. I quickly draw the curtains to a close and escape to the loo to get ready for bed.

I sit on my spotted grey duvet with Bear. Bear is medium size, dark brown with lots of fur. I call my teddy bear 'Bear', just as Holly Golightly calls her cat 'Cat' in *Breakfast at Tiffany's*. Not that I'm anywhere near as glamorous as Audrey Hepburn. But Holly is a lost soul, looking for direction and looking for love. I identify with her completely. I look Bear directly in the eyes.

'Met THREE men today, Bear. Can you believe it?' I hold him up above me. 'Met *three* of them!'

Today's been a good day. Going to bed hungry is just par for the course. Holly would be impressed. Hugging Bear close, I pull the covers to my chin and fall asleep with Tiffany's diamond rings sparkling in my head.

Chapter seven

When I tell Jacquie about all the excitement in my life, she demands we see each other. So Tuesday after work we meet in the Ritzy café in Brixton for a drink. It's bohemian, full of people from all walks of life and an extra helping of lefty *Guardian* readers. We grab a seat outside on the second floor next to the wall covered with film posters. The ashtray on the table is full of cigarette stubs and Jacquie pulls it towards her. She has just flown in from San Francisco, but still looks as glamorous as ever in her silver suit and mauve lipstick.

'God do I hate San Francisco...they won't let you smoke anywhere. Smoking is even banned outside in some places...mad Americans.' Jacquie lights a cigarette, her eyes gleaming. 'So, Sarah...tell me *everything*.'

My story recounts every detail from crashing into Chibu in Selfridges to my first meeting with Sam in the Brixton café, followed by our second encounter in Covent Garden. Of course I can't forget Arthur. I explain how I decided to try out the Internet thanks to Manuele's advice. Arthur and I are writing to each other a few times every day, and it has now been three days since we first 'met'. Even though I've never seen Arthur, given the time we've spent communicating, I know him best.

'Chibu, Sam and Arthur. Bloody hell, Sarah.' Jacquie raises an eyebrow. 'Leave some for the rest of us, won't you? Geesh. With you around, I'll stay single forever.' She laughs, sitting straight up. 'So have any of them called yet asking for a first date?'

'No. But it's Tuesday today and I met them Saturday.' I pause and count my fingers. 'So I'm still OK, right?'

Jacquie blows out some smoke while eyeing a youngish light-skinned black guy who is sitting inside.

'Oh yeah. My bet is that one of them will call tonight. I think Arthur sounds the most interesting. A barrister...how exciting.' Jacquie plays with her diamond necklace. 'Hmm...I wonder which one it will be...Well, which one do you *want* it to be?'

'Well it can't be Arthur because he doesn't have my phone number. But I can guarantee that he'll have sent an email. He sends several every day.' I pause, curling my hair. 'As for the other two...I prefer Chibu really. He's just so gorgeous and perfect.' I cross my fingers. 'Fingers crossed he'll call me. Sam is good too, but those clothes...And he seems pretty young.' I shake my head. 'I don't know how old he is, but he can't be more than thirty. Arthur is great of course, but I haven't met him yet.'

'My money is on Sam calling tonight. Chibu is Nigerian.' Jacquie rolls her eyes. 'It'll take him at least a week to call.'

Jacquie's mother is Ghanaian and her father Nigerian. She's had several years' experience of what she calls 'the late, irresponsible Nigerian man'. I suspect that another reason Jacquie is so adamant that a guy should never get to her is because she spent her childhood watching her father cheat on her mother time and time again. And that will never happen to Jacquie.

'Well, whatever.' I shrug my shoulders. 'It isn't as if I have anything planned for this weekend anyway.'

Jacquie looks uncomfortable. She raises her eyebrows and goes into that 'silent teacher act' that I do several times a day when pupils do things that make me unhappy. 'You did read *The Rules*, didn't you, Sarah?' I nod, desperately trying to remember what Rule I've just broken. Jacquie holds her head in her hands. 'Listen very carefully to me. DO NOT and I repeat DO NOT agree to go out with any of these guys this weekend if they call you after tomorrow. If they call after Wednesday, they don't get a weekend date. And you know why?' Jacquie taps the table. 'Because you have such a busy social life, packed full of men and friends. If they don't book you in time, they miss out.'

'Oh yeah.' Her advice is ringing bells. 'Because I'll look too desperate, right?'

'Exactly.' Jacquie pauses to light up a cigarette. 'Remember, Sarah: men need to feel as if they've worked to get you or they'll never adore you. They want to feel as if you're so in demand that you don't really have time for them. So when you finally make time for them, they think that *you* think they're something special.' She blows out some smoke. 'Don't always pick up the phone. Let them think you're out having a ball. And always make sure you end phone conversations first.' She points her cigarette at me. 'You'll see how quickly they get jealous. Men are just children really.'

Rule Number FIVE: Gotta look busy and in demand. OK. I can do this. It's simple enough. Just think 'BUSY'. I can do that. I'm a BUSY Goddess. Jacquie cuts into my train of thought.

'The other thing to remember is that you need to look the *business*. You've been doing a great job recently of revamping your wardrobe. Make sure you wear something sexy on your dates.' Jacquie pulls her top down to her chest. 'Reveal a little, but not too much. Don't want to look like a tramp. And put on some make-up, Sarah,' she scolds, waving her hand in my face, 'more than just lipstick. Try to make more of an effort. You're pretty really, but you never slow down to make yourself look truly beautiful.'

But what the hell have I been doing for practically three months? Have I not been making an EFFORT?

'Sarah, what about your hair? You could do with a bit more of a funky haircut. You don't have a permanent hair stylist, do you?'

I shake my head.

'Sarah! What kind of a black woman are you? Right. Just a second.' Jacquie grabs her bag and searches through. She takes out her mobile, scrolls her numbers and puts the phone to her ear.

'Hello? Yes, hi. Does Jean-Pierre have any spare time tonight for a haircut? Tell him it's Jacquie. Ask him if he can fit me in. It's for a friend.' There's a pause. 'A cancellation? Great. We'll be with you in ten.'

What? But I haven't even thought about…Jacquie grabs her bag and mine. 'Come on. We're going.' She pulls me up. 'We'll have to take a cab.'

We skip along Coldharbour Lane to the minicab office. '24 hours car hire 071 274 0165' reads the lit sign. The out-of-date area code betrays its age; so do the peeling paint and tatty shutters. Looking up at the several 'For Let' signs, I knock one of the stands outside the Phoenix restaurant. It sells hot jacket potatoes. 'Brixton's Finest', it boasts. As we jump into a cab, a drug dealer winks at me.

'Battersea. And step on it.' Jacquie snaps authoritatively. A police car shoots past us, its siren wailing. Ten minutes later we step out on to the pavement in front of Jacquie's hairdressers in Northcote Road. The pristine pavements and faultless façades make Brixton's shops seem like young special-needs children trying to take their first step.

Black women spend half their lives in hairdressers. The first ever black American female millionaire made her money from black hair products. But Jacquie thinks Brixton hairdressers lack sophistication. They may be open at eleven p.m. on a Sunday, but with names like 'Shaz Hair Studio' and 'Real McKoy Girlz', I suppose I can see why Jacquie avoids them. I grab hold of Jacquie's arm and tug.

'I'm not sure this is such a good idea.'

'Don't be silly. You'll be fine.' Jacquie locks her arm through mine. 'Just trust me.'

Jean-Pierre is a very camp black French hair stylist who has leapt out of a seventies comic strip. A cross between Graham Norton and Trevor Nelson, he wears stretch jeans and a skin-tight white t-shirt, carrying the most enormous Afro on his head and several beaded necklaces around his neck. 'Darleeeng Jacquie!' Jean-Pierre rushes towards us, brushing past the grand display of exotic flowers. 'Ah, ma belle…' He kisses Jacquie on both cheeks, making a kind of 'moowah' sound with each kiss. Jacquie plays her part in the performance, constantly calling him 'sweetie' and whispering in his ear. Tossing his head back, he turns to me. 'Ah? This is she?' He flaps his hand about in the way that only very camp men do. 'Yes. Hmm.' He spins me round. I feel like a life-size doll. 'Hmm. Not much life in this.' He flicks my hair. 'Too stringy.' He laughs.

OK OK Mr Shaft. No need to open fire. I try to talk, but every time I open my mouth Jean-Pierre 'shhes' me, saying that he's thinking and waiting for inspiration. He continually throws his hands up to the sky in a dramatic fashion, each time shouting 'Vas-y, Jean-Pierre!' He looks as if he's in pain. Suddenly he cries out.

'Aha! I haf got it! Ah oui!' He turns to Jacquie. 'Darleeng, you vill just luf what I vill do.'

Hello? Yes…it's me here. I'm the one whose hair you're cutting. Hello? Miss Marie Antoinette? Yes…over here. Don't you think you might want to tell me what you plan to do? Don't you want to ask me what I would prefer? Hello?

I look at Jacquie with desperation. She holds my hand. 'Don't worry, Sarah. I promise, he's a genius with hair. He'll make you look five years younger.'

Younger? I'll go to hell and back to look younger. And I'm always commenting on how Jacquie looks so glamorous. Maybe Jean Pierre can do the same for me? Albert Einstein said that if you're not willing to make a mistake, then you'll never try anything new. Must be courageous to change. But what the hell does Albert Einstein know? Just look at HIS hair! The image of Albert Einstein's hair is enough to make me bolt through the door. But I'm already lying back with my head in the sink with some woman's hands massaging shampoo into my hair. There's no escape. I'll just have to close my eyes and pray.

An hour later, Jean-Pierre swivels me round to face the mirror. Jacquie jumps up and down. 'SARAH! He's transformed you! Just look at you.' Jacquie claps, kissing Jean-Pierre on the cheek. 'Just look at what he's done! You're gorgeous.' It's true. Jean-Pierre has done a marvellous job. I'm a different person. Wow. Fantastic what a haircut can do. My hair has gone from being a bit of a mess to sleek, smooth and shiny. Jean-Pierre stands next to us, chest puffed out, Afro to attention, arms folded, chin up, looking proud. The other hair stylists and Jacquie crowd round to get a better look. Some people even pat Jean-Pierre on the back. Was I really that bad before? Evidently so.

'The rain in Spain stays mainly on the plain.' I feel I should stand up and shout it out. I'm Eliza Doolitle in *My Fair Lady*. All that's missing is Professor Higgins saying: 'SHE'S GOT IT! I THINK SHE'S GOT IT!' Question is: do *I* now have *it*?...God I hope so. We pay out heaps of money, thank Jean-Pierre by 'moowahing' in every direction, and head back to Brixton.

Outside Brixton tube, the *Socialist Worker* people scrutinise us, wondering whether they should try to get new comrades on board. The old black woman who begs by drawing pictures and framing them in foil sits by Iceland on her dirty cardboard boxes, sucking on her comb and making it sing like a harmonica. Jacquie taps me. 'Now Sarah, you have some make-up at home, haven't you?' I nod. 'Good. Go home and try some. You look beautiful. You really do. You'll knock those guys over this weekend.' Jacquie says, winking. 'Anyway, I must run, I have a date later tonight.' Before I have the chance to ask about her date, Jacquie gives me a kiss and disappears down the street. Walking to my flat, I pass one of Brixton's bookshops; the novel *Enduring Love* is in the window. Manuele. Must give him a ring. I wonder what that bizarre phone call was about. I hope he's OK.

I pick up Deirdre's post, and knock on her door.

'Just me, Deirdre!' I holler.

The door opens. 'Hello, dear.'

I hand her the post. 'You well? Look at my new haircut.' I rush my fingers through my hair.

'Thank you, dear. Oh yes, it looks nice, dear.' She squints. 'Would you like a cup of tea?' I hesitate. What if one of the boys rings while I'm down here? Poor thing. She's all alone. If the phone rings, I can always run upstairs and grab it.

'Of course I would. But you sit down.' I push past her into the flat and close the door. 'Go sit down now. I'll make the tea.'

Deirdre hobbles to the tattered patterned sofa in the front room as I fill the kettle with water. Her turquoise cardigan is fraying at the edges and elbows. The flat is dark and small with lots of little ornaments on every surface. The raised wallpaper with funny purple flowers is lifting up near the ceiling and the ledge above the fireplace holds a framed greying photograph of a young man. He reminds me of Harry Belafonte. I have no idea who he is, of course. It's the only photo she has and I don't dare ask.

'Here we go sweetie.' I rush towards her with two cups of tea. 'I put in three sugars, just as you like it.'

Deirdre smiles, crinkling her fragile brown skin, and takes the cup and saucer from me. It shakes slightly in her hands. I sit next to her on the sofa which is covered in that plastic covering that sticks to you when you get up.

'So how are you?' I ask.

'Fine dear. Just fine.' She winces. 'Apart from the arthritis of course. It seems to be getting worse. I went to see Dr Van Den Burg on Thursday and he increased my medication.'

She speaks for some time about the doctor's visit and her aches and pains and I nod respectfully.

'You know, dear, perhaps next time I go to see Dr Van Den Burg, you could come with me.' She smiles mischievously. 'You would do well to meet a doctor like him.'

Even Deirdre's concerned about me. 'That's quite all right, sweetie. Don't worry about me.' I pat her on the knee. 'I'll be fine.'

'Well, I haven't seen a man with you for a while; that's all.' Deirdre looks a little embarrassed. 'And we all need company from time to time, don't we?'

'Yes, maybe you're right.' I grin awkwardly. 'Well, just let me know when you're next going.'

Hopefully she'll forget. We speak for a short while until we finish our cups of tea. Great. I can get upstairs now and wait for my phone call. I take the cups back to the kitchen, wash and put them away. I move to the front door.

'OK then, Deirdre. See you soon. You sure you don't need anything from the shops?'

'Yes, dear. I'm fine for now.' She waves. I shut her door behind me and skip up to my flat.

Following Jacquie's advice, I try out some mascara in front of the bathroom mirror. '*Brrring*.' EEEKS. I wonder if it's one of the boys. I wonder if it's Chibu. My heart beats faster. I throw down the mascara and fly to the phone in the front room. OK, Sarah. Be calm. Think GODDESS. Remember: BUSY GODDESS.

'Hello?'

'Hello, Sarah dear. How are you?'

'Oh. Hi Mummy.' I sigh. Isn't it amazing how mothers always have the most dreadful sense of timing? 'I'm fine. And you and Daddy?'

'We're OK. Your father is coming down with a cold; he hasn't been well. I'm a little worried. He has even stopped his gardening.' Her Jamaican accent resonates on the phone. 'This means he's spending a lot more time in the house with me and he is starting to get on my nerves.'

'But Mummy, he always gets on your nerves.'

'Yes but now it's all the time. He keeps interrupting when I'm watching *EastEnders* and *Coronation Street*. Sometimes I just wish he would hurry up and die and leave me on my own.'

'Mummy! You can't say things like that!'

'Oh dear, you know I'm just joking. But perhaps you might like to invite your father to visit you on his own, one weekend afternoon?'

What? Have my dad spend the afternoon constantly reminding me of everything I'm doing wrong? No thank you.

'Listen, Mummy, I'm sort of waiting for an important phone call.' I pout. 'Do you mind if we speak tomorrow?'

'Of course, dear. Is he handsome?' My mother chortles. 'Remember that boyfriend of yours who had the two cats? My oh my, what a pathetic something or other was he. What man has two cats?'

'Yes, Mummy, I know. He was a bit boring.'

'Boring? That's putting it mildly. I remember your father wondered whether he had been dropped on his head when he was little. I don't know why you can't find a nice boyfriend who will look after you. It isn't that hard, is it?'

'Yes, Mummy, I'm trying. But I'm waiting on a phone call.' I sigh.

'OK, Sarah dear. I'll pray for you. Speak to you tomorrow.'

Annoyed and somewhat disappointed, I hang up and dial Manuele. I'll just find out what happened with that phone call in the café. Two minutes. Anyway, maybe finding my phone is engaged will make Chibu think I'm super-busy with a super-social life.

'Hello?'

'Hi Manuele. It's me Sarah. Just wondering how things are with you…Still curious about that strange phone call in the café.'

'Promise you won't get angry.'

'Get angry? Get angry about what?'

'Just promise.'

'OK OK,' I say eagerly, 'I promise. Now tell me.'

'I've been seeing a married woman.'

'A married woman? You're seeing a married woman?' My voice increases in tempo and tone. 'What do you mean you're seeing a married woman?'

'Just that. I'm having sex with a married woman. Now remember you said you would not get angry, Sarah.'

'What?' I scream. 'What if her husband finds out? Not to mention that it's plain wrong.'

'Now, now, you promised. Anyway, her husband is getting suspicious. That was him who rang my phone the other day when you answered.'

I shake my head in disbelief.

'It's the perfect relationship for me. I get all the sex and none of the emotional commitment. Of course I get a little scared now and then. Especially when we meet at her place. Her husband is a big guy who could easily put me in the hospital.'

'So what the hell are you doing? And you do it at her place! Oh my goodness. You're so going to get caught!'

'But that's part of the excitement. It's racy and ups my heartbeat,' Manuele says, cockily. 'She's lovely.'

Lovely? I've never heard Manuele say a woman's lovely before. Is it because he can't have her? We always want what we can't have. 'Look, I must go,' I sigh. 'I'm waiting for the Selfridges guy to ring. Please be careful with your married affair.'

'I'll be fine. Don't worry. Try to get some sex, OK?'

I go to my computer and log on. As expected, there's an email from Arthur:

Message from 'King Arthur'*: Hi Honey, I'm home! What a day! Someone broke into my car while I was in court today and* *stole the radio. It is such a pain. Anyway, how was your day? How were the kiddies at school? Arthur*

Dear Arthur, I've had a great day. The kiddies were fine, and I just had my hair cut. Now I have a chic layered look that frames my face, blow-dried straight. My friend Jacquie forced me to do it. I don't really know what looks good on me, but she is trying to put some life into my sense of style. Sarah

Message from 'King Arthur': *I'm the same way. I own a bunch of suits, robes, and wigs. I never know what to wear on the weekends. Sounds like I need your friend's help! When I was at school, I was so grateful for that school uniform. Never had to think about what I was wearing. I had a hard time as a teenager. None of the girls ever fancied me. I was top of the class and a bit of a spod. Not sure much has changed! Arthur*

Gosh. I hope he's not another Sam on the clothes front. But he looks rugged in his photo. Bizarre clothes on a rugged guy might be cute.

Dear Arthur, Well, there's more to life than clothes and being popular. I was just the same at school. I like to think I was an ugly duckling. (I.e., now I'm a beautiful swan.) So don't worry about being a spod. Maybe you were an ugly duckling too! Sarah

Message from 'King Arthur': *I certainly hope so. I'm glad you are so confident. Nothing I hate more than a woman who will do anything to please her man and who doesn't know her own mind. As a general rule, I tend not to go out with women under thirty. They're not feisty enough for me. So you just made it into the search I did on the site! Arthur*

Dear Arthur, Well you're a man after my own heart. If thirty is a good thing in your book, then you're a good thing in mine. What happened to that boy you were defending? The one who is always involved in petty crime? Sarah

No one is ringing dammit. Jacquie said one of them would ring tonight.

Message from 'King Arthur': *He spent a couple of weeks in a youth detention centre. He's back out on the streets. But he'll probably be back in court before the end of the month. I don't understand why he doesn't learn his lesson. Anyway, I want to meet the infamous ugly duckling or rather the beautiful swan. What do you say to meeting up for dinner one evening next week?*

Dear Arthur, Yes, we should meet I suppose. But I was thinking about this yesterday and part of me doesn't want to meet for fear that meeting might ruin our relationship! Do you know what I mean? Sarah

Message from 'King Arthur': *I do know what you mean. But we cannot go on like this forever. We must meet. When are you free? Arthur*

I'm in the middle of thinking of what date to suggest, when the phone rings. Jesus. OK, Sarah, move to the phone…Think GODDESS. BUSY GODDESS. You can do this. Just be cool. I leap into the front room. 'Hello?'

'Hi. Is that Sarah?'

'Yes it is.'

'Hi there, it's Chibu. Thought I'd give you a ring and see whether you've recovered from our little tussle.'

Yes yes yes yes yes yes YES. Awhhh…this is brilliant. He called! He called! OK. Stay calm. Can't seem too excited Sarah. Just be cool. And be busy. And end the conversation first. And what else did Jacquie say again?

'Oh…hello there. Yes…I'm just fine. I had my hair cut today.'

'Oh? I hope you're still as gorgeous as you were on Saturday. I'll have to inspect this new haircut. Are you free this Friday to have dinner with me?'

There is a God.

'Uh…I *think* so.' I lie. I have nothing planned for the entire weekend. 'Yes, I think Friday should be fine.'

We chat for about ten minutes. I twiddle with the cord to my stork floor lamp. Following Jacquie's advice, I say I have some work to do and end the conversation. We set a date for seven thirty p.m. on Friday. As he'll be in the area, he says he'll pick me up at home.

I ring Jacquie immediately and tell her. I point out that she was wrong about one thing: Chibu the *Nigerian* called first. Then I ring Georgina. She's thrilled for me. She starts making plans to invite both Chibu and me to her baby's christening. Yeah. Georgina's the only one making sense. Manuele's suspicious of Chibu because he's a man. Jacquie's suspicious of Chibu because he's a *black* man, and worse still, a *Nigerian* black man. Georgina believes he is what he seems to be: A charming, clever, catch of a guy who is one hundred per cent interested in *ME*. So I put on MTV as loud as it will go, and dance to my heart's content.

Chapter eight

My metallic bed is covered with eight different pairs of trousers, six tops, and three skirts, and several pairs of shoes are scattered on the floorboards. I need help. I ring Georgina. She's on maternity leave, so she has time for stuff like this. She heads straight over. I open the front door.

'Thanks for coming at such short notice.'

'Sarah, darling, I'm here now. It's fine. John's been at the hospital since forever, so I have little else to do. You're in good hands.' Her bump pushes out under her silk maternity blouse. Georgina kisses me on both cheeks. 'I may be a happily married *pregnant* woman, but I can still remember how to look glamorous for a date.' God it *irritates* me the way she says that damn word 'pregnant'. I wish I'd called Jacquie instead. Georgina smiles, gives me a hug, and I forgive her instantly. She takes a peek at her watch. 'What time's he coming?'

'Seven thirty.'

'Right. We have two hours. No time to lose. Go have a shower and wash your hair. I'll get some food ready.' She rubs her large tummy.

I do as I'm told. I slap a whole load of conditioner on my head in the hope that it'll make my hair soft and shiny. I take a brand-new razor out of the packet and draw it across my legs and underarms. Perfect. They look great. I look between my legs and feel rather less pleased. My little cat is in need of a trim. Shit. What do I do? Wait a minute, Sarah. Let's not overreact. He's not very well going to see any of this, now is he? It's your FIRST DATE for goodness' sake. Of course. I'm being silly.

I stand in front of the foggy bathroom mirror. God I'm fat. I should have spent the last two days dieting. Oh well. Too late now...

I cover myself in moisturiser as if somehow the process of rubbing will break down some of the fat. I bet we black people are responsible for half the purchases of E45 cream at Boots. No, scrap that...at Superdrug. It's cheaper. Wrapping myself in a towel, I tiptoe into the front room to see what trouble Georgina has got herself into.

On the birch Ikea dining table is a bowl of what looks like 'designer salad' and a plate of fruit.

'Georgina! Where did you get all of this from? My cupboards are empty.'

'Yes, I know they are. That's why I brought all the ingredients with me.' She hands me a plate of salad. 'Come on, eat up. I'm the "date expert". I'll get the hairdryer.'

As Georgina waddles to my bedroom, her hands supporting her back, I stare at the salad. It's just vegetables and lettuce. No big deal. Then why can't I make them? Because there are so many different types of lettuce these days, that's why. Oak leaf, rocket, cos, and God knows how many others. Which one goes with which? How does Georgina know these things? Remember the days when only iceberg existed? Remember when you ordered salad in a restaurant, you knew exactly what you would get? Nowadays, it's anyone's guess. And how can I be so predictably incompetent in the kitchen that Georgina *knows* she has to come prepared? God I hate her.

She returns, and on the table she lays out the hairdryer, four clips, three different types of brush, a comb, a pair of straighteners, and a pair of curling tongs.

'Now you eat and relax. You won't get fat eating salad, so you have no excuse. I'm going to make you look like a star.'

I start munching. Georgina firmly believes that as a woman, eating is necessary before *all* dinner dates. That way, I won't be hungry later and tempted to stuff my face in front of a potential husband. She's right. First impressions are important. The trick is to eat *early* enough so that you can still eat during the date, and to eat *little* enough so that you'll still look *thin* for the date. Thin. Ha! If only. I already look like the Michelin Man.

Georgina spends the next hour tugging at my hair, pinning it up, pulling it down, heating it up, cooling it down. While she works on my head, I paint my nails. Doing my toes is an acrobatic stunt with my legs suspended in the air and Georgina tugging at my hair, but we manage it and my finished pink toes look fab. Georgina stands in front of me with a twinkle in her eye.

'Go take a look.'

I scamper to the large silver framed mirror above my two-seater Ikea sofa. Georgina flicks my hair. 'Lovely, isn't it?' She smiles. 'When I was single, I used to transform my own hair.'

'Yes I know, sweetie. Thank you for helping me out today.'

We head back to the bedroom. I try on everything in my wardrobe two or three times. My French bottom is massive. Finally we decide on the very same bell-bottomed trousers which I threw in Chibu's face, with a sheer ever so slightly see-through black top. On my feet I have a pair of black strappy heels. Sexy, but not vampy. Chic, but not slack. Cool, but not cold. God, I hope he'll like me.

Georgina sits me down at the dining table and places out in front of her all the make-up you could ever wish for. By the time Georgina finishes with me, I'm ready for Hollywood. She takes out some Gucci perfume from her handbag and sprays it in my direction.

'*Voilà*!' She throws open her arms. 'Sarah, you're a princess!' She wraps her arms around me. 'You're so lucky. I wish I could be single again.'

'Thank you, Georgina.' I hug her tight. She's so decent. At the drop of a hat, she rushes over and spends hours making me look right. The fact that she's only weeks away from giving birth hasn't bothered her a bit. She's a tower of strength. I steal a glance at the mirror. Not bad. *I'd* fancy me if I were a guy. I'm not Naomi Campbell, but I'm not Frankenstein either. I'm OK really. At least I *hope* I am.

'Georgina, do you think he'll like me? I mean, what if he only dates white women?'

Georgina opens her eyes wide, placing her hands on her hips.

'White women? If he only dated white women, then he wouldn't have asked you out. Anyway, why are you so bent on being with a black guy? I've never really understood you saying that you're black. Aren't you just half and half? You're not exactly Oprah are you?'

'No, I'm not Oprah. But neither are Halle Berry, Ms Dynamite and Alicia Keys and you'd never say they weren't black.' I'm not as glamorous, but they also find it hard to find a decent man. Now you know we're in serious trouble if even Halle Berry takes a hundred years to find a man.

'But Sarah, being single is exciting and fun.' Georgina squeezes my shoulder. 'You're quite lucky really.'

Clearly she's trying to be kind. How ridiculous. I walk Georgina to the door downstairs and she kisses me on both cheeks.

'Best of luck with your black prince tonight, Sarah. You'll have a great time. I just know it. He's so much better for you than Greg. More spunk. You need someone who can keep you on your toes. You would have just walked all over Greg.' She opens the front door. 'A black guy is best…Greg has probably never even been to Brixton.'

'But maybe Chibu hasn't either,' I reply.

'Oh you know what I mean, Sarah.' Georgina folds her hand over. 'Being mixed-race, a white guy might feel out of his comfort zone with you, but with Chibu, you won't intimidate him.'

'Yeah, it'll be great,' I grin. 'I won't have to worry what his friends or parents think of me. And I'll be able to walk down the road in peace. No more feeling guilty for having given up on black guys.'

'Given up?' she asks, making a face.

'Because so many of them wear loads of gold. YUCK. And the ones who don't, know how rare they are, and just take the piss.'

Georgina chuckles. 'Oh Sarah, you're exaggerating.'

'Oh yeah? How would you know?' I wink at her. 'You've never been out with a black guy...Anyway, it looks like I've found my One. He's perfect. Just what I've been looking for.'

'Yes darling. Must run, taxi's waiting.' She kisses me again on both cheeks and skips over to the black cab. As I turn, I notice the curtains move in Deirdre's flat.

I still have some time to kill. So I log on to 'Love and Friends'. My inbox is full of emails. For the last few days I've been writing to two different guys: Charlie and Jack. I've also set a date with Arthur for next Wednesday. Arthur and I are communicating daily and I'm coming to depend on our interaction.

Charlie's an interesting guy who lives in Brick Lane for the 'culture'. Stick a bunch of Indian and Chinese people somewhere and suddenly the place has culture. He's a social worker; working with people with HIV, and he wants to change the world. He's thirty-four and says he's reasonably fit. There's no photo and Jacquie warned me not to date guys without photos. But isn't that superficial? Shouldn't I only be interested in the kind of person he is?

Brrring. Oh my God. Who could that be? Knowing my luck, that'll be Chibu ringing to cancel. Maybe I'll just let it ring. No. Don't be stupid Sarah, if he's cancelling, then you want to know. You don't want to spend the whole evening waiting for him to show up.

I pick up the phone. 'Hello?'

'Hi. Is that Sarah?'

'Yes it is,' I chirp. 'Who's this?'

'It's Sam'

WHAT? SAM? But it's been a whole week. Hmm…Well, maybe Chibu needs some competition. As Manuele said, maybe he's a dickhead. Who knows? And Sam's so delicious. Might as well keep my options open. 'Oh, hello. Yes, I remember. Nice to hear from you.' I pause. 'Have you had a nice week?'

'Yes, very nice. But I've been working too hard, and I thought I would call and see if you wanted to catch a film tonight.'

TONIGHT? Why do men never plan in advance? 'Oh. That's nice of you.' I twist my hair behind my left ear. 'But I'm afraid I'm busy tonight. How about next weekend? Say Friday?'

'OK, sounds good. I'll ring you in the week to confirm. You have a good weekend.'

'Yeah, you too.'

HOLE IN ONE. On top of the world! Sam actually called. It's just as I predicted. I have men queuing at the door. Who said thirty was the end? Bloody Djamel. It's only the beginning. I'm not going to be the eternal spinster everyone feels sorry for any more. That's right. I'll be Mrs Sarah Somebody. Next week I have a date on Wednesday with Arthur, a date on Friday with Sam, and if all goes according to plan with Chibu, maybe I'll even have a second date for Saturday. One of these HAS to come with eternal happiness. Just call me GORGEOUS. I'm one hell of a Goddess out of control.

Chapter nine

Ding dong. Jesus! Seven thirty already? OH MY GOD. My coat, my shoes, my sequinned bag...What else do I need? Quick. Think quickly, Sarah. Lipstick, lip liner, mascara, eye liner, money, bank card, you never know, he may leave you stranded...OK. Check the mirror. Good. You're all set. Yikes! My keys, musn't forget my keys...*Ding Dong*. Jesus! Yes, I'm coming. I'm nearly there. Just hang on one god-damn minute.

I open the front door.

'Buongiorno, Principessa.' Chibu, his hands stretched out, takes a bow. He's wearing a black classically tailored jacket with a crisp pink shirt. The top two buttons are undone. 'Is my lady ready?'

This has to be a trick. Somebody is having me on. There is no way this guy is for real. No way. They just don't make 'em like this. Men like this only exist in my head. Chibu stands up straight, mouth gaping.

'Wow.' He takes a step back. 'I was on my way here thinking, I hope she's as gorgeous as she was last Friday, especially with the new haircut, and here you are, you're even more gorgeous than before.'

He's good. I have to give him that. I might just faint right here and now. Chibu takes my hand and leads me to his car. It's a little silver Audi TT, those funny round ones that were trendy a few years ago. We jump in and he puts on Marvin Gaye.

'Hope you don't mind some Old School.'

'No no, Marvin Gaye is great.'

We drive to a little Italian restaurant in Notting Hill which Chibu says he loves. He lives nearby but closer to the Ladbroke Grove end. The Kensington side has too many bankers and he's tired of hanging out with City people. Chibu sits up straight as he drives. What a relief. Ever notice how some black guys drive almost lying down? You'd think there was a television in the roof of their car. Chibu's fascinated by the fact that I'm a teacher. He considered going into teaching at university, but decided against it because of the pay.

'I'm a Nigerian you know, I've already disappointed my father by being a banker. A teacher was just out of the question.'

'Really? But banking is so prestigious, well-respected, I mean…shouldn't he be proud of you?'

'You'd think so. And I think he is proud in a way. But every Nigerian father wants all his sons to be doctors. Luckily, my eldest brother bit the bullet and became a surgeon. He now works at Chelsea & Westminster Hospital. When we were young, he wanted to be a pilot but dad just wasn't having it.'

Chibu parks the car on a side street, and before I have the chance to push myself off the car seat, he's waiting by the door to help me out. He grabs hold of my hand, 'Come on,' he whispers, and feeling cold, we hurry along to the restaurant. Above us stand grand and imposing buildings, and I note the number of very expensive cars hugging the pavement. Gosh. Brixton is a far cry from this place. Sometimes I forget what the rest of London is like.

Chibu opens the door and we are greeted by several Italian waiters. The place is small and intimate, with a log fire in the corner, just perfect for an intimate dinner for two. Everyone working in the restaurant knows Chibu. Waiters shake his hand or wave in our direction. I wonder how many other women he's brought here? Am I just some floozy who all these waiters feel sorry for?

The waiter takes us to a table in the corner by the fire, pulls out my chair, and nods at Chibu. 'Buona Sera.' He does a little bow. 'I see we are not dining alone tonight, sir?'

Phew. I'm not a chump after all. Chibu's slightly embarrassed. 'I come here a lot, often on my own after work.' He looks around. 'I work all the time and this place is so laid-back, the food is good and the service is quick, which is a rare find in England.'

I've died and gone to heaven. Is it real? Is it possible I've found my Prince? I order fish, the sea bream, and a side order of mixed vegetables, in an effort to be as feminine as possible. Chibu orders pasta.

'Service is generally much better in America than it is in England, don't you think?' I venture.

'Definitely. It drives me mad the way restaurants are run over here. That was one of the great things about Boston...fabulous restaurants with fantastic service.' Chibu smirks. 'But this place is run by Italians so they manage to reach my high American standards for service while managing to avoid the temptation of serving massive portions.'

'Yeah,' I say nodding. 'I spent some of my teenage years going to school in New York, when my dad's business took us over there; I know exactly what you mean.'

We talk throughout dinner, never having to search for conversation. He loves opera and football. Saturday evenings are spent at the ENO or the Royal Opera House and Sunday afternoons are spent in front of the television supporting Chelsea. I don't know much about either, but I do my best to show interest. 'So why do you support Chelsea?'

'Because they're the best. I used to support Man United, but then Chelsea became the better team.' He nods, smiling. 'What's really important is belonging to the winning side.' I'm slightly taken aback. He winks at me. 'I like pursuing perfection. I suppose it's my favourite sport.' I start to wonder what the hell he's doing, coming out on a date with ME. I try my best to be charming and witty while remaining elegant and poised. I flirt with the tossing of the hair thing, though I struggle with the batting of the eyes. We discuss our favourite films, holidays and television programmes. Predictably, his favourite film is *Pulp Fiction*. Bizarrely, his favourite holiday spot is Chamonix. Gosh. A black man on skis. I went skiing once in my life, but that was on a school trip and I only chose to go because some boy with a brace and freckles was going. Right. I'll have to learn how to ski. Sixteen years on and my life is exactly the same.

'I took my sister skiing last winter but she hated it. It was too cold. She says black people aren't made to hang out in the cold.' He strokes my hand which is sitting on the table. 'My sister thinks that I'm a coconut.'

'So you're white on the inside...' I say jokingly, 'I knew there was something wrong with you.'

'Yeah...because I like skiing and opera. She's so crazy. I try to see her a couple of times a month. She lives in Islington.' He rubs his head. 'But I hate Islington. Too many chain restaurants on the High Street.'

'So you live in Notting Hill for the quirky independent cafés?'

'That, and the fact that it's mixed and cosmopolitan. The race riots of the 1950s were a long time ago. Imagine, Notting Hill used to be crammed full of black people barely able to make ends meet and now it's jammed with brokers and bankers...Ha!' Chibu hoots. 'Nowadays, riots only take place in your neck of the woods.'

'No they don't,' I interject. 'Brixton just has edge to it, that's all. A lot more exciting than Islington, I can tell you...But your sister likes it?'

When Chibu speaks of his sister, it's obvious that he adores her. I begin to realise that she is, of course, like all black women in their thirties... SINGLE. Jacquie once quoted me a statistic that I will never forget: Fifty per cent of black British women will never find a permanent partner. Jesus. How depressing is that? And what are the statistics for white women? They never quote statistics for white women. So if only because of this statistic, I have to know...Am *I* black?

'Don't know why she's single really. She's beautiful, and she can cook.' He laughs.

Gulp. Now is probably not the time to tell him that I live off a diet of canned soup.

'So I bet the boys all sit in the front row in your classroom huh?' He winks at me and I blush slightly.

'No, not really; it doesn't work that way.'

'What do you mean? I remember having a real thing for my English teacher when I was fourteen.'

'And you probably misbehaved more in that class because you were trying to get your teacher's attention!' I argue.

Chibu places his hand against his chest. 'Moi? Misbehave? But I'm such a *good* boy.' We laugh and munch on our food. We talk for some time until Chibu looks at his watch.

'Goodness. Look at the time. It's midnight.' He tilts his head to the side. 'I should take you home before you turn into a pumpkin.'

Oh God. He hates me. He wants to go home. Dammit. Should I have ended the date first? Does the same principle, of ending phone calls first, apply to dates? Bloody hell. I think it does. Now I've gone and ruined everything. Chibu asks for the bill. In the usual way, I reach for my bag as if I mean to pay. As any gentleman would, he tells me to put my bag away. I gloat, thanking him politely for dinner. He is as perfect as perfect gets. And I'm head over heels crazy about him.

Chibu and I sit in the car outside my flat. I look up out of the car window and notice the dozens of Sky dishes stuck to the sides of the houses. A Rasta man struts by, whistling.

'Shall I walk you to the door?' Chibu asks.

God, he's perfect.

'Oh. How nice. But no.' I curl my hair between my fingers. 'No really, it's freezing and it's only a few steps. You stay inside the warm car.'

'But then how will I kiss you goodnight?'

WHAT? How the hell am I meant to answer that one?

Without warning, Chibu leans over from his seat, pulls me into him and kisses me. His lips touch mine softly and then he tugs me in closer and opens his mouth ever so slightly, holding me tight.

God, it's so nice. I haven't been kissed in what feels like AGES. He draws me in some more and we begin to kiss as if we'll never have the chance to kiss again. Taking my face in both his hands, he pulls back slightly, gazing at me. And then, as if he can't help himself, he kisses me again. Oh God this is good. You know that poem? *'Give me a kiss, and to that kiss a score; Then to that twenty, add a hundred more'?* I could kiss him forever. We're all over each other. Chibu is practically in my seat. And then I remember. OH MY GOD, SARAH. Get him off you. Just get him off. You have to get him off. You have to get out of here before all of this gets out of control. I push him back.

'What? What's wrong?' He asks, looking inquisitively. 'Have I done something wrong? Don't you like me?'

Of course I damn well like you…It's precisely because I like you that I can't let you see the lack of grooming down below. BREATHE, Sarah. BREATHE, for God's sake. Maybe I'll disappear into a puddle in the style of the wicked witch of the west. My heart's beating so loud. I wonder whether he can hear it. I stare straight at the floor.

'Sorry, I'm sorry. Uh, thanks for the evening. I mean for the dinner. Uh, thanks for the lift. You know, in the car…beats taking the tube…' WHAT ARE YOU SAYING? Just shut up. Just shut up. Just get out. You have to get out of here. JUST OPEN THE

BLOODY DOOR! Completely disoriented and half-dazed I grab at the door handle. I can't find it. I can't see. I can't feel anything. Jesus. Where is this bloody handle? Just keep smiling, Sarah. Don't look like a prat. Finally, my hand hits the handle and I stumble out with great difficulty.

'Are you OK?' Chibu lowers his head so that he can see me through the door. 'I hope I didn't come on too strong.'

'No, no. I'm fine.' I brush myself off. 'Fine. Must go, that's all.'

'OK…Arrivederci, Principessa.' He does a kind of half salute from his forehead.

I slam the door and march to my front entrance. I turn the key. Dammit. The car's still running. God I wish he'd go away. I stand inside the door, turn, and wave. Finally, he's gone.

I sit on my bed. 'Oh BEAR! Look at what a disaster I am. I just ruined the most perfect evening and now he'll never want to see me again.' Fuck. I was doing so well too, until the car bit. I just screwed up at the end. Now he'll think I'm some neurotic spinster who's so crap in bed that she's scared of inviting men in. Has he been put off for good? Can I still salvage the situation? Will he ever ring again? He said, 'Arrivederci, Principessa'. Does that mean goodbye as in 'adieu' in French? Or does it mean I'll see you again as in 'au revoir'? WHICH ONE IS IT? ADIEU? or AU REVOIR? I have to know. I shoot out of bed, nip to the phone, sit on the sofa and dial Manuele.

'Hello?'

'Manuele, I'm so sorry to ring at this hour, but I have to ask you something.'

'Sarah…? But it is one a.m. I'm with my married sweetheart.'

'What? Where are you?'

'I'm at her place. Her husband is out of town.' He whispers. 'She's upstairs in bed. I've just come downstairs to get a glass of water.'

'Manuele…you're taking too many risks. What if her husband comes home?'

'Oh, stop worrying. Anyway, what are you doing ringing me now? Shouldn't you be having sex?' He asks, sighing. 'Did the Selfridges guy call?'

'Yes and we've just been out and I need to know does 'arrivederci' mean goodbye like aurevoir or adieu?'

'It means "goodbye".'

'No, but which one? Au revoir or adieu?'

'What do you mean *"which one"?* It means "goodbye".' He snaps, irritated. 'What else do you want it to mean? Anyway, I have to go. Nancy's waiting'

I plead with him to give me a couple more minutes and I try to explain the difference between adieu and au revoir. I beg for an answer.

'Well, we have a word "addio" in Italian. No one ever uses it.' He cringes. 'But I suppose this must mean that "arrivederci" is the same as "au revoir". Is that *it* now, Sarah? I really must go.'

YIPPEE! 'Yes yes, that's it, sweetie. Thank you so much. Go have fun,' I say, giggling. 'Give her thousands of orgasms!'

'SHIT.'

'What's wrong?' I ask, worriedly.

'I think that might be her husband at the door.' I hear doors opening and closing in the background. Manuele goes silent.

'Manuele? Are you there? Manuele?' Silence. 'Manuele? Is everything OK?'

'What the fuck is going on?' a man shouts in the background and then I hear a big crash.

'Darling!' screams a woman. 'What are you doing home?'

'SHIT SHIT SHIT.' Manuele shouts wildly. Another crash and then a door slams.

'Manuele? What's happening?' My heart begins to race. Silence. 'Oh my goodness. Manuele? Are you there?' More silence. I'm on the edge of my sofa, strangling a cushion. 'Manuele? What's happening?'

'Who is this?' a man gruffs down the phone.

I jump back on the sofa. 'Who me?' I squeal. 'I'm nobody.'

'Nobody? Just like nobody was fucking my wife. Who is he? What's his name?'

Oh my God. Oh my God.

'What's whose name?' I shriek.

'You think I was born yesterday, do you? Tell me who the fucker is, you bitch.'

'Listen, sir, I don't know who you are or what you're talking about. No need to be rude.'

'I'll tell you what's rude…' he gruffs. 'Tell me who he is…'

'Wrong number.'

'You think I was born yesterday, you bitch?' he yells.

GULP. 'Must go to sleep.' I squeak. 'Sorry.'

I hang up the phone and then take it off the hook. I hug one of the sofa cushions tight. Bloody hell. I hope Manuele's OK. Had better leave the phone off the hook till morning.

I shoot back to bed and hold on to Bear. It's OK Bear. He has no idea where we live. SHIT. Manuele's fancy new phone has my address. OH MY GOD. God I hope Manuele's OK. This guy isn't going to come looking for me, is he? SHIT. I lie in bed with Bear staring at the ceiling. I can't fall asleep; I'm wondering whether Manuele is OK and panicking that the husband might come after me. I try to think of Chibu. He was saying 'au revoir' not 'adieu'. We're OK, Bear. I squeeze him tight. Chibu may call again. We won't be banished to the fifty per cent of the population who never find a permanent partner.

Ding dong. I shoot up straight in bed. FUCKING HELL. Fuck. It's him. Fuck. What do I do? Fuck. I sit still. *Ding dong.* Fuck. Do I open the door? *Ding dong. Ding dong. Ding dong.* OK, OK, OK. Calm down. He can't hurt me. Can he? Fuck. I hide Bear under the covers, jump out of bed and run to the kitchen and seize the biggest knife I can find. I open my flat door. *Ding dong. Ding dong.* OK, OK, OK. I'm coming you idiot. Should I run back to bed? Fuck.

I twist my head round the doorway and peek down the stairs. I push my flat door wide open. I look down at my feet in furry grey socks, and flinch at my flannel puppy dog pyjamas. Can I answer the door looking like this? Do I really want to be found dead in Lassie pyjamas? Ding dong. Ding dong. I creep down the stairs, knife behind my back. As I pass Deirdre's door, it flies open.

'Aarrgh!' I scream, dropping the knife.

'Aarrgh!' Deirdre shrieks. 'Sarah! What are you doing?' She pushes open the door and looks to the floor. 'Why are you carrying a knife?'

Before I can answer, the figure whose shadow we can see through the window, bangs really loudly on the door.

'Aarrgh!' Both Deirdre and I hang on to each other for dear life, terrified. I push her back into her flat. 'Don't worry,' I say nervously. 'It'll be fine. Just go back inside.'

She doesn't argue and pulls the door nearly to a close, but leaves a sliver to keep an eye on me. I bend down and pick up the knife. I tiptoe towards the front door.

'Sarah,' Deirdre whispers, 'what are you doing? You can't take that knife with you!'

BANG BANG BANG.

My insides feel like they're going to leap right out on to the carpet in front of me. Tomorrow's *South London News* will read: 'Single teacher stabbed to death on very night she found true love. She died alone.'

'Sarah! Sarah! Is that you?' The outsider calls out.

Manuele? 'Manuele, is that you?'

'Oh thank God! Open up, Principessa.'

I quickly undo the latches and swing the door open. Manuele is standing on the doorstep, in a pair of trousers and socks, with no shirt. We rush to hug. I pull him in tightly, the knife still in my hand.

'My goodness, are you OK?' I ask.

'Yes fine, he has my phone, that's it. I have my wallet. I need to cancel the phone.' Manuele puts his arm around me and moves us inside, shutting the door. I catch Deirdre winking, as she pulls her door shut.

'But that means he has my address on your phone, dummy,' I grumble.

'Don't worry. We'll cancel it right now,' Manuele says, smiling.

'How did you get here? Did you walk?'

Manuele nods. 'Well, ran more like.'

'Let's get you upstairs then. You must be frozen.'

'Yeah. Can I stay the night on your sofa?' Manuele scrunches his lips together, trying to make himself look cute, as we climb the steps to my flat.

'Of course you can, Mr Casanova. I'll get some sheets. My sofa, is your sofa. You know that.' I tap him on the back and wag my finger at him, 'And you can promise me that you'll never have an affair with a married woman again.'

Manuele shakes his head while rolling his eyes. I push him into my flat, slam the door, and twist every lock shut.

Chapter ten

'Emily Davison threw herself under a horse in 1913 as part of the Suffragette movement for female equality and for the right to vote.'

I stand in front of my sixth form class, reviewing the history of women's rights in Britain.

'Did she die, Miss?' asks Craig, one of the more forgetful pupils.

'Yes, she did. And the question we must ask ourselves is how far women have advanced since this time. In what ways have women's lives changed since 1913?'

My question sparks off a great discussion, prompting these scruffy seventeen-year-olds in ripped jeans and football tops to leap out of their chairs. Things are totally different now, they bellow: women are just like men; they can do whatever they want.

'Yeah, 'cause back then you had to get married even if you didn't want to, but nowadays, nobody gets married, and we girls just have kids whenever we want,' shouts Katie from the back.

'Really? You mean you don't want to get married?' I ask.

Katie shakes her head and Toby sniggers. 'What's the point of getting married? All you're gonna do is get divorced a few years later!' Laughter breaks out, and a lot of muttering. 'Yeah...I'm never getting married.' 'I might just have a baby on my own.' So I ask the class how many of them plan to get married later. To my utter shock, no one puts up their hand.

'You mean, none of you wants to get married? But don't you

want to have children? Don't you want to have families?' I screech. I want to ask the girls: Don't you want to be *Mrs Somebody* one day? They screw up their faces and look at me as if I'm an alien. Katie tries to make me understand.

'But you don't need to be *married* to have children, Miss. We can do that whenever we want. You don't need a *man* for that. I plan to have a baby when I'm twenty-one, but I'm never getting married.'

Zach giggles at my shocked expression. He turns to the class. 'You see, in Miss's day, everyone got married. That's why she thinks we're weird.'

IN MY DAY? What the hell? I'm not *that* much older than you, you little twerp. What's thirteen years? Clearly it's a lifetime. I don't think like these seventeen-year-old girls. All I want to do is get married and all they want is freedom and independence. For me, having a child out of wedlock is a last resort. To them, it's the most natural thing in the world. I wish I could be like them: young, strong, and free of all those damned Prince Charming fairy tales. Somehow I'm caught between generations. There's my mother's generation who got married and stayed married through thick and thin, and there's the younger generation who are cool about everything. We poor gals in the middle have careers and independence, but we lack the laid-back attitude of the truly young. We're like the seventeen-year-olds in terms of our career ambitions but we still hang on to the romantic notion of love and marriage from our mothers' generation. Is it possible to have both?

Later, as I step along the corridor to my office, I consider my sixth formers and I wonder whether the girls might change their minds as they get older. Life on your own? Yuck. I can't imagine anything worse. I pass by Caroline, our Deputy's office. I catch sight of her staring out of the window. She looks sad. Everyone knows she is. She's deeply unhappy. She's a white woman of about forty-eight years, unmarried, without children. She never found the One. She spent her life alone, throwing herself into her work and doing a marvellous job at it. Now, she no longer has the option of having children. At her age finding single men to date makes my feat look like a walk in the park. If *I* think there are no men out there, just imagine what she must think…Men her age only date women *my* age or even younger! So every night forevermore she'll curl up on her own, without even the slightest hope that it might ever change. I shudder, and rush into my office.

I sit thinking about poor Caroline and how she'll never have any children. She'll only ever have the pleasure of inheriting someone else's. Caroline claims she never wanted children. No doubt she didn't when she was thirty-something. But I wonder what she thinks *now*, seeing as the choice has been *taken away*? Maybe now that Caroline *can't* have children, might it be the very thing she wants more desperately than anything else in the world?

I gaze out the window and stare at the pupils running about. They all belong to someone; they all have mums and dads. TICK TOCK TICK TOCK. Suddenly, the fire alarm goes off. Children scream and laugh. Jesus. OK, Sarah. Now think. Procedures. Grab your register. Head to the back of the main playground. Check all the rooms to make sure that all the pupils are out and leave the building immediately.

I head out my office door and do exactly that. Once in the playground, I notice Jessica, the new Science teacher, struggling to control her class. I move my pupils swiftly over to where she's standing and count our classes together. One of the deputies calls me over and quietly explains that the alarm was set off by one of the pupils. There are four suspects. He wants me to play the good cop. We set up a meeting for the end of the day, and I instruct the teachers in my section of the playground to return to lessons. Whenever there's a crisis, it's Sarah to the rescue. I mean at WORK of course.

With my acting role as Inspector Morse's right-hand man over (and with the two culprits caught and punished), I make my way home. As I wander along Brixton High Street, I punch the digits of Manuele's new phone into my mobile. Luckily, that psycho husband never rang. I wonder whether he ever found out where I live? As I press save, I look behind to check that no one is following me. I pass the NatWest machines and stop short of a beggar sitting against the wall.

'Spare some change, hon?' He's an old white man with tufts of hair on his face, wearing a pair of very dirty dungarees. I toss the old man a fifty pence piece as the town hall's clock tower chimes five. Five rings. Maybe that's a sign. It's been five days since I saw Chibu and he hasn't called. Maybe today he'll have left a message on my machine? Need to hurry home to hear the message and then get ready for my date with Arthur.

I'm climbing the stairs to my flat when I hear it. *Brrring* YIKES! Chibu…it might be Chibu…come on, Sarah. Hurry up, hurry up… I jump the steps three at a time, pause in front of the door and shove the keys at the lock. *Brrring, Brrring*, They slip and fall to the floor. Damn damn damn. Quick. Pick'em up, Pick'em up you idiot. Jesus. Brrring. Brrring. I open the door and dash to the phone.

'Hello?' I shout, nearly tearing the phone out of the socket.

'Hello, darling. It's Daddy,' he says in his soft English voice.

'Oh. Hello. How are you?' I mutter.

'You don't sound very excited to hear from your dear dad. Were you expecting a charming young man?'

'Yes. Well, I was hoping it might be.' I sigh. 'It doesn't matter. How are things?'

'Darling, we hardly see much of you these days. We saw this fabulous play at the National last evening…acting was superb. You should have come.'

'Oh Daddy, I'm sorry I haven't been about. I always have so much school work you know and…'

'Your mother and I have been talking...' My father interrupts. 'Though she's been doing more of the talking than I have, of course. In any case, we are becoming concerned about you...'

Oh God. Here comes the 'Are you ever going to get married?' talk...

'...We think that you should get a cleaning lady.'

Do my parents have nothing better to do than to worry about the state of my flat? No doubt they think a clean house will encourage men to think of me as wife potential. Next thing you know, they'll be signing me up for cooking lessons. I scrunch up my face. 'A cleaning lady? WHAT?'

'Yes. Your flat is always in such a mess. I thought I should give you our cleaner's number.' I can hear him flipping through his address book. 'She has an opening at the moment and we've had her for some months now. She is efficient, reliable and very trustworthy.'

If only men could be the same. My dad's sweet. He's sixty-five and my mother's sixty. They're senior citizens now. The idea of having parents who are old enough to be senior citizens is too shocking for words. They met when my mother was a young nurse, just over from Jamaica and my father was a long-haired young hippy trying to make it in the music business. They've been married forty years. I note the cleaner's number, promising my father I'll call her first thing in the morning. My father passes the phone to my mother.

'Hello, Sarah dear. Your father is stepping out and I need to tell you something.'

'Tell me what?'

'Wait just a minute...' She pauses, listening for the door slam. 'You know how I said that he had a cold?' She coughs slightly. 'Well, we've been going back and forth from the doctor's. He's not well.'

'Mummy, what do you mean? Is it serious?'

'I hope not, dear. No need to worry. But I just wanted you to know.' My mother refuses to elaborate. She's prone to drama, so I dismiss what she's saying as being over-concerned and promise to call her later.

I sit on the couch worrying whether there really is something wrong with my dad, but I'm awakened from my daydreams by the phone.

'Hello?'

'Hi. It's Chibu.'

Thank you, God. Thank you. I might have died of grief had this man never phoned me again. So thank you. Thank you for saving my life. We speak for about half an hour. He tells me that a free moment allowed him to steal the opportunity to hear my voice. His week has been hectic, which is why I haven't heard back from him until now. But he's looking forward to the weekend when he hopes he can see me. As it is Wednesday, it's acceptable to arrange a date for a Saturday night, and so I do just that.

'Where shall I meet you?' I ask gleefully.

'As I've been remiss at phoning you, I'll do the gallant thing and pick you up, shall I?'

'Sure, if it's OK with you.' I want to swoon. 'I'll expect you at say, seven thirty?'

'You will indeed.'

When I hang up the phone, I'm on cloud nine. *Brring*. *Brring*. Oh yeah baby…just like the Samaritans on a Friday night…Oh shit. Maybe it's Chibu ringing back to cancel. Oh Jesus. Gritting my teeth, I pick up.

'Hello?'

'Hi, it's Sam. Just ringing to see if you're still on for Friday night.'

Damn right I am. We arrange to meet at the Satay Bar in Brixton for a bite to eat. I hang up the phone, having moved from cloud nine to cloud TEN. YESSIREE…I'm IN DEMAND now. Guys are ringing, begging to see me. Yeah. I'm doing OK. Chibu, Sam and Charlie the Internet guy who I can slot in before my date with Sam. Guys really want me! I have too many men and too little time.

I glance at the clock. Jeepers. Better get ready. I have to meet Arthur at the Bug Bar restaurant in forty-five minutes and I'm still wearing my work suit. I dash to the loo, have a quick shower and throw on something more appealing: a slinky silvery top, dark grey hipsters, and shimmering pointy-toed shoes. I stop in front of the mirror to put on some lipstick. I throw the lipstick in my bag, slam the front door, and head for the centre of Brixton.

No one's in the Bug Bar when I arrive. Believe it or not, the Bug Bar, as well as a nightclub called Mass form the basement of old St Matthew's Church in Brixton. Saturday night frolicking stops at six a.m. in time for 8:00 a.m. Sunday service. Upstairs, the pious pray for the sinners, while downstairs, the sinners do all manner of things.

An evening of seduction awaits me. I'm almost excited. Will I recognise him? I've seen a photo, but might he look different in real life? My first Internet date: I order a white wine at the long, dimly lit bar. A few minutes later, a man enters and walks towards me.

'Hi. I'm Arthur,' he announces, holding out his hand. 'You must be Sarah.'

'Yes.' I take his hand. 'How did you know? You didn't hesitate at all. You walked straight over.'

'Well, you do have a photo on your profile,' he says warmly, 'and it would be hard to forget a face as beautiful as yours. No ugly ducking here…only a beautiful swan.'

Jesus. He's so posh. You know, his voice. He sounds like Hugh Grant with a basket of plums in his throat. As we move to a table, I eye his corduroy dark brown jacket with matching trousers up and down. They seem too big for him and he looks uncomfortable. He is definitely right about the clothes. And I thought he'd be more muscular. He's smaller than he seemed on email. And what about the rugged guy on the photo? It must have been taken years ago. Dammit. Failure #70. I begin to get a little angry. Isn't this just FALSE ADVERTISING? I order Prince Charming and get King Arthur instead. It isn't fair! Can't I exchange him? Can't I send him back to the 'Love and Friends' website and get a refund?

George Clooney flies past the table on a black stallion. I notice the dark stubble on his sharply defined chin. Behind him follows a young Marlon Brando on a white steed. As he gallops by, he winks at me. I stare out into the distance as they ride away.

'Is the spark gone then?' Arthur senses my discomfort. His eyes open slowly like a cocker spaniel's. 'Am I not what you were expecting?'

'No, no. Of course not,' I choke, shaking my head. 'No. I'm tired, that's all. I've had a long day.' Jesus. What the hell am I meant to say? 'You look like a weedy version of Tony Blair, receding hairline included'? Exactly. I think not. Lying is my only option.

We sit down at a table in the middle of the restaurant. We are the only customers. Spacious and empty, with dimmed lights trying to disguise the uneasy atmosphere. The three waitresses stare at us. Oh God. Maybe they know we met on the Internet? Bloody hell. I'm going to die of embarrassment. What if they know? I do my best to ignore the eyes of the waitresses boring into the back of my head. We have lots of polite conversation, order our food and struggle slightly to keep the flow.

'It was easier on email wasn't it?' Arthur tilts his head to the side. 'We always had something to say. Internet dating is a new thing for me.'

SHH! The waitresses might hear you. They'll know that I'm so sad I have to look for love online. I'll never live this down.

Just lower your voice dammit. You may not mind being a sad cyberspace loner, but I do. Arthur doesn't hear my silent requests and continues. 'I think because we've been so used to communicating on the Internet, it's harder to communicate in person.'

Maybe he's right. Or maybe it's just 'cause I don't fancy him. Maybe there isn't a spark. Maybe it's because he looks like a bean pole. I don't feel like kissing him. I don't think he's irresistible. And I don't want to be here. The waitresses return to the kitchen.

'Dating through the Internet is interesting,' I say. It's a bit strange… everything's done backwards.'

'Backwards?' Arthur furrows his brow. 'What do you mean?'

'Well, normally you meet someone, and if you have a spark together, you decide to meet up again. Little by little you discover more and more about each other. With the Internet, you discover loads and loads via email and then you finally meet to discover whether or not there's a spark.'

'So you're saying that there's no spark between us?' He tilts his head to the side. 'I think there is.'

Oh Jesus. 'No no. I'm just very tired. I shouldn't stay too long. I meant that Internet dating is an interesting phenomenon.' I'm annoyed. No fault of Arthur's, but he resembles a balding scarecrow. 'Because people write profiles saying that they're searching for someone who's good looking, or who has a good sense of humour or who likes gardening, when ultimately all that matters is whether or not two people have a spark. People ignore all the so called incompatibilities if there's a spark.'

'Talking of sparks, I saw this television programme the other day all about them,' he says, winking triumphantly. 'This guy was to meet seven women. But he had to put seven t-shirts in order of preference according to how they smelled before meeting them.'

'Let me guess…the women had worn the t-shirts?'

'Yeah, that's right. And of course when he finally spent time with the women and had to put them in preference order as well, without knowing, he put them in the same order as the t-shirts! The programme was claiming that sparks are just instinctive smell.'

'It kind of suggests that we're a bunch of animals, don't you think? We naïvely believe that we have a hand at *choosing* our mate, when in fact we just end up with whoever we instinctively think smells the best,' I say, mockingly.

Arthur blushes slightly. 'Yes, well that was just the claim of the programme. It isn't necessarily true.'

'We're no better than hedgehogs. Or *swans*,' I suggest. 'Well actually, swans stay with the same mate for life, you know. So maybe in the grand scale of things, swans are higher up the evolutionary ladder than we are. We humans must be somewhere down near the hedgehogs.' I tap the table. 'We humans can't even choose our mates!'

Arthur looks slightly shocked. 'Yes, well it was an interesting programme.'

Oh gosh. He thinks I'm crazy. I take a sip of wine and decide to shut up and stick to chit-chat conversation. I discover that Arthur went to Eton, is more English than Prince Charles, and plays squash on the weekends. We don't bother with dessert. I'm tired, so we finish dinner quickly. Arthur insists on paying for the meal and on walking me home.

We stroll past Brixton's main tree with year-round fairy lights. We ignore the reefer odour wafting from the old black men on the benches underneath. They're wearing suit jackets and baseball caps, each with a can of beer in his hand. As we pass by, one of them shows me a toothless grin. Wandering down my street, Arthur kindly pretends not to smell the stewing rubbish in the bins. We pass the boarded-up house next door and stand in front of my flat.

'Whatever happened to that boy who you were defending?' I ask.

'He's back out on the street now, but no doubt he'll be in my care again soon enough.' He sighs.

'Well, thanks for dinner,' I say, politely. 'I had a nice time.'

'I should be the one thanking you,' he says, brushing my chin lightly with his thumb. Goose pimples shoot up my spine. I close my eyes and hope a spark will ignite. But when I open them, Arthur the scarecrow is still in front of me. I lean in, give him a kiss on the cheek, stand back waving, gallop to the front door, and begin to search for my keys. Arthur turns and quickly disappears down the street.

Thank goodness that's over. There was nothing wrong with him. Really, he was fine. But I didn't feel blood rushing to my head. He was polite, intelligent and interesting, but the chemistry thing wasn't there. Where are these bloody keys? I rummage through my bag. I feel bad. He's a nice guy. He's polite, charming and a barrister who wears one of those funny wigs all day. He's an attractive witty guy. So why is there no SPARK? No answer. No more daily emails from Arthur then. We're finished. But we grew close on the Internet. He was my friend. He was a real person with feelings and now I'm going to have to let him down. Oh God. What have I done? Poor Arthur. I roll my eyes. Still can't find my keys. Never thought about this before. Didn't realise that Internet dating could be so complicated.

Rule Number SIX: Gotta meet Internet guys right away to see if there's a spark.

My nails scrape against cold metal in the bottom of my bag. Aha. Here they are. Bloody keys, always getting l…Suddenly my bag is ripped out of my hands from behind. Oh my God. Manuele's psycho husband followed me home.

'Hey!' I screech, whipping round as a boy scampers down the steps towards his bike. 'Give me my fucking bag!'

He has a grey hood over his head. Oh, he's a kid. You little fucker. You can't take my bag. I won't let you. My heart is pounding. There's no time to think. So I jump. I leap from the top of the steps to the hoodlum below. I land on his back, my fingers clawing at his hooded top.

'Give me my fucking bag.'

He falls to his knees next to his bike, with me latched on to his back. Oh my god. What if he has a knife? I let go; he rolls over; and we pause, both on our knees, looking at each other. He's black, with big round eyes, not more than eighteen. I stare at him. His eyes dart about.

'Please,' I squeal.

His gaze gathers pity as he studies me. He looks up at the windows in the abandoned house next door. 'Take it then,' he says, grimacing. He picks himself up and throws the bag at me. And as quickly as he appeared, he hops on his bike and rides away. Jesus bloody Christ. Failure #71. My legs shaking, my heart racing and my eyes blinking, I scoop up my bag and stumble up the concrete steps. As I reach the top, brushing myself off, the door opens and Deirdre steps out.

'Sarah, dear. My goodness, are you all right?' She holds her arms out and she pulls me into her. 'I saw what happened from the window. I'm sorry I couldn't get out in time to help you. I'm so slow these days, dear. These little good-for-nothings on the street should be locked up!'

'Thank you, sweetie. Thank you. Thank you for your help.' We move inside, shutting the front door. 'I should go up to my flat now.'

'But dear, shouldn't we phone the police? Are you OK? Should we report it?'

I shake my head. 'No I don't think so. What's the point now? I have my bag back. I can't believe I got it back.'

'Yes dear, he'll think twice before attacking his next victim. You taught him a good lesson! I'll have to tell Dr Van Den Burg all about it. Why don't you come in and have a cup of tea?'

'No thank you, Deirdre, sweetie. I just want to get into my flat.' I pause, thinking. 'Deirdre, do you know if anyone lives next door?'

She squints. 'Next door where, dear?'

'In that abandoned house: the one with the furniture in front of it.' I tuck my hair behind my ear.

'Oh no dear. The doors are blocked. No one's lived there for years. Why do you ask?'

'No reason really,' I shake my head and then give Deirdre another hug. 'Goodnight and thank you for your help. I'm fine. I'll head up now.' I rub her back and let go.

'Are you sure, dear?' Deirdre asks suspiciously.

'Yes I'm sure. Thank you. I'm fine. Really, I'm fine.' I limp up the stairs and into my flat.

I pick up the phone and ring Jacquie. I tell her everything. Jacquie gasps. 'Bloody hell, Sarah. You have more balls than even me. Well done. Men shouldn't mess with us independent women...Yeah, you made a name for us all tonight, Sarah. Bloody fantastic.'

As I speak to Jacquie I make myself a cup of tea, and try to stop shaking. Jacquie rabbits on about how I'm a modern heroine but all I want to do is curl up in bed with Bear. I hang up the phone and sit on the sofa to watch a DVD of *Ally McBeal*. She's great; always there during times of need. At least I'm not the only thirty-year-old with a disastrous love life who attacks strangers. No chemistry with King Arthur, but tonight I didn't need a Prince Charming to save the day. Maybe Jacquie's right. Maybe this was a success. Somehow, I managed to save the day all by myself. I put my feet up, stretch out, and, feeling proud, I fall asleep to Ally's dancing baby doing somersaults in the air.

Chapter eleven

The Rules probably give strict instructions to never be early for a date. And maybe I missed that bit because here I am at the SW9 Bar in Brixton, ten minutes early for my date with Charlie. Internet date #2. SW9 is a gay bar…well at least a lot of gay people go there. The rare black people who visit the bar are either straight and female, gay and male or indeed a mixture of all four.

I position myself at a table under the colourful painting of an orgy, giving me a direct view of the front door. And then I wait. With no photo on his profile, I start to get a little nervous. Will I recognise him? He said he was of medium height with brown hair and brown eyes. Isn't everyone? And what is the point of telling me the colour of his eyes? Am I really going to get that close to complete strangers to be able to see the colour of their eyes?

I run through all that I know about Charlie. Thirty-four, lives in Brick Lane, is a social worker who works with people with HIV and he wants to change the world. Oh, and he'll be wearing black trousers and a dark brown coat. He sounds interesting. A few minutes later a man walks in. My heart jumps. I look inquisitively, to see the colour of his hair. As he approaches, I notice that it's black, so I return to staring at the entrance. Unlike Arthur, I know little about Charlie and have only exchanged a few emails. No emotional attachment here. No chance of feeling bad. I examine my watch. OK, Sarah…Not more than an hour and a half with Charlie. Must leave enough time to get home and get ready for my date with Sam. The waiter approaches.

'Hi, I'll have an apple juice please.' The waiter turns to go, and I call after him.

'Nah, uh, I'll have a coffee instead.'

When the waiter moves out of the way, a man is standing behind. He's late fifties, with brown hair, wearing tight black leather trousers and a dark brown coat. He has a greying straggly beard that's begging to be shaved off. He sits down on the chair opposite.

'Hi. I'm Charlie.' He takes my hand and shakes it forcefully. 'You must be Sarah.'

'Hi.' I hesitate, confused.

'Yes I know. I'm not thirty-four am I?' He laughs and taps the table. 'No, no I'm not. I just say that on my profile so that you women won't be put off by my age. I'm actually fifty-nine.' He continues to laugh.

WHAT? This guy is a psycho. Failure #72. Get me outta here.

'Oh, I see,' I stammer. 'Yes, I understand. Age can be such a barrier sometimes.'

I don't know what to say and what I really want to do is make a dash for the door. But the manners my mother instilled in me from age one keep me fastened to the seat.

'Yes, age is such a silly thing.' Charlie tosses his head about as if he's a marionette. 'I don't know why people take it so seriously.'

Charlie looks to the bar and mouths the words 'black coffee' at the waiter. I ask Charlie about his work and he launches into a detailed analysis of the care system that's available to HIV patients. I nod politely, 'umming' and 'ahhing' at appropriate moments. Inside I'm praying for a snowfall to suddenly start, for the café to have to close, and for us to be forced to part company. No such luck. He just keeps on talking. Charlie politely asks about my job and so I speak a little about teaching.

'I especially love the naughty ones. They present more of a challenge.'

'Wow. I'm always so amazed by teachers and their dedication.' He cups his chin in his hands. 'Really, I'm in awe of you...'

Now I'm feeling VERY uncomfortable.

'...you see, age doesn't really matter between people. To look at you, you'd think you were at least forty.'

Did he just say what I think he said? Nah, can't be. I must have misheard. 'Sorry?' I whisper.

'Yeah, Sarah.' He insists. 'You come across as being much older than thirty. You seem much closer to forty than thirty.'

OK. I'VE HEARD ENOUGH. That's it. I don't have to sit here and take this. FORTY? I know the Barbie-Bratz-Bitch in John Lewis claimed my smile lines were noticeable, but FORTY? Nah...this guy has gone too far. This is beyond acceptable. My fragile thirty-year-old ego can only take so much...Then I remember my father always quoting Mark Twain: 'Good breeding consists in concealing how much we think of ourselves and how little we think of the other person.' Jesus. I wonder if Twain ever got married?

Charlie must sense me tensing up. He raises his hand as if to say 'wait' and tries to dig himself out.

'No, no,' he stammers. 'Some forty-year-olds can be quite attractive really. Sometimes you can't even tell that they're forty.'

WHUUAT? This guy has lost his mind. My eyes draw into a squint.

'No, I mean that you're attractive and you're like a forty-year-old...'

Yeah. I get it you fuckwit. I look like a fucking forty-year-old. Jesus Christ.

Charlie waves his hands about. 'NO. What I mean to say is that you're very mature, for your age, I mean...you don't sound as if you're thirty. You sound more like a forty-year-old…you know, sensible.'

So you mean I'm boring you rigid? Who is this guy? Why am I here? And more importantly, how the hell am I going to get out of here?

As Charlie continues to drone on, the door of the café opens and I raise my gaze. A young guy in his late twenties walks in. He's blond. He reminds me of Sam. I look back at Charlie and nod as if to suggest I'm listening to what he's saying and return to scrutinising the blond. He moves closer. OH MY GOD. It really is Sam. Dammit. What's he doing here? He's meant to meet me later at the Satay Bar. And now he'll see me out with this psycho granddad. What if he asks how we know each other? I'll have to tell him about the Internet. Oh Lord. I'd rather die. I'd rather a bolt of lightning come crashing through the roof and strike me dead right now than have to admit that I go on the Internet to find men. Instinctively, I dive under the table.

'Sarah?' Charlie leans forward. 'Sarah? Are you OK?'

'Yes. Yes,' I flail, my head bent under the table. 'Just need to get something out of my bag.'

I fumble around in my bag which is sitting on the floor, pretending to look for something.

'I'll…just be a second,' I whisper.

I can see out of the corner of my eye that Sam has approached the bar. He's talking to the bar man. Oh God. How do I get out of this one? Jesus Christ. This is as bad as it gets. Where the hell is that lightning?

'What are you doing, Sarah?' Charlie asks.

SHH, you stupid twit. Don't shout out my name like that. He might hear you.

'Like I said, I'm just looking for something.'

Sam spins and goes upstairs. I'm still under the table. Coast clear, I spring up.

'Found it?' Charlie asks.

'Huh? Oh yeah. No…I mean no. I haven't found it. I was looking for…' I pause, desperately thinking of something to say, '…for a very important key.' I grab my bag. 'It isn't there. I'll have to go. I must go home to find it.' I stand up before Charlie has the chance to say anything. I hold out my hand and he takes it.

'Nice to meet you, Charlie.' I steal a glance at the staircase. I have to get out of here. I have to move fast.

'Yes. Nice to meet you too, Sarah.'

Yeah, I *bet*, you dickhead. Come on, hurry up, finish shaking my hand…But then Charlie looks to the table. 'Hey. We haven't paid for our coffees. It's a couple of quid each.'

WHAT? He wants me to pay for my COFFEE? Charlie puts his hand in his pocket and I hastily dig into my handbag. Suddenly, I hear footsteps in the staircase behind. Fuck. Fuck. Fuck. I turn to the staircase. Jesus. What am I going to say? How am I going to explain this? Oh my God this is so embarrassing. To my delight, a woman appears. Thank you, God. I grab five pounds out of my bag and throw it on the table. 'It's on me.' I force a smile.

'Oh thanks, Sarah. That's very modern of you.' Charlie grins broadly. 'Hope we can do it again. I'll email you.'

Yeah. So that I can kick your head in. Because right now, I'm afraid I don't have the time. More noise on the stairs. It has to be Sam. Jesus. It just has to be.

'Yes, please do.' I start to back out. 'See you.' I throw the hood of my coat over my head just as Sam appears at the doorway and I shoot round, turning my back to him. I pull the hood over my face and charge at the door. It flies open and I zoom out of it.

'But don't you want your change…?' Charlie shouts after me.

I run. I run as fast as I can. I run all the way down the street. Thank you, God. He didn't see me. I wasn't completely humiliated.

Yuck yuck yuck yuck. How awful. Can you imagine being caught on a date with a guy like *that*? I shudder at the thought. I feel like taking a shower. I speed home and do exactly that. After all, I'm to see Sam, and given the close call a moment ago, I want to look the *business*.

The Satay Bar is a bustling Indonesian restaurant which has a mix of people, both black and white, with mostly Indonesian staff. Just down the road are friendly prostitutes and drug dealers, politely offering their services to passers-by. Across from the Satay Bar is a pub called The Prince Albert, a pub-style bar which contains mostly white middle-class youngsters. Round the corner is the Fridge Bar, done in a fancy club-style which contains mostly black people, where they frisk before allowing you in. The Satay Bar seems like the perfect compromise for Sam and me.

I sit at the bar feeling excited. Sam's not an Internet date. I know there's a spark and I know that I fancy him. And most importantly, he isn't a psycho. Then I remember his clothes. God. I'll have to mentally deal with that one. It's Friday evening and the bar starts to fill up. I'm at the bar for about five minutes when a black man wearing several gold teeth and a couple of gold chains approaches. God what is it with the mouthful of gold thing? Is it to spray some testosterone about? Do posh white guys prance around in four-wheel-drives while street black guys strut gold teeth? Are all men predictable?

'Hey, baby.' He smiles mischievously. 'How ya doing tonight?'

'I'm fine, thank you.' I turn to face him. 'And you?'

He seems slightly taken aback and withdraws his hand.

'Oh. You're not from around here, are ya?'

'Yes, I am. I live around the corner.'

'Nah, baby.' He shakes his head. 'What I mean is that you didn't grow up here.'

'No, I didn't. I grew up in North London.'

'North London?' He pauses. 'Ah…so you're a posh bird then, ain't ya?'

Posh bird? Am I posh? Maybe I am to him. But I've never thought of myself as particularly posh. Georgina…now *she's* posh. But me? Miss teacher? Nah.

'Me? Posh?' I laugh. 'No, not really.'

'Uh-uh.' He winks and nods his head. 'I know posh when I see it. You're *wifey* material you are.'

WIFEY MATERIAL? Does that mean he's proposing marriage? What would my mother say?

Just then Sam walks through the front door and rushes over. He's wearing a scruffy t-shirt and dirty jeans.

'Sorry I'm late.' He brushes past the Mr T look-alike and kisses me on the cheek. Then he turns to him and smiles, putting his hand on his shoulder.

'Thanks for holding the fort, mate. I'll take over now.'

The man has a mixed expression on his face of confusion and hurt. He begins to walk away. But as he turns, I hear him muttering under his breath. 'I should've known she'd only go for white guys.'

HEY! That's not true. I go out with black guys all the time. Just because Sam's not black doesn't mean that I don't date black guys. HEY! Who do you think you are…judging me like that? I haven't given up on black men. Just because I won't go out with YOU, you have to get nasty. I want to chase after him. But I don't want to seem like a psycho, so I let it go.

We take a table in the far corner and order some food. Sam is lovely. He keeps moving his blond hair away from his piercing blue eyes. When he looks directly at me, it feels like he's looking at my soul. Sam reminds me he's an artist.

'I spend most of my time in my studio in my flat in Brixton… working, of course. I sell pieces to individuals, restaurants, and banks in the City.'

Sam explains that he's doing relatively well and can live off his earnings. But he doesn't have much to worry about if things take a turn for the worse.

'It's easy for me, you see. If I screw up and end up with no cash, I can always go home to mummy and daddy in South Kensington.' He pauses, chewing on his food. 'Not that I would ever do that. I'd have to be close to starving. But I always have that cushion to fall back on if it's ever needed.' His eyes sparkle. 'My father was a property developer and cleaned up in the mid-eighties during the housing boom. So money's never been a problem for my family.'

'Not like the families of the children I teach then?'

'Nah. Not like them,' he says, shaking his head. 'My parents are divorced. My mother is now a lady of leisure who lunches at a variety of Kensington brasseries.'

Now that's what I call POSH. I'm just middle class.

'I hate the way my parents live,' Sam growls. 'They're so self-obsessed. They love living a rich lifestyle and worrying about what the Joneses are doing next door. Harry and Annabelle Bishop have to be top at everything.'

Sam and Sarah Bishop. MRS Sarah Bishop. Hmm…has a cute ring to it. I nod in agreement and Sam continues. 'I hate Kensington. Like I told you when we first met, I live in Brixton because it's down to earth.'

Sam rarely sees his parents, even though they live in London. Sounds like he really dislikes them. They vote for the Tories and he votes Labour; he produces paintings and they purchase David Hockneys at the weekend.

Dinner finished, Sam leans in and whispers, 'You up for some chocolate cake?'

Gosh. Sure I want chocolate cake. Am I allowed? Will Georgina and Jacquie flip if I tell them I ate chocolate cake on a date? Course, I don't have to tell them. I give in. Boy, is it yummy. Once we've eaten the cake, I lick my lips and fork, scrape the plate, wishing I could ask for another, but reminding myself of Georgina's advice not to come across as a pig.

'So you're a teacher then?' Sam winks at me. 'I'm surprised you're not in PR or advertising.'

'PR?...Advertising?' I frown. 'Why PR?...Why advertising?'

'Because all you women are in PR or advertising these days,' he chuckles. 'You know, the kinds of women who appear in those fluorescent pink and yellow novels in WHSmith, who are always looking for boyfriends.'

I laugh, shaking my head. 'No, I'm a teacher, and I seem to work day and night trying to make my students work even harder. Don't know whether it inspires them though. I think they just think I'm a workaholic.' I pause. 'HEY. You haven't noticed my new haircut!' I run my fingers through my hair.

'Oh.' Sam goes slightly pink. 'Yeah. Well yeah, I hadn't realised. It looks good on you. It does.' He tilts his head to the side. 'I'm not really one to notice haircuts. I'd rather hear about you.'

I smile, blushing. He's sweet. A man outside the window lights up a cigarette and Sam twists his head away in disgust.

'Don't like the smoke?' I ask.

'No no. I gave up smoking a couple of months ago and I'm finding it hard,' he says, rolling up his sleeve to point to his nicotine patch. 'See. Never leave home without it.'

'Really? Do you always have one on? Does it work?'

'Yeah...always. They work a treat. Without these patches, I'd never cope. I hate seeing other people smoke. It drives me mad. You have no idea what it's like being so dependent on something.'

'Well, I think similarly about chocolate if that makes you feel any better.'

'Oh yeah? I feel the same way about sweet stuff now that I've given up cigarettes.' He chuckles. 'That's why I suggested the chocolate cake.'

Phew. He didn't think I was a fat pig then.

'How about we share another one then?' I suggest bravely.

'You're on.'

As we gobble our cake, Sam explains that on Sunday mornings, he coaches an eight-year-olds' football team at Ferndale Sports Centre.

'I feel like I should give something back to the community. You know, having had every modern toy and home tutor when I was young, I feel like I owe the world something.'

'That's very noble of you,' I comment.

'Not really. We had everything…really, we did. My brother and I were at Dulwich College,' he says, wincing slightly, 'and we had access to all the extra-curricular activities you could ever imagine. I just want my Brixton boys to have a taste of what I had when I was younger…Not that football on Saturday mornings is anything like it.'

What a great guy. Maybe he's the One. Maybe it isn't Chibu. Sam is just so nice. Sam cocks his head to one side and winks. 'I'll be back in a sec. Need the loo.'

I watch him walk down the length of the bar in his boots and dirty jeans. Those CLOTHES. They're a serious problem. The rich boy's gone too far with the grunge, trying to remove the Kensington out of his soul. But those eyes…who could possibly say no to them? I wonder what our children will look like? Mixed, or white? Perhaps even Greek or Italian? What'll we call them? Just then, my mobile beeps with a text message. *Hey Principessa. Looking forward to tomorrow night. Cx* Awhh yeah…Chibu is the guy for me. What am I doing thinking about possible children with this blond *boy*, when there is Chibu the man? Hey yeah, that's a point…I don't even know how old Sam is.

Sam returns to the table. He's flushed and his cheeks have turned dark pink. God, I hope he's OK. I wonder what he was doing in the toilet? Sam jogs me out of my thoughts when he asks me if I want anything else.

'No. I'm fine.' I try to smile seductively. 'But I was just thinking to myself that I don't know how old you are.'

'Well, that's an easy one. I'm twenty-seven.'

I start to choke. I knew he was young, but TWENTY-SEVEN? Bloody hell. Are all the available men now YOUNGER than me?

'You're twenty-seven?'

'Yeah. How old are you?'

Oh God. Now what am I meant to say? I can't say I'm thirty: I'll die of humiliation. I'll never get the chance to die miserable and alone because they'll find me dead in the Satay Bar having suffered from complications after a severe bout of embarrassment. So I do as any sensible girl would do: I lie.

'I'm twenty-eight.'

'So we're perfect for each other.' He takes my hand in his and presses his lips against it as if we're in a movie. I smile. God, he's cute.

Sam doesn't own a car. He can't afford one. So he offers to walk me home. Even though he has no money, he insists on paying for dinner. He's the perfect gentleman. We stroll past the Ritzy cinema and notice signs saying: DRUG ACTIVITY PRESENT HERE. We fall about in stitches. The police have little effect on the drug racket in Brixton and their pathetic placards look ridiculous. We amble past the tube and Sam stops to pick up some incense sticks from the Rasta incense guy. The smell of hippy student digs fills the air.

Eventually, we stand in front of my flat and chat for a while. He makes me laugh. He loves films and is always at the Ritzy cinema. I start to wonder why we've never bumped into each other. Then I remember how my film-watching used to take place in front of the television in my jammies. That time in my life now seems far away.

After about ten minutes, Sam gazes down at me as if he's looking at something truly beautiful. He brushes my hair away from my face, and placing his hand behind my neck, he pulls me in gently. Our lips brush together briefly and then he pulls back, letting go of me, and flips his hand through his blond hair. Tossing his head to the side and turning to go, he gives me one last look.

'Good night, Sarah…I'll call you.'

As I dance up the steps to my flat, I begin to wish I'd asked Sam to wait. Searching for my keys, it feels as if someone's watching me. I spin round several times, but no one's there. Must just be the after-effect from what happened the other night. As I open the large wooden front door, I notice Deirdre's bony brown fingers gripping the edge of her door frame, her turquoise cardigan fraying at the edge of her wrist.

'Hello, dear. I see you're a sought-after young lady these days.'

I blush. 'Yes, well, I've been trying, see. I've been making an effort to meet people.'

'Good, dear. I'm glad to hear it. I noticed Dr Van Den Burg flirting with one of the receptionists on Wednesday, so he's probably not the man for you.' She shakes her head. 'Such a naughty man…I was so disappointed. Goodnight dear. And thank you for the milk.'

'No problem, sweetie. Sleep tight.'

I lie in bed with Bear thinking about my two suitors: Sam and Chibu. They couldn't be more different, but I like them both. With one, I'll have black children, with the other, white ones. I think about my friends Philippe and Aicha. They're French and have been living in England for several years. He's a banker in the City and earns a fortune. She's at home with their child. He's shockingly bright and she's extraordinarily beautiful. She's some exotic mix of Arab and black with brown skin and bunches of rich deep brown ringlets on her head. When their baby boy was born last year, they took him to see a new doctor.

The baby was so white the receptionists assumed Aicha was the baby's nanny. Can you imagine having to persuade people you're the mother of your own child? It made me pause to think. Oh, who cares anyway? Chibu's in the lead whatever his colour. There's nothing wrong with him. Sam on the other hand is twenty-seven and thinks I'm twenty-eight. How the hell did I get myself into *that* one? Chibu's perfect. But what if he's too good to be true?

Not to worry: tomorrow's Saturday, I'll be seeing Chibu and he likes me. I have the text to prove it. Tomorrow night, he'll be on a dashing white steed, in full armour, carrying a sword. He's going to rescue me from this life of canned soup, pyjamas and Sky movies. I'm going to be Mrs Chibu Somebody. And finally, I'm going to have a life.

Chapter twelve

'Wow. Your flat looks great. It's so clean.' Jacquie pushes past me into the kitchen, takes a glass off the shelf and pours herself some water.

A little embarrassed, I explain that my father suggested I get a cleaning lady.

Jacquie furrows her brow. 'I hope she rinses the soap suds off the dishes…She's white, right?'

'Yes, well, she's Polish.'

'Well, watch her when she does the washing up. White people never rinse their dishes.' I laugh out loud. 'That's why I don't have a cleaning lady; I like my dishes spotless and squeaky clean.'

'You're mad, Jacquie! Priscilla is great…she's so much better than me, and the flat's perfect for tonight, especially if Chibu wants to stay over.'

Jacquie is furious. Seems I've said the wrong thing again.

'NO NO NO, SARAH. *The Rules* state clearly that you shouldn't rush into sex. Remember, you need to keep them *wanting* you.' She sighs with frustration. 'If you just give it to them right away, then what do they have to work for? This is your second date; try to at least wait until the third.'

Oh. Maybe I should have read more than the first few chapters. God. Didn't realise I should follow procedures. So jumping out of his car was a good thing? In fact, thinking I screwed up the first date, I had a bikini and eyebrow wax. So here we are, a week later, just before date number two, I'm all set and Jacquie tells me that I can't have sex with him. Will I ever get this right? Jacquie lights up a cigarette and pulls an ashtray out of one of the kitchen drawers. We move to the front room and sit down.

'Anyway, Sarah, I haven't told you yet, I've met this really nice guy called Mark.' Jacquie emits a sigh that only comes with being in love. 'He's just a dream. Generous, funny and really good-looking.'

She goes on to tell me that he's thirty-seven, and owns a business that ships materials in and out of the country for foreign correspondents working for the BBC. She met him at some work party with loads of media people. His parents are from Jamaica but he grew up in London. This was her mysterious date from the other day.

'Have you slept with him yet?' I ask.

'No,' she replies coyly, 'but I hope to next weekend.'

Jacquie is excited and I'm happy for her. It's been a while. Jacquie explains that Mark has a sixteen-year-old son but she figures a child of that age won't be much bother. She won't have to play step-mum to him. And Mark's so nice that he makes up for the fact that he has a child. We chat for a couple of hours and Jacquie smokes a few more cigarettes. We talk through all my dates: first the one with Chibu and then the one with Arthur, followed by Charlie and Sam.

'You know, I think turning thirty was good for you, Sarah.' We both laugh. Maybe she's right. Jacquie's always right. And no matter how much older and wiser I become, she'll always be one step ahead of me. That's the funny thing about age. You can't ever catch anyone up. Jacquie stubs her cigarette out in the ashtray and I look at her, wincing.

'You really should stop smoking you know.'

'Nah. It's one of the advantages of being single without children.' Jacquie shrugs her shoulders. 'You're free to do what you want.' She jumps up from the sofa and takes back her coat from the chair beside her. 'I'd better leave you to it then.' She smiles as if she's up to something. 'Make yourself look fabulous before lover-boy gets here. Remember, you're beautiful, Sarah. He's lucky to have you. And don't get too carried away with the 2.4, white-picket fence fantasies. You hardly know this guy.' She leans forward, gives me a kiss on the cheek and backs out of my flat into the main hallway. Running down the stairs, she calls out. 'And make sure you end the date FIRST this time!' I hear her open the front door. 'Hey Sarah, something out here for you!'

I shuffle downstairs and find a packet of chocolate digestives on the doorstep with a note that says: '*For Sarah*'. How bizarre. I wonder who they're from? Chibu? No wait, maybe they're from Sam seeing as he likes chocolate? I rip them open and devour two before making it back up the stairs. I put the biscuits away, dash to the loo and mentally lay out my preparation timetable. I have two hours. No time to lose. Once showered, de-fuzzed and moisturised, I pull out my knickers drawer. It's filled with deliciously new sexy items. French knickers, g-strings and hipsters, all garnished with lace and frills. I still have a number of good old Marks & Sparks cotton pants of course. I can't possibly throw out *all* of them.

But now I'm the *new* Sarah. I cast the Marks & Sparks pants to the side and pick up my favourite new g-string. It's pink and black and so very very little. I've never worn such a thing; only ever seen them hanging up in sexy lingerie shops. You know, on days when feeling sorry for myself, stuffing my face with a bag of Millie's cookies, I'd wander through Knickerbox silently sobbing, wishing I had a reason to buy something. Finally there's a reason, and this g-string will guarantee me the confidence of a GODDESS. But I'm not supposed to have sex with him. A horrible pair of knickers will help me to resist temptation. Sexy knickers on the other hand are just an encouragement. I look at the Marks & Sparks cotton pants. What am I to do? Jesus. Why couldn't Jacquie have stayed a little longer? I hold up the sexy g-string. It's *so sexy*. I even have the matching bra. I shut the knickers drawer, put on the practically non-existent g-string and dare not look in the mirror for fear of feeling embarrassed.

Seven thirty. Perfect. I'm just on time. I stroke my lips once more with my 'Steamy Scarlett' lipstick and sit on the sofa. Half an hour later, I'm still sitting there. I keep looking at my watch as if somehow it'll speed Chibu's arrival. I'm worried. I'm worried because he hasn't called. I'm worried he isn't coming. And I'm worried he's been a figment of my imagination. I play with the remote control and zap through all the channels. I pause on a re-run of *Sex and the City*. The girls are talking about what it feels like to be stood up. I think better of it and swap over.

Ding dong. Thank God for that. Bloody hell. Talk about giving me a heart attack. I jump up, grab my coat and bag and skip down to the door.

'Buongiorno, Principessa.' Chibu throws open his hands as if he's singing a song. Then he squeezes me round the waist and kisses me squarely on the lips. 'God, you're gorgeous. You get better looking every time I see you.' I can't help but blush. And I giggle a little. But then I catch myself. 'HEY! You're late, you are!' I frown and peer at my watch. 'You've kept me waiting nearly forty minutes!' Chibu draws me in and kisses me on the forehead. 'I'm a *black* man.' He laughs. 'Just following BPT.'

Bloody Black People's Time: I've probably lost three years of my life thanks to BPT. I smile forgivingly. Chibu explains that we're going to a little Lebanese restaurant in the West End. It's another one of his favourites. Youpee. I love going to Middle Eastern restaurants. The staff always assume I'm from the Middle East and give me special treatment.

We park the car near Covent Garden and jump out. Chibu takes hold of my hand. 'I hope you don't mind take-away.'

Take-away? We're having TAKE-AWAY? 'No, no, of

course not,' I choke, wondering where we'll be eating our foil-wrapped cuisine.

'Do you like falafel?' Chibu asks.

'Yes I do.'

'Great, because they do these brilliant falafel sandwiches.'

SANDWICHES? We're eating take-away sandwiches for dinner in the street? What the hell? We walk into a little Lebanese take-away. The fluorescent lights above the mirrored wall flicker. The man behind the Formica counter is broad, wearing a white apron, with a short sharp haircut. He smiles at Chibu, clearly recognising him. Chibu approaches and shakes his hand. 'Hey, Latif. You well?'

'Oh, I'm divine,' he camply sings, bending his hand at the wrist. 'Dead in here tonight though.' He examines me, wagging his index finger. 'She's a beauty…Treat her well, you rascal you.'

'Oh I will,' Chibu says, smiling seductively. 'She's a real find…Give us two falafel sandwiches will you? Oh, and a couple of Cokes?' Chibu glances at me for approval and I nod.

The man hands Chibu the sandwiches, and off we go, returning to the car. So do we eat these sandwiches in the car or in the street? What kind of a date is this? We drive for a little while and finally park on Waterloo Bridge. Chibu takes me by the hand and pulls me towards the Strand. Should I ask where we're going? A park bench? The river bank?

A short walk later, we turn into Somerset House. I'm so taken aback by its beauty that I nearly stumble. The stately eighteenth-century building almost pales in comparison to the fountains in the courtyard, jets of water in geometric lines, spurting directly upwards at different heights. Sometimes they're low down and sometimes sky high. Some lines have yellow lights, others red, and some even green or blue. The place is empty. Chibu claims a metal table and a couple of chairs, and places our feast across the table.

'Come on, eat up!' He takes hold of his sandwich.

I sit down and start munching. 'I don't believe you're not

eating meat. Men always eat meat.'

Chibu laughs. 'I'm a twenty-first-century kind of guy.'

We chuckle and talk about how delightful the place is. He explains that he visits Somerset House regularly.

'The skating rink will be up next week. I try to come at least once a year. You ever been?'

'No.' I shake my head.

'Well, I'll have to bring you back here then.' He winks at me. 'I'll take you skiing AND skating. You'll go from principessa to ice queen.'

I giggle and chew on my food. I chomp, trying hard not to let the sauce drip down the side of my mouth. Lady-like, Sarah. Remember to look SEXY. But the sandwich is falling apart in my hands. The task is becoming almost impossible. I'm busy trying to stop all the bits from falling, when Chibu leans over and brushes the side of my chin.

'Just a piece of wandering lettuce, that's all.'

I blush. As I struggle with the sandwich, I struggle on my seat. A very expensive and ropey item riding up my bottom is causing me serious distress. I try sitting on the left cheek, then I move to the right one. No difference. I move to the edge of my seat and rock about. No change. I so badly want to stuff my hands down the back of my trousers and rip the bloody thing off. Whose idea was it anyway to start wearing g-strings?

Once I finish my sandwich, I scramble around for a napkin. Mustn't lick my fingers in front of him. Black guys always have such a thing about hygiene and manners. I wipe my hands.

'Do people ever tell you you're good-looking?' I ask.

'Yeah. All the time, but it doesn't mean much to me. In fact, it's almost off-putting.' He puts his hand on his chest. 'I'd prefer it if people said I was a nice person. But they never do.' He goes on to explain that because he's goal-oriented, sometimes people find him ruthless. 'I just wish people weren't so scared of me. I'm a nice guy. I think it's because people find it difficult to categorise me…they prefer to put things in boxes and I don't fit into any of the boxes they've seen before.'

You can come play in MY sandbox anytime you like. I tilt my head to the side. 'You're quite sweet really. A bit of a softie underneath.' Chibu blushes slightly, hanging his head in embarrassment. How cute.

'So do you like chocolate digestives?' I ask, hinting.

'They're OK I suppose, though chocolate isn't my thing.'

Oh. Sam must be the mysterious chocolate-giver.

'I leave soon for Nigeria, for Christmas, you know. Can't wait,' Chibu says, smiling. 'When my parents retired, they moved back home…well, like so many other Africans and West Indians have done.'

'Hmm. Well my mother isn't going anywhere, seeing as she married an English man,' I say pointedly.

'Oh no, of course not. So your parents are still together, eh? So are mine…Pretty uncommon these days.'

'Yes it is,' I agree. 'My parents are old-fashioned. They're even worried that I'm still single.'

'My parents are just the same. My dad in particular is very worried that I haven't found a woman to marry yet.' He rolls his eyes. 'He's convinced that London is a bad influence. I know when I go home next week, he'll have dozens of women lined up for me to meet.'

'Really? Does he want you to marry a Nigerian?'

'Oh yeah.' He pauses, wrinkling his nose. 'Definitely. Not just a Nigerian. An Igbo woman. I have to marry an Igbo woman.'

'You mean as opposed to a Yoruba woman?'

'Yeah, but also as opposed to *any* other kind of woman. I just have to marry an Igbo Nigerian.'

Oh. Here's the catch. Maybe this is Chibu's way of telling me that he'll never marry ME. Maybe he's just trying to let me down easily. Maybe this is the end.

Chibu takes my hand in his. 'Not that I'm going to of course.' He smiles, winking. 'Well, I *might* marry an Igbo woman, if the woman who I choose happens to be Igbo. If not, so be it.' God he's wonderful. I hold on to his hand tightly. 'I figure I've been rebellious in everything else.' He says, kissing my hand. 'If I was willing to disappoint him and become a banker, then I should be willing to disappoint him in other things as well.' This man is as perfect as perfect gets. Here I was worrying about what white boys' parents might think of me, when maybe I should have been worrying about the black ones.

'Come on!' Chibu shouts, jumping up and grabbing my hand to drag me to the fountains.

'What are you doing?' I cry. 'I don't want to get wet!'

'Don't worry, just run between the fountains and you won't feel a drop!'

We dash between the colourful jets of water, catching a slight spray of mist while holding hands. Every time the jets change height, I yelp, prompting Chibu to clasp my hand. Bliss. This is paradise. This is the man I'm going to marry. Chibu's footballer legs negotiate their way through the maze of water, with me skipping behind, hanging on to his hand for dear life.

We're getting ready to leave, when Chibu remembers our rubbish on the table. 'I'd better go pick that up. Can't leave the place in a mess.'

He saunters back to throw it out. 'Beep beep.' I take a peek at my mobile. It's as if my phone knows exactly when my dates are out of earshot. '*Can't wait to see you again. Hope you're feeling better. Arthur x*' Arthur? God. I thought he'd take the hint. I stare at the phone, trying to think of a plan. How can I let him down gently?

'Oooh. A secret admirer?' Chibu throws his arms around me from behind. 'Who's my competition then?'

'No one.' I say, shaking my head. 'No one important.' I quickly shove my phone in my bag. 'He's no one of any interest.'

122

'Oh really?' Chibu deliberately makes an exaggerated face to suggest he doesn't believe me. 'Sounds like I have *lots* to worry about.' He points at my bag. 'Strange men texting *my girl* when we're out on a date. Ha! I might just have to take out my sword.'

Did he just say MY GIRL? Did he? Did he really? Am I really HIS GIRL? Am I finally someone's GIRLFRIEND? What a wonderful evening. I should be paying for this date.

We sit in Chibu's car parked outside my flat.

'We've been here before, haven't we?' Chibu puts his hand on the door handle, winking. 'So this time, I'm walking you to the door. Haven't come all this way for nothing.'

'That might not be a bad idea. I was mugged a few weeks ago on my doorstep.'

'What?' Chibu strokes my hand. 'What happened? Are you OK?'

I tell the story of my heroic exploits and no sooner have I finished than Chibu jumps out of the car and appears at my side to open the door.

'Principessa, I'll be your guardian angel for tonight,' he announces, holding out his hand as if we're in a Jane Austen novel, and helps me to my feet. I glance at the top window of the boarded house. Nothing. We walk to the front door. OK, Sarah. Remember: however tempting it may be, however much you want it, send him away. He mustn't come upstairs. Remember Jacquie's advice. Remember *The Rules*.

I'm all set to thank Chibu for a lovely evening when he takes my face in his hands and kisses me. It's soft at first, then hard, and I feel my knees give way. Putting one arm around my waist, he holds me up. We continue to kiss for what seems like ages.

Suddenly he pulls back, holding my face in his hands. 'Take me upstairs, Sarah.' Oh no. No! Jacquie said no. I'm not ready for this. I haven't slept with a man in so long. Will I remember how? What if I screw up? What if he never comes back? No.

No. No. I back up, putting my hand against his chest. 'No. I mustn't. I just can't.' He tugs at my collar and kisses me again. I melt into him like women do in Hollywood films. He feels so nice. I feel like a little girl. His strong arms hold me tightly, wrapping me completely. I could snuggle beside him forever.

Maybe Jacquie doesn't know what she's talking about. Maybe I could take him upstairs. At least my bikini wax and g-string would get seen... And I should definitely get some kind of payback for wearing this g-string all night. We don't have to have sex...he could just sleep in my bed. Chibu and I continue to kiss on the front doorstep. Deirdre is bound to be watching this. What must she think of me? I have to stop this. God I want him. But I don't want to lose him later because of what I might do now. Jacquie will *freak* if I have sex with him tonight. I catch myself and push Chibu back.

'I must go. I really must go,' I say, shaking my head. I'm sorry.' I kiss him on the cheek. Chibu looks frustrated and pauses before speaking, as if deciding what to do.

'Well, I always say nothing's worth doing unless you do it one hundred and ten per cent.' He shrugs his shoulders. 'And if you're not really into it, then we can't get anywhere near that target.' He pauses, rubbing his hand against his shaved head. 'Tomorrow then.' Chibu grabs hold of my coat by the neck and pulls me to him, kissing me softly. 'Come to Brighton with me next Sunday.'

Am I dreaming? Brighton? With the most perfect man on earth? Why not just lasso the moon and pull it down for me?

'OK. Yes. Yes.' I'm stammering. 'I mean, yes, of course. I'd love to.' I smile non-stop. 'School holidays will nearly have started by then.' I giggle. 'Yes. I'd love to. Come round in the morning, around eleven.' I kiss him on the cheek. 'I'll be waiting.'

And with that, I open the front door, and glide inside.

Chapter thirteen

The week passes quickly with Chibu and I emailing each other all the time. I count the days down till Sunday. Finally, one morning I wake up and Sunday has finally arrived.

I pour myself a glass of Tropicana smooth-style orange juice. I hate orange juice with bits in it. It's nine o'clock, and Chibu's coming at eleven. I rush back to the bedroom and make the bed. Tonight will be the night; no doubt about that. I snatch Bear off the bed and hide him in the wardrobe. It's just for tonight. I hope he'll forgive me. I shower and get ready in a way that has become routine. Transforming into a Goddess is familiar. I enjoy observing myself in the mirror, developing into something that is almost attractive. If only I could be a little bit thinner...Just shave off a little from my hips and backside and I'd be happy. Oh well. It'll have to do. As I put on one of my many g-stings, I cringe. No choice about it. The day's going to end with sex and I have to be prepared. My bottom, à la française, in a g-string. Crazy. But Jacquie says men are VISUAL creatures. They like what they SEE. A g-string is a definite requirement. Sex it is then. But do I still remember how to have sex? Am I any good at it? What if Chibu has a dreadful time and never wants to see me again?

I start to panic. So I jump on my bed and ring Georgina. Who else would be up at ten a.m. on a Sunday morning? Georgina sounds flustered. The washing machine won't work and she has a ton of washing to do. Her cleaning lady has gone away for Christmas and John has been at the hospital for the last thirty-six hours. She's clearly fed up, but in her usual upbeat way, she switches back to her habitual happy self. I tell her about my worries.

'What if I'm crap in bed, Georgina? I mean...' I hesitate. '...what if I don't know how to do it any more?'

Georgina laughs. 'It isn't something you forget, Sarah. It's like riding a bike.'

But her reassurance isn't convincing and I go on about how I've forgotten everything and how I'm sure I'll lose him forever. Finally Georgina sighs...then silence. 'Georgina? Are you there?' I wait. 'Georgina?' Has she hung up the phone out of exasperation?

'Yes, I'm still here. Look, Sarah. You're being silly. Lots of people don't have sex for periods of time, but they always remember how to do it.' She pauses. 'John and I haven't had sex for months.'

WHAT? Oh my God. For *months*? Does she really mean *months*?

'But that's different. You're pregnant,' I argue.

'The reasons might be different, but the outcome is still the same.' Georgina bangs the washing machine. 'Sarah darling, I really must go. I have to sort out this bl...' she catches herself, and continues, '...washing machine.'

'Of course. Good luck with it. I'll let you know how it all goes.'

At 11.10, the doorbell goes. It's him. Gosh. It's him. OK, Sarah. Think GODDESS. Grab your bag. Check the mirror. That's it, Sarah honey. You look fabulous. Stand up straight. That's it. Think 'NAKED'. Come on. Let's go. I tear downstairs and open the front door.

'Shall I compare thee to a summer's day? Thou art more lovely and more temperate.' Chibu is standing against the railing with a single rose in his hand.

I laugh and continue for him. 'Rough winds do shake the

darling buds of May, And summer's lease hath all too short a date...' I grin. 'How does the rest go?'

'No idea, babe. I only learn Shakespeare to impress the girls. He smirks, handing me the flower. 'Let's go.' Taking my hand, he pulls me along to the car.

We drive for a couple of hours and talk about all sorts of things. Chibu tells me about his ex-girlfriend of eighteen months from a few years back. She's Chinese of all things, and has some fancy-smancy position as assistant director at Proctor & Gamble. So he likes his women intelligent. Can I do genius? Sure. I'm smart. Think Einstein, Sarah. Think Einstein. Her name was Anne and she was thirty-one. She owned a flat in St John's Wood. They spent many weekends there and Chibu found it boring in the extreme.

'I used to wonder whether we would've lasted so long if we'd seen more of each other...we were always so busy working. It was the perfect relationship for me: not too time-consuming.' He says, staring out at the road ahead. 'I liked her so much that I nearly bought her a ring.'

'So what happened?'

'I don't know. I chickened out. I was only thirty-two. I got cold feet. Maybe I was too young. Back then I wasn't made that way.'

Hmm. I wonder if he's made that way now?

'Have you had other serious girlfriends?' I probe.

'No...Anne was it. Sometimes I think that maybe I made a mistake. Anne was good for me...'

Dammit.

'...She kept me on the straight and narrow. I liked being a good boy. Now I knock about with all sorts of women,' he says, breaking into a grin. 'Just look at who I'm hanging out with today!'

Smiling, I whack him on the arm. Chibu hollers.

'So how about you? You ever been serious about anybody?' he asks.

127

'Yeah. I had a boyfriend called Djamel. We were good together.'

'So what happened?'

'Well, he was a Muslim. In the end, there were too many cultural differences. And I couldn't possibly convert. My mother—a Born Again Christian—would keel over if I converted to Islam.'

Chibu perks up. 'Your mother's a Born Again? That must be rough.'

'Yeah. To say the least.' I roll my eyes. 'Not that we split up because of her. I just hadn't realised how much Islam meant to Djamel when we first started seeing each other. As time went on, he became more involved with the mosque and his views became more apparent.'

I'm a fighter but even Sarah, Goddess of the Night, is bound to lose a war with Allah.

Chibu and I continue talking of how people change over time and how it's difficult to sustain a relationship amongst all those changes. We discover that neither of us has much experience of long-term sustenance. Our relationships never last more than a few months.

'So who was that guy who isn't so important texting you last night, then, eh?' Chibu nudges me with his elbow.

'Oh. No one really. Just some guy I met on the Internet.'

Jesus. Did I just say that out loud?

'On the Internet?' Chibu's eyes open wide. 'You mean you meet guys on the Internet?'

'Yeah. Nothing wrong with it,' I snap defensively. 'Just another modern way of meeting people…"Love and Friends". That's the site. It's fantastic. You should try it sometime.'

Chibu gapes at me. 'Me?' He puts his hand on his chest. 'On the Internet? Nah. No thanks. Anyway, don't need to. I've already met the woman I want.'

We park the car near the beach and walk to a restaurant by

the pier. It's a funny little fish and chips place with large heavy wooden tables, each adorned with a Heinz ketchup and bottle of vinegar. It's packed: families everywhere. We don't care. It's warm and frankly if we were on the moon, I'd be happy. We sit at a table with a view of the sea. The restaurant's loud and we have to lean in to hear each other. Halfway through eating I notice Chibu smiling at one of the little girls waddling past our table. She beams back. She's lovely. YIPPEE…good sign. He likes children. Maybe he's ready to have his own little ones. He's thirty-five after all. Maybe I've caught him at exactly the right age. I wonder whether he'd be willing to move to Brixton? Probably not. Well, I could live in Notting Hill. Hmm…What would be my route to work?

'Sarah? Are you there?' Chibu waves his hand in my face. 'You with me?'

'Yes. Yes. Sorry.' I point to the sea. 'I was just taken in by how beautiful it is.'

'It's great, isn't it?' He chews on his food. 'Well at least the view is. Fish and chips isn't my favourite. I prefer it raw. I eat sushi every other day.'

What is it with bankers always eating sushi?

'Actually, my favourite food is Suya,' he continues. 'It's a Nigerian kebab and it's delicious. I hate all that fast food stuff like McDonald's. You ever read *Fast Food Nation* or seen *Super Size Me?*'

'I've seen *Super Size Me*. Pretty scary what all that McDonald's food did to that guy.'

'Tell me about it. I won't touch the stuff. Well, every now and then I allow myself some McDonald fries. They're too good to give up entirely.' Chibu winks. 'Let's get out there. Let's go have some fun'

We finish lunch and head to the pier. We walk along holding hands, pausing every now and again for a kiss. It's like an old Cary Grant film; a picture perfect day.

'So, you ever cheated on a girlfriend?' I smirk.

'Moi?' Chibu places his hand on his chest. 'Nah...No, really. I never have. Of course that doesn't mean that I'm always monogamous.'

'What? Yes it does! So you've cheated on girlfriends then!' I smack him lightly on the arm.

'No. I always tell them what's up. Honesty is the best policy...That way I can't be accused of any wrongdoing. She has to agree to the terms if she wants to hang with me.'

'Well that's the strangest way of doing things.' I raise my chin. 'And who are these women who agree to your terms anyway? You sound like this friend of mine. I don't get men. I've only ever had one boyfriend at a time.'

'Really?' Chibu laughs. 'You should get out more.'

We reach the pier and ramble down the length of it together. Candy floss, rock candy and postcards line the boardwalk. It's cold and windy, so we hold on to each other tight. To get warm, we jump in a car in the Haunted House. The platforms creak as the man in a skeleton costume pushes a black lever to the floor. The three-minute ride is completely silly and not scary at all. But I make clever use of it and at every possible opportunity, I bury my head in Chibu's chest. He wraps his arms around me, carefully kissing me on the forehead every time I shriek. That done, we move into the arcade arena. We play several games. We race each other on the cars and we compete at shooting several different types of alien invaders. I'm the better driver. But he annihilates me on all the shooting games. Boys always know how to shoot. Is it a skill they're born with? As we approach Ace Driver, an unshaven white guy of about forty with straggly black hair pushes ahead of us and grabs the steering wheel.

'Hey, mate!' Chibu says authoritatively. 'We were about to use that.' But the man ignores us and puts his money into the machine. 'Hey!' Chibu shouts, moving to stand in front of him.

'What's wrong with you? I'm speaking to you.' But the man continues to play as if we don't exist.

'Look, just leave it. No big deal. There are lots of other games,' I whisper, trying to pull him to another machine. Chibu's arm is rigid against his side. He tugs away from me.

'But that's not the point,' he mutters, making a fist. 'Who does he think he is? I'd like to punch his lights out.'

'Look, it's Whack-a-Mole!' I point excitedly to the other side of the room. 'Lets go play that. I love that game. Bet I beat you…'

'What? You beat ME? No way!' Chibu rushes forward to get to the game first. Phew. That was a close call. I detour round, trying to take a short cut. I pass the man on Ace Driver who turns to look at Chibu dashing away.

'Fucking black bastard,' he mutters, stepping down on the accelerator. I shake my head, wondering whether I heard him properly. I pause in my tracks.

'Hey!' Chibu shouts over from the machine. 'What you doing?'

'Coming!' I yell, and I charge at him, ripping the Whack-a-Mole hammer out of his hands.

Eventually, we have thousands of yellow tickets falling out of our pockets. We're having such a good time I barely notice the old Madness song sounding through the intercom:

'It must be love, love, love, nothing more, nothing less, love is the best.' Chibu pauses and takes hold of the lapels of my coat, pulling me into him. 'Hey.' His face is nearly touching mine and he looks right at me. 'I think it *must* be.' Jesus. Did he just say what I think he said? Did he really? What else could he mean by that? OH MY GOD. Well, *if music be the food of love, play on! Play on!* I really am going to get married!

Suddenly it starts to thunder and then CRASH. The rain comes pouring down. Chibu tilts his head to one side. 'What do you say we cash in our tickets, and go find ourselves a hotel?'

He glances at his watch. 'It's six already. And I don't want the day to end just yet.'

A hotel? Gosh. Well why not? Why not have sex in a nice hotel instead of my bed? Yeah. It might be really romantic. Maybe we could go back to the same hotel for our honeymoon.

'A hotel?' I try to look coy. 'But that would mean we'd...' I twirl my hand round in circles.

'Yes. It would.' Chibu pauses to give me a peck on the lips.

'But seeing as I wanted you from the moment I saw you in Selfridges, I figure I've been pretty patient.' He smiles. 'Anyway, with all these guys after you on the Internet, I have to get my moves in pretty fast before my competition takes over.'

I burst into laughter. Competition? He's clearly never met Arthur the scarecrow. Gulp. What if *my* moves are totally out of date? I curl my hair around my left ear and Chibu takes my hand. We head for the desk to present our tickets. We have enough to get a giant white rabbit with floppy ears. Chibu hands it to me. 'For you Principessa.' He winks, chuckling. 'I already have one called "Sugarkins".'

Is he joking? Does he really have a stuffed rabbit? What guy owns a stuffed rabbit called Sugarkins? Maybe an ex-girlfriend gave it to him? What if he brings all his girlfriends to Brighton pier and wins stuffed rabbits? What if I'm just one more girl in a long line of suckers? Am I being a chump? And here we are on our way to a hotel. Oh Jesus. Maybe this is a bad idea. I hold on tight to the giant rabbit. He's enormous and I can just about get my arms around him. Chibu jumps about trying to get sight of my face. I move the rabbit to one side and unblock the view.

'Ah. There you are,' he sighs. 'God dammit. You're just so beautiful. I can't even go a few minutes without seeing your face.'

Oh oh oh. Maybe I'm being silly. He's lovely. It must be love love love. It must be. It must be. Get me to that hotel. We sprint outside into the rain and Chibu holds the giant rabbit over our heads. We fall about with laughter as we run, trying hard to avoid the puddles. When we arrive at the car, we're soaked through and so's the rabbit. We throw him in the back and jump in.

'Don't worry, I know a lovely little place just outside of the city, over there.' Chibu points into the distance. 'I'll have you warm and dry in no time.'

An hour later, we're sat by the fire, draped in a couple of hotel robes sipping champagne in a cosy little room in the cosiest of hotels. He certainly has good taste. The hotel is small and refined. The kind of thing you might find in a film starring Helena Bonham Carter, straight out of the nineteenth century.

What a difference a guy makes. That day I locked myself out of the house in the café with Jacquie, the rain made life difficult and downcast. With Chibu, the rain is a delightful part of our picture perfect day. It's brought us closer and I now feel as if I've known Chibu for years. We lie on the soft white wool carpet, chatting.

'I think it's great you're a teacher. It's such an important job. I went to my local comprehensive as a kid,' Chibu sighs, rubbing his head. 'What an experience. Supply teachers in and out of lessons. Kids way out of control. Sometimes it was pandemonium.'

'Some schools have a tough time,' I say, nodding.

'That's an understatement!' Chibu raises his voice. 'In my school if you weren't seriously determined and talented, you were finished.' He twists his hand into a fist. 'The only route to success was to be the best…whatever the cost.'

So that's why Chibu's so bent on being goal-oriented. He's one of *those* black guys. The type that will succeed no matter what. And no one will ever stop them. Chibu rubs a towel over my head. 'Can you believe that idiot at the arcades today? What a jerk. What the hell was his problem anyway?'

Do I tell him what I overheard? 'Well he was just an idiot. Let's forget him.' I squeak, wondering whether I'm doing the right thing.

Chibu jumps up. 'Yeah, you're right. Anyway, I have to make a couple of phone calls.' He walks to the sofa on the other end of the room. 'Have to sort out being late for work tomorrow.' He rolls his eyes. 'Some of us aren't as lucky as teachers whose never-ending holidays are about to start!' He sticks his tongue out at me and takes out his phone.

As Chibu chats work stuff on the far end sofa, I warm myself by the fire and gaze at him. Here I am at this beautiful hotel with *my* boyfriend. *MY BOYFRIEND*. After all, he said I was his girlfriend last night. He's perfect. I wouldn't change a thing about him. With guys, there's always *something* that isn't quite right. But Chibu couldn't be better if I'd made him myself. Maybe thirty isn't so bad? It just depends on how you look at it. Chibu waves in my direction with the phone still glued to his ear. 'Why don't you order some room service? Get me something with chicken.'

I leap to the king-size bed and pick up the stylish phone by the lamp. I ring the front desk and ask for a couple of cold chicken sandwiches and a large bottle of still mineral water. Might as well try to keep the calories to a minimum. Chibu's about to witness the carnage created by other Machiavellian calories. All I can do now is hope that the light is dim enough to hide the cellulite crawling up my bottom.

'Hey.' Chibu sits next to me.

'Hey.' I reply, turning to face him. Come on, Sarah. Think GODDESS. You'll be fine. Remember you have a sexy g-string on and he'll love it. It's like riding a bike. Just like riding a bike. 'This will be OK, won't it?' I look at the floor.

Chibu pulls my chin up and kisses me. 'Babe, just trust me.' So I close my eyes and do as I am told.

Chapter fourteen

OK, no number two...just number one. Can't do number twos in the same vicinity as a guy until you're married to him. I'll just wait till I get home. I stand up from the toilet, draped in a towel, and punch Jacquie's number into my mobile phone and put it to my ear.

'You'll never believe where I am.'

'Sarah, it's six thirty in the morning.' Jacquie sighs. 'I've only just woken up.'

'I know. I'm sorry. But I'm in a hotel in Brighton with *you know who*,' I screech in my whisper. 'I finally did it! Manuele will be so proud of me.'

'Chibu?' Jacquie pauses, thinking. 'You had sex?' She claps. 'Wow. Was he any good?'

'Damn right he was good.' I pause and listen out for noise from the bedroom. 'He was great. Jesus, Jacquie. I forgot sex could be this good.' I move towards the bathroom door to check that he's still sleeping. 'You know his...well you know, his...LUNCH BOX is just the perfect size; not too big, not too small and he knows how to move so that it's just so...ooh...it was so good! I tell you Jacquie. I could *so* marry this guy.' I open the door.

'Oh could you now?' Chibu is standing on the other side of the door with a towel wrapped round his waist.

Fuck. Fuck. Fuck. I drop the phone. 'YIKES!' I fumble, trying to pick up the phone, gripping my towel around me, while keeping my gaze on Chibu. 'I was just talking to myself.' I cough. 'I mean, I was talking to my friend

Jacquie...I was having trouble sleeping.' Phone in hand, I curl my hair around my left ear and simper awkwardly.

'OK. Well hurry up in there, babe.' Chibu turns, walking back into the bedroom. 'We have the drive back ahead of us.'

STUPID Sarah. STUPID. Everyone knows it's *the* cardinal sin to mention marriage in front of a new boyfriend. Bloody hell. He'll probably be put off for life. STUPID Sarah. Really STUPID.

Rule Number SEVEN: Gotta make sure your man never knows what you're really thinking.

As we leave, we step over the chicken sandwiches sitting on the tray outside our room door. We didn't quite get round to eating them. We jump in the car and Chibu takes off like a shot.

'Hey, Principessa.' He looks over at me and winks.

'What's your last name?' I ask.

'It's Okoru. So what's with you telling your girlfriends that my dick is only medium size, eh babe?' he chuckles, grabbing his crotch. 'Other girlfriends have always told me that it's ENORMOUS. I have a rep to protect, you know.'

'Yeah? *Enormous*?' I giggle, making a face. 'Well, what can I say? Your ex-girlfriends should get out more.'

What is it with guys and their obsession with having big lunch boxes? Don't they realise that it HURTS when they're too big? Yuck. Yuck. Yuck. Thoughts of Alex, a boyfriend of mine at Cambridge dance in my head. He was Welsh with curly black hair. He also had the most gigantic packet I have ever seen. To this day, I am certain the main reason I am slightly bowlegged is because of his constant persistence in the middle of the night.

Chibu winks at me. 'Babe, you can't go round saying that kind of thing. I'm a *black* man remember.'

'So that means you have a big one? You black guys are always strutting around as if you have something delicious hidden between your legs. ' I chuckle. 'Yeah right. Some white guys carry packed lunch boxes too you know.'

'Oh do they now?' Chibu shakes his head. 'Bigger than mine?'

'Well, what can I say? I suppose your mother forgot to give you an extra sandwich in case you got hungry at break time.'

Chibu's eyes open wide. 'What? No white guy is bigger than me. I guarantee it.'

Dring dring. Chibu answers on his hands-free set and our conversation comes to an end. Every few minutes he reassures work by saying, 'I'll be there in a bit' or 'see you in twenty', and each time he drives a little faster. He's preoccupied, so I stare out of the window at the beautiful countryside. Lovely country houses... I wonder whether we'll have one. Soon I'll be Sarah Okoru. Has a nice ring to it. *Mrs* Sarah Okoru. What will my signature look like? I knew I'd be *Mrs Sarah Somebody* soon enough.

As we near London, Chibu explains that he's to leave for Nigeria on Friday and has too many work commitments to see me beforehand. I'm disappointed, but I understand. He's a hardworking black man and failure's not an option. I'm not about to complain. It certainly beats the number of wasters I've met in my time. He drops me in front of my flat and speaks through the open window of the car.

'I had a great time.' He taps the steering wheel. 'I'll call you before I fly.' He reaches to the back of the car, picking up the giant rabbit. 'Hey, you forgot our friend the rabbit.' He opens the passenger door and shoves the rabbit at me. I take hold of it and slam the door.

'I love your silver car,' I giggle.

'Silver? It isn't silver. It's *pearl* grey.' He winks. 'Got that? Pearl grey, for a *pearl* of an owner.' He waves. 'Arrivederci, Principessa.' I wave back as he drives off down the road.

He's wonderful and I'm madly in love. As I skip up the steps to my flat with the rabbit bouncing about in my arms, I notice something move in the top window of the abandoned house next door. 'Hey!' I shout. 'Who's there?' But he's gone. Or maybe I didn't see anything in the first place. I wonder whether the guy who tried to steal my bag lives up there? I stare at the window for a few minutes, then move inside. I gallop to my bedroom, place the rabbit on the floor in the corner, snatch Bear out of the wardrobe, and jump on the bed.

'We did it, Bear. We did it. I'm his GIRLFRIEND.' I toss Bear in the air and scream, 'Don't be jealous, Bear. Rabbit wants to be your friend.' I pause. No…not Rabbit. I'm not lost like Holly Golightly any more. Chibu rescued me. I'm a GODDESS. Prime City. I look in the mirror and hold the rabbit next to me. 'You, Mr Rabbit, need a real name.' I lean over at Bear. 'What shall it be?' But he doesn't answer. 'I know,' I shout. 'Let's call him Brighton.' Yeah. That's perfect. Brighton and Bear. Even they make the perfect pair. I roll over on the bed and grab the phone. I try calling both Manuele and Jacquie, but their phones are turned off. They're busy working. Even Georgina's phone is off. I've just spent the night with the most gorgeous bloke on the planet, and I can't tell anyone! I lie on my bed. I'm so happy. My mother will have grandchildren now. I've beaten the clock. I've won the bloody war.

I lie there for a while when the doorbell goes. HEY! Maybe he's come back. Maybe he got out of work. Maybe he just *had* to see me. I jump to my feet and check myself in the mirror. I skip down to the main front door in my socks. I fiddle with the lock for a moment, and then, grinning, I swing the great door open. A man is holding some flowers.

'Are you Sarah?'

WAHEY! Flowers for ME?

'Yes I am.'

'These are for you.' The man hands me the flowers. 'Could you just sign this for me please?' He flaps a piece of paper about. I sign, thank the man, and close the front door. How did Chibu arrange these so quickly? God, he's good. He sent me FLOWERS! I really *am* in an old Cary Grant film!

I charge up the stairs and dash to the kitchen. I throw the

flowers on the counter and rip the card from the plastic. The staple fastens the card to the envelope and I struggle to remove it. The flowers are beautiful...Just beautiful. I wonder what he's written? Will he call me Principessa? Or better yet, will he call me 'his girl'? Come on, Sarah, hurry up with this damn card...I turn the card over and read: 'To Sarah, the prettiest of princesses. King Arthur' Arthur?...WHAT? Arthur sent me flowers? Can't the skinny Prince Charles take a hint? What's with this guy? Isn't it funny the way flowers from the *right* guy send you over the moon, but flowers from the *wrong* guy make you sick? Oh God, do you think he also left the digestives? I should've told Arthur from the start that I wasn't interested. I never made that clear. Now he's sent me flowers. I wouldn't like it much if our positions were reversed.

Rule Number EIGHT: Gotta treat the guys I don't like as I would like to be treated.

I put the flowers in a vase and place them in the front room. They're stunning. I log on to the Internet and go to the 'Love and Friends' site. OK, so I'm a coward. I can't bear the thought of telling him face to face. Especially after he sent me flowers. I just can't.

Message to 'King Arthur': *Thank you for the lovely flowers. You really shouldn't have. At the moment, I'm a bit busy with things. Christmas is coming and I don't know if I will be able to see you. But thanks for the flowers and I'll see you in the New Year. All the best Sarah.*

There. That should do. I'm about to press SEND, when I read the message again. No, Sarah. You're not being straight with him. So I delete the 'I'll see you in the New Year' and replace it with: 'I hope you meet someone nice on this site.' There. That's better. He can't possibly misunderstand that. I press SEND just as the phone starts to ring. Oh God. Please don't let that be Arthur. Oh God. What will I say? Especially as I've just sent him this email? I move slowly towards the phone.

Brring. Brring. Maybe I won't answer it. Yeah. I could just let it ring...No, Sarah, it could be Chibu. You HAVE to answer it...

'Hello?'

'Hi, Sarah. It's Sam.' He pauses. 'I figured you'd be on holiday from today.'

'Oh hi, Sam. How are you?'

'I'm really well. Just sold a painting to the Royal Bank of Scotland. For some good money too.'

'That's great. Well done! You been out to celebrate?'

'Yeah. Went clubbing in Brixton Saturday night and then spent Sunday recovering from a hangover,' he says, excitedly. 'We had a drinking competition and I downed a number of tequilas. I was pretty good. Got second place.'

White guys love getting pissed. Rare to see a black guy doing that. Then they're sick in some corner of the street. It's disgusting. And what happened to his eight-year-olds' football team? I deliberately avoid telling Sam about *my* weekend and move the subject on to what we'll do during the holidays. We're both to spend Christmas with our families and Sam is dreading it. Hanging out in Kensington with his café society mother and his corporate lawyer brother who's flying in from New York is too much. He can't wait until the New Year. I'm feeling much the same.

'On the one hand the holidays are good because they force you to spend time with your family,' Sam chuckles, '...and on the other they're terrible because they force you to spend time with your family.'

'I know what you mean.' I pause. 'Sam, this might sound a bit strange, but did you leave a packet of chocolate digestives on my front step the other day?

'Chocolate digestives? No. Someone must be watching over you! Wish someone would leave me some chocolate digestives, might just help me to give up these damn cigarettes.'

I like Sam. He's funny, charming, and we certainly have a

spark. But he's twenty-seven; he thinks I'm twenty-eight, and his clothes...he's such a rebel. Friday and Saturday nights are spent in a nightclub drinking into oblivion even if it means abandoning a bunch of eight-year-olds. And what about our date when he turned pink after being in the loo? He was probably doing a line of cocaine...bored rich boy out for a bit of fun. He's also white, whereas I prefer boys black...I think. Anyway, it doesn't matter. Chibu's my boyfriend and I don't have eyes for anyone else.

'So Sarah, when are you and I going to hook up?' he asks.

'Well, I'm quite busy at the moment, preparing for Christmas and all, then I'm away in North London for a week.' I pause trying to think of what to say next. 'So I'm not really sure when I'll have the time.'

'OK then. If you want to hook up in the New Year, give me a ring.'

I agree and we hang up. After all, I'm *Chibu's* girlfriend now. I won't be calling Sam ever again. I charge to my bedroom and grab Brighton the rabbit. I fall on the bed with my arms wrapped around him. Mrs Sarah Okoru. My initials will spell the word 'so'. Hmm. Not ideal. But it won't matter. Mrs Sarah Okoru.

'And our children can play with YOU, Brighton.'

I squeeze him tight. Hmm. So neither Chibu nor Sam left the biscuits. Was it Arthur? Seems strange that he would send flowers *and* biscuits. Oh well, guess it must have been him.

I stare at the phone. Wish I could call Chibu. But I'm following Jacquie's advice. Look how far it's got me already! It nearly has me down the aisle. I'll have to wait for him to chase. Sometimes I feel like I'm waiting forever. Wish I could fast-forward time. Wish I could fast-forward to the end of the book. Wish I could fast-forward to the day that Chibu and I get married and live happily ever after.

Chapter fifteen

Still have a thousand things to do before Christmas. When the hell will I get it all done? The plan is to spend just over a week in North London with my parents and I only have two days to prepare. Psychologically, I've been preparing for weeks. Realistically, this isn't enough. My retired, bored parents are bound to give me the 'Why aren't you married yet?' talk and we're bound to argue.

As an only child, I'm their only hope for grandchildren, for another lease of life. Without grandchildren, all they have to look forward to is a life filled with hospitals, wheelchairs and medication. Their happiness hinges on *me*. But I can't even look after my *own* happiness, let alone *theirs*. Talk about pressure. I lie on my bed for a while trying to come up with a solution. At least *this* year I'll be able to tell them I have a BOYFRIEND. Chibu rings me every day. He's lovely, and he's mine…But *marriage* is what my parents want. They want to see a *ring*. They won't care that he adores and misses me. They'll want a wedding date. Should I lie? Bloody hell. The phone interrupts my train of thought.

'Hello, baby.' Chibu makes a soft kissing sound. 'How's your day?'

'It was fine, thanks. You all packed for your trip?'

'Yeah yeah. Nigeria's going to be great. Two whole weeks of sun.' He chuckles. 'I'll think of you in the rain and freezing cold.'

'Yeah. And think of me stuck up in North London with my crazy parents.' I add, 'I'll miss you, you know.'

'Me too, baby. Me too.' We talk for a little while about how we'll miss each other when I hear the phone ring on Chibu's end in the background. 'Look, I'd better get back to work. I just wanted to hear your voice before flying tomorrow.'

'Oh. OK. I know, you're busy. Have a good trip...Oh, and think of me!'

'You know I will. I'll ring you when I'm back.'

He's so wonderful. Mummy and Daddy are going to love him. They won't be able to help themselves. And he'll give me a ring eventually. Then there'll be grandchildren. Mummy and Daddy can baby-sit on Saturdays. That way Chibu and I can spend some time alone together. Chibu's mother will have to fly in from Nigeria to see the grandchildren. Hmm. I wonder how often she'll be able to visit? I take Bear and hold him above my head. 'What do you think, Bear? You won't be jealous of the children, will you? 'But he doesn't answer, so I put him down and pick up my stack of still-to-be-written Christmas cards. Imagine, next year I'll be signing 'Lots of love, from Sarah and Chibu' ...or should I say 'Chibu and Sarah?' Both have a lovely ring to them. We're made for each other. Imagine, next year the writing of Christmas cards will transform from being a chore into a pleasure. I start scribbling Deirdre a Christmas card. Hmm. Will have to get her a present too. Maybe I'll get her a new cardigan.

Two hours later I lick the last envelope and paste it shut. It's for my Uncle Cyril in California. I troll through my address book looking for his address.

Ding dong. Eight p.m. on a Thursday evening. Wonder who that could be? I head downstairs and swing open the great front door. It's Chibu. 'Hey, Principessa. Had to see you before flying tomorrow. I left work early so that I could drop by and say hello.'

AWWHH YEAH...He's mine. All mine. Forever and ever and ever. Shit. Wait a minute, no make-up on. No G-string on.

I'm totally unprepared. Fuck. I throw my arms around Chibu and kiss him all over his face. I grab hold of his hand and drag him up the stairs. Right. Must get him upstairs and dim the lights immediately. Thank God Priscilla came by the other day and tidied up. Saved by Priscilla. Must remember to get her a gift to say thanks.

'Wow. You sure seem pleased to see me,' Chibu squeaks, as I pull him into the flat.

'You bet I am. It's so nice of you to drop by. You've made my day.' I beam, turning off the main light and switching on a little lamp.

We sit down on the sofa. Chibu places his hand on the back of his head and sighs. 'I'm so tired. Work is crazy at the moment. But I had to see you. Com'ere.' He tugs at my chin and kisses me gently. 'You have a nice place. It's cute. Will I be allowed to see the bedroom, tonight?' He winks and kisses me again.

'Yes. Of course. Hang on just one minute.'

I kiss him lightly on the lips and run to my bedroom. I dive into my panties drawer and pull out a fancy black velvet bra and red lace g-string. I quickly rip off my clothes, slip them on and re-dress. He'll never know. He'll just think I wear this sexy stuff all the time. I fly back to the front room and throw myself at him.

'So how are you then?'

'I'm OK I suppose.' Chibu hangs his head. 'Tried to get a taxi straight here from work tonight. I should have arrived earlier.'

'Oh, you didn't drive here?'

'Well I had to in the end. Couldn't find a taxi willing to take me.'

'You mean they were all full?'

'No. I mean when I said I was going to Brixton and they put two and two together...black man... Brixton...they drove off.'

I sit up straight. 'They did? Bloody idiots...I'm sorry.'

Poor Chibu. He looks angry. Must change the subject.

'So how's work been?' I snuggle into his chest.

Chibu wraps his arms around me. 'Same old thing. I work twenty-four hours a day. These maniacs never stop.'

I sit up slightly, looking suspicious. 'But isn't it just that you want everything to be perfect, so you work until it is?'

'Well partly, but banking's like that...people work like crazy. Of course, you're right. I can't let anyone prove themselves to be a better workaholic than me.' He grins.

'Would it really hurt you to be second best once in a while?' I ask, timidly.

Chibu pushes me off him. 'You know when I was at Harvard Business School, I went to lunch with a bunch of white American guys in one of my classes who had all been to top private schools. One of them let it drop that he thought I was there because the university had to fill their quotas.'

'Quotas? Quotas for what?'

'Quotas for African-Americans...Some universities in America are required to take a certain number of African-Americans.' He claps his hands. 'So this idiot figured that because I was black, I had to be some kind of token offering. Nothing to do with my intelligence or accomplishments...I was there because the university was forced to take me.'

'Was it true?' I whisper.

'Hell no. I demanded to know what this guy's scores were in each of his classes and I had him beat in every one of them,' Chibu smirks. 'The fucker thought he was better than me, well he had another think coming. Ever since then, I figure if I'm always number one, no one can ever doubt that I'm where I am because I deserve to be.'

Chibu is agitated and I rub his shoulder to calm him down. Must change the subject.

'Do you like me as much as I like you?' I ask.

'Well I'm here, aren't I? You have no idea how unusual this is for me. I think I like you too much actually.' Chibu strokes my cheek with the back of his hand, but pulls back suddenly. 'Anyway, I don't know why you would want me to be second best. You're a woman. You're meant to find power and success attractive.'

'Well, I never said I *wanted* you to be second best. I was just thinking about your work life balance, you know...maybe you'd be happier working less. I wouldn't mind if it meant you were happier.'

Chibu grins. 'What? Oh and I suppose I'd be happier with a woman less beautiful? Women want powerful men and men want beautiful women. That's the way it works.'

Is that all chemistry is? The more powerful the guy, the more intense the thunderbolt? Is there no such thing as the One? But doesn't that mean we'd all be chasing the same men? Hang on a sec...*are we*? I try to speak, but he grasps my face, kissing me hard. Pulling back, I blush. 'What time is your flight tomorrow?'

'Early. Very early. I'll be gone before you get up. My stuff is packed, but I'll have to go via my house to pick it up.'

'Then we don't have any time to waste,' I say bashfully, kissing him. Chibu grabs hold of me, kisses my neck and starts to unbutton my top.

God this is good. God, I'm in love. God, I'm so grateful. Thank you. Thank you. Thank you...Shit. BEAR. Where is he? Oh Jesus, how embarrassing. I hope Chibu doesn't see him. Chibu's hands disappear behind my back and I screech in delight. I cross my fingers on one hand, hoping I've left Bear hidden somewhere on the floor and with the other, I help by undoing my bra.

Chapter sixteen

I sit at my parents' dining table, eating breakfast. The house is exactly the same as it was the day I left for university, twelve years ago. An old Victorian house with about four flights of stairs near Belsize Park, the creaking wooden floors and my mother's antique furniture give the place the feel of a museum. To me, it now feels small. When I was little, the dining room was HUGE. Like a giant Neanderthal I clump around a house which was once the size of Buckingham Palace.

In his day, my father owned a recording studio which did pretty well. He recently sold it and took his retirement. My mother was a nurse all her life, working at Paddington Hospital in the children's ward until six months ago when she too retired. I have bored retired parents in desperate need of entertaining grandchildren.

It's Boxing Day and Christmas has gone off without a hitch. On Christmas Eve, we watched the customary *It's a Wonderful Life* and my mother cried at the end as she always does. We open presents on Christmas Day, and no one mentions a word about me not being married; eight days down, one more to go; so far so good.

Perhaps I've got away with it this time. Perhaps they've taken pity on me seeing as I'm thirty. In any case, I have my trump card: Chibu. We've been together for four weeks. When I checked my phone service yesterday, there were TWO messages from him saying he missed me. Chibu is my beautiful bona fide boyfriend. I chomp on the dumplings and saltfish my mother made for breakfast. It's delicious. Her Jamaican food is the best part of being home. As I break my second dumpling in half, my parents sit themselves down on the other side of the table and fill their plates. My father is greying badly now, but he wears glasses which help to disguise the many lines across his face. He remains slim, and his whitish beard covers any sagging on his neck. My mother is a dark black woman, and looks much better for her age than him. She wears a colourful house robe with rollers in her hair. There's an odd silence. I look up at them from my plate and my mother sighs.

'Sarah, dear, your father and I want to talk to you.'

Oh God. Here it comes. My father clears his throat and holds his hand out as if he's about to give a speech.

'Sarah.' He pauses as if he's trying to find a delicate way of saying what he wants. 'Sarah, your mother and I think that you are getting old.' His posh English voice rings about the room. Great dad. Brilliant start. Just what I want to hear. I glance up from my plate with a look of disbelief.

My mother tries to help him. 'No no, Sarah dear. Your father just means that you really should have marriage in mind. Don't you think?'

I work hard to keep myself from exploding. I force my fingers into a fist and hit the table.

'Yes I know I need to get married,' I say, abruptly. 'And I'm trying. I even have a boyfriend now.' I gloat triumphantly. 'His name is Chibu. He's thirty-five, and he's great.'

'Chibu?' My mother screws up her face. 'Chibu? What sort of name is that?'

My father taps my mother's hand to calm her. 'It's Nigerian, darling, Nigerian.'

My mother jumps up. 'Nigerian? You want to marry an African?' She's hysterical. 'An African? My mother would roll over in her grave.' She pauses. 'And is he a Christian? I bet he's one of those Muslims too.'

Jesus bloody Christ. Why didn't I just keep my mouth shut?

I dated Djamel for months and never mentioned him to my parents. Imagine, I thought Chibu was my trump card. In fact, it was the worst thing I could have said.

'Now now, dear,' my father taps her hand, 'Sarah should be able to go out with whomever she wants, we've always said that.' My father winks at me. 'And anyway, don't they say the blacker the cherry, the sweeter the juice?'

WHAT? The blacker the cherry? Clearly my father has been watching too many Blaxploitation movies. My mother throws her hand in front of my father's face. 'No, Sarah. Don't you listen to your father now, you hear me? A white English boy is what you want. They won't take off with no other woman, you hear?' She wags her index finger at me. 'Not like those Africans.'

I turn to my mother, my hands forming two perfect fists on the table. 'So who do you want then?' I'm irritated. 'How about a Jamaican?'

My mother lifts her head. 'A Jamaican?...Have you gone and lost your mind, child?'

Things are getting heated. My father straightens his glasses. 'Now, now. That's enough. It's just that we worry about you Sarah. You are always on your own. Maybe you aren't looking in the right places.' He clears his throat again. 'The first thing you need to remember is that you want to find someone who you have something in common with...'

Thanks, Dad. Thanks for the ground-breaking advice. Hadn't thought of that one. You're a bloody genius.

'...If your mother and I had realised how little we had in common when we were married, then we might have thought twice about it.' He looks at my mother. 'Yes. Had I known that your mother would be so involved with the church, we would never have married.'

My mother turns to me, 'Yes, Sarah. If I had known he would be dragging me to the opera and the theatre in my old age, I would never have married him.'

They both nod at each other, and I gape at them in shock. Maybe familiarity *does* breed contempt. All my life my parents have argued incessantly. Is that what people do when they're in love? And if you don't argue with your other half, does that mean you're *not* in love? I think about my ex-boyfriends. The ones I argued the most with were always the ones with whom I had the biggest sparks. Is it really a toss-up? Is it *either* a spark *or* friendship? Can't I have *both*?

'But dad, I want to find someone to hang out with who is also my soulmate.' I pause. 'I want to find LOVE.'
My father peers at me from over the top of his glasses. 'Love? What's love?' He chuckles. 'Don't tell me that you believe in *love*, Sarah?'

'Yes. Of course I believe in love, Daddy.' I stop to think. 'What about Romeo and Juliet, Catherine and Heathcliff, Scarlett O'Hara and Rhett Butler?'

'Exactly, Sarah. They're all characters from books and films. They're not real people.' My father's eyes glint condescendingly. 'Love only exists in books, dearest.'

POW. Side kick to my ribs. My mother knocks my father on his shoulder.

'Your father is being silly, Sarah. Sure love exists.' My mother smacks her fist against her hand. 'But you're meant to run into it by accident; you're not supposed to look for it the way that you do, Sarah dear.'

Run into it by accident? Why do people always say that rubbish? Any other sphere in life and people will tell you to pursue your goal. If you're hungry, they'll send you to a restaurant; if you want a pair of shoes, they'll send you to a shoe shop. But when it comes to love, they believe in fate and mystery and tell you to just stay at home and never meet a soul and then, magically, Prince Charming will suddenly appear. WHAT BOLLOCKS!

'That's rubbish, Mummy.'

'But you need a man who will stand by you.' My mother clasps her hands together. 'Like a nice Christian boy. There is one at the church I know. I told him about you.'

WHAT? A date with a Born Again Christian? I stand up from the table and kick my chair back.

'Look, this conversation is over.' I push my chair in, muttering, 'I have a boyfriend now. So I'm OK. Just leave me alone.'

I fly upstairs to my old bedroom and slam the door. Failure #73. I feel as if I'm sixteen. I'm being rude to my parents out of frustration of being told what to do. I sit on my dated bed and wish Bear was with me. The aged flowery wallpaper I chose at fourteen is beginning to peel at the edges. The pinkish furniture has faded into peach and my ancient teenage romance novels line the bookcase. I miss Chibu. My mother appears at the door.

'Sarah dear, I don't want to upset you. We just want you to be happy.' She pauses and smiles imploringly. 'But you need to bring Jesus into your life.'

I gaze up at my mother from the bed. I've heard this speech a zillion times.

'Because the Lord taketh when it is your time.' My mother holds her index finger in the air. 'And I want you in Heaven with me. You're my daughter. Please, Sarah.' She holds out her hand.

I roll my eyes and take my mother by the hand. 'I don't believe in God, Mummy. You need to accept that.'

My mother looks like she might cry. 'OK, Sarah. He will reveal himself to you when He is ready.' She holds her hands above my head. 'Let me just plead the blood of Jesus over you now. I plead the blood of Jesus over you, so that one day you may find a husband.'

I sit quietly on the bed, wondering how long this will take. I also wonder whether God might hear my mother's desperate cries and send a bolt of lightning crashing through the house with Chibu attached to the end of it. No such luck. No bolt of lightning. No Chibu. Just my mother droning on. Come on, Mummy, you're meant to have direct access to God…why am I still single?

Some fifteen minutes later, my mother seems satisfied, kisses me on the forehead and moves to the door. I take her hand in mine.

'Mummy, what was it like marrying a white man and then having me later on?'

My mother sits down on the bed beside me. 'Well, Sarah, it was no easy thing you know. My parents thought I was mad. But your father, you know, he was so charming.' She blushes. 'He swept me off my feet.'

'But Daddy just said that you don't love each other.'

'We must love each other, Sarah. We just can't get along, that's all.' My mother strokes my hair. 'He's all I have. I don't know how I would live without him.'

I hug my mother tight and she continues to stroke my hair. She tells me about walking through the streets of London in the sixties. How she held hands with my father and how people would stare. Sometimes people even laughed. But she was a brave woman. She told me about how once, after I was born, she even received some hate mail through the door. The letter told her to take her mongrel baby back to the jungle where we belonged. And you know what she did? She just tore it up and went about her business.

'I don't understand these white people. We black people have been here since the eighteenth century and some even since Roman times and they still can't accept us.' My mother pauses, shaking her head. 'Never told your father though. Didn't want to worry him. To this day, he doesn't know about that letter.'

'Wow, Mummy, you're outstanding.'

'I'm not the one you should admire, dear. It's your father.'

My mother smiles. 'You know how you've never met your grandparents? On your father's side?'

I nod. 'Yes Mummy. But they're dead.'

'No. They're not dead.' My mother bows her head. 'They just stopped speaking to your father when he married me.'

I look up at my mother, my mouth gaping. My mother wipes her eyes as if she's trying to hold back the tears.

'You see, Sarah. Some people are willing to turn their back on their own flesh and blood for love.' She strokes my face. 'Your father's just joking when he says he doesn't love me.'

Wow. I have grandparents I've never met. Wow. I can't believe it. My dear old dad decided to marry my mum with or without their blessing. Gosh. He must have been into my mum BIG TIME. Extraordinary how you grow up thinking your parents did everything wrong, and then later you're astounded at how much they did right; especially as it gradually becomes clear how bloody impossible it all is.

'You know why I want you with a white man, Sarah?'

'Why, Mummy?'

'Because I want you to be with a man who is just like your father.'

I give my mother a huge hug. 'Maybe you're right, Mummy. I'm always worrying about what other people will think about my choice of boyfriend...always worrying about what his parents will think of me. But you're living proof that even if people hate you, not only can your relationship survive, it might even get stronger.'

'Uh-huh.' My mother strokes my hair.

I sit up. 'Yeah. Who cares what random people on the street think? What matters is whether I'm happy. A man's colour shouldn't matter.'

'No. It shouldn't, Sarah dear. Though I still think a white one would be best, just like your father.' She pauses, thinking. 'Then again he did spoil you rotten. No other man will match

153

up to him in your head. I always used to tell him to stop treating you like a princess.'

Hmm. I wonder whether women with attentive fathers always have trouble finding good men? Maybe their expectations are too high. Maybe Daddy's little girl needs to grow up and deal with reality. My mother winks at me. What you need is a man you can train to do what you want.' She shakes her head. 'Men aren't so good at showing their feelings. Look at your father...can't even admit he loves me.' I place my head on her lap as she continues. 'Sarah, men enjoy being manipulated. Years ago, before you were born, when we were struggling financially, I used to pretend I had a bad back so that your father would do the hoovering.' I sit up as my mother breaks into a smile. 'He loved hoovering. He was happy because I needed his help and he enjoyed taking care of me.' She strokes my hair. 'You see, Sarah, it gave him the opportunity to show me that he loved me and it also made him feel more of a man because I depended on him for something.'

I giggle. 'Yeah right, Mummy! And let's not forget, you didn't have to do any of the hoovering!' We fall over together on the bed laughing.

Incredibly, my father never suspected a thing. Even when my mother's back ailment magically cleared up a few weeks after they had enough money to hire a cleaner, he still thought my mother was as honest as the day is long.

Rule Number NINE: Gotta be manipulative.

I'll always believe in the search for my soulmate; no matter what anyone says. Just look at what my parents have done. Just look at what my *mother* has done. My soulmate could be white, black, Indian, Chinese; whatever. When you're with your soulmate, anything is possible. Just need to find the One meant for me. God I hope it's Chibu.

'Sarah, remember how I said that your father was ill?'

'Yes, but he seems fine.'

'Don't tell him I told you. He made me promise not to say anything.'

'Tell me what?' I ask, frowning.

'They found a tumour.'

I spin my head round and grab my mother by the arm. 'A tumour? What do you mean? Where?'

'In his chest, near his lung. They're doing tests at the moment. I'm so scared.' My mother puts her hand on her lips. 'What if he dies? What will I do? I can't live without him.' I pull my mother to me and hug her. I hug her harder than I've ever done before.

'Don't worry, Mummy. I'm sure it'll be fine.' I rub her back. Will it be fine? Fuck. My father with cancer? Fuck. I don't even dare say the word. 'Mummy, when will we have the results of the tests? Will he have to have an operation?'

'They said they would ring in a few days…and yes, I think they may have to operate.' My mother bends forward, hugging me again. 'Please don't tell him I told you.'

'Don't worry. I won't say a word.'

My mother kisses me on the forehead and shuffles downstairs. I lie on my bed for a while thinking about my father and how short life can be. Could my mother end up like Deirdre, all alone in her old age? What would she do all by herself? Could my dad really die?

I bounce up and look in the mirror. Daddy's going to be fine. How silly. How can my dad die? That would make me unbelievably old. I peer at my reflection. If something were really wrong, then they would rush him to hospital right away. Wouldn't they? They wouldn't waste time on tests. And he doesn't look ill; he looks fine. He couldn't possibly have cancer. My father can't go and die like that. I'm not old enough. That would happen on some Channel 5 film, not real life. I look in the mirror and force a smile. Daddy's going to be just fine.

I notice something shiny in my hair. So I brush it away. But it doesn't move. So I brush my fingers through my hair forcefully. It still doesn't move. So I look a little closer. OH MY GOD. Right there on the top of my head in plain view for all the world to see is one shiny GREY HAIR. How the hell is this possible? I know I'm not nineteen any more, and the bitch at John Lewis said I had smile lines, but GREY HAIR? Maybe I really am old enough to have dead parents. I start to cough. I start to hiccough. Then I can't breathe. Oh my God. Is my father really going to die? I think I'm hyperventilating. I can't cope. AARRGH!

'DADDY!' I shout as loud as I can.

My father comes charging up the stairs. 'What's wrong darling?'

I rush to him, throwing my arms around him as I did when I was a little girl. He holds on to me tight. I want to cry. I want to be six years old again when my father bounced me on his knee and read me bedtime stories. Tell me you're going to be OK. Tell me you're not going to die. Tell me that I can stay a kid forever. Standing together, my father's grey hair tickles the side of my face. I stare at him in horror.

'Sarah, what's wrong with you?' he asks.

I promised Mummy I wouldn't tell. 'Daddy, I just feel so *old* these days.' I sigh. 'I just feel so *old*.' My father looks at me with pity in his eyes, and finally, he speaks:

'Well, Sarah…if *you* feel old, just imagine how *I* feel.'

He's right. Thirty's young. I have my whole life ahead of me. Here's my father facing a fork in the road of life, knowing that death may be imminent and he's standing tall. How extraordinary. I want to be just like him. So with my father standing next to me, I turn to the mirror, trap the grey hair between my fingers, and give it a mighty tug.

Chapter seventeen

'Wheatgrass juice for you, madam?' I stand in the café in the entrance to the Virgin Active gym in Clapham. Manuele suggested we meet there and get fit together. A young woman shoves a tiny plastic container (no bigger than a twenty-pence piece), holding some dark green goo in my direction. 'It's only £2.95 and will completely clean out your system,' she trills. NEARLY THREE QUID? You mean to tell me that those few drops of wheatgrass juice are capable of revolutionising my internal organs? FOR £2.95? How the hell do you get any juice out of wheatgrass anyway? It's just a piece of grass.

The counter is stuffed with healthy cereal bars and various fruit juices. Hmm. I wonder whether Arthur was the one who left those chocolate digestives? Flowers *and* digestives? Just seems too over the top. Hmm. Must ring Mummy later. Inconclusive tests? What can she have meant by that in her message? Jesus. I can't believe my dad could have cancer.

'Ciao, Bellissima.' I snap round and Manuele kisses me on both cheeks. 'Long time no see.'

'Yes, well that's because you're always so busy with your many girlfriends,' I sneer.

'Now do not be jealous, Sarah.' Manuele winks, stuffing his current novel into his jacket pocket. 'You know that *you* are my favourite girl.' I laugh and give him a hug. I haven't seen Manuele for a couple of months. Not since he nearly got caught by that married woman's husband. Abandoning our usual hit of caffeine, we order a couple of waters. Finding a seat takes some doing. It's late-January and the gym is packed full of super-keen people seriously dedicated to their New Year's resolutions.

'So I take it you haven't seen that married woman since the night you stayed at my flat?' I ask, grinning.

'Nah.' Manuele shakes his head, smiling. 'Nah…That night pretty much ended things for us. But it was good while it lasted.' He gulps his water. 'So what happened with that guy from Selfridges and that guy from the café?' He pauses and scans me up and down. 'Have you finally had SEX, Sarah?'

I'm excited. For once, Manuele will be proud of me; I have a success story to tell. I tell Manuele how Sam is gorgeous but young, fun but unreliable, and sexy but badly clothed. I haven't heard from Sam since before Christmas, and I'm unlikely to see him in the near future. Manuele makes a face as if to say he's disappointed with me. But he has no idea that I'm saving the best for last. I tell it slowly, building up to the crescendo. I tell him how Chibu rings me non-stop and quotes Shakespeare. I tell him that incredibly, Chibu calls me Principessa as well as his girlfriend. I tell him about the giant rabbit and the pier and how we stayed in a hotel in Brighton and had incredible sex.

Manuele pats me on the arm. 'Wow, Sarah. I thought you might stay single forever. And now you have a boyfriend. Wow. That's great. So when do I get to meet him?'

'Well, I'm not sure. He's pretty busy at the moment…' I make a face, '…especially at weekends. I don't even get to see him. So I don't know.'

'I thought you said he was calling you non-stop?'

I hesitate. 'That was before Nigeria. Since he's come back, he's been too busy. Work is full on for him at the moment, one weekend he was working and the others he's been away.'

'Where does he go at weekends?' Manuele asks, puzzled.

'His aunt lives in a village near Manchester and he goes to visit her.'

Manuele scrunches his brow. 'How long since you last saw him?'

'We had a drink after work a week ago.'

Manuele gives me a look of pity. I shake him by the shoulder. 'What's wrong? There's nothing to worry about. He's just busy.' But Manuele remains silent. 'Manuele! What's wrong? Do you think he's giving me the run-around?'

'Well, Sarah.' He pauses as if he's trying to find a nice way to put it, 'Yes. He's a bad-boy like me. He's doing exactly what I would do. How do you say? Oh yes…WHAM, BAM, THANK YOU, MAM.'

Clearly he didn't think too hard about putting it nicely. *I'm in a boxing ring and my opponent gives me a powerful knock to the jaw. Down I go, my shoulder hitting the canvas. Thud. My head shakes violently from the impact and my body bounces about. I'm down for the count. 1...2...3...4...5...6...Come on, Sarah. Get up. Get back up and fight, honey. Manuele's wrong. Prove it to him.*

'NO. You're wrong. He's busy, that's all. And he said his aunt is ill.' I lie. He never said any such thing. But I'm sure she must be ill. Why else would he visit her all the time?

'Don't be naïve, Sarah. The man is playing you. His aunt is ILL? Don't make me laugh.'

Now I'm getting angry. 'NO. I told you. He's busy. Everyone gets busy now and then.'

Manuele frowns. 'Look, Sarah, I guarantee you, ring him now. Tell him that you want to see him this weekend for a coffee to catch up. Anyone can spare half an hour. See what he says. I guarantee you, he'll turn you down.'

'Fine. You're being silly. But I'll ring him. Of course he'll meet me for coffee.' How could he not meet me for coffee, right?

I take out my mobile phone and dial Chibu's number.

'Hello?'

'Hi, it's Sarah. I was wondering whether we could meet this weekend for a quick coffee. Just half an hour. I could come to wherever you are.' I hesitate. 'I know you're busy, but I haven't seen you in so long and…I miss you.'

Chibu clears his throat. 'Look, Sarah; I don't really have the time…I told you, I'm pretty busy at the moment. I may be working this weekend, and if not, I'm going to visit my aunt.'

'Yes, I know you're busy. But just half an hour. Just to catch up.' Manuele gives me a look that says, 'I told you so.'

Chibu shouts to someone in the background telling them to hold fire and that he'll be there in a sec. 'Look, Sarah; I'm unbelievably busy right now. I'd love to see you. Really, I would. But I can't get a moment's peace here.'

I feel a lump begin to gather in my throat. 'Yes, but I really need to see you. Please. Please, Chibu. I really need to see you.'

'No. I don't have the time. I just can't see you right now.'

'Well it doesn't have to be right now. How about tomorrow? Or tonight? Just fifteen minutes. I could drop by your house tonight if you like.'

I can see Manuele wincing out of the corner of my eye and I start to feel sick.

Chibu sighs. 'No. I can't possibly spare the time.' Chibu calls to someone in the background. 'Yeah, hang on a minute will you?' and then returns to me. 'Why don't I give you a call when I have some free time?'

I know what that means. 'What do you mean?' I can feel the lump in my throat growing and I tense up. Manuele is looking at the floor. 'I don't understand. I just want to see you for fifteen minutes. I don't understand.'

Chibu's getting irritated. 'There's nothing to understand. I'm busy with work. I'll call you when I have more free time.'

'So what does that mean?' I raise my voice. 'What have I done wrong?'

'You haven't done anything wrong. I want to see you. Really, I do. But I just can't right now.'

'You can't spare FIFTEEN MINUTES?' I yell, nearly in tears.

'No, I can't. In fact I've spent far too much time on the phone with you right now.'

I take a peek at my watch. We can't have been on the phone for more than five minutes. Why is he doing this? Why humiliate me like this? I survey the room. Manuele's cringing, desperately trying to show some sympathy. Other people in the café stare. They're staring at a hysterical woman shouting into her phone.

'Too much time on the phone? WHAT? If you don't want to see me any more, then you can just say so.'

'I can't do this now, Sarah.' Chibu coughs. 'OK then. I don't want to see you any more. I'm sorry.' And he hangs up the phone. Failure #74.

WAIT. I didn't mean it. I didn't mean for you to say so. NO, WAIT. Please don't end it. You're meant to be my One. You're meant to be the man I'm going to marry. Oh Jesus. This can't be happening. Oh God. Why are you doing this to me? I sit in my chair, lower lip quivering, phone in hand, looking at Manuele, unable to speak. Manuele stands up and moves over to give me a hug. He remains holding me for some time, while I fight to hold back the tears. The people in the café try hard not to stare at us. Finally, Manuele sits back down.

'I'm sorry, Principessa. I hate that I was right. Your Mr Big is a waste of time and does not know what he's missing.' He motions with his hand. 'Just forget him and concentrate on the next one.' His use of the word 'Principessa' feels like he's putting salt in the wound. How can I think about anyone else? Chibu's meant to be my One. How can he do this to me? What about the grandchildren?

'That's easy for YOU to say,' I whimper. 'You're the dog of the century. But I don't even know where to start. Are all you guys dickheads?' All the good men were taken at twenty-five. The ones left in their thirties have been left for a *damn good* reason.

My phone rings. 'Hello?'

'Hi, baby. It's me. I'm sorry.' Chibu sighs. 'Look, I do want to see you. But this weekend is out of the question. Let's meet for a drink tomorrow night after work, OK?' GRAND SLAM. He loves me after all.

'Yes. That would be lovely. Thank you. Thank you. Just a short drink. I can't wait. The same bar as last time? Seven p.m.?'

'Yes, Principessa. I'll see you there.' Chibu makes a kissing sound and hangs up the phone.

I turn to Manuele with a look of victory on my face. 'HA! You see, I told you. I told you he would see me. You see. Everything's going to be fine.'

Manuele winces at the ground. 'No, Sarah. He's meeting you tomorrow. He's not meeting you this weekend. Do you not understand?' Manuele shakes me by the shoulder. 'Something is happening with his weekends.'

'I know. His aunt. His aunt is ill,' I reply.

'Oh stop it. There is no aunt. If Chibu is visiting his aunt this weekend, I'll marry the next girl I go out with.'

'You mean you think he's lying?' I pause. 'You mean you think he might be married? Or maybe he has children? Or maybe both?'

'Yes. Exactly. I wonder which it is.'

I shake my head. 'You're being silly, Manuele! You've been watching too much *Coronation Street*.'

'OK, fine. Don't listen to me if you don't want to. But listen to this at least.' Manuele takes my hand. 'Sarah, you're too *nice*.'

TOO NICE? Who's ever heard of being too nice? That's the most ridiculous thing I've ever heard. I gape at Manuele incredulously.

'No. Listen to me.' Manuele taps the table. 'You are too nice to these guys and you are too keen. You must be tougher and *sexier*. You know…Act like you don't care.' I continue to gaze in his direction with a puzzled look on my face.

'OK. I tell you what. You must be like Samantha. You know, from *Sex and the City*.'

WHAT? SAMANTHA? Is Manuele telling me to go to bed with a different man every night? Who the hell would ever have the time or energy to sleep with as many men as SAMANTHA?

'But, Manuele, I don't want to sleep with lots of men. I want a BOYFRIEND.'

'Look. It doesn't matter what you want. The point is that Samantha doesn't take any shit off men.' Manuele sips his water. 'That doesn't mean you have to have sex with lots of men. Though it wouldn't hurt to find a few more bed partners…' He rubs his hands together. 'Whatever the end goal is, you must learn to *act* like Samantha.' He pauses. 'You need to show that YOU are in control…OK. Let's try it, repeat after me: *Hi there, sexy. You are looking HOT tonight.*'

'Do you really think he's lying about his aunt?' I whimper. Manuele grabs my sleeve and tugs.

'Forget Chibu. Come on, Sarah! Pretend that you're in a bar and you see a guy you fancy. And so you say: *Hi there, sexy. You are looking HOT tonight.*' He does his best to put on a sexy and sultry voice, batting his eyelashes and looking seductive as he speaks. So I try to imitate. We have to go over it several times until finally I reel it off in a way that satisfies him.

'*Hi there, sexy. You are looking HOT tonight.*' I toss my head and curl my lips. I'm sexy and confident. I'm a real little *sex kitten*…just like Samantha! It's almost fun.

'That's it, Sarah! Now whenever you speak to a man, you must think, how does Samantha speak to men?' He taps the table. 'You need to ooze confidence in the way that Samantha does.'

Rule Number TEN: Gotta act like Samantha Jones.

I bat my eyes. 'But what about Chibu?' I'm starting to panic slightly. 'Do you think he's married?'

'Forget him, Sarah. You need to take *control*.' He twists his hand into a fist. 'You need to be like *Samantha*. Men LOVE women who are in control and who know what they want.'

Manuele goes on for a while about Samantha and how her confidence is what is most appealing about her. If I look like a wounded puppy then guys are bound to take advantage. I sit there, taking it all in. But as I listen, the seeds of doubt that Manuele planted take root and begin to sprout.

'Remember what Thatcher used to say, Sarah.' He shakes my shoulder.

'Thatcher? *Margaret* Thatcher?'

'Yes. She used to say that you shouldn't wear your heart on your sleeve. You should wear it *inside* where it functions best.' Manuele pauses. 'Just like Samantha.'

I'm gripped by a vision of a cross between Samantha Jones and Margaret Thatcher. It's not a pretty sight.

'What made you so cynical, huh Manuele?'

'Me, cynical? I am just realistic.'

I toss my head to the side. 'Did some girl break your heart at school? Nothing to be ashamed of. You can tell me.'

'Well if you must know, her name was Sophia. We were twelve years old. I was so nice to her. I spent my pocket money on her, carried her books for her, walked her home from school.'

'So what happened?'

Manuele's hand tightens on the table. 'She dumped me for another boy in the class. He was a real bastard and never did any of the things I did for her, but he was the one she wanted.' Smiling, he continues. 'We always pass the nice ones over. It's human nature. I figured it out at age twelve and you, Sarah, are learning it at age thirty.'

'No need to remind me of my age, you know!' I shout. 'And

I still haven't learnt it really. I'm sure you have it all backwards. Samantha has nothing to do with anything.'

Manuele tries to persuade me and speaks of a Spanish woman he's seeing called Maria who has the 'Samantha act' down pat. He takes my hand and drags me to the changing rooms.

'We could always go swimming...' He smirks. He knows I hate swimming. I can't see the point of it. How the hell can it be such brilliant exercise when whales are hugely fat?

'OK OK. I'll see you in the gym,' I say, resignedly, as Manuele shoves me through the doors to the women's changing rooms.

I climb on to the cross-trainer closest to the televisions. There are dozens of them in rows, each lumbered with a whitish pinkish flabby body whose arms flap about. Manuele climbs on the one next door and I watch as he ogles the attractive women in the room. The machine asks for my weight. Bloody hell. As if I need reminding. If I were happy with my weight, then I wouldn't be at the gym, now would I? I make a random guess and punch in sixty-seven kilograms. Yuck. When the machine asks for the length of time, I punch in twenty-two minutes. Apparently the first twenty minutes of a workout doesn't actually burn any calories. It's only *after* the initial twenty minutes, that you start making a difference to the FAT. I figure that for today, two minutes of fat burning will suffice. Away we go. I plug in my earphones and tune into MTV. This is almost fun. Little Kylie's twirling her bottom in the cameraman's lens, and I figure this will make for reasonable inspiration. As I chug along, I imagine her bottom in place of mine and thoroughly enjoy every minute of the fantasy. Manuele chugs beside me, smiling. Three minutes down. Nineteen to go.

Chibu, married? Is that possible? Am I just his mistress? It's true I've never seen his flat. At about four minutes, I feel tired. MTV doesn't seem so much fun any more. And Kylie has turned into Blue, who are rather less inspirational. How the hell am I meant to do another eighteen minutes of this? I know. Let me talk to Manuele. It might help get my mind off this madness. So I turn in his direction. WHOAH. As I turn towards him, I nearly lose my balance, swaying back and forth. Jesus. How do I stay on this thing?

Catching my balance, I speak. 'Hey Manuele, I forgot to tell you that Georgina had her baby boy a week ago. His name is William. William James. Nice, huh? Manuele met Georgina about a year ago when he played the part of my date at one of her infamous dinner parties. Manuele glances over in a nonchalant way. 'If you like that kind of thing.' Well actually, if you think about it, we should all be in mourning. Georgina's baby is a boy. Just one more player to add to the long list of players already here on earth. In thirty-five years, William will be another Chibu breaking some woman's heart.

Manuele tells me about the various women he's seeing at the moment. He speaks about Maria the longest. She's thirty-three years old. I'm astonished. Normally, Manuele only ever chases girls under the age of twenty-five.

Nine minutes now. Jesus. I'm going to keel over. How the hell am I meant to meet men at the gym when I look like a hamster drowned in sweat? Manuele continues to talk about Maria. She works in PR for some fancy art company. She lives in Pimlico. He thinks she's the bee's knees.

Suddenly, a voice interrupts our conversation. 'Sarah? I thought it might have been you…Hi.' I look up, and lo and behold, it's Sam and his dreamy blue eyes.

'Sam!' I jump off the cross-trainer, nearly falling off. I hang on to Sam's arm to get my balance. Jesus. I have to look attractive. Smile, Sarah, smile. Forget Chibu. Come on, stand up straight. Think 'NAKED'.

'I forgot you go to this gym.' I brush my hair away from my face. 'I'm just here doing my routine workout, as you can see.' I twist my hair behind my ear. 'Though it's been a little while since the last time I was on one of these cross-trainers.' I can feel the sweat pouring off my brow. It's so embarrassing. I wipe my forehead with the back of my hand. But it doesn't seem to make any difference. I'm sweaty, smelly and fat...certainly in comparison to Sam. He is an Adonis in his gym wear, demonstrating muscles I had no idea existed.

Sam raises his eyebrows. 'Oh? So how long have you been on this thing?' He moves towards the touch pad on the machine to check the time.

WAIT. Twelve minutes...not exactly Olympic standard stuff. And I'm already covered in sweat. Must stop him. Can't let him know I'm a couch potato who lost her way into couch potato hell. I jump ahead and slam 'CLEAR' on the pad. The screen goes blank.

'Heh heh. Yeah. Well, don't want you knowing that kind of top secret information. Don't know what you might do with it, now do I?' I explain.

Oh Jesus. Didn't Sartre say that Hell is *Other People*? Yeah. But didn't he cheat on his wife all the time?

'Oh I see...' Sam hisses with an air of suspicion. 'You're one of those mad fitness freaks who is massively competitive aren't you?'

'Yeah. I'm a real fitness freak.' LIAR LIAR PANTS ON FIRE. Oh God. If this isn't hell, then I'm certainly reserving a place in the dungeons of darkness for the whole of my afterlife with the lies I've told today.

'Then you must come upstairs to the Body Pump class I told you about. It starts in five minutes.' Sam rubs his palms together. 'If you love fitness, then I guarantee you'll love this class.'

Now you've done it, Sarah. You've really done it now. If he sees you in this class, he's bound to know that you've been lying. You'll make a complete fool of yourself. I look to Manuele for help. But his eyes are glued to MTV. Beyoncé's dancing about in a bikini. I have no chance.

'Well I'm not sure whether I can really. I'm here with my friend Manuele and he won't want me to take off without him.' I say, huffily.

Before I realise what he's doing, Sam taps Manuele on the shoulder.

'Hey, mate…would you mind me borrowing Sarah for an hour upstairs in the Body Pump class?'

I try my best to tell Manuele 'no' with my eyes and draw them tight. *Come on Manuele…Please understand…*

'No. Not at all. Take her. Go have fun.' Manuele winks at me, his earphones still plugged in his ears. *Knife in hand, I creep to the shower curtain as the water beats down. I rip it back and Manuele whirls round, startled. I hold the knife high above my head, ready to pound it down on Manuele's soft white flesh. He grabs hold of my arms; we struggle. Manuele twists my hands round my back and pushes me towards the gym studio, laughing. A loud deep voice echoes above: 'Welcome to Lucifer's dungeon of horror.' The cackling is so piercing, I have to cover my ears.*

'Here's a barbell, Sarah.' Sam hands me a long black rod and a couple of clips. 'The weights are over there.' He points to the wall. The walls are covered in mirrors, from the ceiling to the smooth oak flooring. I randomly choose some of the smaller weights and adjust them on my bar. The other class members know what they're doing. I stand still at the back, looking awkward and out of place. Sam goes up front. I suppose he's trying to give me some space. Thank God. At least he won't see me humiliate myself. I gaze at the super-fit women up front who are carrying three times my weights. How did they get like that? Were they born that way?

Our instructor is about twenty-five and extremely fit.

Looking at her makes me want to run away. I'll never be like her and frankly it seems ridiculous to even try. She beams from ear to ear.

'Hello, everyone! Welcome to Body Pump forty-eight.' She smiles again. 'My name is Melissa and I'll be your instructor today.' She scrutinises the room. 'Anyone *new* today?' I hesitate and then sheepishly put up my hand. I'm the only one. Sam looks behind and gives me a little wave. Then he mouths the words 'See you after'. I nod in agreement. Melissa tells me to keep the weights light and gives a demonstration. She looks like an acrobat in the circus. God help me. I'm a lamb being sent to the slaughter.

Loud music booms out of the speakers. You mean I have to exercise to a beat? 'Take it down for two.' Melissa bends forward holding her barbell. Two? What's two? Jesus. I pick up my barbell and realise that everyone else is moving the other way. So I try to redress myself. I keep starting and stopping. My barbell is going in every possible direction apart from the right one. AARRGH! This is just bloody impossible. Take it up. Take it down; whatever it is, I can't do it.

After three or four minutes, Melissa puts her barbell down and begins swapping weights. So does everyone else. Thank God that's over. Thank God. Sam didn't really notice. I'm spared complete humiliation. I wonder what happens next. Melissa speaks into the mike attached to her earpiece. 'Right. That's the warm-up done folks. Easy bit done. Now on to squats.' THE WARM-UP? This woman is crazy. I can't cope. I just can't. Those women up at the front are another species. I'm not like them. And neither will I ever be. Failure #75.

Sam's busy changing the weights on his barbell. I look to the right. I look to the left. I put my barbell down and flee out the back door. I escape down the stairs past the gym and into the changing rooms. I don't look for Manuele. I empty out my locker and I run all the way home.

'Hello, dear.' Deirdre is standing in her doorway wearing the new pink cardigan I gave her for Christmas. 'It fits well, doesn't it?'

'Yes it does. It looks beautiful on you.' I do my best not to cry. Deirdre must sense something's wrong as she doesn't invite me in for tea. I quickly say goodbye and run upstairs.

I lie on my bed with Bear beside me. We are silent for some time. I try to ring home. No answer. Gosh, what about my dad? It starts to rain. The drops beat more and more heavily against my bedroom window. I think of the rain in Brighton and I stare at Brighton the rabbit. When I named him there was a sparkle in his eye. Watching him, the sparkle disappears. Chibu can't be married. He just can't be. So I haven't seen him for the last few weekends. He's looking after his aunt, that's all…Oh Jesus. He must be married. It's the only thing that makes any sense. I roll over on my side and close my eyes. Am I ever going to get married? Is there already a Mrs Chibu Okoru? I think of my mother and her desire for grandchildren.

What's wrong with me? Why won't anybody love me? Why must I always be alone without anyone to help me through the tougher times like now? My dad may have cancer and I have no one to talk to. I'm not a bad person. I'm nice to people and I work hard. All I want is a boyfriend. That's all. I don't need riches or fame. I don't need a nice car or a fancy house. I just want a guy to call my own. Is that too much to ask? Tears start to fall and I bury my head in my pillow.

Come on, Sarah honey, we need to think positive. Maybe I'm wrong. Maybe God will take pity. Maybe Chibu's aunt really is ill. And maybe that which goes down will indeed go up again.

Chapter eighteen

'RAW! Look at MISS!' Vishnu is standing at the door to my classroom, looking at my outfit. Pupils start to gather by the doorway, some giggling, some pointing and all staring. I'm wearing the school uniform. It's Charity Day when pupils give £1 to charity and in return get to wear their own clothes. The pupils are forced to wear this ridiculous uniform every day. I'm trying to show some solidarity. My crested jacket and tie coupled with grey skirt and black clumpy shoes are enough to create a scene.

The school day shoots by and I find myself in two meetings after school which seem to last an eternity. Caroline the Deputy is chairing one of them. She drones on about results, saying she isn't pleased with the performance of certain departments. We know who they are of course. But we're too polite to point them out. We just sit in silence. Work harder. Work longer. Yes, we know. Work miracles. And then amongst all the miracles, Sarah, try to find yourself a husband too.

By the time we've finished it's six fifteen. Dammit. Meant to meet Chibu at seven. I'll have to go straight there. I jump in the loo to sort out my face and leap in front of the mirror. Staring back at me is Pippi Longstocking. Bloody hell. The uniform. My hair is tied in pigtails with red and white ribbon attached. I've even drawn fake freckles on my cheekbones to heighten the effect. Oh my God. I sat in that meeting looking like THIS? I peek at my watch. 6.20 already…no time to go home. Dammit. I begged Chibu for this meeting. I can't possibly cancel.

171

Suddenly it hits me. SAMANTHA JONES. A school uniform would be just up her street; wouldn't it? Chibu is bound to love it. Maybe he'll find it sexy? Maybe it'll give me the upper hand? Yeah. That's right. Maybe he'll even want to meet up with me this weekend.

I whip on some lipstick and mascara, snatch my bag and skip out of school. OK. You'll be fine, Sarah. Think posture. Think Naked. Think Samantha Jones. You're in control. You call the shots. Think SAMANTHA JONES.

I march to the bar. The streets are packed with people wearing suits and sharp shoes. The beautiful cream buildings with fancy glass windows scream wealth. The City is a foreign country to me. My pigtails and fake freckles stand out a mile and I feel a little self-conscious. I open a large glass door and catch sight of Chibu by the bar. He's the only black guy in there. The bar is modern, silver and black, with long geometrical lines. I sneak up behind him and whisper in his ear.

'Hi there sexy, you are looking HOT tonight.' I curl my lips, keeping a clear image of Samantha in my head. Chibu shoots round. He's wearing a spotted blue shirt and grey suit and tie.

'Hey there.' His innocent smile metamorphoses into a naughty grin as I flick my pigtail in the sexiest way I know. 'Wow. You are something else, Sarah. Totally unpredictable.' He leans over and kisses me squarely on the lips. 'I like the new look...Sexy as hell.' SLAM DUNK. The Samantha-skills are working. I toss my head to the side and wink at him. 'I thought you might like it.' I lick my lips. 'So how are things?' Chibu talks about his day and how busy he is. He can't stay long, he says. 'You know, I only made the effort to come out because it was to see you. No other woman would have me doing this.'

So should I be grateful? You're in control, Sarah. Come on. If you're his girlfriend, then he should treat you like his girlfriend. Expect more. Demand more. Accept nothing less.

'Well I've also been stressed recently you know. My dad has been ill with a tumour and they've been doing tests at the hospital. It's been a difficult time for my mum and I'm trying to be as supportive as possible.'

Chibu squeezes my hand. 'God, Sarah, I didn't know. I hope he'll be OK. When will you know what's wrong?'

'Not sure really. We ring the hospital every day and my parents keep going back for more tests. I can't wait until they come up with something conclusive.' Chibu leans in and kisses me gently on the cheek. I knew it. He loves me after all. He's just been distracted recently and my Samantha school uniform has snapped him back into my grasp. Phew.

Twenty minutes later, Chibu announces that he has to return to work. 'Sorry, babe. But I did say it would be short.'

'Yes I know, you sly thing you.' I draw my finger across his chest slowly, keeping my gaze glued to his brow. 'How about we meet up this weekend for another short drink?' Well said, Sarah honey. Don't you dare walk outta here without a weekend date.

Chibu scowls. 'No. I can't. I'm going to see my aunt.'

'Is your aunt ill?' I ask.

'No. But I have to visit her this weekend. That's all.'

'Well, what time do you return on Sunday?' I plead. 'We could meet then if you want.'

'No. I can't. Too much work.' Chibu rubs his head. 'Weekends aren't good for me at the moment.'

Gulp. Manuele's right. Married. He must be married. Oh Jesus. I can feel my stomach doing somersaults inside. Why doesn't he like me? Why am I not enough? Fucking dickhead. The fucking son of a b...

'Hey Sarah.' Chibu squeezes my arm. 'Don't look so sad. You're damn sexy in that uniform. I'll see you soon.'

'No you won't,' I mutter. 'You call this a relationship?' I can feel myself starting to boil with rage. 'This is just a waste of my time.' That's right, Sarah. You tell him, Samantha. You give him what he deserves,

'Hey, Principessa. Calm down, baby. No need to get so excited.' Chibu winks at me. 'We'll see each other next week.'

'You patronising, arrogant, self-obsessed, vile, good-for-nothing snake!' My voice is getting louder. 'Don't you tell me not to get excited!' I jump off my stool and stamp my foot. 'You treat me like crap as if I'm some client at work.' I sense feel the tears beginning to well up in my eyes as I start to shake. Chibu is feeling more and more uncomfortable as people begin to look round. 'I only want to see you for a drink this weekend. Just a little drink!'

'Look, Sarah. There is no need to overreact. I can't meet you this weekend.' Chibu grabs my arm and pushes me towards the door. 'For that matter I can't meet you for the next three, or even four weekends. This is how I am. I'm extraordinarily busy at work. You can take it or leave it.' He shrugs his shoulders and tilts his head to the side. We pause in front of the door. Oh God. Why is he so mean? Why is he doing this? Come on, Sarah. FIGHT. Where is Samantha? Come on, Sarah. Don't let the side down. Don't cry. Whatever you do, don't cry. Tell the mother-fucker what you think of him.

The tears start to roll down my face and I can feel them burning as they slowly dissolve my fake freckles. People in the bar are trying not to look, but they can't help themselves. Chibu is mortified. He opens the door while putting on his coat and pulls me out with him. It's cold and starting to rain, but he doesn't care. I rub my cheeks to hide the tears, but the more I rub the faster they appear. Come on, Sarah. Tell the mother-fucker what you think of him.

'But, I don't understand,' I whimper. 'I just don't understand. I thought you said that you...well, I thought that maybe you...' I gaze up at Chibu, begging for some confirmation that he cares.

'Look, I care, sure I do. But I'm busy. I really like you, Sarah, but perhaps you need a guy who can pay you more attention.'

Oh God, no. No. Don't end it. Please don't. Please don't dump me here in the middle of a sea of suits. I grab on to the lapels of Chibu's coat. 'No, wait. I don't want anyone else. I want you,' I sob, wiping my face. 'I want you. Only you. Please. I just want to see you on the weekends. How do I know you're not married?'

Chibu's jaw drops open. He throws my hands off him and steps back. 'MARRIED? Where the hell did THAT come from?' He starts to back up. 'Nah, nah.' He shakes his head. 'This is too much. Do you have any idea what I had to do to get out of work to come here tonight to see you? You're crazy. I tell you what, Sarah, let's call it a day. OK?'

'What? Call it a day? Wait. I didn't mean it. I just meant that if you're never around on the weekend it looks a bit funny, that's all.'

'Yeah, well I don't care what you meant.' Chibu moves forward and takes me by the arms. 'Listen very carefully. It's over. It's over for good. I don't want this any more.' And then, without so much as a goodbye, he turns. He strides off in the rain down the street. Failure #76. The rain accelerates into a downpour and I stand entirely still. I watch Chibu disappear into the distance. My pigtails feel heavy on my head, soaked in water and dripping on my face. No one can tell I'm crying. The rain is a shrewd disguise. I watch the various people rush past me in their suits, holding umbrellas over their heads, not noticing my silly uniform, not seeing my tears, nor feeling my obliterated sense of self.

Eventually I walk away with the rain still falling hard on the pavement before me. I kick the pavement as I trudge. No more Mrs Sarah Okoru. I don't suppose there was ever any possibility of a Mrs Sarah Okoru. The rain is pelting down. And I begin to wish that it might just pelt me straight into the ground.

Chapter nineteen

'Take Jesus into your life!' A black man waves a bible in my face.

'Jesus!' I step back, slightly shocked.

'Don't take His name in vain now!' The man grins. His name? Whose name? God's name? This man's here every day at seven a.m. shouting about Jesus. Maybe he thinks it's his job. He loves it so much, he does it for free.

I walk past the flower stall in front of Brixton tube. It's inundated with people. The three people working there are rushed off their feet. The whole of Brixton is buzzing. People rushing every which way. It makes sense really. Today is Valentine's Day. February fucking fourteenth. The most dreaded day of the year. At the tube, various people are shouting about God and eternal damnation.

'Your time is up!' yells a youngish bearded black man over and over.

'Jesus is Lord!' sings a beautifully made-up light-skinned black woman time and time again. Each politely waits their turn. Leaving the harmonious a cappella behind, I walk into Woolworths on the High Street in search of a baby card for Georgina. Have to pretend I'm happy for her. No. Don't mean that. Of course I'm happy for her. I'm greeted by a sea of red balloons, all marked with 'I love you'. I twist my face sideways and march blindly past. The cards section is packed with people. I can't get through. So I go round to the back of the aisle. It's only the Valentine's section that's heaving. Both men and women, black and white, young and old, are buying their loved ones a Valentine's card. The chocolate section is practically empty. I deliberately face the baby cards straight on. I don't want to catch anyone's eye. I don't want anyone feeling sorry for me because I'm not buying a Valentine's card. Every now and then, I take a peep at the people in the Valentine's' section out of the corner of my eye. They look happy. And I hate them for it. Having found a suitable card for Georgina, I notice a card in the joke section. *'Fuck Love. All you need is a great pair of shoes.'* I pick it up and march to the till. Great. I'll stick this on the inside of my front door, so that every day when I go out, I'll see it, and I'll remember that all I need is a great pair of shoes. That's right. Just a great pair of shoes.

As I approach the till, I notice the security guard looking uneasy thanks to a bunch of young black men crowded together by the entrance. They're dressed in a range of hooded tops and trousers that sit on their hips. They're wearing baseball caps. One of the kids is white, but you have to look hard to notice. He's dressed in that urban style, with a headscarf tied around his head and he's wearing lots of jewellery: a young Ali G. As I stare at him, he glances over at me and a smile breaks out on his face.

'Miss, man!' He lightly punches his buddies. 'Hey look, it's Miss!' He points in my direction. Silly me. I didn't realise. They left school a couple of years back. Come on, Sarah. Remember their names... The white boy is Jake...and then Ashley, Kyle, Samir...oh yeah, and Kofi.

'Hi boys!' I call out. They aren't boys any more. But they'll always be boys to me. The security guard moves behind the group and 'encourages' them to leave by holding his arms out and sweeping them towards the door. The boys peek over their shoulders at me.

'Happy Valentine's Day, Miss!' they holler. 'Make sure your man buys you flowers!' How sweet. They assume I have a boyfriend...Fat chance of that. Dumped by Chibu two weeks ago and no hope of ever meeting anyone new. I've spent two weeks in and out of tears, back in my jammies, watching Sky movies round the clock. At least I've been going to the gym.

Out on the High Street, men are carrying flowers and chocolates. The queues outside the Barclays Bank machines are massive. You love-sick fools. Why don't you go do something useful? I bet half of you have mistresses anyway. Yeah. Your poor wives and girlfriends. I feel sorry for them. You're just a bunch of liars. Yeah. Just a bunch of jerks. I know, I'll run up to the first guy in the queue and push him backwards so he'll fall against the one behind. These unfaithful evil men will fall like dominoes and find themselves flat on the ground.

Lacking the nerve, I head to Sainsbury's instead. As I weave my way through the crowds on the pavement, it feels as if someone is watching me. I twist round. Nothing. Two policemen swagger by. One's black, the other white. The black one has a bit of a tummy on him. Both are in their thirties but the white guy has lost some hair on top. The white one nudges the black one and points at something in the sports shop window. The black one's eyes light up and he whispers something to his partner as if it's top secret. I wonder if they're friends. I wonder how long they've worked in Brixton. I wonder whether they like it. Are they married? Are they going to spend tonight with their women or will they have to work until late? Is there lots of crime on Valentine's Day?

Sainsbury's too is filled with flowers and balloons and I ignore it all. I aim straight for the Ready Meals section. It's strangely deserted. Single Brixtonites are too scared to leave their houses for fear of execution. The vegetable lasagna is my favourite; only four minutes in the microwave and totally edible. I throw it in my basket, with some orange juice and milk and head for the biscuits. I need some reinforcements to get through a day like today: warm milk and chocolate biscuits. I glance behind me. Hmm, I could have sworn someone was there. Anyway, chocolate digestives, chocolate chip cookies, chocolate-coated shortcake...and then I grab some Belgian chocolate Häagen-Dazs ice cream out of the freezer. My armour for my war with Valentine's is complete. Victory will be mine.

I stand in the queue and wait. As my eyes glance over the various other chocolatey items, I notice a cute guy wandering through the aisle ahead, heading straight for me. He's about six foot, with sandy hair, like David Beckham. He's wearing a long dark blue coat and black loafers. He's lovely. And he looks straight at me. I twirl round to see if he's looking at someone else. There's only an old man there. My eyes clock what he's carrying...some pasta. No flowers. No card. No chocolates. Maybe he's one of the few brave singletons who have decided to go to war today.

I'm wearing a woollen hat. I look like a twelve-year-old. I reach up and pull it off and quickly run my fingers through my hair. Jesus. Maybe coming out today wasn't such a bad idea after all. Just stay calm, Sarah. Think NAKED. Try to look approachable. Smile. The man advances slowly, still looking in my direction. He has a slow controlled walk, as if he's a model showing off some clothes. He looks right at me and smiles. Shivers go up my spine. OK, Sarah. Stay calm. Think Goddess. Think Samantha Jones. I stand perfectly still. Eventually he approaches, and I smile at him. But he stops short of where I am. Just in front of me, he bends down and slides under the blue elastic strip that demarcates the queue area. Then he takes hold of the woman with reddish-brown hair standing ahead of me in the queue and kisses her.

Oh. Oh I see. Jesus, how embarrassing. He wasn't looking at me at all was he? No. He was looking at the woman he loves. And now he's kissing her...on Valentine's Day. Failure #77. I bite my lip and inspect their basket of food. No Ready Meals in there. I quickly move the stuff in my own basket around so that the orange juice hides the ready meal vegetable lasagna. I should have stayed at home. As I stand in the slowest moving queue in history, I pull my woollen hat over my forehead, snatch a *Marie Claire* magazine off the shelf and throw an extra large packet of M&Ms into my basket.

I take a detour on my way home to pick up some vitamins at the health food store on Atlantic Road. I stroll past the Lebanese shops selling Afro hair products and briefly consider picking up some cocoa butter. The bookshop on the corner nearly persuades me to stop, but I continue nevertheless. The smell of fish and raw meat fills the air and discarded fast-food paper boxes and broken bottles crunch beneath my feet.

Stepping out of the health food shop with two large glass bottles filled with funny shaped pills in hand, the sushi restaurant on the other side of the road catches my eye. I can't help but think of Chibu. *Dring dring*. I scramble about in my bag, grip my phone, and glue it to my ear. It's Jacquie. I tell her I'm going home to hide. Defeat by Valentine's is inevitable.

'Don't be silly, Sarah.' She commands. 'I've booked us a manicure with Tendai at three p.m.'

'But I don't think I want to…'

'Now now, Sarah. I hear a defeatist attitude. I'll see you at the beauty salon at three.'

'Well I don't know…'

Jacquie sighs.

'Well, OK then,' I whimper.

It's impossible to say 'no' to Jacquie. There isn't any point in trying. I open the main front door and pick up my post off the side shelf; none for Deirdre, poor thing. You never know, maybe Chibu will use Valentine's Day to patch things up. I quickly sift through. One red envelope stands out in the pile. WOW. Maybe he wants me back. I rip the card open . 'Happy Valentine's Day, dear! Chin up. We still love you. Next year you might even have a husband who will love you too. Love,

Mummy and Daddy.' Jesus Christ. Failure #78.

Deirdre opens the door. Her pink cardigan brings out the pink in her hair.

'Hello, Sarah dear. Would you like a cup of tea?'

'Yes, sweetie. Look, I've brought you some vitamins.' I hand her one of the bottles. 'My mother is always saying that they're good for me. Can't do any harm I suppose.' I shrug as she takes the bottle and opens the door for me.

'Thank you, dear. I'll put the kettle on.'

'Now now, you know the routine.' I lead her to the front room and nip to the kitchen to fix the tea.

'Bring the biscuits which you gave me, the ones with the sugar on top,' Deirdre orders. 'They're in the cupboard.'

I return with a tray of biscuits and tea and place it on the coffee table. I sit next to Deirdre on the sofa. Harry Belafonte's look-alike framed in a rusty silver frame stares down at us.

'So Sarah, have any of your young men asked you to marry them yet?' Deirdre sips her tea.

'Marry them? Well, it might be a little too soon for that,' I chuckle.

'Too soon? But in my day boys asked after a few weeks, certainly after a few months…Has no one asked you yet?'

'No. Not yet.' I take a biscuit from the tin and chomp on it.

'Well, Dr Van Den Burg looked lonely last week when I saw him. I don't think he had any plans for today. I knew I should have introduced you to him.' She sighs. 'No matter, as it's Valentine's, maybe one of your boyfriends will ask you today.' Even Deirdre knows it's Valentine's. Gosh, poor thing. She's all on her own. Must change the subject.

'Anyway, I have other things on my mind at the moment. My father is very ill, you know.'

'Really, dear?' Deirdre puts her hand on my knee. 'What's wrong? Is he in hospital?'

'Well, they've found a tumour and they might have to operate. I have to phone home today to find out whether the operation is necessary.'

'Oh I'm sorry, dear. I'm so sorry to hear that. You had better head upstairs and make that phone call then.' I stand up.

'Yes, I should. Thank you for the tea. I'll just rinse out my cup.' I wash and put away my cup and head for the door. Deirdre places her tea down and tries to stand up.

'No no. Stay where you are. Enjoy your tea and biscuits,' I say quickly. 'See you soon.'

I position the Valentine's card on the fireplace and ring my parents. My mum picks up.

'Is Daddy there? Can you talk?'

'He's upstairs. It's OK. He can't hear me.'

'So…what did the doctor say?'

'He's fine, Sarah. He doesn't need an operation.' My mother screeches in her whisper. 'He's going to be just fine.' I can almost see her smiling through the phone.

'Well, thank goodness. Oh good, Mummy. I'm so happy for you.'

'I know. I don't know what I would do without him. I don't know how I would grow old by myself. We've planned to see a play tonight to celebrate. The things I do to make him happy!' She pauses. 'Oh, that's him coming. Take care, dear.'

'Love you.' I run downstairs and bang on Deirdre's door. She opens quickly.

'Deirdre! Good news! He doesn't need an operation!'

'That's wonderful, dear.' Deirdre squeezes my arm.

'I'm so relieved. I was so worried.' I jump up and down. 'And I couldn't let my mum know how worried I was because I didn't want to worry her even more.' Deirdre nods and opens up the door. I walk in and sit on the sofa with her beside me.

'My mum was so worried.'

'I can imagine, dear.'

'She just said to me on the phone how she was scared of growing old alone.' As the words come out of my mouth, I want to pull them back in.

'Yes, I can imagine,' Deirdre replies. 'It can be tough on the ones who get left behind. There's always one who gets left. Finding a spouse doesn't guarantee eternal companionship.'

'I'm beginning to see that now.' I squeeze her hand. 'It must be harder on days like today, is it?' Deirdre gazes at Harry Belafonte above the fireplace. 'He was my life. His name was Fred. We were married three years and a bit, two months and a half to be exact.' She goes quiet, staring at the photograph.

'What happened?' I venture.

'A car accident. He was on his way home from work. He was a salesman for a company that doesn't exist any more. He was crossing the intersection when a drunk driver came out of nowhere, and hit him. He died instantly.'

I cover my open mouth with my hand. 'Oh my goodness. That's so awful. I'm so sorry. I'm so sorry. That's just so awful.' I shake my head, my hand still covering my mouth. 'I can't imagine what you went through.'

'Well, Fred was the love of my life. I couldn't replace him. So I've been on my own ever since…been on my own since the age of twenty-four.'

'Since you were twenty-four? Wow.' I put my head in my hands and start to laugh. 'Gosh. I thought I had it hard still being single at thirty. I was dumped recently by my boyfriend and I've been so upset. But you're awe-inspiring.'

'Not really, dear,' Deirdre smiles. 'I had no other choice, that's all. You're right to be worried at your age. It's important to find the one for you. Even though Fred isn't here in person, he never really left me.'

I look at Deirdre with big eyes and turn to Fred. Fred and Deirdre. I wonder whether they'll meet in heaven. I stay with Deirdre for a little while and listen to her tell me all about

Fred. Her face instantly brightens whenever she says his name. I listen intently to her many stories, and hope that one day I might meet my Fred too.

2.55 p.m.: I am walking to Tendai's beauty salon. Jesus. I'm late. TICK TOCK TICK TOCK. As I skip along, I read the sign posted outside one of Brixton's many churches: 'Jesus said: I am the door: By ME if any man enter in, he should be saved. John 10.9' Bloody hell. I wonder if Jesus can save me from Jacquie and Tendai?

Tendai is a very large Zimbabwean woman, probably nearing forty, but looks closer to thirty. Her fattish face plumps out the wrinkles. She's been in England for most of her life and has a ten-year-old daughter. She works every day of the week. She is one of those single mothers who has given up on men and who does everything on her own. She doesn't have lots of money, nor a great education. But she has determination, like so many other young black women in Brixton. She's remarkable and has managed to give her child the life that she deserves.

Jacquie's outside the door when I arrive. She's wearing low heels, casual slacks and her hair is tied on her head.

'Sarah!' Jacquie kisses me on the cheek. 'Come on. Tendai will have us looking beautiful in no time.' She takes me by the hand. 'I've booked us in for a manicure *and* a pedicure.'

I make a face as if to say I'd rather be having a root canal.

'Sarah, you're being silly. Valentine's is just like any other day.' Jacquie pushes open the door of the salon and we take a seat in the waiting area. Everything is white: the walls, the counter, the chairs and the shelves. I suppose the idea is for it to look as clinical as possible.

Jacquie tells me that she split up with Mark, the good-looking thirty-seven-year-old Jamaican with the shipping company. She explains that while he was perfect on paper, in reality, there was something missing. 'You mean the sex wasn't any good?' I ask.

'No, Sarah. It wasn't even that. He was fine. Nothing to write home about, but he was fine.' Jacquie tilts her head to the side as if she's looking for an explanation. 'I just didn't feel *crazy* about him. He was a great catch really; a decent black man with a good job, a good sense of humour and a full head of hair,' she laughs. 'I should have been over the moon. But I wasn't. When the spark isn't there, it just isn't there.'

Tendai marches in, dressed in a white coat, with her braided hair tied back in a bun and tells us that she and her assistant Efia are ready for us. Efia is a very quiet girl. She's young. She can't be more than nineteen. She's dark with sharp chiselled features. Her long relaxed hair is tied in two bunches, lying lifelessly on her back. My guess is that her parents are West African, maybe Ghanaian.

I wonder whether she comes from a large family? I wonder whether she's the youngest child? I'll never know. She's perfectly silent. I choose light pink as a colour; Jacquie chooses deep red. The pedicure is lovely. It's the kind of pampering that makes you feel like a girl. As Efia massages my feet, I almost forget that it's Valentine's Day.

'So we're both single then, Sarah! Or have you and Chibu finally tied the knot?' Jacquie winks at me. 'Dammit. I wish I could smoke in here.'

Tendai glances up at Jacquie. 'Uh-uh.' She shakes her head. 'Not in here. You need to stop smoking those cigarettes.'

'Yes yes.' Jacquie rolls her eyes. 'I know. I will do one day.' She smiles and looks at me. 'So, Sarah, tell me…what's happening with all your boys?' I explain that I've given both Sam and Arthur the cold shoulder. Then I tell her how Chibu dumped me in the rain while I was wearing a school uniform. Jacquie squeezes my arm and gives me a sympathetic look.

'Why didn't you tell me?' she asks.

'Because I didn't want to disappoint you. I thought I was going to marry him.'

Tendai looks up at me, puzzled. 'Chibu? Are you going out with a *Nigerian*?'

'Yes. Well, at least I *was*.'

Tendai jumps up from her seat. 'Oh my goodness! Do you know where your credit cards are?' Jacquie and I burst into laughter.

'No, girls. Stop laughing,' Tendai pleads. 'I am being serious you know. Where is your wallet?' Tendai insists I pull out my wallet and show her all of my credit cards. As all the cards are there, she sits back down, a little more relaxed. Suddenly she jumps up again. 'But does he have the key to your front door?'

'No, Tendai, he doesn't. Not that it would matter.' I shake my head, chuckling. 'He's not like that.'

Tendai sits down muttering to herself about Nigerians and how they're all a bunch of crooks, while Jacquie and I laugh and laugh. I keep telling Jacquie how much I miss him; how I can't understand why he suddenly dumped me, hoping she'll give me some expert advice on how to win him back. But she shakes her head and says it's over.

'Sarah, he's probably married. Why else would he never be around at weekends?' Jacquie says, shrugging. 'And even if he's not lying, the man's a dickhead. He treated you shabbily. You need to forget him. He's gone and he isn't coming back.'

'But why?' I demand, frowning. 'I want an explanation. I want to know why he changed his mind. I hate not knowing if he was lying, if he was just playing me all along. I feel like sitting outside his flat until he comes home so that I can demand an answer!'

Tendai winks. 'Just trust in God and He will make it right.'

Yeah yeah, I know. That's why your man took off and left you to bring up your child on your own. Because God was taking such good care of you.

Efia quietly rubs my hands and files my fingernails. She doesn't utter a word. Both Tendai and Jacquie, however, are filled with advice on how to pick yourself up after a guy walks all over you. We discuss everything possible about relationships and how to get over one that has failed. According to them, the number one thing to do is forget about Chibu. Number two is to get involved in extracurricular stuff. So I butt in and explain that I've been going to the gym. Jacquie stares at me suspiciously.

'*You*, Sarah?' She pauses. 'You've been going to the gym regularly?'

I feel proud. I have indeed been going regularly. Since the disastrous first time event with Sam, I decided to brave it and tried again. I've been going at least three times a week for the last fortnight. I feel at ease on the cross-trainer and I have a weights routine for the gym area. The huge number of thirty-something guys is another motivational pull and I can't get enough of it. Jacquie's happy for me. She claps her hands. Tendai wrinkles her forehead. 'Stop that!' She grabs Jacquie's hands and places them back down on the table. 'You will ruin everything.'

Now the third thing I have to do is find another guy. And there we have a problem. There's no one. 'I'm just too old,' I cry. 'The average marrying age in this country is twenty-eight, you know.' I look at the girls with desperation. 'That means that most people are in their "soulmate" relationships by the age of twenty-five or -six…Admitting you're thirty when you're single and female is like admitting to impotence when you're married and male.'

Jacquie tilts her head to the side to show sympathy. 'I know. I blame it on feminism.'

Tendai perks up. 'Feminism? What does feminism have to do with anything?'

'When we women hit thirty, the playing field changes. Suddenly, guys we would have balked at when we were twenty-two become serious possibilities.' Jacquie says, laughing. 'And the guys know it too. As they get older, they become more attractive, whereas we become less so.'

Gosh. I knew Jacquie had to care about this stuff. 'Yeah yeah, but what does it have to do with feminism?' I ask.

'Well, the reason there is suddenly this new phenomenon where so many women are unmarried and in their thirties is because we grew up in the age of feminism. In the eighties, it was all about careers and education. Our mothers never talked to us about getting married.'

'So that's why my mother never told me to grab one of those gem guys at university?' I ask.

'Exactly. Our mothers were swayed by the feminist argument that financial independence was what mattered.' Jacquie tilts her head. 'So you work like mad at school and build a fantastic career…and you figure the right guy will come along. And then one day you wake up and suddenly you've moved from being the pitcher to standing in the outfield.'

The room falls silent. Jacquie is agitated. 'Well if it ever gets really bad, we can always move to New York,' she shouts. 'Apparently women aren't considered old over there until they hit their late thirties…Move to New York, and we'll feel twenty-two again!'

'Great. You're telling me that I have to move countries?' I hoot. 'What about *now*? I need to find another guy right now, and there isn't anyone!'

'Sure there is,' Jacquie purrs reassuringly. 'What about Arthur?' She pauses, raising her chin. 'I always liked the sound of him. And you could probably get him back if you tried. There is something sexy about a guy who needs a woman's help to fulfil his potential. You could take him clothes shopping.'

Maybe Jacquie's right. Maybe I didn't like Arthur initially because I was obsessed with Chibu. He's a nice guy after all. Maybe I should give him another chance.

'Call him *now*,' Jacquie orders. 'Go on Sarah. Call him!'

I take out my address book and dial his number on my mobile. Arthur is surprised to hear from me. I suggest we meet up. We arrange a date for the following Saturday at my place for one p.m.

'By the way Arthur, this might sound a bit strange, but did you leave a packet of chocolate digestives on my doorstep?' I ask, furtively. Jacquie looks at me and frowns.

'No, Sarah, I sent you flowers, remember?'

'Yes, I do. And they were very lovely. Thank you. See you Saturday.'

I hang up the phone. Jacquie is happy, having managed to patch things up for me.

Tendai smiles in my direction. 'Well, anything is better than that *Nigerian*.' We all start laughing again.

'Oh, Tendai, you're exaggerating,' Jacquie howls. 'Let's face it: whether the guy is black or white or even Nigerian isn't really the point. Just think of all the black women who only date black guys because they think these guys will understand them better.' She pauses and winks at me. 'But are these guys, *any guys*, ever going to understand us women? Whether they're black, white or blue, the undeniable fact is that they're all MEN...the dumbest species on the earth.'

I raise my eyebrows to the sky. 'What? Is that you speaking in there, Jacquie? You're the one who only dates black guys.'

'Yes, well maybe I've been a tad short-sighted in my youth. Perhaps I'll give white guys a try in the future.'

I stare at Jacquie and try unsuccessfully to figure out whether or not she's joking. The manicures and pedicures finished, Jacquie insists we meet later for a drink at the Satay in order to show off our glamorous feet and hands. We arrange to meet at eight p.m. I skip off home, forgetting that it's the most dreaded day of the year.

7.50 p.m.: I'm actually looking forward to tonight. Jacquie's right. Valentine's is just like any other day. No big deal. I'm bound to dazzle a guy or two with my new manicure. And my great pair of open-toed shoes will show off the pedicure. I wonder who it was that gave me those chocolate digestives?

It's cold, and I'm running so quickly that I hardly notice the protesters gathered outside the Ritzy cinema under the sparkly tree. White kids wearing sunglasses, beaded necklaces and bandanas are holding signs asking cars to honk and show their support: 'Honk and make cannabis legal!' All that's missing is a guitar with flowers tied to the strings.

I open the big glass door of the Satay Bar. A large black bouncer stands in front of me and puts his hand out. 'Are you in a couple?'

'No, I'm meeting a friend here for a drink.'

'Sorry. Tonight only COUPLES are allowed in.' He pushes me back. 'It's Valentine's Day'.

'But I've told a friend that I'd see her here at eight,' I protest. 'She might be waiting inside.'

'Not if she's on her own, she ain't.' The bouncer sniggers.

You mean, ugly, twisted fuckwit! What woman would ever want you? You look like you've eaten one too many KFCs. As I stand there, two other women appear, and the bouncer tells them that they can't enter either. They look bewildered. So I start shouting.

'THIS IS DISCRIMINATION AGAINST SINGLE PEOPLE! I DEMAND JUSTICE! I DEMAND EQUALITY! I WANT EQUAL RIGHTS!' The whole of Coldharbour Lane turns round to look at me. The bouncer rolls his eyes.

'Hey, lady. Chill, man. Just chill. I don't make the rules, I just enforce them.'

Yeah. And you probably eat them too. I throw my fist up in the air. '*Damn* Valentine's Day. *Damn* the Satay Bar. And *Damn* YOU.' I storm off down the street. Failure #79.

I look across to Brixton town hall and note a massive

billboard saying 'Brixton Shall be Saved'. I send Jacquie a text to say that I want to stay at home. The bottom of the billboard reads: 'Stop the Gun Crime'.

Oh if only I had a gun right now. I run quickly, storm inside my flat and throw myself on the sofa. To hell with these people and their Valentine's bollocks. It's all just a big commercial trick to get people to spend more money. At least I'm not falling into that trap. Who needs a bunch of flowers from a guy in order to feel special? All I need is a great pair of shoes. Churchill says that *'in wartime, truth is so precious that she should always be attended by a bodyguard of lies.'* My war with Valentine's is no different. I march to the bedroom and put on my jammies. I stomp to the freezer and take out the Belgian chocolate Häagen-Dazs ice cream. And then I tune into the Sky movie channels. *Casablanca* is just finishing. Humphrey Bogart is in the middle of his speech where he says, 'We'll always have Paris.' I think of Chibu and wonder whether we'll always have Brighton. Will we? Or more to the point, did we *ever* have it?

I drive my spoon deep into the Häagen-Dazs bucket and draw out a huge mouthful of ice cream. And I continue doing so until I've eaten the entire thing.

Chapter twenty

It's nearly one o'clock. Arthur will ring the bell any minute. This is going to work. It has to. Sparks aren't necessarily *instant* things, are they? Arthur and I need a new 'space'. 'Friendly' has to change to 'Sexy'. I spray some perfume on. Sex will do it. We have to have sex. Then I'll view him differently. He'll transform from a *scare*crow into *Russell* Crowe. I'll see him as more of a man. Maybe he'll be really good in bed and I'll find him irresistible? Yeah. Sex it is. I stuff Bear in the wardrobe.

'Ding dong.'

I leap downstairs and open the front door. 'Arthur! Hi.' I give him a kiss on the cheek. He looks the same. Very white, a little on the skinny side, receding hairline and a distinct resemblance to Tony Blair. He wears the same dark brown corduroy jacket but this time with corduroy cream trousers. He looks like some of my old Cambridge tutors.

Sex with Tony Blair. Gulp. How does Cherie do it? Come now, Sarah: sex isn't only about the physical. I can get over this hurdle. I have to. I have to get Chibu out of my head. And my mother will be dead happy seeing me with a white guy.

'So how are you?' I ask with a glimmer in my eye.

'Not too bad, thanks,' Arthur steps in and closes the door. 'I must say I was slightly surprised to hear from you.' We walk up the stairs. 'I thought you felt we lacked a connection.'

'Oh really?...Nah.' I toss my head to one side. 'I was just busy, that's all. And you know, I never told you about how I was mugged the night you dropped me off at my flat.' Arthur hesitates,

192

putting his hand on my arm. 'What? You were mugged? Oh my goodness.' He puts his hand to his forehead. 'I knew I should have waited until you went inside. My goodness. I'm so sorry. Are you all right?'

'Yes, yes. No problem. I even got my bag back!' I chirp. We enter my flat and I recount the escapade in more detail. We move into the front room where we sit on the sofa. There's an elongated silence.

I jump up. 'Shall I get you some tea?'

'Oh. Yes, please. Black, no sugar,' Arthur says, awkwardly. 'You have a nice flat. It's very,' he hesitates, 'comfortable.' What does he mean by that? Maybe he means it's small. Maybe he thinks it's a mess. Maybe he doesn't know what else to say. I make two cups of tea and return to the front room.

'So how has work been lately? Had any difficult cases come your way?'

'Oh, it's fine. Just fine.' Arthur lightly taps his knees as he looks around the room.

'Have you been busy?'

'No, not more than usual.'

'Well what ever happened to that kid you were defending? Did you get him off?' I ask, persevering.

'Funny you should ask.' Arthur perks up a little. 'I'm defending him again at the moment. He's in another spot of trouble. Actually he spends his time squatting in empty houses in Brixton.'

'Oh really? How funny. There's a house down the street that I think is squatted. So what did he do this time?' I ask.

'Oh, nothing much.' Bloody hell, if only the real Tony Blair could be dumbstruck in a similar fashion. I try a variety of conversation tactics. But he just won't bite.

Jesus. Why are white guys so shy and awkward? Why are they always so scared? By the look on his face, you'd think I was Godzilla. Come on…don't give up that easily. Don't throw in the towel like that. Remember, you're a GODDESS. GODDESSES don't give up. A police car siren sounds in the distance. I peer over at Arthur. He's sitting straight up on the edge of the sofa with his hands folded on his knees. His tea is on the coffee table. It's now or never.

'Arthur…' I say coyly. 'It's a bit cold in here, don't you think?' I rub my arms.

'Cold?' Arthur makes a face. 'Really? I feel quite warm.' Oh bloody hell. Come on DUMMY…'Hmm. Maybe…' I kick my shoes off under the table, and curl my legs up under me on the sofa and turn to face him, thinking of Samantha. 'Have you ever watched a porn film?'

Arthur coughs uncomfortably. 'A porn? Uh, well, uh…' He coughs again, running his fingers through his hair.

'Well, have you?' I flick my hair to the side and gaze seductively in Arthur's direction. 'We could look at one right now if you like.'

Yeah, right. If I had one. Why did I say that? Dammit. Am I coming on too strong?

Arthur taps his knees. 'Well maybe we should get a move on?'

Oops. 'A move on?' I throw my hair back. 'A move on indeed…' I coo.

But he does nothing. He sits still, looking at me. OK, Sarah. Think. What would Samantha do…?

So I do the only thing I can do. I jump on him. I feel like an eagle descending on its prey. He's startled at first and moves in an awkward fashion. But he slowly relaxes, giving in to me, and begins to kiss me properly. It's a nice kiss…smooth and drawn out; his tongue slipping in and out of my mouth with ease. It's nice.

We kiss for a while and his hands start to wander up my top. Great. Just what we need. I'm determined. Sex is inevitable. But there's something not quite right about Arthur. He doesn't *smell* right. Not that he smells *bad*. He just smells *funny*. He doesn't smell RIGHT. Thoughts of seven women, and seven t-shirts come to mind.

Right. Had better look like I'm enjoying this.

'Hmm. Hmm. Hmmmm.' I squeeze him tight.

KABOOM!

'What the hell was that?' Arthur jumps up, throwing me off. 'It sounded like a gun shot!'

'No no. Just a tyre blowout I think. Don't know really.' I scratch my forehead. 'I hear that noise all the time, but I don't know what it is.' I pause. 'Anyway, where were we?' I lean towards Arthur, but he puts his hands up in front of him.

'Well, maybe we should go out. It's a lovely afternoon and we don't want to get *too* carried away.'

WHAT? I'm not giving up now. Sex HAS to happen. I ignore what he said, and jump on him again. Gradually, I can feel him giving in to what is only natural. So I trail my hand along his shirt, until I reach his belt. I undo the belt as delicately as I can. He's still with me. We continue to kiss. He's mine…all mine. I can do whatever I want. Just call me Samantha Jones. I push my hand beneath his trousers and reach the top of his pants. He doesn't move an inch. Yeah baby. Just come to mama. Sarah-come-Samantha has something for you…I push my hand a little lower.

Jesus Christ. My hand stops dead. It's scared to go any further. It's big. No, that's an understatement. It's bigger than anything I've ever felt before. It's HUGE. Images of shooting pain pass through my head. Chalk scrapes along a blackboard. A car screeches to a halt. YOUCH. YOUCH. YOUCH. And then the dull thudding, over and over and over…till you think it won't ever end. And all the while you have to pretend you're enjoying yourself. And every time you moan, it's because you're in pain. Uh-uh. Not for Mr Scarecrow man. Not for Tony Blair. So I draw my hand out and pull back. Failure #80.

Too late. Arthur has changed his mind about going out. He lays me back on the sofa and pulls himself on top of me. Oh Jesus. Now what do I do? He kisses my neck. I scan the room over his shoulder, trying to think of an excuse. I started this and now I have to stop it. Come on, Sarah. Think. Can I say I left something on the stove? Nah. Think. You're a clever girl. What about I left the tap running in the bathroom? Crap. Come on, think of something. QUICK. Arthur starts undoing the buttons to my jeans and pushes his hand below. Suddenly, I hear someone fumbling with keys at the door to my flat. Then the door opens.

'Sarah! 'Tis me, Priscilla!' MY CLEANING LADY! Saved by my Polish cleaning lady! Thank God. I push Arthur back. 'Oh my goodness. It's Priscilla, my cleaning lady. I completely forgot she was coming.' Arthur looks like I've told him it's my father instead. He turns even whiter than he is naturally and scrambles to do up his belt.

Priscilla stands at the entrance to the front room, suspicious. She's a plump woman in her forties, with a short, dated haircut and hoop earrings. 'Hallo, Sarah. I will start in de bedroom.'

'Yes, yes, of course,' I gasp, rearranging my clothes. I wave at her. 'We're about to go out.' I point at Arthur. 'This is Arthur by the way. A friend. You know, a *new* friend. I mean, he's just not an *old* friend. You know, he's, well…a friend.' Oh God, Sarah. Shut up. Priscilla nods in Arthur's direction and waddles to the bedroom. I turn to Arthur and suggest we go. He jumps at the opportunity and stands up. We put on our coats and shoot outside. After a very bad start to the day, I propose the pictures. No speaking to each other there. We won't even have to look at each other. No doubt feeling similarly, Arthur thinks the Ritzy is a brilliant idea.

The Ritzy is a funny cinema; it's part artsy/bohemian, part mainstream. Rumour says it started out being entirely the artsy kind, and then reality dawned when the managers realised they were in a black neighbourhood. It seems the majority of black Brixtonites want to watch Martin Lawrence and Chris Rock. Most of the Chibus of this world tend to live north of the river. But in order to satisfy the Sams of Brixton's trendy side, the Ritzy plays cheap double bills of so-called arty films on Saturday and Sunday afternoons.

Luckily, we're in time for the second film. It's *Pulp Fiction*. We've both seen it, but we're happy to see it again. Feeling bad for the earlier episode at my flat, I insist on buying the tickets. Arthur reluctantly agrees, saying he'll get something to eat from the café upstairs while I get the tickets and will meet me inside. I prop myself up at the counter. Tickets bought, I swivel round with my head bowed, looking at them for the screen number. Let's see, screen number 4. Hmm. I wonder whether the boy who Arthur is defending is the one who…

'Sarah…Sarah.' A man grabs hold of my arm. I look up. It's Chibu. Chiselled face and shaved head.

'Oh.' I draw back slightly. 'Oh. Hello.' *BATTLE STATIONS EVERYONE! Gunmen to my right. Swordsmen to my left. Snipers, stay hidden. I'll call when you're needed. Get ready to rumble…THIS IS WAR.*

'Hi, Sarah.' Chibu smiles. 'You here to see *Pulp Fiction* too?' He puts his hands in his pockets. He almost looks embarrassed, shrugging. 'I saw it was playing here, so I couldn't resist…You know me.'

No, I don't know you, you fuckwit. I *thought* I knew you and then you broke my heart. If you're so busy, how do you find time to go to the cinema? You worthless, lying, scumbag. I hate you. I really really hate you. 'Well actually I'm on a date.' I smile, smugly. 'He's already gone in. I really should get in there myself,' I pause. 'It was nice seeing you.' I move to walk away. Well done, Sarah. Victory is yours.

But Chibu takes hold of my elbow. 'Look, Sarah, I'm sorry.' He tilts his head to the side. 'I'm sorry I disappeared...I was busy, and I needed some space. It's just that I liked you, see...' He squeezes my elbow. 'I'd like to see you again.' GULP. *Gunmen and swordsmen are dead. Snipers? Where are you? I need your help here. Do you hear me? I NEED BACK-UP. URGENTLY.* I scowl in Chibu's direction. He squeezes my elbow. 'Please?'

'Well, you know my number.' With that, I snap my arm out of his grasp and march past the popcorn counter to the cinema screens. Bad move, Sarah. That was the same as saying 'Yes, I'm madly in love with you, all is forgiven, and please treat me like shit again.' Jesus. What the hell happened to SAMANTHA JONES? I scamper to my seat in the dark. Arthur is already sitting in the middle of the cinema. With Chibu close behind, I move quickly. When I sit next to Arthur, he smiles at me. He resembles a scarecrow more than ever before. Bloody hell. Things are going from bad to worse. I face the screen and pray that Chibu will sit somewhere in the back so I won't be distracted by him. One of those ads for Orange Mobile phones comes on and I stare at the screen as if it's the most interesting thing I have ever seen. Please don't let him come this way. Please, God. Please let him sit behind. Please, God. Please.

There are some small mercies. Chibu sits in the back. But it doesn't make any difference. I hardly notice a thing on the screen. The whole time I'm thinking about Chibu, Arthur and us all being in the same cinema *together*. Pretty weird stuff if you ask me. Uma Thurman, John Travolta, not even Samuel Jackson can catch my attention. Chibu is sat somewhere behind me. I can think of nothing else. What happens when the film finishes? Do we head out the doors when the credits roll? Or do we wait and pray that Chibu leaves first? What if we run into him? Do I introduce them? Do I really want Chibu to meet Arthur the scarecrow?

'And I will strike down upon thee with great vengeance and furious anger those who attempt to poison and destroy my brothers. And you will know my name is the Lord when I lay my vengeance upon thee.' God, I want to be like John Travolta and Samuel Jackson. *I hear scuffling in the back... then arguing. A policeman taps me on the shoulder. I twist round. 'Excuse me, Miss, but we have him where you want him, right over there.' He points over to Chibu who is struggling in his seat as another policeman fights to keep him pinned down. 'Here's my gun, Miss.' He hands me a pistol. 'Do what you like to him. He deserves it.' I look up at the policeman, eyes beaming. I take the gun and point it at Chibu resembling a rabbit in headlights, about to beg for mercy.*

'Come on, Sarah, let's go.' Arthur nudges me in my seat. The credits are rolling. Oh Jesus. Here we go. Let the games begin. I'm frozen to my seat. I sit entirely still. Arthur stands and picks up his coat from the empty seat next to him. I've been so preoccupied that I'm still wearing mine. Oh God. I'll have to get up too. I stand up from my seat and move slowly in the dark to the aisle. I can feel Arthur pressed up against me, urging me to move faster. As we leave the cinema, I look around hurriedly. No sign of Chibu. He's gone. Phew.

We walk out into the bar area. I deliberately walk slowly, to give Chibu enough time to get out of sight. I squint in the bright light. The metal in the room seems to shine, and my eyes have trouble adjusting. There is no sign of Chibu. I'll be spared the utter humiliation of having to introduce him to Arthur. We approach the glass doors to leave the building.

'Sarah!' It's Chibu calling from behind. Jesus. Keep walking? Pretend I didn't hear? Is that feasible? Turn, or run?

Chibu taps me on my shoulder from behind. Dammit. I should have run. I twirl round. 'Hi,' I smile. 'Did you like the film?'

'Yeah. Always do.' Chibu winks at me. 'So you off to do something fun?' He turns to Arthur, expecting to be introduced.

'Oh,' I hesitate. 'I'm sorry. This is Arthur. And Arthur, this is Chibu.'

They shake hands and nod politely. God. Arthur looks so scruffy next to Chibu. Old jeans and tatty white t-shirt, next to Chibu's slick black slacks and black buttoned shirt. Must white guys who read the *Guardian* always dress as if they're going to Glastonbury? I push the glass doors open, and we move outside.

Bloody hell, Sarah. Come on. Get yourself out of here. *Say* something. *Do* something. Just get the *hell* out of here.

'Anyway, must dash. It looks like rain…' I point to the sky. They look up. There isn't a cloud in the sky. Failure #81. Arthur stares at me with a confused expression on his face. Chibu sniggers. Bastard. He *knows* I'm uncomfortable. And he's enjoying it.

I wave in Chibu's face. 'See you.' I peer at Arthur as if to say 'come on' and we walk away. As we stride off, Chibu calls after us.

'I'll ring you soon.'

I march past the graffiti façade of the Ritzy as if I haven't heard him. Two large black women are shouting at each other in front of KFC. One throws her fist in the air as if she might hit the other one. 'And Jesus walked!' sings the twenty-strong Korean choir, dressed in white robes with their hands pointing to the sky. Their music is deafening. A middle-aged bearded black man hands me a flyer. It reads 'Professor Bamba. Serious African medium. Twenty years' experience in Haiti. Protection against bad spirits. Definite and immediate return of your loved ones…One hundred per cent.'

One hundred per cent? What, like he's going to bring back only fifty per cent? Only head and torso, but sorry, honey, legs and feet have to stay in the grave? I screw it up and throw it in the bin, walking determinedly to the tube. Poor Arthur has to run slightly to keep up with me. 'I think I'd better be going then.' He snuffles awkwardly. 'Thanks for the film. It was nice to see you.'

Rule Number ELEVEN: Gotta remember that SPARKS don't grow with time.

Arthur kisses me on the cheek and says he'll call me. But I know he never will. He knows it too. Arthur brushes my chin lightly with his thumb. I almost feel attracted to him. Almost. He spins and jogs down the stairs to the tube. He looks pretty sexy as he skips the steps two at a time. Too bad we don't have any chemistry. Too bad his lunch box is so packed.

I scan the other men on the stairs and street. I wonder how many sandwiches they're carrying? Can't tell. Wish I could rip off their trousers to check out the merchandise. Out of the corner of my eye I notice a young black boy wearing a grey hooded top and torn jeans climbing the staircase. Hey...he looks like the boy who tried to take my bag. Didn't Arthur say that the boy he was defending lives in Brixton? The boy turns away from me as he leaves the tube, wandering down the street.

Dammit. Can't see his eyes. I remember his eyes.

I start to follow him. He swaggers, hands in his pockets, in the direction of my flat. I step swiftly and quietly behind. His trainers are torn and dirty and the bottom of his jeans drag along the ground. Eventually he reaches my street. Aha! Knew it. I wonder if he's the one in the old abandoned house? I watch from the crossroads as he bends down before the overgrown hedge which surrounds the old house. He spins round. YIKES. I leap behind a parked car. I kneel down. Jesus. Did he see me? What if he comes to get me? Should I stand and run? Stooping in the gutter, I try to calm my nerves and study the sewer water washing some old newspapers down the street drain. Finally, I pop my head up over the car. He's disappeared. Thank goodness for that.

I run to the hedge. I push away some of the branches until a hole gradually appears. He lives in the house! I knew it. I knew I'd seen someone in that window. Do I follow him?...I wonder what it's like to live in a house with a tree growing through the roof? I push the branches wide and start to push myself through.

'Sarah? Is that you, Sarah?' Bloody hell. I recognise Deirdre's frail and shaky voice immediately and jump up, quickly pushing the branches back into place. She hobbles towards me, carrying a bottle of milk.

'What are you doing snooping around that house? There could be rats in there. You should be careful.'

I jog to her side and take the milk from her hands. 'Don't you scold me: you shouldn't even be outside. I could have bought this for you.' I put my arm through hers. 'Come on, let's get inside.'

'Thank you, dear. You're always so good to me. You'll come in for a cup of tea, won't you?'

I nod and we hurry to our building arm in arm. No chemistry with Arthur, but Deirdre and I look after each other. As we step inside, I wonder what I'll learn about dear Dr Van Den Burg over our cup of tea. I squeeze her hand as I put away my keys and then I shut the door to the big cold world outside.

Chapter twenty-one

It's lovely stepping into a dazzling clean bath. Priscilla makes everything shine. Even the bath bubbles sparkle in the light. Simply divine having a cleaning lady. What took me so long to get one? I love Sundays. Haven't brought any marking home. Nothing planned, and nothing to do. How wonderful. I pop the bath bubbles with my fingernails and imagine life with a husband who will fetch me cups of tea and tell me I'm beautiful. Wonder if Chibu will call…No need to wonder about Arthur. I'll never see him again. But what am I to do now? I need a plan. I can't have Chibu as my only option. It'll give him too much power. I need some more men.

Bath finished, I log on to 'Love and Friends'. The Internet is the perfect place to accumulate any number of encounters with delectable male items without even the inconvenience of stepping outside. Six emails in my inbox. WOW. I start to troll through: two Indian guys and two white ones. And two emails from Charlie …Charlie, the psycho granddad. I click delete without even reading them. White guys and Indian guys. Hmm…I want a guy who can make Chibu feel threatened. Faced with Arthur, Chibu laughed. Black guys are never intimidated by white guys. I suppose they figure they have small lunch boxes. But when Chibu met Arthur, it was like David meeting Goliath. Chibu came out on top. Absolutely no white guys. Indian guys? Hmm. Imagine Salman Rushdie makes a play for Mike Tyson's woman. Is Mike worried? Yeah, right. The only way to make Chibu regret is to find a black guy just like him.

I turn to the search engines, and put in a detailed search for men between thirty and forty. I have a choice between Afro-Caribbean and African. Let's try African. Make my mother stew a bit. In any case, Chibu's rival has to be well-mannered with a decent job. Statistics point to the Africans. And under no circumstances must this man wear gold. So, African it is. Great. Twenty profiles. Just my luck. None have photos. But the first of the bunch seems promising:

Black-Eyed Pea

A black man with a dangerous laugh. Want to tussle with me? I like cosy restaurants and fast cars. I never have the time to meet the woman of my dreams. Neither have I done this on the Internet before. There's a first time for everything I suppose. I'm a bad boy who needs a little taming. Are you the woman to do it? If you like my profile, then drop me a line.

Thirty-five, single, no kids, no divorce. Sounds great; just the perfect competition for Chibu. I scroll down.

Occupation: I work in the City, in banking.
Education: Degree level. Do you really care?
Religion: None.

Sounding more and more perfect by the minute…Yeah. You just wait, Chibu. I'm going to find myself a hot good-looking guy who'll make you wish you never messed up.

Languages Spoken: Some French.
Music Enjoyed: Blues and Old School.
Sports and exercise: I go to the gym and I used to play lots of football.
Interests and activities: Working. And opera.

Opera? What's with these black men liking opera? What ever happened to black guys liking rap and hip hop?

Newspapers and magazines: When I have the time, the Financial Times *and* Wallpaper.
Books: Nick Hornby, Tony Parsons, Tim Lott.
Favourite Films: Pulp Fiction.

Pulp Fiction? Chibu's favourite film is *Pulp Fiction*. This can't be...? Nah. But it sounds just like...? Of course not. Don't be silly, Sarah. Chibu is far too busy to be on the Internet looking for a woman. My eyes wander back up to the start of the profile: *'I never have the time to meet the woman of my dreams.'*

Fuck. I read on:

***Enjoyable evening out**: A little cosy restaurant.*
***Favourite Dishes:** I like Italian.*

Jesus. It *is* him. I start to feel sick:

***In another life**: Aristotle*

But it CAN'T be him. He said he'd never go on the Internet to find a woman. No way. Not Chibu. He's so busy. He doesn't have the time to do this kind of thing. He never said he loved Aristotle. It can't be him. I'm being silly:

***Personality**: Charming and complicated.*
***Ideal Holiday**: Skiing.*

Oh my God. Skiing *and* opera? I sit there, staring at the screen, trying to recover from the shock. It has to be him. How many black men are there who ski, like Italian food, and opera, and love *Pulp Fiction*? Bloody hell. So that's why he was so busy and unavailable at weekends.

I sit for a while feeling gloomy. I stare at the computer screen until those funny squiggly lines appear in my vision. I twist my hair round my fingers several times over, and bite my bottom lip. Staring at the ground, I pull my feet on to my chair and hug my knees hard enough to eventually cut off the circulation in the lower half of my legs. Then I look back at the computer screen and draw back from Chibu's profile. He only knows about this site because of ME. He even laughed at the idea. Now he's on that site, meeting other women. Fucking bastard. All men are a bunch of FUCKING BASTARDS. Make him pay. He can't get away with this. He can't walk all over me. Sarah, Goddess of thirty years, is not about to be taken for a fool. I have to make him suffer. I start to think. As my mind lingers over various malicious projects, the phone rings.

Brrring. I lean over and pick up. 'Hello?'

'Hi. It's Chibu.' Oh Jesus. I'm not prepared for this. Is it his profile or not? If it is, would he be calling me? Should I tell him? No. Just be cool, Sarah. Be cool. Don't mention a thing. Think naked. Think SAMANTHA JONES.

'Hi there.' I pause. 'So the man has decided to crawl out of his office and have some fun has he?' I try to imitate Samantha as best I can.

'Yeah. Yeah I have.' Chibu takes a deep breath. 'Look, I was wondering whether you might like to meet up sometime?'

'Ahhh. Well, that's a pretty complicated question, now isn't it?' I chuckle. 'I mean, given everything that's happened, I think it'll take a little more convincing to get me to say yes.' I curl my lips as I speak. It almost feels *good*.

'Oh really?' Chibu sounds surprised. 'OK. Well I'll give you another call in the week and see if I can persuade you then.'

'Fine by me. Have a good weekend.' BRILLIANT, Sarah. You were brilliant. Well done. Maybe it isn't him on the Internet after all.

I march back to the computer and return to the homepage of 'Love and Friends'. I have to know. I click on 'Create new profile', and put a plan into play:

GLAMOROUS

I'm 29, and I still haven't met anyone I like much. I love to ski and I have people over for dinner parties all the time, but everyone I know is married or getting married! Blondes are meant to have more fun, but I don't seem to fit that mould! I like the theatre and cinema and I love walking in the countryside. I'm want someone who is fun but sensible and who wants to hang out. I look forward to hearing from you.
Occupation*: I'm a GP in West London.*

Education: *Studied Medicine, obviously!*
Religion: *Christian*
Languages Spoken: *None*
Music Enjoyed: *Classical*
Sports and exercise: *I play tennis and I ski. I also like walking.*
Interests and activities: *The cinema and theatre. And I love having dinner parties.*
Animals and Pets: *None.*
Newspapers and magazines: The Telegraph
Books: Brick Lane *was wonderful.*
Favourite Films: Pulp Fiction
Enjoyable evening out: *Restaurant. Cinema. Theatre.*
Favourite Dishes: *All kinds.*
Ideal Holiday: *Skiing.*
In another life: *Florence Nightingale*
Personality: *Kind, generous and understanding.*

That done, I turn to AOL and set up another email account: 'Andrea'. I've always liked the name Andrea. Kinda like my mum pretending to have a bad back. What's a little manipulation between friends? No man's going to humiliate me. I'm Sarah, sexy, sultry and sophisticated. The old Sarah Chibu met at Selfridges is long gone. He doesn't know who he's dealing with now.

Message to 'Black-Eyed Pea': *Hi there. I see you like* Pulp Fiction. *Isn't it a great film? I've seen it dozens of times. So do you eat Royales with cheese, or is McDonald's not your thing? Andrea*

I press SEND. I return to my inbox, or rather I should say 'Sarah's' inbox, called 'Firecracker' and begin to pen a response to one of my four suitors. Some minutes later, I return to Andrea's inbox 'Glamorous' and Black-Eyed Pea has already responded. I click open the message and wait impatiently.

Message to 'Glamorous': Pulp Fiction *is my favourite film. It is a joy to come across a woman who has it listed as her favourite too. Most women like films like* Casablanca *and* Love Story, *don't they? Are you not much of a romantic then? By the way, I prefer Big Macs myself. Black-Eyed Pea*

Dammit. He didn't say his name. I want a NAME. But he responded quickly. Chibu is unbelievably busy with work. He'd never respond to some woman he didn't know so fast. It took him *ages* to return my phone calls. Maybe I'm being paranoid. I try again.

Message to 'Black-Eyed Pea'*: Why do you call yourself Black-Eyed Pea? Are you West Indian? Or is it because of that pop group 'Black-Eyed Peas'? And no, I'm not a romantic. I'm told that I'm a bit of a man-eater. You still want to tussle with me? Andrea*

He responds immediately.

Message to 'Glamorous'*: Of course I want to tussle with you.. No, I'm not West Indian. But it sounds cool to pretend that you are, doesn't it? It's the Jamaican guys who give all of us black guys a 'cool' reputation. So I thought 'Black-Eyed Pea' was better than 'Lagos' or something equally boring. I'm Nigerian. Black-Eyed Pea*

Aha! Of course you're Nigerian, Mr Black-Eyed Pea. You also live in Notting Hill and you're bloody well called Chibu.

Message to 'Black-Eyed Pea'*: Yes, but what is your NAME? Mine is Andrea. I live in Knightsbridge. I'm a doctor. I work far too much, so I thought this would be a good way to meet people. But you won't even tell me your name! Andrea*

I sit on the edge of my seat, waiting for his email.

Message to 'Glamorous'*: Dear Andrea, My dear, Names are so unimportant. 'A rose by any other name would smell as sweet.' Black-Eyed Pea.*

SHAKESPEARE? It HAS to be Chibu. I want to rip the computer out of the socket and throw it to the ground. I'm going to tear him limb from limb. OK, CALM, Sarah, CALM...He's not inside the computer, now is he? And the only way you'll get revenge is by taking it slow.

Message to 'Black-Eyed Pea': *Dear Mr Pea, Indeed it would. But how wonderful that it has the name of 'rose' so that we are able to refer to it with ease. Andrea*

Come on...play ball...

Message to 'Glamorous': *Dear Andrea, You're a persistent woman, aren't you? I like that in a woman. I'm a bit of a rascal. Need a strong woman to keep me in line. The name is Chibu, and the pleasure is mine.*

BINGO. I knew it. Ha! I was right! Oh Jesus. I'm right. It really *is* him. Oh fuck. I stare at the screen. What a lying scumbag. 'Fucking fucking bastard! I fucking hate the lot of you! You fucking bastard scumbag men!' I scream. Oh gosh. I'd better be quiet. Poor Deirdre's going to wonder what the hell is going on.

I stand up and bang my fist on the table. REVENGE. Who the hell does he think he is, waltzing into my life, turning it upside down and then waltzing out again? I actually thought I could MARRY this guy! What's with all the lies? Why do MEN lie like that? AARGGHH! OK, OK, OK. I need to stay calm. I need to play it right. Come on, Sarah. I know you can do this, honey. Chin up. No one knocks you down. Stand up and fight. Do it for ALL women. Do it for women EVERYWHERE. On behalf of all the women who have been messed around by bastard men. Make this one pay. Make him wish he'd never been born.

So I return to sending emails back and forth between Andrea and Chibu. Chibu tells me, or rather he tells *Andrea*, lots about himself. Stuff I already know, of course. And I, or rather *Andrea*, tells Chibu all about herself too. I base her character on Georgina, but make her a bit scarier. Manuele says 'edge' is attractive, so I give it to Andrea. Chibu eats it up like a baby.

We spend hours emailing each other. As the deception continues, I begin to feel more and more comfortable as 'Andrea' and I enjoy knowing that I have Chibu just where I want him. Not that I have any idea what I'll do next of course. Have to figure out a way to make him pay. Turn the 'player' into the 'playee'. Remember, Sarah: revenge is a dish best eaten *cold*. Just take your time.

That night I find it hard to sleep; I keep playing over different plots in my mind. It's all so devilish that I find it rather exciting. Watch out, men; the new Sarah is here. VICTORY will be mine. Chibu will pay. And we women will have our revenge.

Chapter twenty-two

'Don't look so despondent, Sarah; this is going to be fun!' Jacquie puts her arm through mine as we slip amongst the streets of Soho. 'Speed-dating is meant to be the most modern way of meeting men these days. In just one night we'll *both* find a boyfriend.' Since splitting up with Mark, Jacquie has made it her mission to find another boyfriend. She's become a little like me. I think she's finally realised that she's nearly thirty-six years old. So powerful is the realisation that she has decided to completely overhaul her search criteria. That's right. Jacquie is excited because for the first time ever, she has decided to consider white guys. She figures white women have it easier. They have a larger pool to choose from, so there are bound to be more choice guys. Having always restricted herself to only four per cent of the population, access to the full one hundred per cent is like taking a kid to Hamleys toy shop for the first time. Jacquie is convinced that tonight we'll meet a pool of gems. Vain hope that is. I've been dating white guys for years. They're just as hopeless as the black ones. Remember how Carrie was so scared of returning to singledom in New York that she moved all the way to Paris with the Russian guy who didn't even want kids? Jacquie and Carrie have one major thing in common. When you're over thirty-five, you'll do just about anything not to be single. The future is not bright. Nor is it orange. It's more like a mixture of mauve and olive green.

We step into the bar and get some drinks. The sleek lights above create a mystery about the place. We are half an hour early. The place is packed with ordinary people having a drink after work. It's the bar *downstairs* where the speed-dating is taking place. Jacquie explains to me that we are attending a 'standard' speed-dating event. Speed-dating events cater for all sorts of people. There are Asian ones, Jewish ones, and Muslim ones. There are events for people working in the media and for people who only want to meet those who earn at least thirty grand a year. There are even 'Sugar Daddy' speed-dating events, where as a man you have to be rich and over fifty, and as a woman, you clearly have to be young and beautiful.

'Black speed-dating events are rare,' explains Jacquie, 'black men don't go for this kind of thing.'

'You mean they don't HAVE to do this kind of thing,' I smirk. 'They have so many women chasing them that no effort is required.'

My phone rings. 'Hello?'

'Hello, darling. Your mother is driving me batty with concern over you. Are you well?'

'Yes, Daddy, I'm fine. How are YOU?' I cup my hand over my free ear.

'Oh, just fine. But your mother is driving me mad. She insists we see this evangelist healer this weekend.'

'A healer? Why?' I say with worry. 'Are you OK? I mean, are you both OK?'

'Yes, darling. We're just fine. But some woman at her church told her this man has great charisma and makes people in wheelchairs walk. So now she wants me to go with her. What a bore. Anyway, what are you up to?'

'I'm out with Jacquie, speed-dating.'

'Speed-dating? What's that?' I explain to my father about the four-minute dates, the ringing bell, and how it's a brilliant way of meeting more than twenty guys in one evening.

'But, Sarah, it's so crude. It sounds like you're a piece of meat hung up in Brixton market.' Absolutely. Good deals on oranges, tomatoes and potatoes. Special reduction on thirty-something Sarah as she's soon to reach her sell-by date! Somewhat deflated, I tell my father I'll ring him later and hang up the phone. We sit amongst the very young crowd and sip our glasses of white wine. Everyone looks about twenty-four, and nearly everyone is white. I feel like I'm back at university, but as someone's older sister. I take the opportunity to update Jacquie on my love life. First I explain that Arthur and I are through. Jacquie is disappointed.

'Oh no! But I liked Arthur. He seemed nice from what you said.' She lights up a cigarette. 'What a shame. He was a good catch.' Jacquie raises her eyebrows when I tell her about his you know what.

'A big DICK?' she screeches.

'SHHHH!' I flap one hand about wildly and with the other, hold one finger over my mouth. How embarrassing.

'Oh who cares, Sarah?' Jacquie throws her hands up. 'Hmm. I didn't realise that some white guys have big dicks too…' She laughs. 'Every woman wants a big dick. That's why black men have such an easy time getting white women into bed…Hmm. A white man with a big dick. What a treat!' I totally disagree, but I'm not about to argue the size of men's packets with Jacquie and her loud voice in the middle of a very crowded bar. So I change the subject and tell her all about Chibu. I mention the Ritzy and him phoning me the following day. I tell her about the 'Love and Friends' website and the invention of Andrea. Chibu and Andrea have been communicating for two weeks and have become great friends.

'Sarah, you talk about "Andrea" as if she were someone you know.' Jacquie taps her packet of cigarettes. 'You do realise that this is now moving into the domain of Bunny Boiler action, don't you?'

'Bunny Boiler action?' I'm confused. 'What's that?'

'Bunny Boiler…people who boil bunnies.' Jacquie rolls her eyes. 'You know, *Fatal Attraction*?'

'Oh. You mean you think I'm like a stalker?'

'Yes, Sarah. You've turned into a psycho,' Jacquie sniggers. 'What happens when Chibu wants to meet Andrea?...Have you thought of what you'll do then?' True. Haven't thought through the complications of it. '...and have you considered that Chibu might be so horrified when he finds out that he might never speak to you again?'

'But I don't care about that. I know it won't work out between us. I want to humiliate him.' I twist my hand into a fist. I want revenge...Revenge for us all.

We glance at our watches. It's time. We head downstairs. The woman in charge introduces herself as Sandy. Sandy is pretty with flowing blonde hair and long eyelashes. Her tailored pink suit tries hard to disguise the fact that she can't be more than twenty-two. Her heels click against the floor as she walks and she speaks in a high-pitched voice.

'Ladies, you sit at the tables and gentlemen, you get up and move to the next table when I ring my little bell.' She tinkles her bell, giggling. 'I will ring the bell every four minutes so you guys had better impress quickly! On your card you can either tick or cross each candidate and later when you return home you can enter your ticks on our website.' Sandy beams, opening up her arms. 'And remember everyone, our website is www.speeddater.com. So don't forget the website www.speeddater.com! Then tomorrow you'll receive via email the email addresses of those people who also ticked you!' She squeals. 'You only get an address if you've both ticked each other!' I notice a dreamy guy sitting near Sandy. He has short dark brown hair done in that electric style, gelled in different directions. He glances over at me and smiles. I smile back. Maybe this isn't such a bad idea after all. Except the men are spineless jellyfish and not enough of them have come along. There are fifteen men and twenty women. So for five of the dates (essentially twenty minutes) we women will be twiddling our thumbs. Oh well. Everything can't be perfect. I'm beginning to feel a little excited. Who knows, maybe I'll get lucky. I wonder who that cute guy is. Just have to cross my fingers...

'Right, ladies, here are your badges, now go to the table that matches the number on the badge.' Sandy hands me a badge, grinning uncontrollably. Number THIRTEEN. I uncross my fingers. Does God not like me or something? Did I do something to Him?

We move to our assigned tables. Jacquie is sat round the corner from me and I can't see her. My number thirteen badge, clearly stating SPEED-DATING, stands out rather awkwardly on my chest. I might as well have a big sign across my forehead marked LOSER. Well, it doesn't really matter. Only speed-dating contestants are in the downstairs bar area. Nothing to be embarrassed about. And soon I'll get to speak to that yummy guy. Sandy skips over and explains to me that for the first five dates, I'm free to twiddle my thumbs, but she assures me of an evening choc-a-block with 'hot dates' after that.

I sit in my chair, looking around, feeling excited. My dreamy guy is chatting to Sandy and I can see him glancing over in my direction periodically. Sandy shakes her big bell and the dates begin. I turn around and notice that I'm sitting next to the loos. Great. Number thirteen and next to the toilets. Two women trundle down the stairs and pass me to answer the call of nature. They stare at my badge and point. 'Hey look! It's speed-dating.' Giggling, they push open the door to the toilets.

As time ticks on, more people pass, staring, pointing and sniggering. A big bell sounds. A short stunted fat man waddles out into the middle of the ring. People from the stands above applaud. 'And now for the most horrific, most shocking, most terrifying act of all...' I hear a drum roll, 'Sarah, the single thirty-year-old!' Someone pushes me forward and I find myself stumbling into the centre of the ring, blinded by a beam of light beating down from up above. I squint, and look out. People are jeering and pointing. I turn away...

DING-A-LING. Date ONE is over. There is movement and a little confusion as the men change tables.

'Hi there. How are you?' I look up and my dreamy guy is standing next to me.

Jesus. OK, Sarah. Stay calm. Think Goddess. Think NAKED. 'I'm well, thanks. You enjoying this evening?'

'Yes, it's going really well.' He winks. 'Hope you meet some interesting men tonight.'

Huh? Is he gay? 'Yes, well uh, yes, I hope so too,' I stammer.

'Right, well maybe I'll catch you later.' He waves and jogs up the stairs. Gosh, I'm such a disaster. I can't even get a guy's attention at a speed-dating event which is packed with men wanting to meet single women. Hmm. Maybe he went to get a drink? Another woman passes, staring at my badge. OK, enough. Dunce cap off. Ripping off the badge, I hurry over to the other women who are waiting for the men to catch up.

A young white woman of about twenty-five, quite pretty, with long straight black hair turns to me. She's carefully made up and manicured, wearing a stylish/casual beige suit. 'We might as well go home now, don't you think?'

'Go home?' I peer at her inquisitively. 'What do you mean?'

'Well, they're not exactly worth sticking around for, are they?' she snaps haughtily.

'But we haven't even spoken to them yet.'

'There's such a thing as PHYSICAL attraction you know,' she replies, cocking her head. Arthur versus Chibu. Maybe she's right. But still, can't just write them off like that. Can you? It seems too unfair. I sit and chat with three of the women. Everyone is depressed. They complain about the men at the event and about men everywhere. Why are these women so bitter? Oh yeah, Chibu. One too many Chibus in your life and you could easily get bitter. REVENGE. But why are they even here?

'Girls, I really think we need to be more positive,' I announce. 'I know the dating world is pretty harsh, but if we lose heart, no one will ever find us attractive.'

Rule Number TWELVE: Gotta remember to never get bitter. No matter what. Most of the women nod in agreement. The pretty one with long dark hair just rolls her eyes.

DING-A-LING. YIKES. My first date. Right, Sarah, remember to sit up straight and smile. Think NAKED. I put my badge on, rush back to my seat and take out my scorecard and pen. I hope four minutes will be enough time. Matthew, Number One, sits down. He's medium height, with olive skin and short brown hair. He's quite attractive, with big round eyes, like a white Tiger Woods, but less goofy looking.

'Hi. I'm Matthew.' He holds out his hand and I shake it. 'So you're Sarah.' He eyes me up and down. 'And how old are you?'

WHAT? That's a bit quick. Bloody hell.

'I'm thirty,' I squeak.

'THIRTY, eh?' he sniggers. 'Well, you'd better hurry up then. You only have a couple of good years left.'

'Sorry?'

'But you're not as bad off as some, mind you.' He scans the room. 'I think some of these women are actually FORTY.' He starts to laugh, holding his stomach. 'That's just too old. They should have given up and stayed at home.'

He's an ordinary-looking thirty-something guy. Nothing special. Ten years ago he was probably awkward and desperate for a girlfriend but now he's calling the shots. Nevertheless, I'm not going down without a fight.

'How old are YOU?' I demand.

'Me? Well, I'm thirty-three, but I'm a man. Not the same thing.' He wags his finger. 'No biological clock.'

'You're right, it's different. It's harder for me.'

'Yeah,' he yawns, 'you women have such a hard time finding men...I feel sorry for you.'

I tilt my head to the side. 'That's so good of you, Matthew, so thoughtful…it's so difficult for us women, which is of course why I am speed-dating,' I say, grinning. 'But as you're a man and have it so easy meeting women, why ever have YOU had to come to speed-dating to meet someone?'

'Well, I just thought…well, I thought it might be interesting…'

'My guess is that you've been here dozens of times and you still haven't found anyone.' Matthew's face turns a pale scarlet and I know I'm right. 'Even in my position, as desperate as it is, I wouldn't touch you with a bargepole.'

STRRIIIIIKE. That's it, Sarah. Give 'em as good as you get. Matthew is dumbfounded. I look at Sandy, wondering how long it'll take her to ring the bell. I never thought four minutes could feel like such an eternity.

DING-A-LING.

'It was a pleasure meeting you.' I hold out my hand and smile in the way that they do at McDonald's. Matthew shakes it and moves on.

I cross my scorecard and turn my head to Miles, Number Two. Oh my goodness. This guy's wearing a white bowtie. He really is. A white bowtie and the penguin suit to match. Miles is black. He's jet black with a short neat haircut. He looks about forty and has clearly had bad acne as a child. Miles introduces himself as a Trinidadian who has spent over twenty years in Helsinki.

'Really?' I chirp. 'So you speak Finnish then?'

'I do. Not that it's much use to me here.'

Miles speaks a bit about Finland and its fantastic hospitals, social programmes and education system.

'So why did you move to London then?' I ask. And do you know what he says?

'Because I'm tired of Finnish women. All they want to do is sleep with me because I'm a black man.'

My jaw drops in astonishment.

'It's true: all they want to do is see the size of my black dick…A man can only take so much sex you know.'

You mean they actually wanted to have sex with YOU? I burst into hysterics and double over the table. Miles joins me and I laugh so much that I nearly cry. Bloody hell. They must have wanted some black booty BIG TIME. Because I'm sorry, there is no possible world in which I could ever have sex with YOU.

DING-A-LING. Wow. Never thought I could laugh so much in four minutes. Another cross goes down on my card. Two disasters, another thirteen to go. I glance up from my card, and in front of me stands Patrick.

I shake his hand and watch him sit down. He's short; at least he seems short from where I'm sitting. He has long dark brown hair in a pony tail. He's in his early thirties and his glasses give him a bit of an intellectual look. If only he could cut the hair, he mightn't be so bad.

'God am I glad to see *you* here.' He winks. 'You're gorgeous.' I blush slightly. Maybe this guy deserves a second look.

'Well, thanks,' I say perkily. 'This is fun, tonight, isn't it?'

'Only now that I've met you.' He takes my hand. 'You're just my thing.'

Hmm. Well maybe these guys aren't so bad after all. Things are looking up.

'That's very sweet of you.' I curl my hair around my ear with my free hand. 'But I'm sure you say that to all the girls.'

'Nah. No way. Only the black ones.'

I withdraw my hand.

'You're all so sexy. You know how to move and you're all so beautiful.' He groans, making a fist. 'And your behinds are just so tight.'

OK. Yup. That's enough. I've had my fill here. Thanks very much for a lovely evening. Must be running now. Come on bell…Fucking well RING. But there is no such luck. TICK TOCK TICK TOCK…Sandy is talking on her mobile phone.

Has she forgotten us? Am I to stay talking to this Jungle-Fevered Tarzan Twit all night? Patrick goes on to tell me about a few of his black ex-girlfriends and compares them to his white ones. He loved the black ones because they were well-endowed. He hates 'model types', as he likes something to hold on to.

'Yeah…because you black babes know how to grind those hips…'

DING-A-LING.

THANK THE LORD. I want to beat Mr Tarzan into the ground. Instead, I smile and shake his hand. These guys are going from bad to worse. I start to think that the woman who said we should go home was right. I scan the room for the delicious man I noticed at the start of the evening. I can't see him anywhere. I've obviously given him too much of a fright. The dates continue. And as each date passes, I hate Jacquie more and more for dragging me out to this farcical attempt at finding a boyfriend.

When it finishes, Jacquie comes dashing round the corner. She puts her arm through mine and hurries me up the stairs. As soon as we are out the doors, she shows me her scorecard. There lie fifteen perfectly formed crosses. I show her mine. Exactly the same. We fall about with laughter in the street.

'Did you speak to the jungle-fever guy?' I ask.

Jacquie raises her eyebrows. 'That's it for me and white guys.'

'But there were a couple of black guys there tonight and an Indian guy…and remember there was that one who looked mixed…anyway, he wasn't white,' I argue.

'So what are we saying then, Sarah?' Jacquie squeezes my elbow. 'That all men are hopeless whatever their colour?'

'Yeah. I think we are.' We laugh and laugh.

It starts to rain and we start to run, arm in arm to Tottenham Court Road. Jacquie gives me a nudge. 'Hey,' she whispers, 'who needs a boyfriend when you have girlfriends like us?'

'Damn right,' I reply. And arm in arm, we jog down the steps into the tube.

Chapter twenty-three

I sprint down the hill away from school in a hurry. I'm to meet Georgina at the gym at five and I haven't left myself much time to get there. This is one meeting I don't want to miss. I'm planning to ask Georgina a favour. One of my GCSE students, Rita, calls after me.

'So who is it you have the HOT DATE with Miss, huh?' The girls around her giggle. 'Who is it that you *fancy*? Is it Mr Philips?' Some of the girls turn their heads in embarrassment. Mr Philips is one of the Art teachers. He's young and relatively attractive and I regularly eat lunch with him in the canteen. Of course he also lives with his girlfriend. The kids added two and two, and got five, an experience regularly repeated in their Maths lessons.

'Don't be silly, Rita. I'm going to meet a friend.'

But Rita isn't having it. '*Uh-huh*, Miss? YEAH RIGHT!' By now Rita is shouting. 'We've seen how you look different these days, Miss. Before you was all mash-up and now you're all POW.' Rita throws her hands open. Some of the other girls start nodding and saying 'Yeah, yeah.' Rita turns to her friends. 'Her hair is all styled now and she wears trendy clothes, man.' She pauses. 'What we wanna know is…who's the MAN?' I laugh. Part of me is rather pleased that they've noticed my efforts to look more attractive. At least *someone's* noticed. If only some single thirty-something guy might notice too. I wave at the girls, telling them that I'll see them tomorrow and jump on the bus.

Sitting on the bus, I notice a couple of young black women

221

at the back, eating chicken from one of those imitation KFC places on every corner of South London. Black people love their chicken, don't they? Next to them is an old Indian couple by the window, late sixties perhaps. They're grey and wrinkled and look slightly cold. They've been to Sainsbury's. There are too many bags for one old woman to carry, so her husband came out to help. I stare at them. That's what I want. That's what love is. Love is looking after each other.

As the old woman pulls at her husband's coat, trying to do it up properly, I start to wonder what she would do if he weren't around. Maybe she'd order in from Meals on Wheels. Maybe she'd just buy less at Sainsbury's. Or maybe she would give up eating altogether and one day we would find her all shrivelled up, frozen cold, having died because there was no one who loved her enough to accompany her to the supermarket. The bus turns the corner and I glance at my watch. It's six minutes to five.

I hurry into the café at Virgin Active. I'm five minutes late. I stride quickly towards Georgina who is draped in expensive baggy gym wear designed to cover every inch of fat. She sits by the wall, with a couple of glasses of water, holding William, surrounded by baby stuff.

'Oh Georgina!' I clasp my hands together. 'He's grown so big since the last time I saw him.' William seems enormous. He's nearly two months old and resembles a giant doll in a pair of jean dungarees. No doubt he is perfectly normal looking for his age. But what do *I* know? Not only have I never had a baby, there isn't the slightest possibility that I'll ever have one. I smile and look as interested in him as possible. Georgina is terribly proud of him. She beams from ear to ear. Her whole life is about William now. Whether she goes out or stays in depends on him. What time she goes to bed, gets up, eats or relaxes, depends on him. She and John can't go on holidays any more. And she is yet to have a proper night's sleep.

Hearing all her stories makes me worry for her slightly. It also has me wondering whether this baby malarkey is really for me. Maybe I'm better off without one. I like being able to sleep through the night and I like going on holiday. But Georgina is overjoyed. This is the first time she's meeting a friend out of her house in over two months. She's excited.

'Sarah, darling, you're so lucky.' She smiles at me. 'You have so much time to yourself. Thank you for inviting me out today. It's such a treat!'

A treat? Going out is a treat? Maybe I really *do* need to rethink this baby thing.

'Mind you, I've just hired a nanny. So I'll be able to get out more now.' Georgina pauses, gulping her water. 'I need to get to the gym more often. I've become so fat.' She's right. She's much larger than she used to be. But then she was extremely slim before. Now she looks kind of like ME. I point out to her that by saying this, she's basically calling me fat too.

'No, Sarah, just look at you.' She disagrees, pointing at me. 'In the last two months, you've lost a lot of weight. You look fantastic now.' I glance down at myself and then stand up. It's true. I've lost some weight.

'I suppose going to the gym pays off.' I hoot gleefully. 'Yes, exactly.' Georgina nods, getting up. 'I'm going to put William in the crèche and I'll see you in the changing rooms.' Off she goes.

I'll ask her the favour later. I finish off my water and start picking up a few baby toys that Georgina has left behind. As I do, I notice a very beautiful redhead dash through reception in a tight baby-blue body suit, her hair tied in a pony tail. Boy, that woman is amazing. Not quite there yet.

'Don't tell me you've had a *baby* since the last time I saw you.' I swivel round, toys in hand. It's Sam. Even better looking than I remembered. I glance at the toys leaning against my chest. 'No. They belong to a friend…HEY!' I smile. 'Great to see you.' We both hesitate slightly and then give the other one a peck on the cheek. Sam stands back and tosses his floppy blond hair to the side. God, he's cute.

'So the fitness freak is back working out again is she?' What's with me pretending all the time? Isn't that what I hated about Chibu? I'm sick of it. Come on. Be different. Be bold. Be me. 'No, Sam. Actually I'm not a fitness freak at all.' I make a silly grin. 'When you saw me here, that was my first time at the gym in months.'

Sam smiles. 'Yeah. Well, that was kind of obvious. I just didn't say anything.'

Oh Jesus. How embarrassing. OK, ground…now would be a good time to open up…

Sam winks. 'But that was *then*. This is *now*. And from the looks of it, you've certainly turned into one.' Sam stands back, examining me. 'You look like one sexy kitten.' Wow. He just saved the day. Gosh, he's nice. I wonder whether I still have a chance here?

'So you still wearing your nicotine patch?' I rub my hand down the side of his arm.

'No, not any more. I think I finally managed to kick the habit. What a relief.'

'Ah, but are you still eating chocolate?' I ask mischievously.

'Yeah, course I am. But I'd be a fool to give that up. Bloody delicious it is. You still eating chocolate cake, I take it?'

'Oh yeah. Most definitely. Couldn't get through a day without it.'

'You do know what chocolate is meant to substitute, don't you?' Sam sniggers.

'Yes, but I'm a girl. Girls always eat chocolate. You're the one to worry about. Any guy who admits to liking chocolate must definitely be in need of something.'

We laugh. Sam is so sexy in his gym kit; my stomach somersaults a dozen times. He tells me about an art gallery in

New York that has agreed to show some of his work. He's thrilled. It's a huge deal for him. It'll mean more exposure.

'That doesn't mean you'll move to New York, does it?' I ask worriedly.

'Nah.' Sam waves his hand. 'Of course not. I love London.'

Thank goodness for that. And maybe he could love me too? OK, Sarah, just play it cool and maybe he'll forgive you for ditching him before Christmas. Maybe there is indeed a God.

We speak about New York and compare it to London. He loves roller-blading in Central Park, and he's crazy about Greenwich Village.

'If ever I have enough money, one day I'll buy a brownstone in Harlem and do it up,' he says dreamily.

'And what will you do with all the space?'

'Fill it with my paintings of course!'

'Oh I see. So you object to your parents filling their house with paintings, but you can do what you like, huh?'

'But I'm not David Hockney!' Sam laughs and so do I, as I curl my hair around my ear. Perfect. Just perfect.

'Well anyway, I should run,' says Sam, 'my girlfriend is waiting on me upstairs.'

OK, so maybe not so perfect. Girlfriend? 'Yes, of course, uh yes, um…definitely,' I stammer.

'Sarah! Here you are. I've been looking for you all over the place.' Georgina marches into the café.

She's slightly flustered. She looks at Sam and I introduce them. They shake hands.

Sam takes a step back. 'I'd better go work out then.' He waves. 'It was good to see you Sarah. Till the next time.' He whirls round and jogs away. Georgina grabs me by the arm and sits me back down at the table where we were sitting.

'Who was THAT?' she demands, trying hard not to scream.

'That was SAM. You know, the one I told you about…the artist who lives in Brixton.'

'That was *Saaaam*?' Georgina grins with excitement. 'Wow, Sarah. He's *gorgeous*.' She looks like she might wet herself.

'I know he is. He was great. I really messed that one up.'

'No you didn't. Just go ask him out.'

'I can't. He has a girlfriend now. I just waited too long I suppose.'

'Oh, I see what you mean. But it makes him even more attractive, doesn't it?' She laughs. 'Oh, Sarah, darling, I wish I could have one too.'

'One what?'

'A cute guy.'

'But you have one… John.'

'Yes of course I do. But I mean that I want a date with a guy I don't know who is charming and funny.' She pauses. 'You don't know how lucky you are to be single.'

Divine. Now's the time to ask. First I explain about Chibu and *Sarah*. How he called a few times, asking to meet up, but that he would have to do more than just 'ask' to get back into my good books. Then I tell her about Chibu and *Andrea*. The more I tell, the more Georgina draws closer to hear.

'And that's where *you* come in, Georgina.' I pause. 'I need you to play the part of Andrea.'

'Play the part of Andrea?…What do you mean?'

'Andrea and Chibu have been communicating for three weeks and he has asked to meet her. I've tried putting him off, but I can't do it for much longer.' I take Georgina's hand in mine. 'So I need you to go on a date with Chibu and pretend to be Andrea.'

Georgina stands up. 'You want me to do *what*?'

'Look. I know it sounds a bit kooky. But you're the one who said you wanted a date with a charming funny guy.' I run my fingers through my hair. 'Now you have one. Or at least *Andrea* has one.' Georgina looks at me like I've finally flipped and sits back down.

'Go on, Georgina…it'll be fun…only one evening and it'll

be easy as I've based Andrea's character on you,' I squeeze her hand. 'A blonde doctor who lives in Knightsbridge.'

'Sarah, you've gone mad. I know he was a bastard to you, but you're going too far.'

'Maybe. But I need to see this through.' I smirk devilishly. 'I want revenge, and you're the only one who can help me win it.' I gaze at Georgina imploringly. 'He's sexy and will make you feel like you're the most beautiful woman on the planet. I promise you'll have a good time. He may even make you feel like leaving John!'

Georgina tilts her head to the side. 'Maybe I could do the *one* date. I've never been out with a black guy before.' She smiles. 'John's always working. It would serve him right...Of course, I'll do it for *you*, Sarah.' HOME RUN. She's going for it. My plan is in motion. I update Georgina on information that has passed between Chibu and Andrea. Georgina is secretly enjoying the mystery and intrigue, taking notes of the various things she has to remember. 'We're all set.' I say, licking my lips. 'All you need to do is get him to fall for you, or at least like you. Then we'll throw it all back in his face. He's a dead man. He doesn't know who he's dealing with.'

Suddenly, Georgina gasps. 'What will we do with William? The nanny doesn't do evenings.'

'Oh don't worry,' I say casually, 'I'll look after him at your house while you're on the date.' Georgina is slightly dubious, but once I assure her that I'll take good care of him, she agrees. My plan is ingenious. Georgina will get what she wants: a date. I will get what I want: revenge. And Chibu will get what he deserves: sheer and total humiliation. That'll teach him not to mess with a supreme Goddess. No one's going to mess with Sarah, Goddess of the Night, ever again. Of course I have no idea what the next step will be. But I know one thing: Chibu will pay; revenge will be mine, and its sweet taste will sizzle on my tongue forever.

Chapter twenty-four

I'm standing in Georgina's front room, peering out the side of the window, from behind the heavy cream wool curtains. 'Sarah! Move from there!' Georgina shoos me away with her hands. 'Chibu will be here any minute. We don't want him to see you, now do we?' I shake my head and dutifully move away from the window. Chibu is to pick Andrea up at eight and take her to a lovely little Italian restaurant in Notting Hill. Bastard. I feel sick.

Georgina points upstairs. 'I've just put William down, so he should sleep through until I get home. And remember: nappies are in the third drawer. And his clothes are in the light blue chest. Spare bottles in the fridge.' She shakes her head. 'Not that he'll need feeding of course...'

'Don't worry, Georgina,' I interrupt. 'I'll take good care of him.' I grin. 'Now *you* remember your name is *Andrea*. Be tough. Don't fall for his charm. He's a dickhead, OK?'

'Yes, Sarah, darling. You've told me already. Now if William wakes up, he likes playing with his rattle. It's on the side table in his room.'

'Yes, I know, Georgina, I know.'

A car beeps outside. The enemy is in our midst.

'Remember to phone me if there's the slightest concern with William.' Georgina drops her keys in her bag and moves to the front door.

'I'm so excited, Georgina!' I clap my hands. 'We're going to get him! Remember to be sexy. Remember he has to find you irresistible!'

'OK, Sarah, the things I do for *you*,' Georgina kisses me on both cheeks. 'Wish me luck.' She rushes her fingers through her hair. 'I'm quite nervous really...I haven't been out with a man in *years*. Take good care of William.'

'You'll be fine, and so will we.' I cross my fingers. 'Good luck. Make him pay!' I wave goodbye to Georgina from the front room. To be honest, I'm worried for her and scared she might screw up. I'm sending a bunny to battle with a bulldog. I wait a minute and eventually give in to the temptation to peer out of the curtains. At the end of the road, I catch a glimpse of the silver Audi...oh sorry, I mean *pearl*-bastard-grey. Fucking dickhead. God, I hate men.

I sit down on the front room sofa and turn on the news. Let's see, they should take about twenty-five minutes to get to the restaurant...What must they be talking about? Will he make her laugh? I wonder whether she'll like him? God I want to be her. I want to relive the excitement of thinking that I've found my 'One'. But...Georgina won't be thinking of Chibu like that. She's just playing a part. So if your date isn't the 'One', does that mean you can't feel excitement? Is it only the possible fulfilment of marriage expectations that makes a thirty-something woman feel a sense of thrill?

I look at the television. Jesus. Bombs are blowing up people all over the world. Perhaps I'm being frivolous and self-obsessed in thinking that getting married and having a family is the most important thing in life. Some people in other parts of the world are just trying to survive the day and be thankful for tomorrow.

My eyes wander up over to the fireplace and I catch sight of a framed photo of John, Georgina and William: a real and genuine family. To hell with the rest of the world. Sure I care if people are dying. But I want a family too. My eyes tune back to the television.

Miraculously, Channel Four's news presenter starts to

transform. I blink. Chibu is sitting at a café terrace in Knightsbridge eating his lunch. Georgina and I are chatting and strolling along on the pavement. As I get closer I notice that he's fat. He's unshaven and his clothes look like they need a good wash. I, on the other hand, look stunning: I look fit: the gym is clearly paying off. My hair is shining in the sun. We approach Chibu's table. He looks up from his food, wretched and uncomfortable. We stare straight at him and then we start to laugh. We just laugh and laugh and laugh.

KABOOM! What the hell was that? I shoot to the window and scan the street. Nothing. WHUAHHHH...Oh my God! WILLIAM. It woke him up. I bound upstairs and stand over this wrinkly squidgy baby, screaming his little heart out. What do I do? Pick him up? Just leave him? What if I break him? Oh, Jesus. Georgina's going to kill me. Why the hell didn't I listen to her instructions? The screams get louder. I grab his rattle and wave it in his face. Come on, William, shut up. Just shut up. *Please* shut up. But the wailing doesn't stop and he looks like he's turning blue. So I pick him up and put him on my shoulder like I've seen Georgina do so many times before. I start jumping. Not quite sure why I start jumping. Something tells me I need to jump. He continues to holler. So I gently swing him about and make funny faces. Then I shuffle up and down the stairs, putting a skip in my step. But he keeps screaming. Should I call Georgina? But that would ruin the whole plan of humiliating Chibu. Then it hits me: a very unpleasant smell coming from William. So *that's* why he's crying.

OK, Sarah, change the nappy. Easiest thing in the world. Women do it all the time. So can you. Now what did Georgina say again? Hmm. Maybe this isn't as easy as it looks. How the hell do I do this? I move to the changing table and place William down. His face looks like it might explode. And I'm beginning to wish he would. How can something so small make so much noise? How can something which was once relatively cute be so objectionable now? Bloody hell. Maybe baby-making isn't for me after all.

I scrunch up my nose and remove William's nappies. Yuck. Yuck. Yuck. I can't believe Georgina does this several times a day. Beurrk…I troll through the blue chest. There are thousands of baby items everywhere.

How many products does a tiny baby need? Georgina has a baby and suddenly she's opening up a franchise of Mothercare.

I find a nappy, some baby wipes and do a botch job, but in the end, William is clean and eventually stops wailing. Well, he stays silent when I hold him. If I try to put him in his crib, he shrieks. So I take him downstairs and we both sit on the sofa, flipping through Georgina's millions of Sky channels. Great. A re-run of *Desperate Housewives* where the blonde one is interviewing nannies.

'Perfect for us, eh William?' I hold him out in front of me and speak in 'baby-talk'. 'Hello, cutie. Take a look at the little baby-waby on the television.' Unfortunately, he sees neither the significance of the programme nor the coincidence of it being on. Let's face it, neither would most men of any age. Can't blame the baby for being a boy. They just aren't as on the ball as us girls. Luckily, an hour later, when I try putting William in his crib, he's clever enough to fall asleep. He knows his Mummy will soon be home and that he'll get into trouble. For that matter, so will I.

A couple of hours later, Georgina walks through the front door. I jump up and shoot over to her in the hall.

'William is fast asleep…So how was it?' I ask eagerly. 'Are we all set to make a fool of him?' Georgina doesn't respond right away. She takes her time removing her coat. 'So, Georgina…So? What happened?'

'Did everything go well with William?' she asks.

'Yes, just fine. No problems at all. He slept straight

through,' I lie. Georgina looks at me, then hikes upstairs to check on William. I stand in the hall waiting. A few minutes later, she walks past me in silence into the front room. Bloody hell. She's in shock. What the hell can have happened? Why the hell won't she answer me?

'GEORGINA!' I shout. 'What's wrong with you? Tell me what happened!' She sits on the couch and I perch next to her. We sit in silence. Has something dreadful happened? My God. What if Chibu figured out she wasn't Andrea? What has he done? He wouldn't have attacked her, would he? Oh God. Bunnies don't win battles with bulldogs. Fear begins climbing its way up my spine. I jump over to the kitchen, pour a couple of glasses of white wine and return to the sofa. Georgina remains absolutely silent.

'So?' I ask, expectantly. Georgina turns to me. And then suddenly, she starts to cry. I lean over and give her a hug. Oh God, forgive me. What have I done? What has Chibu done? Poor Georgina. I hold her tightly which prompts her to cry some more. We sit for a number of minutes, in silence. Finally, she pulls back.

'I'm sorry, Sarah.' She wipes her eyes. 'I'm being silly. But it's just that I had such a lovely time tonight.'

Lovely? I feel a lump in my throat. But I smile and try to forget it. 'Well, that's a good thing, isn't it?'

'No, Sarah. You don't understand.' Georgina wipes her face again. 'I *loved* being out with a good-looking black man, and I *loved* pretending to be single.'

'So what's wrong with that?' I ask, trying to ignore the envy in the pit of my stomach.

'Everything. Don't you understand Sarah?...Don't you see how lucky you are?' She shakes me by the shoulders. 'Don't you see that being single can be *wonderful*?'

I look at Georgina with eyes big enough to swallow the world.

'You can go out with men whenever you want. I can't. You can go off skiing for the weekend at the drop of a hat. I can't. You can spend a day in a health spa whenever you feel like. I can't. You can go drinking in sophisticated places and meet interesting men. I can't.' She pauses and holds her head for a moment. 'The last time I had that kind of freedom was when we were at university...when I didn't have any real money to be able to do any of those things.'

WHAT? Georgina speaking so candidly? Georgina not happy? All this time while I've been thinking that *she's* the lucky one, she's been thinking the same about *me*?

'But what about John?' I insist.

'Sure John is lovely, and I'm very lucky to have a husband like him. I wouldn't change him for the world.' Georgina takes me by the hand. 'I don't envy you *Chibu*; I envy you your *freedom* as a single woman. You have freedom *with* money. Those of us who married young have never had that, and never will.'

Georgina takes a sip of her wine and then continues, almost wincing as she speaks. 'You also have the freedom to experience new things, Sarah...Chibu's the first black man I've ever been out with. I've never kissed an Italian or an American. And I never will. What if sex with John is not the best possible sex? What about sex with Chibu?'

Fuck me. Georgina and Chibu had SEX? How could they? Where? His car? The loos in the restaurant? But she was only gone for a couple of hours...I feel like punching her.

'So what happened with Chibu?'

Georgina beams, gazing out into the distance. She then tells me that our devious plan worked like a charm and that Chibu never suspected that Georgina was anyone other than Andrea. But frankly, I don't care any more. All I want to know is how the hell Georgina's just done the business with my ex-boyfriend. So I wait impatiently for the answer. Georgina tells me that her date with Chibu was the most perfect date in the world, thanks to his charm, his humour, and his cheeky grin. 'And then in the car at the end, Chibu kissed my cheek.' She pretends to shiver. 'Sarah, it gave me goose pimples. I felt like I was sixteen!'

'Just a kiss?'

'Of course just a kiss.' Georgina looks shocked. 'What do you take me for, Sarah? I'm married remember?' Georgina continues talking, going over details and I listen in silence. And every time Georgina shrieks with glee at how glorious her date was, I want to slap her. She must notice, because finally she puts her hand on my shoulder.

'What's wrong, Sarah?…Why the long face?'

I push her hand away and stand up, folding my arms.

'Because I know that I asked you to go on this date. But you weren't meant to enjoy yourself. You already have the life that I want.' I stamp my foot. 'Not only do you have it all, but you have to take what little I have too.'

How dare she. How dare she like him. How dare *he* like her. How dare they. How fucking dare they. I thought Chibu and I had this mind-altering SPARK when in fact he clearly has them with every woman he dates.

'But Sarah, I don't understand. You wanted me to pretend to be Andrea and I did as you asked.' She looks at me helplessly. 'I did what you wanted. I only…'

'You liar! You didn't do this for ME. You did it for *yourself*.'

Georgina looks down to the floor. 'You're right. OK. Yes. Yes, you're right. I'm sorry. But how could I help but like the date?'

'It isn't fair!' I wail, stamping my foot as the tears roll down my face. Georgina jumps up and holds me against her.

'It's OK, Sarah. I'm sorry. I'm sorry.' She pats me on the back. 'But I don't understand why you're so upset.'

I take a deep breath. 'You have this perfect life with the perfect husband and the perfect baby. I just don't understand why you're so excited over this date with Chibu.'

'Perfect life?' Georgina gasps. 'You think my life is *perfect?*' Tears start to gather in her eyes. 'My life is wonderful...well, sort of, and I can't complain. But I haven't felt like I did tonight in *years*. I felt *excitement*. I felt butterflies in my stomach. I felt like a schoolgirl again.'

I'm totally confused. 'But you of all people, Georgina... *you* have what all of us want. You have what all of us single girls spend our time searching for. You have a guy who loves you.'

'Yes, I do,' Georgina smiles. 'But I also have a husband I hardly ever see because he's always at the hospital. We have our fair share of problems. I have a baby who has totally taken over my life and I only have boring household tasks to keep me entertained every day.' She laughs. 'I'm *really* lucky, aren't I, Sarah? I can see how you might envy me.'

'I suppose I see what you mean...Still. You're married. Being single, I feel so OLD these days. You don't know what it's like. Before it was easy finding a boyfriend, and there was no pressure because babies were a thing for the future. Now I feel like an old used Lada which survived a couple of car wrecks and is trying to compete with the newer models.'

Georgina stares at me in amazement.

'OLD? You don't know the *meaning* of OLD, Sarah. Do you know what makes people feel old? Having a husband and a baby. Not having any kind of freedom to go out or go on holiday. Never wanting to have sex any more feels old!' Georgina shakes her head. 'Sarah, the irony is that the thing that you're looking for is the very thing that *really* makes people feel old.'

Shuffling sounds outside the front door. Georgina and I dart round. Chibu. He's come back. Oh my God. He can't catch me here. Should I hide? What should I do? Where can I hide? The front door opens. Georgina wipes her face with the back of her hand. I rub my eyes to disguise the fact that I've been crying. I eye the kitchen wondering whether there's enough time to make a dash for it. In walks John. Thank goodness for that.

'Hello, darling.' John slides over to Georgina and gives her a peck on the cheek. 'Hi, Sarah, how are you?' he asks, turning to me. He's unshaven and his hair is a mess. He's wearing his hospital scrubs under his coat and his eyes are heavy with fatigue.

'Fine, thanks,' I answer. John takes a step back. 'Looks like you've been crying, Sarah.' He glances at his wife. 'You too, darling. What's wrong?…What's happened here?'

'Nothing,' Georgina snaps, 'we're fine. Nothing to worry about.' She pushes away the hand that John was resting on her arm.

'But you're not fine,' he insists, examining her. 'Why are you wearing that outfit? I thought you were staying in tonight.'

'Well you were wrong. I went out with Sarah.'

GULP…No wait, John. Not true. I forced Georgina to go out with Chibu. My fault. All my fault.

'You put on THAT to go out with Sarah? Where did you go? And who was here with William?' John's getting cross.

'Stop asking me so many questions. You're always bothering me with your petty jealousies. You're not even meant to be home now,' Georgina retorts.

'Shift ended early…What jealousies? While I'm working day and night, you're out doing goodness knows what.'

'Sarah's here. This isn't the time to have this conversation.'

'Not the time? Well when is the right time then, Georgina? At midnight when you would normally be in bed, you're wearing a fancy dress, in tears, flustered, and I don't have the right to ask WHY?' he bellows, turning around to walk out of the room. 'I'm going up to bed. Join me if you want, otherwise there's always the spare room. It sees more of you these days than I do.' He walks towards the door. Trudging up the stairs, he spins round. 'Sorry, Sarah. See you soon. Goodnight.'

Georgina leans back in my direction. 'See what I mean? Marriage isn't everything.'

I rush to her and give her a huge hug. 'I'm sorry, dearest. I'm so sorry.' I rub her back and pull her into me. Georgina has rumbled my world.

She's right. Being single and free is something that should make me feel *young*, not *old*. All this time, I've been wrong. I have my whole life ahead of me, filled with choices and decisions and adventure. Instead of dreading it, I should be looking forward to it. My dear, dear friend Georgina. I've known her forever yet all this time I haven't really known her at all. Finally, after so many years, perhaps without even realising, just by being honest with me, my dearest friend has changed my life forever.

Chapter twenty-five

I pick up my barbell and stand at the front of the Body Pump class. 'Welcome to Body Pump. My name is Danni and I'll be taking you today.' She looks at me. 'Hi, Sarah, how are you?' Danni's small and cute with short black hair. She speaks with an Australian accent and looks a bit like Danni Minogue.

'Fine, thanks. Haven't seen you in a while,' I reply.

'No. I've been on holiday. Have to get back in the swing of things. I see Body Pump is having an effect on you. Slim-fitting Nike shorts and sports top...' She nods, pointing to my thigh. 'I'm impressed. Not so long ago, you wouldn't have been seen dead in that. I even see some muscle there.' As we run through the first couple of routines, I move from track to track with ease, changing my weights accordingly. It's almost simple.

Danni winks at me. 'You should really increase those weights again. Looks like you're having too easy a time.' I blush and look behind at the others. I catch sight of a young woman at the back, in the corner, who is struggling with her weights. She's about twenty-three, carrying a little too much fat for her small frame, draped in baggy clothes. She is, as I once was, shabby, nervous and intimidated. Wow. Back then I was intimidated by women like me. I've gone from being a Gruesome Gym Goblin into a Glamorous Gym Goddess.

At the triceps curl exercise, I am on all fours, bending my hand-weight towards my back. Danni calls to the struggling young woman in the corner.

'No! Not like that. Keep your back straight.' She sighs. 'Your arm, watch your arm...it should be level with your back.'

238

While Danni contorts herself at different angles in order to demonstrate what she means, the rest of us continue with the exercise. With an air of desperation, Danni turns to me.

'Look at her.' She points at my arm. 'Do the exercise with your arm and back straight...like this lady here.' Who *me*? Is she really pointing at *me*? YIPPEE! I'm the model student! I'm the success story! Hit them for six. For once in my life, I'm doing something right. I feel like the teacher's pet and grin all the way to the end of the class.

Class over, I'm happy to see that the young woman at the back persevered. I run up to her.

'I was exactly like you when I started. Actually, I was worse. I ran out of my first class in tears.'

Her eyes open wide. 'Really? But you're so fit and you carry so much weight on your bar.'

'Trust me,' I say, reassuringly. 'It wasn't always this way. You'll get here too.' I smile, and skip out of the studio down the stairs.

'I see the sexy kitten has just come out of Body Pump?' Sam leaps in front of me.

'Sam!' I look up and giggle. 'Yes. I have...where were *you*?' Sam shrugs his shoulders and bends down to kiss me on the cheek. 'Oh, I was late. Been working too hard. So I worked out in the gym instead.'

He's so cute in his tight-fitting gym wear that I curse fate for allowing him to have a girlfriend. We move down to the bottom of the stairs and stand against the window which shows off the pool.

'You've been coming here a lot recently, haven't you?' I ask, flirtingly.

'You're one to talk! Yeah. Well this football team that I coach...' He pauses. 'Oh yeah...I told you about them?...' I nod. 'Well, it hasn't been happening for a few months.' He pauses again and flips his fingers through his blond hair. 'So I've been trying to make up for the lack of exercise by coming in here more often.'

So that's why he wasn't at football practice that Sunday. He didn't abandon those boys at all. You're such an idiot, Sarah! Why the flipping hell did you let this one go? And now he belongs to someone else.

'It's my birthday next week.' Sam boasts. 'I'm going to be twenty-eight. Same age as *you*.'

Oh Jesus. Forgot I told him I'm twenty-eight. What the hell is wrong with me? Why am I always in such a mess? I grin.

'Well actually, I kinda lied.' I cock my head to one side. 'I'm not twenty-eight at all. I'm thirty.' Great, Sarah. Well done you. There. It wasn't so bad. If he decides that I'm too old for him, well more fool him.

'WHAT? You're thirty?' Sam twists up his face. 'Oh my goodness…had I known, I would never have spoken to you.' He pauses and holds his head in his hands. 'Goodness knows how you cope with being *that* old. I bet you don't even enjoy sex any more, huh?' I laugh. How come I only realise how great this guy is now that he's found a girlfriend? Dammit. I notice the nicotine patch on his arm.

'Hey, I thought you said you didn't wear those any more.' I toss my hair to the side.

'Yeah, I didn't, he says shyly. 'But then I got stressed and started smoking again. This is my second attempt.'

Oh how cute. If only you didn't have a girlfriend. Sam peeks at his watch.

'Well, I have a friend I'm supposed to meet up with and in any case, I don't want anyone to see me talking to any *thirty-year*-olds…' He looks around mischievously as we stroll down the corridor.

'See you, Sarah.' He winks and strides towards the men's changing rooms. Wait a minute. Maybe he isn't with his girlfriend any more? Who knows? I mean, maybe it isn't going very well? And I know *The Rules* say I shouldn't do this… but what the hell, there are exceptions to every rule.

'Hey, Sam!' He turns around. 'What you doing later on this evening? Do you want to meet up for a drink?' He approaches, drawing his eyebrows together. Damn. Maybe I shouldn't have said it. What kind of a woman tries to take another woman's man?

I stammer. 'Uh, well, I mean if your girlfriend doesn't mind.'

'Yeah.' he walks up to me smiling. His hips knock sexily from side to side. 'I'd like that. Don't worry about my girlfriend. She's not exactly my girlfriend any more…'

KNOCKOUT. We arrange to meet in front of Brixton tube at four. Then I skip down to the women's changing room, grinning all the way.

I meander down my street and glance at the top window of the old house. No one. I wonder whether that boy really lives there. I need to know. I steal behind the house and push away the branches in the hedge. I climb through the hole. The garden is filled with weeds and long blades of grass. I follow the trodden path to a broken window in the back wall of the house. I climb in.

'Dwain…Did you get anything?' A woman's voice calls from upstairs. Bloody hell. Maybe I should get out of here. I eye the staircase at the edge of the room. There are giant holes in the floor and small shrubs are growing inside. I negotiate my way around the debris and dirt and climb the stairs. 'Dwain?…Babe, did you get it?' the woman shouts again. I open the door at the top of the stairs. A young pregnant woman is lying on an old dirty mattress. She's white, with a boy's cut of blonde hair, skinny arms and high cheekbones. Startled, she pulls a tatty blanket over herself. 'What the hell? Who are you?' she scowls.

'Oh. I'm sorry. My name is Sarah.' I hold out my hand and quietly approach her. She deepens her frown and pulls the blanket up to her neck.

'What are you doing here?'

There is a beat-up television in the corner. A pile of clothes lies neatly against the far wall and a few tattered books are heaped by the side. I pull my hand back and place my gym bag on a plastic chair covered in graffiti.

'I live next door, and I thought…'

'Yeah, I know who you are,' she interrupts, 'but how'd you get in here?'

'Through the back. I saw your boyfriend come in once.' I scratch my head. 'Listen, I know this might seem an odd question, but I'm just wondering whether he ever tried to steal my handbag.'

The woman throws the blanket off and stands up with some difficulty, showing off her round belly. 'Who do you think you are? You come into my home and accuse my boyfriend of stealing your bag? Just get out of here before he comes back.'

Jesus. Maybe I should go. I start to turn. I stop. No, I'm not giving up that easily.

'I see you're about to have a baby. Congratulations. How much longer to go?' I ask, enviously.

'Just a week now.'

'Oh wow. You're so lucky. I'd love to have a child. How lovely. What's your name?'

'Tina,' she hesitates, blushing, 'I watch you all the time, going and coming from your flat.'

'Oh really? I've always felt someone was watching me.'

'You won't tell anyone, will you? I don't know where we'd go. We don't have anything else. Dwain's already been in court so many times.' She struggles in trying to sit back down on the mattress.

'Here, let me help you.' I take hold of her arm. She sits

down, legs spread open. I sit next to her. 'Don't worry, I won't tell anyone. I only came up here because I was curious.'

We sit for a little while, talking about the house and her pregnancy. The house keeps them warm and the pregnancy gives them hope. I don't ask how they get money to survive. As we talk, I gather her boyfriend begs and steals to get by. His name is Dwain and he does odd jobs here and there.

'I don't know how you manage with so little,' I squeak. 'And you seem so happy.'

'Well, we aren't as lucky as you. You have your flat and job. You're a teacher, right?' I nod. 'And you have so many boyfriends. You have a brilliant life!'

My life, brilliant? 'Yes, well, I suppose it depends on how you look at it.' I pick up a torn picture off the floor of Tina and Dwain. 'So your boyfriend's black, eh?'

'Yeah. I prefer them black. White boys just don't do it for me,' she giggles. 'But I'm worried about bringing up a black baby. Dwain says there's so much stuff about racism that I don't understand.'

'Oh, don't worry about it. You'll figure it out together.'

'You see, I'm Jewish,' she says, 'so our baby will be both Jewish and black.'

'How nice. Really, you shouldn't worry. Mixed-race children have it good.' I gesture at myself. 'Look at me. My father's white, my mum's black, and as you just said, I have a brilliant life!'

'You really think so?'

'I know it,' I wink, patting her arm.

I stand up. 'I should be going. It was nice to meet you, Tina.' I hold out my hand and she takes it. I reach into my bag and pull out some notes. 'Here, have this. That's my baby present to you.' I hand her the money. Maybe there are more important things in life than getting married. Some people are just trying to survive the day.

'Thank you. I told Dwain you were a kind person. And we

shouldn't steal stuff from kind people. That's why I left the biscuits on your doorstep, to say sorry. Well, seeing as you like chocolate.'

So you were the one. Of course.

She stuffs the money in a pillow. 'But don't come back. He wouldn't like it. I won't tell him you were here.'

'You won't tell *me what*?' Dwain is standing in the doorway, grey hood covering his head and a knife in his hand. His bright eyes stand out against his black skin. He growls at me. 'What are YOU doing here?' He pauses. 'Don't answer that. Just get the fuck out.' He motions to the doorway with his knife.

'I'm sorry.' I hold my hand out in front of me. 'I didn't mean any harm.'

'Just get the fuck out!' he yells, waving his knife in my face.

'OK OK!' I push past him and into the corridor. 'Sorry. I'm really sorry!' As I run out of the house, I can hear Dwain shouting at Tina. Tina yells back. Gosh, close call. I hope Tina will be OK.

I rush down the street to my flat. I'm approaching my door when Dwain speeds up behind me. 'Wait a minute,' he gasps, stopping to catch his breath. I twist round. In that moment of silence, I can hear Tina groan from inside their house.

'Tina...she's pregnant,' he whispers.

'Yes, I know. Is everything OK?'

'No, I mean, yes; I mean she's pregnant...I mean I think she's in fucking labour.'

'What?' I start to head back to their house. 'Is she OK?' I can hear her screaming from inside.

'It's too early, man. She's not due for another week.' Dwain pushes the branches open in the hedge and his eyes dart about in panic. 'Man, we have to get to the hospital. Shit. An ambulance! Do we need one? I mean, do you have a phone?'

'Yes, I have a phone. Don't worry, I'm sure a week early won't mean anything.'

We run up the stairs to the bedroom and I rush to Tina's side. 'My waters broke, Sarah. This is it.' She lets out a blood-curdling scream in between her gasps of air.

Fuck fuck fuck. 'OK, stay calm everyone, we're going to be fine,' I say, grabbing my phone from my bag. 'We just need to get to the hospital.' I call Brixton cabs. 'Look, I need a taxi right now. No black people's time, you hear me? I need it now. For the hospital.'

'Thank you Sarah, thank you,' Tina sobs. I hang on to her hand as Dwain paces around the room.

'I know!' I yell. 'I can call your lawyer, Dwain. Maybe he'll be able to help with this.' I scroll through my numbers to find Arthur.

'My lawyer?' Dwain's voice raises in pitch. 'How you know my lawyer?'

'Just coincidence, I guess. Why don't you help get Tina outside while I ring?' Dwain obeys, helping Tina to stand while I dial Arthur's number. 'Arthur! Thank goodness you're there. It's Sarah. No time to explain, but I'm with that boy you were defending.' Dwain and Tina make their way down the stairs.

'How's that?'

'Long story. He lives in the abandoned house in my street.'

'Really? Mikey lives on your street?'

'Mikey? Who's Mikey?'

'The boy I was defending.'

'But his name is Dwain.'

'Who's Dwain?'

'Your delinquent.'

'My delinquent is called Mikey, not Dwain.'

'He is? But that doesn't make any sense. Is he about five foot ten?'

'Yes.'

'And does he wear a grey hooded top?'

'Yes.'

'And is he black?'

'No. He's white.'

'He's white? What? But all this time, I thought he was...'

BEEP. The taxi honks outside.

'Sorry, Arthur. Sorry to bother you. I have to go. No time to explain. Look... have a good life, OK?' I hang up the phone and charge downstairs. Dwain is helping Tina into the taxi. I run round to the other side. 'Turns out I don't know your lawyer after all! Shall I go with you?'

'No, Sarah, I think we'll be fine,' Tina's eyes sparkle as I push my arm through the window and squeeze her hand. Dwain nods as if to say thanks. I shoot round to the taxi driver, hand him some money and order him to take them to the nearest hospital.

'Good luck!' I shout, waving, as the taxi hurries down the street. I stand, staring out into the distance until the car completely disappears and then head back to my building.

I enter my flat and find it lovely and clean. Priscilla has just been, and the place smells of soap suds. I put my gym kit away, sit on my bed and ring Jacquie. I have so much to tell her! I've been trying her for days and she hasn't returned my messages. She's seeing a new guy. He must be something else. This disappearing act isn't like Jacquie at all. Her machine picks up and I leave another message. Then I log on to the computer as Andrea. It's only been a few days since Andrea's date with Chibu, but he's keen and has already written her an email. So much for his being busy. I double click on it and wait for the message to appear.

Dear Andrea, It was good to meet you the other night. I wonder whether you might like to meet up again? Let me know... and don't break my heart...Chibu.

What a dickhead. Mister, I-have-a-rabbit-called-Sugarkins. Make yourself look vulnerable and sensitive and the women start queuing up. Then when they get too close, just cut 'em loose, like a fish which is a little on the small side. Who the hell does he think he is, treating women like that? I've had enough of this. I'm not wasting my time on him any more.

Dear Chibu, I'm not into phoney guys. I like them real. So I don't like you. Stop playing games and grow up or you'll continue to live in the cold dark dungeon that you have learnt to inhabit. Good luck with your life. You're going to need it. Andrea.

I press SEND. I wonder what Chibu wants out of life. Love? Sex? Will he ever look after his woman the way Dwain does? Anyway, not my problem. Chibu is a thing of the past. He left me a message the other day (that's *Sarah*, not *Andrea*), but I haven't returned the phone call. And neither will I ever return his phone calls. We all become slightly insane when we get dumped by a guy: some women dye their hair, others take a fabulous trip to some exotic destination. I, it would seem, construct entire new beings and pretend to be them. But I don't need to see Chibu suffer to feel better about myself any more. Why would I? Tina's right; maybe my life is brilliant. Gosh. I hope they'll be OK.

Yeah. I'm Sarah, thirty-year-old Goddess who has her whole life ahead of her. If a guy doesn't see that, then I don't want him. Perhaps my date with Sam will be blissful. Perhaps it will be excruciatingly dull. Either way, I'm a single gal, free as a bird and I'll fly with whomever I want.

Chapter twenty-six

'Hi!' I jump in front of Sam as he stands gazing at a couple of Brixton's ticket touts hassling the public in front of the tube.

'Hey. How are you?' he asks, kissing me on the cheek. 'Let's go. I've an idea.' Sam is wearing a pink collared shirt, drain-pipe jeans and Adidas trainers. He left the coat and boots at home. Sexy, sexy, sexy. Sam takes me by the hand and leads me across the street. A 59 bus appears and we leap on.

'So where are we going?' I inquire, sitting at the top in the front of the double decker.

'You'll see,' he winks. 'Hey, look over there.' Sam points out the window at an accident down below on Brixton High Street. The participants are shouting and are close to blows. As we drive past, a policeman grabs one of them.

'The drama never stops in Brixton. Every day, there's something to keep us entertained,' I chuckle.

'That's why I like it,' Sam sniggers. 'Anyway, it's been a while since we've been out. What've you been up to?'

'Work's been keeping me busy; looking forward to the summer holidays...we have six weeks off you know!'

'Yeah, yeah, I know. And normally I would envy you, but with the success I've been having in New York, I could probably afford to take off a couple of months too.' Sam flops his hair to the side. 'In fact, I've been thinking of doing just that. Maybe go travelling or something.'

Sam and I move on to discuss our favourite spots around the world.

'Barcelona is great because of the Picasso museum. And the

248

only problem with Tokyo is that it's even more expensive than London,' Sam comments. 'Flats are so small, they make living space in London look...'

'Ahh!' I shriek. The branches from a nearby tree scrape over the bus window, giving me a fright. Sam rubs my back ever so lightly, allowing his hand to slip further towards my waist.

The bus stops in front of Parliament and Sam leads us in the direction of Westminster Pier.

'Are we going on a boat?'

'Yup. I thought it might make a change from a Brixton bar,' Sam says, excitedly. 'I'll get tickets for a round trip.' He joins the queue at the end of the platform, while I take a seat on a nearby bench. Uncharacteristically, the sun is shining brightly in the sky. It almost feels warm enough to take off my coat. Parliament stands magnificently as if it's been painted on to a canvas and the river below glistens under the rays of sun, warming its chilly waters: another picture perfect day.

Dring dring. EEKS. My mobile. Gosh. Now where did I put it? My pocket? No. *Dring dring*. EEKS. My bag. Must be in my bag. Quick, Sarah. It'll ring off before you get to it. Hurry up dammit. *Dring dring*. Bloody hell. It's in here somewhere...My hand scrabbles around in the bottom of my bag. Must clear this out when I get home. What the hell is all of this stuff anyway? Ah. Is this it? Yup.

'Hello?'

'Ciao, Bella. How are you?'

'Oh, Manuele! I'm fine. Nice to hear from you. How are you?' He wants something. He never rings me.

Manuele coughs slightly. 'I am fine, I am fine.' He pauses. 'But you see, Maria my *girlfriend* is giving me a little *trouble*.' Maria his girlfriend? Giving him trouble? Manuele ringing *me* for *help*? This is unbelievable.

'What do you mean, she's giving you *trouble*?' I ask, suspiciously.

'Well, she wants to meet my friends. And as you know, Sarah, I never introduce my girlfriends to my friends. It makes things too complicated.'

'So what's the problem?'

'Well, she wants to meet my friends. And I...' He hesitates. 'Well, I kind of like her...'

WOW. Manuele has a heart after all.

'...and so I am wondering whether she could meet you and maybe some of your friends too. My friends are all players. I do not want Maria to have a bad impression of me. You are my only wholesome friend, Principessa.'

Bowl me over. Manuele cares about the impression he's giving this woman? He actually wants her to like him? My God. And she's THIRTY-THREE too.

'I know!' I exclaim. 'I'll have a dinner party and I'll invite you and Maria.'

'That would be perfect, Principessa. Do you know how to cook?'

'Not really,' I respond, 'but I'll learn. Let's make it next Saturday for eight.'

'Well OK, Sarah. But you will not mess it up will you? I do not want Maria to have to eat burnt cat and fried squirrel.'

'Don't worry, sweetie. It'll be fine. I promise.'

'OK, Principessa. See you then. And...grazie.'

Yeah. Why shouldn't I have a dinner party? I'll just learn how to cook.

'Got the tickets!' Sam charges over. 'All set?' I notice a cigarette in his right hand.

'I thought you had quit.'

'Yeah, well I had. But then I slipped up again.' Sam takes a last drag and flicks the cigarette away. 'I think I need to accept that I'm hooked.'

'Oh well,' I sigh, 'can't win them all, I suppose.'

Sam grabs my hand and pulls me on to the boat. The boat is

jammed with plastic seats, all very beaten and worn, and for the most part, empty. We stroll past and stand by the stern against the railing and look out at the Thames. I gaze at Sam and his cute face as he winces in the sun. Why has it taken me so long to notice how scrumptious he is?

'Would you like to come to a dinner party next Saturday?' I tuck my hair behind my ear.

'Where? You mean at your house?' Sam furrows his brow. 'You sure you know how to cook?'

'Yes. Course I know,' I lie. 'What black woman can't cook? You ever had jerk chicken and rice and peas?'

'Had jerk chicken once at Notting Hill Carnival… spicy. But can't say I've eaten rice and peas.' Sam nudges me. 'So will you show me some real Jamaican cooking?'

GULP. I have no idea how to cook rice and peas. Don't worry, Goddess-Sarah can just ring Mummy and she'll sort it out.

'That's right. My place on Saturday. You can meet some of my friends. I'll also get a chocolate cake just for you.'

'Sounds good.'

The boat moves smoothly along and we pause to take in some of the beauty of London. I turn back to Sam.

'So do you go to Notting Hill Carnival every year?'

'Yeah, basically. My friends always drag me along. Though I'm not its greatest fan.'

'Why not?'

'Well…I like the food and the atmosphere, but it can get really crowded.' He pauses. 'And then when white guys like me start dancing, black guys can get pissed off.'

'Black guys get pissed off? What do you mean? You mean 'cause you can't dance?' I smirk.

'That's just it.' He shakes his head. 'The thing is that I CAN dance. And I've known black guys to muscle me out of the way because I'm stepping on their turf.'

'What? Stepping on their turf? Oh don't be silly.' I wave my hand. 'You're exaggerating.'

'Oh yeah? What would you know?...Not that it's ever been a huge problem or anything. I get why they're pissed off. Remember when I went to the loo at the Satay?'

'Yeah...'

'Well that guy who was chatting you up before I arrived tried to start a fight with me.'

So that's why Sam turned pink that evening. 'What?' I touch Sam's wrist. 'What did he do?'

'He pushed me up against the wall and told me that I should keep my hands off you and who did I think I was and how I'm just a little white boy etc.' Sam flips his fingers through his hair. 'So I pushed him off and we got into a bit of a scuffle.'

'I can't believe it. The nerve of him. How dare he. Why didn't you tell me?'

'Didn't want you to think I was a trouble-maker...didn't want to put you off going out with me,' he grins. 'Anyway, no big deal. He was just jealous.'

I burst into laughter. 'I'm glad you're so confident.'

'Well I'd have to be to go after a woman as beautiful as you, wouldn't I?' Sam slides his arm around my waist and pulls me into him. The wind picks up slightly as the boat passes the Royal Festival Hall and blows my hair over to the side. Sam takes the opportunity of a clear path to kiss me gently on the lips. I look up at him with big round eyes as he lets me fall back to my original stance.

'Wow.' I say breathlessly. 'So, uh, well...wh...what were we saying?' I shake my head. 'Oh yeah, Mr T from the Satay Bar.'

'Most black guys are obviously not like him,' Sam protests. 'But there are a few who can make us white guys feel uncomfortable. Though the guy I feel most sorry for is the black guy who can't dance. Because we all expect him to be an expert and you women see him as a failure.'

Sam moves his hips a little, sidling up to me with his hands on my waist. Hmm. This guy wasn't joking when he said he could move.

'Don't be silly. We women don't expect black men to dance well...well maybe we do...' I draw my eyebrows together. 'Don't know. Maybe. Nah. It's just everyone. You know. It's society.' I shrug my shoulders. 'Like how we think blonde women are dumb and cheap. It's just a stereotype.'

Sam seems to be more interested in moving his hips next to mine than in what I'm saying, but I continue nevertheless. 'I have this theory that the reason black men always go out with blonde women is because they have one major thing in common.'

'What's that?'

'They're both stereotyped by society. Like you said, black men are expected to be good dancers, good in bed and great sportsmen. Blonde women are meant to be stupid and easy and great clothes shoppers. So I figure black men and blonde women are drawn together because of how we view them.'

'Do black guys really go out with blonde women more than with other types of women?'

'Well actually, I've no idea whether that's true,' I chuckle. 'My friend Jacquie is always complaining about it so I've kind of assumed that they do.'

'But aren't you just stereotyping again?' Sam laughs. 'You're as bad as everybody else!'

I giggle and nod, agreeing. Don't know about most white guys, but this one certainly isn't out of his comfort zone when talking about race. How lovely. Sam takes me in his arms and pauses to kiss me. The kiss is harder and longer and I lose my balance, forcing me to grab on to his arms to stay upright. Sam holds me close and we gaze out at the water. We stay silent for a few minutes, wind whistling, sun shining. But then I pull back.

'I should really go to the loo.' Hell, Sarah. What did I go and do that for? 'I'll be back in a sec,' I shout, flying off in the direction of the toilets. Talk about totally unsexy. Kodacolor kissing moment and I turn it into Kodacolor crapping moment. AARRGH.

Greenwich appears and I can feel the boat starting to rotate. I dive into the toilets and while washing my hands, I look at the mirror. Not too bad. Could be better. But not too bad these days. I move closer. YOUCH. A pimple at the end of my nose. Fuck. Where the hell did THAT come from? I poke at it, trying hard not to make it any angrier, fearing it might turn into the jolly green giant. Fuck. Why do pimples always appear when your life is hanging in the wind? No, Sarah, you're being silly. He's just a guy. You're a Goddess. No big deal. I inspect the pimple. FUCK. No cover-up in my bag either. Have the world and the kitchen sink in my bag, but no cover-up. Jesus. OK. Calm down. Maybe he won't notice. Goddesses get pimples too. Get out there and think naked and he won't even notice that it's there.

I march back out to the deck. The boat has already turned itself around and is returning to Westminster Pier. As I approach, Sam takes hold of my hand and pulls me close to him. 'Hey. You were gone ages. Did you get lost?'

'No, no.' I shake my head. 'Just slow, that's all.'

Sam squints in my direction. 'What's that?'

Oh God. 'What's what?'

'That.' Sam points at me.

What do I say? Do I make a joke about it? Oh God. He moves closer.

'Uh, well, I don't know. What's what?' I stammer.

'That thing, right here, right over…' Sam draws me in and kisses me firmly. Our tongues play about with each other's and I fall against his chest. We kiss for what seems like an eternity, until finally the strength of his hold gives way. Pulling back, I speak courageously.

'Wow, that was nice. I thought you meant this pimple on my nose actually.'

'Pimple? What pimple?' Sam chuckles and kisses me again. 'You women are mad.'

We wander along the deck. Every now and then Sam points out a dazzling piece of architecture and gives me some historical background. As we pass the Tate Modern, he brushes my arm.

'Must take you in there one weekend. Such a great place. Some Saturdays I go and hang out for most of the day. Not just 'cause I'm an artist. More because it's so peaceful and it's a wonderful place to think.'

'I've been a couple of times, but never with anyone who understands art.' I flinch. 'Like that upside down piano whose keys jut out every few minutes, while making an incredibly loud noise. Don't get it. I just don't get it.'

Sam laughs. 'Well just because I'm an artist doesn't mean I necessarily "get" stuff. I'm like you. And modern art is open to interpretation. To be honest, my favourites are the historical big guys...like Van Gogh and Picasso. Van Gogh because of the way he painted landscapes. The paint he used was so thick! And Picasso was a genius of course.'

'Why?'

'Because he was always coming up with something new. The man was out of the ordinary. He had the courage to be unusual.'

As Sam speaks, I stare at his well-defined chin. Lovely jaw, lovely smile. I've hit the jackpot. The boat sails on, and we chat on, and frankly, I could stay chatting forever.

Some while later, we find ourselves back where we started, in front of Brixton tube.

'Great seeing you.' Sam winks at me. 'I'm looking forward to Saturday night.' He pops a sweet in his mouth.

God he's cute. 'Yeah, me too.' I smile. 'I had a really good time today. Thanks.'

'My pleasure.' Sam slides his hands around my waist and pecks me on the lips. 'It really was a great day. Shall I walk you home?' Before I have the chance to answer, someone pushes me apart from Sam.

'Who the hell is she?' screams a woman with red auburn hair and blue sparkly eyes. Hey…that's the woman who dashed past at the reception in the gym the other day…the sexy one in that blue gym outfit.

Tears are running down her cheeks.

Sam jumps back. 'Karen! What are you doing here?'

'More like, what are you doing with HER?' She points her finger at me and frowns.

'But Karen, we broke up, remember? I'm entitled to go out with whoever I want.' Sam looks over at me and grabs my hand. 'Sorry, Sarah. Let's get out of here.' Sam pulls me behind him and leaves Karen standing in front of the tube.

'Fucking bastard!' She calls out after us.

We stop outside Sainsbury's. 'I'm sorry about that. Don't let it bother you. She's just a little upset about the break-up,' Sam explains.

'Don't worry,' I purr. 'We all have baggage at our age. I don't mind. And hey, it makes us fit right in with standard Brixton behaviour.' We walk a little further and then I pause. 'No need to walk me home, Sam. It's kind of you to have walked me this far, but I don't want to take you out of your way. It's still light out and I'm pretty good at saving the day on my own.'

'What?'

'Don't worry, I'm being silly. Head on home, I'll see you Saturday.'

'You sure?' I nod. 'OK, see you Saturday.'

Sam saunters up the High Street and I watch him move

amongst the people on the pavement, until he has completely disappeared. Then I turn and walk towards my flat. The streets are strangely quiet and the warm air seems to whistle past me as I step. What an ex-girlfriend to have. Gosh. I'm glad I don't have that kind of baggage. I bet Chibu has tons of women who feel that way about him. I wonder whether he responded to Andrea's email? I can check on the Internet when I get home.

I stop dead in my tracks. No. Chibu's over now. Forget him. I start walking again. The sun is setting in the distance. Right. Dinner…must make something fabulous. I'll invite both my white and black friends. Let's see…Manuele and Maria, Georgina and John and Jacquie with her new black mystery man…oh, and Sam of course. I'm a cosmopolitan woman living in a cosmopolitan city. I stroll past the Brixton Academy – a concert hall – and I notice that Madonna is playing. There's a woman who knows how to be sexy. She's over forty and any man would die to get to know her. Hmm. Can't wait for my dinner party. I'll have to find a recipe and buy the ingredients. And I'll have to get some flowers for the table. It'll be great. Glamorous Goddess Sarah will be the perfect hostess.

I arrive at my doorstep and find a packet of chocolate digestives. The note says: *'It's a baby girl. Tina and the baby are fine. Dwain'*. I rip open the packet and devour a biscuit. Sometimes life just has a way of making you smile.

Chapter twenty-seven

Avocados to start with salad…with lots of different types of lettuce. Fine. Then some salmon…everybody likes salmon. I saw Nigella Lawson make a salmon dish once on television. It's all coming together just fine. Mummy would be proud. I cheated with dessert though: a chocolate cheesecake from Sainsbury's which Sam should love. Also cheated with the rice and peas. Picked it up this morning from my mother, but plan to pass it off as my own. Oh well. They're my friends. They'll forgive me. After all, it's my *first* dinner party.

I put on a black silk and sequin dress and a g-string without even thinking. These days I've become so used to them that ordinary underpants feel uncomfortable. Strappy heels, a pair of diamond earrings, some mascara, and *voilà*. Simply scrumptious. My *derrière* is now the size of England and I feel right at home.

The flat sparkles and the daffodils from the corner shop brighten the room. I put the salmon in the oven and am in the middle of filling bowls with mixed nuts and expensive crisps when the doorbell rings. I jog down the stairs and swing open the big door. It's John and Georgina. We climb the stairs. I wonder whether Georgina told John what really happened that night? I sit them down in the front room.

'Sarah darling, you look lovely and so does the flat.' Georgina's eyes dart about. 'Have you moved things around?'

I shake my head. 'No. It's amazing what a few flowers will do.' I shrug my shoulders. No need to mention Priscilla…I might as well take the credit for all her hard work. Everyone else does the same, right? 'Would you like a drink?'

They nod and ask for some wine. As I hand them their glasses, I notice how tired they seem. Exhausted, more like. Georgina is especially worn out.

'We've left William with the new nanny,' Georgina sighs. 'But I'm worried about him. He hasn't been sleeping properly and I'm not sure I trust this nanny.'

John strokes Georgina's hand while winking at me. 'Early night tonight, I'm afraid.' The doorbell goes again and I disappear downstairs, returning with Manuele, Maria and Sam. Sam is scrumptious. His white linen shirt presses against his torso and his black linen trousers hug his bottom. I wonder if he's ditched the long black coat?

'You look fantastic, Sarah.' Sam crunches on a sweet in his mouth and leans in to give me a kiss.

'Well, thank you,' I grin. 'Let me introduce all of you.' I remind Sam and Georgina of their encounter at the gym, and introduce John. Manuele met Georgina and John when I once persuaded him to be my date at one of their dinner parties. They say their hellos and he introduces Maria. Maria is beautiful. She speaks with a strong Spanish accent. She has straight black hair which curls up at the ends and her long eyelashes make her look dreamy and mysterious. She holds on to Manuele's hand tightly. Or perhaps it's Manuele who holds on to hers. In any case, they are clearly glued to each other like Siamese twins.

'She's lovely,' I whisper in Manuele's ear. He smiles, knowingly. I catch Manuele gazing at Maria from time to time. He contemplates her like she's the most precious thing in the world. He's clearly in love. When she speaks he hangs on to her every word as if he could capture each one in the air and hide it away in his pocket. Manuele in love: how is that possible? Then I remember *When Harry met Sally*. Sally's ex-boyfriend wasn't the non-marrying type, he just didn't want to marry *her*. Men always say they don't want to get serious until they meet the woman they want to get serious with. Manuele has simply met that woman. He has met the one who all of us women hope to be: the one he'll love and adore and who he'll probably marry. I leave them to chat amongst themselves and shoot into the kitchen to continue my cooking. Georgina insists on helping me and I welcome her expertise. The others pass the time chatting in the front room.

DING DONG. 'Ah, this must be Jacquie,' I declare. 'She's bringing some mysterious guy with her.'

'Oh good. I'm so glad I finally get the chance to meet Jacquie. I've heard so much about her.' Georgina smiles. 'I'll set the table for you.'

I skip downstairs and swing open the great front door. Jacquie is propping herself up against the doorframe. I can't believe it. I almost faint. Arthur is by her side. He's wearing a sleek dark grey Armani suit and black square-toed leather loafers. His slick new haircut takes ten years off his face. His usual 'uncomfortable look' is gone. Arthur has turned into a swan.

Jesus Christ. 'Hi!' I holler.

'Hello, Sarah,' Jacquie says coyly, and turns in Arthur's direction. She's wearing a black sleeveless chiffon blouse and slim-fitting trousers. 'I won't bother introducing the two of you, as you already know each other.' I turn my head in Arthur's direction and he looks sheepishly at me. We both nod and mumble 'yes' and 'hello' while shaking hands.

'Well, come in!' I say gleefully. Arthur's Jacquie's date? This is ludicrous. I lead them into the front room and introduce everyone. Georgina hands Arthur and Jacquie a couple of glasses of wine and they sit next to Maria. I grab Jacquie by the hand and insist on her help in the kitchen. She follows me through.

'OK. Start talking. What are you doing with ARTHUR? How did you meet him? Why didn't you tell me?' I roll my eyes. 'I thought you didn't go out with white guys? What the hell is going on?' I check the salmon in the oven.

'Well I changed my mind... about white guys I mean.' Jacquie smirks and lights up a cigarette. 'I always thought Arthur sounded like a good catch. And when you told me about his *dick*...' She smiles devilishly. 'How could I resist?'

'WHAT? You mean you're going out with him because he has a *big dick*?'

'No. That's what prompted me to pursue him. I know you think he's a scarecrow, Sarah, but I like him. And you have to admit he looks good, now that he's with me, eh?' Jacquie winks. 'Each to his own you know.'

'But you don't like white men,' I insist.

'Yeah. I *didn't* like white men. Now I do.' Jacquie lowers her voice. 'There's a lot more to Arthur than what he looks like. He gets me, you know? Anyway, I got us subscriptions at the gym. Plan is to take him three times a week. He'll look like a god by the time I'm finished with him.'

I raise my eyebrows incredulously.

'Look. There are issues, dating a white guy, OK? That's why I didn't want to do it.' She rolls her eyes and blows out some smoke. 'I have to have dinner with his white barrister buddies next weekend and do all of that posh white English talk that I hate. Doing it for work is one thing, but doing it while out with your boyfriend's friends is a whole new ball game.'

I start the finishing touches on the salad. Jacquie stubs out her cigarette and begins helping, continuing her gabble. 'White people do some strange things in bed you know, Sarah.'

'Like what?' I ask.

'Well...they suck each other's toes...yuck.'

'Is that all?' I giggle.

'No. What about *anal* sex? Black people don't do that shit...' I burst out laughing. 'What if he wants to have *anal* sex?' Jacquie twists her mouth sideways as she enunciates the word 'anal'.

'You can always say no,' I shrug, 'but not all white people

do it you know, Jacquie. Anyway, why put yourself through all this angst?'

'Because he's worth it.'

WHAT? Scarecrow man is worth it? Jacquie goes on to explain that when you really like someone, you make sacrifices to be with them and you don't mind. But I'm not really listening.

'Wait a minute. Wait a minute. You still haven't explained how you met him.'

'Well, that was easy,' Jacquie answers. 'I went on to that "Love and Friends" website, created a profile and looked him up. The rest is history.'

Jacquie made a profile for herself on "Love and Friends"? HUH? What is it with all these people listening to me talk about the damn Internet and then signing up as if it was their own idea? I peer at Jacquie. 'So he's your *boyfriend*?'

'Yes, I suppose he is. You don't mind, do you, Sarah?' Jacquie puts her hand on my wrist. 'You did say that you didn't like him.'

'No. No of course not. I can't believe you're with a white guy. You, of all people, Jacquie! Don't you feel guilty?'

'Guilty? Guilty about what?' Jacquie blows out some smoke.

'About being with a white guy. About giving up on black men.'

'Why is that *my* problem? I dated black men for years because I thought they were better suited to me...' She leans in, whispering, 'And to be honest the dick size is a big thing with me.'

I laugh. 'Oh. So you don't feel guilty about not holding up the side and not being true to your own?'

'No! Do black men feel that way about us? Bloody hell, Sarah. Finding a good man is nearly impossible whatever his colour. If you find one, hang on to him because if you let him go, you may never get another chance.'

Hmm. Maybe Jacquie's right. 'But why didn't you tell me?' I ask, scowling.

'You thought he was repulsive. Even *I* have my pride.' Jacquie touches my arm. 'It's OK, isn't it?'

I shake my head. 'I don't mind at all. It's a little weird. But I haven't had sex with him. I suppose that takes the "ickiness" away.' Extraordinary: while I find Arthur repulsive, Jacquie likes him enough to make him her boyfriend. Do powerful women always end up with weak guys? Maybe they don't need someone to take care of them the way the rest of us do? Is there really someone out there for everyone? Is there someone out there for me?

We pick up the various dishes, and move into the dining area to lay it all out.

'OK! Dinner everyone!' I exclaim. My guests move to the dinner table, including Sam, who takes a short detour to give me a peck on the lips. 'Where's the rice and peas?'

Jesus. The rice and peas. I run back to the kitchen and a second later appear with a bowl in my hand.

No need to tell him I just heated it up in the microwave. White lies won't hurt anyone.

'How's the food?' I whisper to Sam who is sitting next to me.

'Delicious.' He beams. 'Had no idea you were such a good cook.'

As we eat, I notice Arthur, who is sitting on my other side, catching Jacquie's eye and smiling. It's as if they share something that the rest of us don't quite understand. At one point, Jacquie leans over and whispers in Arthur's ear. He pulls back and brushes her chin lightly with his thumb, smiling. I remember him doing the same to me. But Jacquie purrs with delight when he does it to her.

'So, Arthur, how are you?' I ask, chomping on salmon. The others are making conversation amongst themselves.

'I'm well, yeah, pretty good, thanks. Though I'm still wondering about that strange phone call the other day.'

'Oh yeah, well, I just confused your white delinquent with

my black mugger. That's all. You said your guy lived in Brixton and I put two and two together and got five.'

'You seemed pretty stressed when you rang.'

'Yeah. We were rushing his girlfriend to hospital because she was about to have a baby.'

'And did she?'

'Yes she did. She had a baby girl.'

Just then, the doorbell rings. Who could that be? Jehovah's Witnesses? Or maybe it's my mother? No doubt she wants to know what my friends think of her rice and peas. Bloody hell. She'll make a total fool of me. Fuck. As I push my chair back, Manuele shoots up,

'Sit down. You have done enough, Sarah. I will open the door.' He quickly darts out of the flat and down the stairs to the main door. Suddenly Manuele's a gentleman? I hope Maria sticks around a while. But now I can't warn my mother to keep her mouth shut about the rice and peas. I sit back down and quickly eye everyone's plates. They've all finished their food. Great. They must have liked it. I'll just have to own up that my mother made the rice and peas.

'Ze food was excellent, Sarah.' Maria blushes as she speaks.

'Yes, Sarah,' John adds. 'It was delicious. I think you're an even better cook than Georgina.' He leans over to kiss his wife on the cheek.

Manuele appears at the door. FUCKING HELL. Just behind Manuele, appears...Chibu.

'Chibu!' I jump up from the table slamming my fork down.

'Hi, Sarah.' He looks slightly embarrassed. 'I'm sorry to disturb you. I didn't realise you had people round.'

I glare at Georgina who follows the cue and turns her head slightly to the left so that her face is out of Chibu's sight. 'That's OK,' I say hurriedly. 'Lets talk in the kitchen.'

Dumb Sarah. Dumb thing to say. Now he'll stick around. Fuck. Fuck. Fuck. Well what was I meant to say? I had to get him out of the front room. At least he won't see Georgina.

I lead Chibu into the kitchen. 'I'm sorry to have come over unannounced.' He touches my arm. 'It's just that you haven't responded to any of my messages.'

I turn to face him, folding my arms across my chest. He stands back and stares at me.

'You look fantastic. God. You look stunning.'

I raise my eyebrows. 'I don't have all day, you know.'

'Oh. It's just that you're so lovely looking. OK. Yes…' He puts his hand up. 'I'll get to the point.' He raises his head. 'Look, Sarah, I know I hurt you. I'm sorry. I was just worried about moving forward with you, that's all.'

I wrinkle my nose and tighten my arms in front of me.

'I really like you. I feel like a prick for messing you about. Please don't tell me to fuck off.'

Oh God. Maybe I'm being too hard on him. Maybe he really means it. Then Andrea comes to mind. 'Look Chibu, I'm having dinner with my friends. I can't talk to you about this right now.' I go to walk out of the kitchen and he gently grabs my arm. I have to get him the hell out of here. He mustn't see Georgina. We can't get found out. I need to get him down that staircase.

'OK, OK. But promise you'll call me,' he pleads.

'I'm not promising you anything.' I pull my arm away from his grasp and storm back to the front room.

'There's the door.' I point at the front door next to where we are eating, which leads to the large staircase downstairs. Chibu stuffs his hands in his pockets, frowning. 'But Sarah…'

I open the door for him. 'Goodbye, Chibu.' He sighs and moves in to give me a kiss on the cheek. His cheek brushes mine when he suddenly pulls himself back up. He turns away from the door, and faces the front room. 'Let me just apologise to everyone for disturbing their dinner.' He walks towards the dining table.

Jesus Christ. Everybody take cover. He walks right up to the table. DIVE UNDER THE TABLE, GEORGINA! I want to shout as loudly as possible. But I just stand there, panic paralysing every limb.

'Sorry, everyone, for barging in like…' Chibu's eyes land straight on Georgina and he stops dead in his tracks.

'…Andrea!' He pauses. 'Andrea? What are *you* doing here?' Chibu looks at me and then looks back at Georgina and then back at me again. I can see his mind ticking at full speed. I stand deathly still, frozen with fear. Georgina sits still, not knowing what to say. John looks confused and stares at Chibu, frowning. Oh God. She never told him. He has no idea who this guy is. Fuck. We're all dead. This is a fucking disaster. Everyone sits in silence.

Chibu flinches at Georgina. 'Andrea, what are *you* doing here?'

John is increasingly irritated. 'Hey, mate, her name isn't Andrea, it's Georgina; you must be mixing her up with someone else.'

I have to do something. Come on Sarah…THINK! But I can't think of anything. It's one great big mess and there's no way I'm getting out of it.

'Chibu, I think you'd better go,' I seethe, pointing to the door.

He turns to me. 'You mean, you and Andrea or Georgina or whatever the *fuck* her name is *know* each other?'

'Yeah. That's right. So I think you'd better go.'

John stands up. 'Look, mate, I told you, her name is GEORGINA. Why do you keep calling her Andrea?'

Oh my God. Poor Georgina. I've never seen John get angry like this before. He's really pissed off. He's going pink. This is all my fault. Oh, Jesus. Forgive me, Georgina. The table is transfixed by the scene. Georgina tugs at John's shirt and asks him to sit down.

Chibu stares at her furiously. 'ANDREA! Will you answer me? What are you doing here?'

John turns red. He looks like he might hit Chibu. 'No, mate.

YOU answer *ME*. Why do you insist on calling my *wife* ANDREA?'

Chibu is bewildered. I jump in between them.

'Look, I think you should go...just LEAVE, please.'

But Chibu moves to the side to make eye contact with John.

'Your *WIFE*?' He shakes his head. 'Well just a couple of weeks ago she went out with *me* on a date.'

Oh, Jesus. What have I done? Enough said. Game over, everyone. Hands up. We've been caught. OK OK. Just don't send me to prison. Forgive me, Georgina. John peers down at Georgina with a look of confusion on his face. Then he glares at Chibu, grabs hold of his shirt collar and shakes him. 'You lying piece of shit. Don't you talk about my wife that way.' Chibu grips John's arms, trying to pull him off. The two of them fall back away from the table and hit the floor.

'Let go of each other!' Georgina yells, standing up from the table. John and Chibu struggle around on the floor.

'Her name is Georgina!'

'No! Her name is Andrea!'

Not knowing what else to do, I throw myself on top of them and try to prise them apart. I flap my arms about. 'STOP IT! LET GO!' Miraculously, it works, and they let go of each other. Wiping his brow, John stands up. Chibu pulls up his collar and flattens out his shirt, moving away from John.

'Look Chibu...just get the hell OUT. Nobody wants you here.' I jump up and point to the door. Chibu looks back at Georgina and then at me, shakes his head and sighs; then he hangs his head down and walks out, slamming the door behind him.

I sit down at the table, so does John, and we all stay in silence looking at each other, listening to Chibu on the stairs and the great big door slamming downstairs. John is steaming.

'Sorry about that everyone,' I smile, blushing. 'Anyone for more salmon?' I pick up the serving spoons.

'MORE SALMON?' Manuele screeches with laughter. Sam

makes a sympathetic chortle and takes the serving spoons out of my hands, returning them to the dish. John stands up, snatching Georgina's hand. 'Look, we have to leave.' But she tears her hand out of his grip. 'NO. I'll explain.' She takes John's hand back in hers, pulls him down in his seat, and begins. She tells them everything: my dates with Chibu, his treatment of me, the invention of Andrea and her own date with him. Of course, she only recounts the facts, leaving feelings and thoughts aside. As she speaks, I glance at Sam. I'm a psycho. I admit it. But that was then. This is now. I've learnt my lesson. Please, Sam. You're too good a catch. I promise I won't boil your bunny. I look at Sam imploringly and he smiles at me. I mean you're the one with the psycho girlfriend at the tube. It just means we have a lot in common.

Georgina emphasises that she was doing me a favour and explains to John that she hadn't told him the truth on the night he caught us because she didn't want him to get jealous. Everyone listens in amazement. Manuele and Jacquie burst into laughter. Even John seems appeased. Sam is slightly shell-shocked but gradually joins in. Eventually our faces are wet with teardrops from all the laughing.

I wonder what John and Georgina will talk about when they get home tonight? Will this have a dramatic effect on their relationship, or none at all? And will Georgina ever forgive me? What a fiasco. I make Glenn Close look positively tame.

My first attempt at being a grand society hostess. The food went down well. The conversation flowed smoothly and I looked as glamorous as can be. One thing is for sure: everyone will take away the same thing: Sarah, thirty-year-old Goddess gives Jerry Springer some serious competition.

Chapter twenty-eight

Two weeks have passed since my dinner party and I haven't seen a soul. I've been busy with work and so has everyone else. Let's face it, with both Manuele and Jacquie 'in love', I won't see them half as often. Sam too has disappeared. I suppose he's freaked out by the revelation that I'm an axe-murderer in disguise. Maybe his psycho ex-girlfriend looks perfectly sane next to me. It's Sunday afternoon; the streets in Brixton are quiet. Remarkably, the sun is shining brightly and it's warm enough to go out without a jacket. On my way to the gym, I'm jogging past some children playing ball in the street, when my phone rings.

'Hello?'

'Hey, Sarah, it's Sam.'

'SAM! Hi! I was beginning to think I gave you food-poisoning and you were quietly dying somewhere.'

'Nah, nah,' Sam chuckles, 'but I'd like to talk to you.'

'Well, I'm on my way to the gym now,' I say, tentatively.

'OK. How about we meet at Virgin Active café in quarter of an hour?'

'Right...done. See you then.' I press the red button on my phone. He wants to talk to me? What guy says he wants to 'talk'? Oh boy. Break-up time. Sam thinks I'm a psycho.

I jog on zestfully, in a navy cotton shirt and pink wide-cut cords, very much aware of the irony that I'm hurrying to take part in my own execution. Running past Clapham Common, I notice Sam in front of me in a t-shirt and jeans. 'Sam!' He doubles round. 'Sarah...Hi!' He kisses me on the cheek. Bad sign. VERY bad sign. Maybe I can plead temporary insanity. Sam leads me to the park by gently pushing my elbow in that direction. We walk along one of the paths that cut through the Claphamites lying in the sun on the grass. A family has set up a barbecue. A couple lies asleep across each other. A dog shoots past and brushes my leg.

'Long time no see...How are things?' I ask.

Sam hangs his head. 'Fine, fine. Everything's going well.' He's clearly uncomfortable and I want to put him out of his misery.

'You wanted to tell me something?'

'Yeah, yeah, I did.' He glares at the ground.

'So?' I say, pointedly. Sam looks at me with big round eyes in silence. I sigh. 'Look Sam. It's OK. I understand. After what you saw at my dinner party, I don't blame you for backing out.' I tuck my hair behind my ear. 'I understand, so no need to feel bad.'

Sam stops dead in his tracks. 'What are you talking about?' He shakes his head. 'I wanted to speak to you today because I've decided to move to New York.'

I take a step backwards. 'You're moving to New York?'

'Yeah. That's why I haven't been in touch.' He flops his hair to the side. God, he's sweet.

'My paintings have been selling so well that I would be mad not to move. But I really like you and I'm sorry that I have to leave now, when things are only starting up between us.'

Just my fucking luck. 'So when do you go?' I ask, trying to smile.

'Well that's the thing,' he says grumpily, 'I go on Saturday... and I wanted to see you one last time and explain.'

God, I've been stupid. 'It's my fault, you know. We took so long to get it together because I was an idiot. That'll teach me.'

Sam twists his face to show he doesn't understand, but I continue nevertheless. 'If I missed out on a good thing it's because I waited so long.'

'Well, it's nice of you to say that.' Sam blushes and runs his fingers through his hair.

'No, it's true,' I insist, touching his arm. I feel a nicotine patch. 'Ah...I see you're trying again?'

'Yeah. Third time lucky I hope.' Sam puts his hands around my waist and draws me in, kissing me softly. 'Sorry, Sarah. Sorry my timing is so off.' He winks triumphantly, stepping back. 'But I tell you what, you'll have to come to New York and have a drink with me there...Once I have a flat and a phone number, I'll give you a ring.'

'Sounds like a plan,' I exclaim. 'Good luck then. Say hello to the Statue of Liberty for me.'

Sam looks at me wistfully, bends down and kisses me on the cheek. 'You bet I will.' Then he turns and cruises towards the High Street.

Wounded, I trudge in the direction of Virgin Active. The sun hides behind the clouds as if it wants to show respect. Well, that should teach me. So stupid Sarah. So stupid. If I hadn't waited so long...oh well, Daddy would say spilt milk and all that. Have to pick myself up and try again. I'm a Goddess. And goddesses don't get knocked down. Goddesses get back up and fight. So I march to Virgin Active with energy and determination.

My workout done, I jog back to Brixton. At my flat, I pick up a book on encouraging children to answer questions in the classroom and snuggle on the sofa to read. DING DONG. Bloody hell. Sam? Is he going to come back à la Hollywood and tell me that he's not going anywhere after all? Might I get a happy ending? I jump off the sofa, run downstairs and open up the great front door. Chibu. Bloody hell. Should slam the door in his face. I take a step back and notice Deirdre peering out of the curtains.

'Hi, Sarah...Can I come in?'

I put my hands on my hips. 'No, you can't come in.'

I go to shut the door but Chibu blocks it with his hand.

'Look, Sarah. I'm sorry.' He bites his lip. 'I'm really sorry.'

'You play hide-and-seek with me, refuse to meet up for one measly drink, then you dump me in the rain… not to mention ruining my dinner party. You're a fucking dickhead. I don't have anything to say to you.' I try again to slam the door, but Chibu's hand remains steadfast.

'Please, Sarah. Please just hear me out. Let me in for a minute. I'm sorry…OK? I'm sorry.' Chibu tilts his head to the side and makes a sweet face. Oh gosh. Maybe I'm being too harsh. I open the door and he walks inside. We travel up the steps to my flat and I show him to the sofa in the front room.

'Do you want a drink?' I ask, irritably.

'No thanks, just sit with me.' He pats the spot next to him on the sofa and I obey. He sits, elbows on knees.

'Look, Sarah, I've come to say that I'm sorry.' He shrinks, shaking his head. 'Not that I'm the only one who should be apologising…that whole Andrea/Georgina person invention was seriously fucked up. Tell me, when Andrea and I were emailing, was Georgina responding, or was it you?'

'It was me,' I say, triumphantly.

'Jesus.' He puts his hand on his forehead. 'You are one fucked-up cookie.'

I feel myself boiling inside. Who the hell does he think he is telling me that *I'm* fucked up? What about *him*? But he speaks before I have the chance to explode.

'But I kind of like that about you. You're unpredictable,' he declares. 'I have to give it to you. You got me. I have to admit that. You really got me. But it was really fucked up.' As I listen to Chibu describe me as some insane stalker, I know he's right. Somehow I've gone from being a perfectly normal person to some mentally unstable whacko who steams rabbits for lunch.

'So what I don't understand is why you're here now.' I squint coldly at Chibu. 'We're finished. We were finished long before Andrea anyway, and now "we" are just irretrievable; if there was ever a "*we*".'

'Really?' Chibu looks worried. 'I was hoping that…Well, I really like you Sarah.' He takes my hand in his. 'I want to see you again.'

I pull my hand away. 'Do you think I'm stupid?' I pause. 'You've already played me once. And it was my mistake to have believed you. But I'd have to be stupid to make the same mistake twice.'

'Believed me? What do you mean?' Chibu queries. 'I never promised anything. We saw each other a few times and had a good time together and suddenly you're talking MARRIAGE in the loo of the hotel in Brighton. That really freaked me out.'

'I said that I *could* marry you…because I thought you were pretty fantastic…and you led me to believe that you were serious about me.' I twist my hair around my left ear. 'You implied in everything you said and did that I was more than just a bit of fun. And you *knew* I liked you. And then you refused to see me at the weekend.'

'But I liked you too.' Chibu holds his head in his hands. 'I liked you too much perhaps. And I had so much work on and you were totally unwilling to understand. I went to so much trouble to organise getting out of work for that last drink with you. But it wasn't enough. You even accused me of being married! I can't get involved in something that might compromise my time.' He pauses and looks at me. 'Time is money, you know. I'm not some rich white boy who has had everything handed to him on a plate. I've had to work hard for everything I own. I didn't get to where I am now by fooling around.'

'You think 'cause you're a black man you have the right to treat your girlfriends like a chore?' As the words come out of my mouth, an image of the racist unshaven straggly haired guy at the Arcades jumps into my head. I pause for a moment, thinking. 'Get over it.' I shout. 'Don't you see? The joke is on you. You're the one who'll end up heartbroken and deserted at eighty-five. You keep working like a madman to prove that you're the best. Keep putting in a hundred and ten percent and see where it gets you.' I hold my head up. 'And go find yourself another woman who you don't have to spend any time on. Because I'm not that woman. And I'm clearly not the woman for you.'

Chibu grabs my hand, his eyes pleading. 'But that's just it. I think you could be.' But then he drops my hand and puts his elbows back on his knees. 'The thing is that you women always want us men to become things we don't want to be…You like me because you think I'll be a good provider, I have a good job and I know how to behave myself in public.' He holds his head in his hands again. 'You women never understand that all we men want is to be ourselves, with no pressure to look after you or commit to you forever. We want to feel *free*.'

There's that word '*free*' again. Everyone wants to feel *free*. At least women who are married or men who are running in the rat race want to be free. Those of us who are as free as birds like infamous thirty-something single women are desperate to tie ourselves down as soon as possible and abandon our freedom to the wind.

'I liked you because you were charming and nice. I don't want you to look after me; I can do that just fine on my own, thanks very much.'

'Bullshit. You women don't want nice guys. There are thousands of NICE guys out there. You liked me because I was a bit of a bastard and all you women want a bad boy who you can tame and then marry.'

Hmm. Hugh Grant's character in *Four Weddings* was adored the world all over for that very reason. Is he right? Have I been pursuing prick-men? Is that why my relationships never work out? I make a face. 'Who do you think you are? I might want commitment, but as for long-term commitment, well that's something that comes with time, if both people want it.'

'But I don't want to have to transform myself or to start planning a wedding.' Chibu turns to face me. 'It's hard to meet women I like, you know. Finding a woman who is attractive *and* intelligent and also fun and laid back is nearly impossible.' He smiles gently, tilting his head to the side. 'So I got used to moving from woman to woman. But you were different. We were good together.'

I listen carefully to what Chibu is saying. Is it really hard for them too? Nah. It can't be as hard as it is for us. For one, they can have children at sixty. But maybe he deserves another chance?

'Sarah, I wouldn't keep coming here if I didn't think you were something special worth fighting for. You have flavour… there is something different about you. The other women I meet are just regular.'

'And if Andrea had been real, would you still be chasing me?' I retort.

'Andrea? Bloody hell, Sarah. Andrea was one of many women I have taken out. You and I were finished. I was perfectly entitled. I didn't do anything wrong there. We went out once. We had a nice time. You and I had something much more profound.'

'So why wouldn't you see me on the weekend?' I probe.

'I told you. I was visiting my aunt.'

'You were visiting your aunt every weekend for a month? What do you take me for?'

'OK OK. I needed space to think and work. Her place was far enough away to escape, but close enough to get some work done. And one of those weekends I stayed in London. I just didn't want everything to get out of hand with us…I wanted some time to myself. Maybe I should have explained that to you, but I didn't know what to say really. And I had an enormous amount of work.'

'You had too much work?' I roll my eyes. 'Do you think I'm stupid? Why were you never around on the weekends?'

Chibu leans his head back and massages his skull as if he is preparing himself for something significant. 'The thing is, Sarah, well, when I returned from Nigeria, this woman who I once went out with...well, we never went out, we kind of had a fling a couple of years ago...well, she lives up in Manchester. I met her at a Man United match once.'

'You mean you were seeing her on the weekends and seeing me during the week?' I interrupt, folding my arms in front of my chest.

Chibu puts his hand up. 'No! No, not at all. I used to go up to Manchester to watch the occasional match and as my aunt lives nearby, it was convenient to stay there. Helen, that's her name...well, we had a short fling a couple of years back.'

'And...?' I say impatiently. 'What the hell does two years ago have to do with now?'

'Well, when I came back from Nigeria, she phoned to say that she has a fifteen-month-old boy and that I'm the father.'

My jaw hits the ground. 'What?'

'Her kid...she said I was the father.' Chibu pulls himself up on the sofa. 'So I went up there for a few weekends to see her and the kid.'

'What?' I shake my head. 'But why didn't she tell you this two years ago?'

'That's what I wanted to know,' Chibu smirks. 'But she said because we weren't involved, she hadn't wanted me to know, and then recently she changed her mind.' He pauses and I move to the edge of the sofa. 'So I tried to get to spend time with the kid. His name is Jack. So I couldn't be here on the weekends. And you were giving me such hassle. And I had so much work.'

'Well, why didn't you just tell me?' I ask.

'Tell you?' Chibu raises his voice. 'How could I tell you I suddenly had a child I had no idea even existed before?'

'I thought you said that honesty was the best policy. Remember? I thought you always tell women the truth.'

'Yeah, you're right. But that's with women I don't care about. With you, it was different, so I didn't tell the whole truth.'

I sit and listen quietly.

'Please, Sarah. Just one more chance.' He puts his hands together. 'I promise. You won't regret it.'

'Why do you think you have the time for me now? You're a new father, that's a pretty major adjustment.'

'Oh, that's just it. I insisted we have a paternity test done. I mean, she's white and the kid was brown, so I figured he was probably mine.' He grins, knowingly. 'But then later I thought it's not as if I'm the only black guy on the planet...so I insisted.'

I move back on the sofa. 'And?'

'The results came back a few days ago.'

'And?' I ask, eagerly.

'Well, I'm not his father.' Chibu widens his smile, clapping his hands together. 'He's not mine. I've never felt so relieved. I'm free. I'm free to do what I want. And what I want is you.'

I think over what he's saying. I sit in silence. Then I finally speak. 'You don't get it do you?'

'Get it?...Get what?'

'We've gone too far in the wrong direction to ever go back. Kid or no kid, you still treated me badly. We were something else before Christmas. I was someone else. You changed that. We can't go back to what we were.' I twist my hair around my ear. 'Even if I tried to believe and forgive you, I'd never really trust you.' I stand up from the sofa. 'You're not the guy I thought you were. And so, quite simply, I don't want you *enough*.'

Rule Number THIRTEEN: Gotta remember what you're worth.

Is THIRTEEN unlucky? Is the glass half-empty, or half-full? It all depends on how you look at it.

A disco ball spins round in the centre of the room. I'm

wearing a disco catsuit. There are thousands of women around me. We start to sing. 'I used to cry...but now I hold my head up high...Now go, walk out the door... just turn around now...'Cause you're not welcome any more...You think I'd crumble?...You think I'd lay down and die?...WILL SURVIVE.'

I walk Chibu to the door. His sexy footballer legs propel him forward, his chiselled face looking at the ground. As he trudges to his car, I catch sight of Deirdre behind her net curtains. Then she pushes the curtains to the side and mouths the words 'well done' in my direction. He is definitely cute. But I want something infinitely more wonderful than that.

There are thousands of men out there. I remember once reading a magnet in a shop: 'Why get married and make one man miserable when I can stay single and make thousands miserable?' Yeah. Why indeed? No more Sam. No more Chibu. Freedom is what everyone wants and I'm lucky enough to have it. I won't give it up for just anyone. I'm Sarah, Glamorous Goddess, thirty-years'-worth, who can dazzle any guy's world. Welcome to Sarah's new attitude. Only the most extraordinary of guys, white, black or purple, will ever be eligible to board this racy rocking new roller-coaster and I'll be the one to choose him.

Chapter twenty-nine

I sit in the Lounge café in Brixton munching on hummus and pita bread with Georgina. The Lounge is a comfy café which serves any number of fresh juices. It has a large mix of people, black, white, straight, gay, old, young, and is an exceptional Brixtonian establishment in this respect. It doesn't have a dominant clientele. Some of the customers even read the *Telegraph*. Georgina sips her fresh orange juice quietly. I tell her about Chibu's escapades in Manchester and his visit to my flat.

'Georgina, you know I'm sorry about the whole Chibu thing, don't you?'

'Yes, I know, Sarah darling.' She pauses. 'Anyway, I was the one who said yes.'

'But maybe I shouldn't have asked,' I simper timidly. Georgina goes on to explain she's glad it happened. It forced a conversation between her and John that should have taken place a long time before, but that neither of them was brave enough to face. They were honest with each other. She told him about her marriage anxieties and he told her about his.

'In fact, I'm really grateful to you.' Georgina puts her hand on my arm. 'John and I are much closer now because of what happened.'

What a relief. I haven't ruined my friend's life after all.

I notice a well-built, clean-shaven white man sitting in the corner in a suit. The suit can't hide the fact that his chest must be ripped underneath. You certainly wouldn't want to get on the wrong side of him.

Georgina sighs. 'I don't know what I would do without John. He's the one thing I can count on. Every night, he's the one I say *goodnight* to.' She squeezes my arm. 'Don't worry Sarah, you'll soon find a soulmate too. Just don't give up.'

Yeah. I'll find him all right. Confucius says: 'Our greatest glory consists not in never falling, but in rising every time we fall.' Oh my goodness...Bear! God. He's still in the wardrobe. I stuffed him in there before my ridiculous attempt at sex with Arthur and I never took him out. Poor Bear. He's been in the wardrobe for weeks. Imagine that.

'Come on, Sarah, let's go. Our tickets are for half-past.' Georgina stands up. 'Is Jacquie meeting us there?' She is indeed. The plan is for the three of us to ride the London Eye together...my two best friends and me. I invited Manuele but he's spending the day in the park with Maria. He's actually thinking of moving in with her. No doubt they'll get married next year. We pay our bill at the counter. The owner of the café, a young Nigerian guy, does a double-take when he sees me. 'Sarah? My goodness. I hardly recognised you. You look great.' Slightly embarrassed, I tuck my hair behind my ear. 'Thanks. I've been making an effort recently.'

'Well, whatever you're doing, keep it up, it's working!' He winks.

The suit guy in the corner of the café is becoming heated and all three of us look over to see what's going on. Suddenly he leaps up from his chair, as if he might hit the scrawny man opposite him.

'You think I was born yesterday, do you?' He growls.

GULP. My heart nearly disappears into the pit of my stomach. I grip Georgina's elbow and push her towards the door.

'Come on, let's get out of here.' Maybe it's Manuele's psycho husband, maybe it isn't. But I'm not taking any chances. We fly out the door in a hurry. We walk to Brixton High Street to catch a bus. It's hot and we hold our coats in our hands. Marks &

Spencer is buzzing with people and the colourful vibrant market is in full swing. Some shout about the price of tomatoes, others shout about Jesus and everlasting life, while the Nation of Islam guys do their best to sell their newspapers. 'Sister, man; come, come, sister…help a brother out.' People crowd the streets.

I notice a woman dressed in black on the opposite side of the street. It's Tina. She's carrying a baby. Dwain is standing next to her, his arm wrapping them both. She looks over at me, beaming. I smile back. Gosh, I hope they'll be OK.

We board the 159 bus and take a look upstairs, but there isn't any room. Luckily, there are still two places free downstairs, and we sit. It's a sunny day, and the whole of London has decided to come out to top up their tan. As we sit down I spot an withered black woman who followed us into the bus. She's wrinkly, bent over and resembles a dried-up raisin with hair as white as can be. She must be over ninety. Deirdre might look just the same in twenty years. Georgina and I stand and offer her our seats. The old lady peers up at us, her eyes sparkling.

'Thank you, girls. You are kind.' Her Nigerian accent is still strong. She holds on to the railings and with some help from Georgina, the old woman manages to sit down. 'You young people are more and more polite these days.' Then she looks straight at me. 'My my…you look just like my granddaughter. So young. So so young…' She stares out of the window in a daze and goes quiet. I turn to Georgina to continue our conversation when the old woman speaks again.

'My husband and I moved to London in the fifties. Then we had four children. I now have twelve grandchildren and three great-grandchildren.' I smile, gazing at the woman's wizened face, as she becomes more animated.

'Chinua and I saw the world together. We moved house four times and every second of July for fifty-five years, he never forgot my birthday. Sadly, my Chinua died last year.' The old lady tilts her head to the side, wagging her finger. 'You're only young once girls. Don't waste it. Before you know it, you're my age, all by yourself with a walking stick, struggling to get on the bus.' The medieval lady smiles. 'Enjoy your youth.'

'I'll be sure to do exactly that,' I respond, grinning. She closes her eyes and sighs, leaving a smile on her lips.

I suppose so; we're young and she's old. It's a matter of perspective. Being thirty could mean I have my whole life ahead of me – perhaps even the best part – just like Daddy said. In comparison to this old woman, even my father is young. We get off the bus on the bridge and walk towards the London Eye. I turn to Georgina. 'There is nothing either good or bad, but thinking makes it so.'

'More *Shakespeare*, Sarah?' Jacquie shouts out, hugging me from behind. 'When are you ever going to give up on the Shakespeare quotes?'

'HEY! Jacquie!' I whip round. 'Where'd you come from?'

'Was on the bus behind you.' She looks at Georgina and they swap their hellos. 'So nothing is either good or bad, huh?'

'Yeah,' I say proudly. 'For instance, before you thought white guys were bad and now you think they're good. ' The three of us stroll amongst the crowds by the river bank. People are dressed for summer, eating ice creams and riding bicycles.

'Damn right I think they're good.' Jacquie chuckles. 'Fucking *divine*, I'd say. Apart from the pub-drinking and the having-no-rhythm thing on the dance floor, of course...'

'I know white guys who can dance,' I respond, looking across the Thames.

'Really?' Jacquie roars. 'Maybe we could introduce them to Arthur...They'll never be perfect, Sarah. There's always something that doesn't quite fit. The question is whether the missing bit is something you can live with.' She laughs. 'Who would ever have thought I would end up with a white guy?'

'So which is best, white or black?' I giggle.

'How would I know?' Jacquie shrugs her shoulders.

'Arthur's the only white guy I've been out with. And he's so kind. We fit together like pieces in a puzzle. And I haven't had to compromise on you know what...They say that white guys are small, but I tell you Arthur is seriously well provided for...' She makes a fist. 'And boy does he have some bedroom skills!'

'Shh!' Georgina leans in. 'That old couple behind us... they're listening to us!'

'Well what do YOU think Georgina?' I say naughtily. 'Who makes a better mate? A black guy or a white one?'

'I don't know. The only black guy I ever went out with was Chibu. I suppose he was smoother than most white guys. I don't know. He was sexy. But maybe that was just him.' Georgina blushes. 'Anyway, you're the expert Sarah...you're the one who has been out with lots of both. What do YOU think? Are black guys better in bed?'

The three of us huddle in together as we join the queue for the London Eye. 'Hmm, well, some black guys are really rubbish...just like some white guys. And some white guys are really good. But they say black guys on average have bigger... you know what...' I whisper.

Jacquie throws her hand up. 'Well, I for one can tell you...'

'Yes, yes, we know, we know...ARTHUR...' I groan, and the three of us howl with laughter.

'If only all guys, white or black, could have dicks like Arthur,' Jacquie yells, 'we'd all be in heaven every night!'

The surrounding conversations stop dead. Everyone pauses to stare at us. How embarrassing. Must change the subject.

I shake my head and sigh. 'I just hope I don't run out of time trying to find the right one, whatever his colour.'

Georgina seizes my arm. 'Don't be silly. You have plenty of time. Some women look better in their thirties than they did when they were younger! She nudges me. 'Just look at Princess Diana. At nineteen, she was insecure and awkward and at thirty-six she was magnificent. She improved with age, and so will you.'

I clasp Georgina's hand. 'Yeah, you know, I think you're right.' I turn to Jacquie and ask for an update on Arthur. Jacquie lights up a cigarette and explains to us that she and Arthur are going strong. He's intelligent, charming and kind. They both love to travel and have already planned a holiday to the Seychelles. Jacquie loves to talk and Arthur loves to listen. While I can't see Arthur as anything but Dorothy's right-hand man, to Jacquie he's a sexy clever catch-of-a-guy. I wonder whether Jacquie will marry him? Arthur certainly isn't like any of her ex-boyfriends, nor is he the type I would have imagined her with, but she's never been so excited over a guy.

'You should see him these days,' Jacquie laughs as she puffs out some smoke. 'The gym is really paying off. He has some serious muscles now. And he's just so well-read!'

How extraordinary. One minute you're single and in a flash your life is changed for ever.

'So, Jacquie, you might end up with mixed-race children!' I exclaim, grinning. 'Just like me!'

'No. I'll have black children…Black children who are also mixed-race.' Jacquie winks at me.

'Just like you.'

Dring dring. Dammit. I rummage around and latch on to my phone.

'Hello?'

'Sarah, dear. It's your mother.'

'Oh hi, Mummy. I'm just with Georgina and Jacquie. We're about to get on the London Eye. How's Daddy?'

'Oh, he's fine, just fine. He gave me such a fright. Don't know what I would do without him,' she says, thankfully. 'Of course if he weren't around, I wouldn't have to see *The Marriage of Figaro* this evening and wouldn't that be a relief!'

'Mummy! You mustn't say things like that!'

'Oh, I'm only joking, dear.'

'Anyway, I'm with my friends right now.'

'If you're busy, then we can speak later, dear. Well, tomorrow I suppose. Tonight I'll be bored to tears sitting uncomfortably in darkness.' She sighs. 'The things I do for him...'

I promise I'll ring her later and hang up the phone.

'You know what?' I flip my hand through my hair, winking at Jacquie and Georgina. 'I don't think I need a man to be happy.'

'Of course you don't!' Jacquie shrieks. 'You're a brilliant, successful, beautiful woman...Why would you need a man to be happy?' Jacquie makes a face. 'Hey, you're only THIRTY, Sarah. They say that thirty is the new twenty-five. And you look *fabulous* these days. Like I said, I think turning thirty was GOOD for you. You're in your prime.' That's right. Prime City. The Barbie-Bratz-Bitch at John Lewis was just trying to sell face cream after all.

'So what will you do for your thirty-first?' Georgina nudges me.

'Don't know yet,' I say pensively, stepping into the moving pod. 'We'll have to go out and celebrate.' I pause. 'I'll be turning thirty-something, so we'll have to celebrate me being young and single. I might just get addicted to it.'

'That's the way to think...you're learning, Sarah...you're learning,' Jacquie chirps.

The three of us move to the side of the pod to see the view. As we do, I notice a cute guy with short dark hair, gelled out in different directions sitting on the benches in the middle. He has a little nose and delicate features. He's sharply dressed in a white collared shirt that shows off his tanned skin. He has a choker beaded necklace round his neck. He smiles at me as we brush past him.

'Hey!' Georgina tugs at my arm. 'That man likes you.'

Jacquie taps me. 'He's cute, isn't he?' Jacquie looks down at his beat up brown loafers. 'Well, minus the shoes.'

Oh no. Been there, bought the t-shirt. I don't give a hoot what his shoes look like. I glance quickly at him. 'I'm sure I know him from somewhere. Is he looking over here?' I clasp Jacquie's arm.

She surveys the pod as if she is just taking in the scene. 'Yeah yeah. He keeps noticing you. He likes you, Sarah. He can't stop looking in your direction.' So I swivel round, catch the man's eye and give him a large smile.

Suddenly, on the other side of the pod, two young men explode at each other. They're about eighteen or nineteen years old. One is black and one is white. The twenty people in the pod shoot round to look. 'I'm gonna fuck you up, you mother fucka.' The white one grips the black one by the collar and pushes him up against the glass of the pod. Some people shriek. So do we. Everyone from that side of the pod starts to edge away. The two young men continue to fight with each other, shouting. Both over six foot and heavily built, yet they throw each other about the place like dolls.

'You fucking bitch. You understand?' The white boy screams loudly and then pummels the other boy in the stomach.

We're terrified. We stare in silence, not knowing what to do. The two young men crash against the glass.

'My GOD!' a woman shrieks. 'They'll break the glass!'

Jacquie and Georgina each hold on to one of my arms. I notice that the man in the sharp white shirt has moved to the edge of the pod on to our side. Now where do I know him from? No time to search my memory. The boys are tumbling around the pod. I look at them. Then I look a little closer. My God! It's Kofi and Jake! I've known them since they were eleven years old. Kofi has Jake's head under his arm, blocking off his air supply. Bloody hell. All this fuss and it's just Kofi and Jake. I march up to Kofi and grab him by the shoulder. He stares at me and snarls: 'What the fuck?' I stare straight back and sternly command: 'Let go of Jake NOW.' He lets go instantly. The two of them stand back with their hands up as if I'm pointing a gun at them.

'Sorry, Miss. Sorry, Miss. Sorry, Miss,' they mumble.

'That's OK boys.' I hold out my hand, smiling. 'It's nice to see you.'

They take turns shaking my hand, both grinning awkwardly. Kofi blushes. 'Yeah, nice to see you too, Miss.'

Jake follows with: 'Yeah, Miss, man. Good to see you. I hope your boyfriend bought you flowers on Valentine's Day.'

Gosh. Woolworths on Valentine's. Seems like decades ago. There's silence. Then the others in the pod start applauding. I spin round. They cheer and clap in my direction. The boys wave at the crowd in an apologetic way and take a seat. Everyone appears very relieved and I nip over to where Jacquie and Georgina are standing. Georgina gives me a hug.

'Well done, Sarah!' Jacquie jumps up and down. 'No one messes with YOU, huh?'

I chuckle and say that it's nothing.

'It's not *nothing* at all,' comes a voice from behind. I twirl round. It's the man in the white shirt. 'I'm impressed. I can see you're a woman who isn't to be messed with.'

'That's right,' I say, triumphantly.

'Some view isn't it?' He points to the glass.

'Yes it is.' I pause. 'Don't I know you from somewhere?'

'Yes. We met once, speed-dating in that bar in Soho... Remember?'

My mouth gapes open. 'Oh yeah! You're the guy who disappeared before we started!'

'That's because I wasn't there to date; I own the speed-dating company. I was just there training Sandy.' The man holds out his hand. 'My name is Derek, Derek Thomas.'

'Pleased to meet you.' I shake his hand. 'My name is Sarah.' I pause. 'It's Sarah *Spencer*.'

'Hello, Sarah Spencer; that's a nice name. It sort of has a ring to it...as if you should have your name in bright lights outside a theatre.'

Ring or no ring, my name is Sarah Spencer and I like the way it sounds.

'These are my friends Jacquie and Georgina.'

They shake hands and then Derek speaks for a little while about the view and the wonder of London. He's well-spoken, charming and has a glint in his eyes.

I like him.

'So are you girls busy this evening? Would you like to get a drink together?'

Hesitating, I tilt my head to the side. 'You know, Derek, I would love to have a drink, but we're having a girls' day out and it'll no doubt continue till late tonight...'

Jacquie looks at me and draws her eyes wide.

'But another time would be great.' I take a pen and paper out of my bag and write down my phone number. 'I know you probably have a mobile phone, but I'm an old-fashioned kind of girl, and I like to do things in an old-fashioned kind of way.' I wink, handing him the paper. Just then Big Ben chimes three times. It's three o'clock. Three o'clock and I'm on top of the world. Derek takes the paper and puts it in his top pocket. He pats his shirt as if to suggest he'll keep it safe, says it was nice to meet us, and sits back on the bench. The three of us return to the edge of the pod and gaze out into the distance. Success #1.

'Well played, Sarah.' Jacquie squeezes my arm. 'He'll be dying for you now.'

'But I wasn't playing,' I say indignantly. 'We already have plans. I also have to pick up some milk for Deirdre. Some things are more important.' I pause and smile. 'And if he calls, I'll think about seeing him another time.'

Both Jacquie and Georgina look at me as if I've lost my mind. And perhaps I have. At least I've lost my old way of thinking. I link arms with my friends as the Gherkin building flashes in the sunlight. I pull them in close. 'Who's up for Häagen-Dazs afterwards?' I grin mischievously. 'I'm buying.'